THE THIEF OF JOY

THE THIEF OF JOY

STACEY MURRAY

This edition produced in Great Britain in 2024

by Hobeck Books Limited, 24 Brookside Business Park, Stone, Staffordshire
ST15 0RZ

www.hobeck.net

A CIP catalogue for this book is available from the British Library.

ISBN 978-1-915-817-29-7 (ebook)

ISBN 978-1-915-817-30-3 (pbk)

Cover design by Jayne Mapp Design

Printed and bound in Great Britain

ARE YOU A THRILLER SEEKER?

Hobeck Books is an independent publisher of crime, thrillers and suspense fiction and we have one aim – to bring you the books you want to read.

For more details about our books, our authors and our plans, plus the chance to download free novellas, sign up for our newsletter at **www.hobeck.net**.

You can also find us on X/Twitter **@hobeckbooks** or on Facebook **www.facebook.com/hobeckbooks10**.

For my mother, Jessie

CHAPTER ONE

The brain was a strange old thing, she thought, watching the clock, willing it to go faster. All those years when she'd had nothing to look forward to, Fridays had still always felt different – even smelt different – from the other days.

But today there was a reason for the 'Friday feeling'. Tonight she was going for drinks and dinner at the new Italian in town. She was going out with Daniel.

She slammed the front door behind her and raced up the stairs. She had twenty minutes till Daniel came to pick her up. Twenty minutes to change out of her uniform into her denim tunic-dress that showed just the right amount of cleavage. She would wear it with black tights and ankle boots and stick a cardigan in her bag; it was a mild enough day at the moment, but the mid-September nights could get chilly.

She pulled the brush through her newly dyed black hair and smoothed the starchy fabric over her hips in the mirror.

Something was missing. The outfit was too plain, too boring. It needed something else. A silk scarf around her neck? No. Too ageing. She was thirty-nine, not sixty-nine. A pendant maybe. Or some earrings.

Poking around her jewellery box, she found the Art Nouveau silver brooch – a gift from her mother on her birthday. 'It's a Rennie Mackintosh design,' her mother had said, in her Miss Jean Brodie accent. 'It wasn't cheap, you know.' She fished it out and pinned it to the left of her neckline, hoping for a hint of sophistication. But it wasn't right and she took it off, pricking her finger in the process.

She sucked away the blood and chose another: a hare made from amber crystals that her daughter, Chloe, had bought for her at the school bring-and-buy sale. It was an odd-looking thing – the creature looked positively possessed – but she fastened it to her dress, front and centre. It would be a conversation-starter. A chance to talk about Chloe. She was keen for Daniel to meet her. Something casual to begin with – an ice cream or hot chocolate in town one weekend – to give Chloe a chance to get used to him. To the idea of her mum having a 'boyfriend'. And then, if things went well over the next little while, they could book to go away for a few days over the Christmas holidays. To a cottage by the coast, just the three of them. Maybe to Whitby. Daniel had just been there on that stag weekend with the lads. He'd loved it and was keen to go back again...

She sprayed herself with her best 'Pomegranate' perfume and wondered how Chloe was getting on. Tonight was a big deal for her too: her first ever sleep-over, staying at Ruby's house. She should call to check she was OK. In a minute.

She rummaged in the wardrobe for her boots, to find them covered in a perfect layer of dust. With no time to clean them properly, she pulled them on and wiped each one down the back of her other leg, transferring the dust to her tights.

Her phone rang out on the dressing table. That would be Chloe now, checking in with her, just like she'd told her to. It would have to be short and sweet...

But no, it was Daniel. Surely he wasn't stuck at work: a music teacher's hours were nothing if not predictable. He was probably lost and ringing for directions – all the streets round here looked the same.

She pressed the answer button. 'Hiya!' she smiled. 'Which is it, then? Are you lost – or running late?'

'Is... Is that Roz?' said the voice on the line. Not Daniel's.

'It is,' she replied. 'Who's this?'

'It's Luke. I'm a friend of Daniel's.'

'Oh. Right,' said Roz. 'Is everything OK?'

'Ah... Well... No,' he said. 'I'm afraid it's not.'

CHAPTER TWO

Roz sat on the couch, staring at the wall. The sun had disappeared now, draining the room of its colour.

She should have called to cancel the restaurant, but hadn't trusted herself not to blurt it out: *I'm very sorry. We won't be able to make it tonight because my boyfriend has died.* But it didn't matter now. It would be clear they weren't coming. Some other couple would be sitting in their place.

Her phone sat silent on the coffee table. She was scared to touch it again, but she couldn't sit here all night and not tell another soul – couldn't physically contain it. She'd have to try calling Kate, even though it was the weekend and she'd be busy.

Roz jumped when Kate actually answered, her voice as clear as if she was in the street outside, not nearly two hundred miles away in London. From the rumble of the traffic and the clack of her heels on the pavement, she was dressed up and hurrying somewhere.

'Holy shit!' said Kate, when Roz told her. 'How did...? What caused it, do they know?'

'They think it was an aneurysm,' said Roz, her own voice thin and fragile.

'An *aneurysm*?' Kate repeated the unfamiliar word. 'What, is that like a stroke or something? I thought that was an old person's thing?'

'Not exactly,' Roz sighed, reaching for the tartan throw that hung over the back of the sofa and pulling it round her shoulders. 'It's when a blood vessel swells up and then bursts in your brain. Basically.' This felt surreal, like she was floating high above herself, watching herself speak. It was wrong to be talking about Daniel like this: she should've been telling her best mate how the date went – about their plans for Christmas – not describing how he died.

'Oh. Right,' said Kate. 'So... Was it, like, some sort of congenital thing?'

Was it? Roz had no idea. She raked through her memories of Daniel, trying to unearth something, some clue from what he had said.

'I mean, was he born with it?' said Kate, as if Roz hadn't heard her the first time. 'Something in his family?'

A wave of helplessness rose up in Roz. 'I really don't know,' she said. 'He never mentioned anything.'

'Yeah,' said Kate. 'It's not the sort of thing you come out with when you've just met someone.'

Roz bridled at this. 'That's a bit unfair. I hadn't *just met* him.'

'Ah, look, I'm sorry,' said Kate. 'What I meant was... I know you two were getting close and everything, but it's not like you'd been together a long time. You hadn't really had a *chance* to find out these things.'

Oh God, thought Roz. Kate was trying to be all sensitive now, which was making things worse. She was regretting calling her at all. 'No, *I'm* sorry,' said Roz. 'I can see this isn't a good time. Maybe I should let you go and—'

'No, no. It's fine,' Kate insisted.

Roz hesitated. It wasn't ideal – trying to talk to Kate as she weaved through the after-work crowd, random sirens screeching in the background. But she didn't have anyone else.

'So,' said Kate. 'Where was he when it happened? Were you with him?'

'No,' said Roz. 'His friend...' She closed her eyes, recalling the awful conversation. 'His friend Luke went round to his flat this morning to pick up some gear.'

'Some *gear*?' said Kate. 'Uh-oh.'

'No,' said Roz sharply. 'Musical gear – an amplifier and stuff. They're in a band together.' She paused. '*Were* in a band... And Daniel was apparently saying he had a terrible headache – the worst he'd had in his life. He'd called in sick to work. And then Luke called an ambulance, but by the time they got him to hospital it was too late. They'd already given Luke his belongings – his phone and that – to look after, and so he called Daniel's parents and then my name popped up on it. A reminder about tonight. We were supposed to be going out...'

'Fu-uck,' was all Kate could say.

Roz carried on. 'There'll have to be a post-mortem, Luke said. To confirm the... cause. But he said they seemed pretty sure.'

'Oh God,' said Kate softly. 'This is so shit for you, Roz. I know how much you liked him. I'm so sorry. I really am. I don't really know what to say...'

Kate's sympathy had pierced through the shock and Roz began to snivel. She glanced at the door to check it was closed; she didn't want Chloe to hear her upstairs. But she was forgetting... Chloe wasn't there. She was safely tucked up at Ruby's.

'Listen, Roz,' said Kate. 'You sound like you need somebody there with you. Do you want me to come home for a visit and see you? So we can talk face to face. I mean... I can't this weekend. We're going down to...' The line was breaking up. 'But I could come up next Friday after work?'

Next Friday? thought Roz. A whole week.

'Oh bugger. I just realised I can't,' said Kate. 'I've got dinner that night with some of my personal training clients down at Canary Wharf. But I could come up on the Saturday morning. It'd have to be a flying visit, but I'm worried about you and it'd be good to—'

'No. No. I'm fine,' said Roz, trying to keep the shake out of her voice.

'You don't sound very fine. Couldn't you go and stay with Fiona for a couple of days?'

'Not really,' said Roz. The idea of going to stay with her younger sister hadn't even occurred to her. 'And anyway, she's in Alderley Edge now...'

Kate whistled. 'Very posh... Although it's not *that* far. You could still go over and see her. Tomorrow, I mean. Once you've had some sleep.'

'Ugh,' said Roz. 'You know what Fiona's like. Spends every waking hour at the office.'

'Not at the weekend, surely? Even God had a day off!'

'I wouldn't be so sure.' Roz laughed bitterly. 'She's just been made a partner at her law firm in Manchester. She earns a shitload, but they expect their pound of flesh in return.'

'Or you could give your mum a call?'

'You reckon?' scoffed Roz.

'Sorry. I wasn't—'

'Although maybe you're right. Maybe I should ring Fiona.'

'Excellent,' said Kate. 'And you'll do it right now? As soon as I've hung up?'

'As soon as you've hung up.'

'Promise?'

'Promise!' Roz smiled in spite of herself. Kate had always been a bossy cow.

'Right. Well you take care of yourself. I've got to go now – I'm late – but I'll call you in a day or two, OK?'

'OK,' said Roz. 'Where are you off to by the way?'

'The Dorchester... Sam's up for a TV award.'

'Oh,' said Roz. 'Exciting.'

'Not as glamorous as it sounds. Quite boring actually. Now listen, I'd better run. Sam'll be wondering where I've got to. Speak soon, OK?'

'OK,' said Roz, to the sound of the line going dead. 'Speak soon.'

The Pomegranate perfume was making her nauseous, and calling Fiona was the last thing she felt like doing. It had been weeks since they'd talked – months since they'd seen each other in person at that meal for their mother's birthday.

It was properly dark now, as Roz kicked off her boots and curled up on the couch, pulling the tartan throw over her head. She closed her eyes and tried in vain to stop the thoughts from churning. This morning at work, as she'd been counting down the minutes till she saw him, Daniel had been fighting for his life. And while she was upstairs preening herself in the mirror – planning out their future – he was lying on the slab in the hospital, already cold.

CHAPTER THREE

Ruby's dad dropped Chloe back at home the next morning and Roz had never been so pleased to see her.

'Ow!' Chloe moaned when Roz threw her arms around her, squeezing her tight. 'Are you OK, Mum?'

'Of course I am,' said Roz, straightening her clothes and smiling. 'What kind of question is that?'

She'd never dumped her baggage on her daughter – unlike some – and she wasn't about to start now. Chloe knew nothing about Daniel and never would. But the weight in Roz's body, the pressure in her head – they would have to come out somehow. She'd have to talk to someone and it would have to be her sister.

~

Roz lay awake in the pre-dawn of Sunday, thinking, planning... She wouldn't cold-call Fiona and drop the bomb-shell like she'd done with Kate. She'd drive over and see her in Alderley Edge – on the pretext of calling in to see the new house – then tell her when the moment was right and the family were out of earshot. As Kate had said, even Fiona wouldn't be working on a Sunday.

Several hours later, when the sun had seen off the last wisps of morning mist, Roz and Chloe went out to the car.

'Can I sit in the front?' asked Chloe, opening the passenger door. 'I measured myself. I'm tall enough now.'

'No,' said Roz firmly. 'I told you. Not till you're twelve.'

'But that's ages away!'

'No it's not. It's only two years. Less than two years...'

'But—'

'But nothing,' said Roz. She wasn't taking any chances, not today.

Chloe slammed the door shut and got in the back.

'Here's my phone,' said Roz, handing it to her from the front. 'You can navigate to Auntie Fiona's.' It was only partly because she was unsure of the route – mainly to stop Chloe sulking.

The climb out of Buxton took them along the notorious 'Cat and Fiddle' road, which crossed the moors in a series of bends used by bikers as a ready-made race track. Several sets of them had roared past already as Roz kept a steady pace and tried to ignore the wilted tributes tied to lamp posts, fleeting memorials to lives taken too soon. Like Daniel's.

She replayed the last few weeks in her mind – again – for something she could've done differently, some sign she'd missed that things weren't right. The last time she'd seen him – in town for a coffee during her lunch break – he'd looked fit and tanned in his mirrored sunglasses, buzzing for the start of the new term and the prospect of taking the school orchestra to a competition in Cardiff. He'd always been so enthusiastic about everything – big things and small – which was one of the reasons she'd fallen for him so fast. He was the antidote to all the world's moaners and miserable gits, and in a just world, he'd be here in the car with them now. She'd be taking him to Fiona's to show him off. But no. All that energy extinguished, just like that. By something so small and silent and invisible. He'd never complained to her about a headache, but then he hadn't complained about anything much. Nothing she could remember. But it didn't stop her rewinding to the start and re-running the tape. Till she got to that day again – the day they'd met for coffee. The last time she would see him – that she hadn't known would be the last time.

'Mu-um.' Chloe tapped her on the shoulder from the back.

'Yes, love?'

'Can we go out for tea next Saturday? To Nando's?'

'Eh? Where's that?' said Roz, eyes fixed on the road. 'I don't think we've got one in Buxton...'

'It's in Stockport,' said Chloe. 'And can Ruby come too? She's been there loads of times and—'

'Look, can we talk about this later?' Roz snapped. 'I'm a bit busy at the moment.'

'Sorry,' said Chloe and folded her arms.

'No, I'm sorry, love. It's just... I need to concentrate, OK?'

'OK,' said Chloe and they carried on in silence for a while.

'Where do we go at the end of this road?' Roz asked eventually, even though she knew from the road signs.

'You need to turn... right,' said Chloe, checking the phone.

'Thanks, love. You're doing a great job,' said Roz, and was rewarded with a smile.

Soon the peaks and valleys and twisty roads gave way to the flatlands, big skies and open feel of Cheshire. The traffic was slightly quieter now and Roz felt calm enough to switch on the radio. Ten minutes later, following Chloe's directions, they were turning into a leafy cul-de-sac and crawling up to the last house.

'Wow!' said Chloe as they passed through the grand stone gateposts of the red brick mansion.

Roz parked her little Corsa next to Fiona's Range Rover with the private number plate, feeling the wealthy crunch of tyre on gravel. 'Wow indeed,' she muttered.

'Roz?' exclaimed Fiona, opening the door. She would fit right into the 'Cheshire Set' with her high blonde ponytail, skinny jeans and pale pink angora sweater with white stars on the front – a world away from Roz's black layers and leggings. Roz ran her hands through her hair, conscious she looked worse than usual after no sleep.

'We were, eh... We were just passing and thought we'd call in,' said Roz, shooting Chloe a look to stop her saying different.

'Come in! Come in!' said Fiona, oblivious. 'Let me take your jackets and things. That's a pretty anorak, Chloe...'

And they stepped into the 'brand-new' smell of the spacious hallway with its black and white floor tiles, navy blue walls and stained glass window at the top of the landing. All the way up the stairs there were professional-looking framed photographs of Fiona, her husband Ian and their three kids – some individual shots, most of them together.

The effect was so perfect that, when Fiona ushered them

through to the kitchen-diner, Roz was desperate to find fault with it. But it was impossible. It was like something from a magazine: one wall was exposed brickwork, with the rest of them bright white; a rectangular central island ran the length of the room with high leather stools on either side; a range of copper pans and most of John Lewis's utensil department hung from ceiling hooks above; and the wide windowsills were dotted with vases of fresh lilies and white candles in huge glass holders. Fiona pointed out a few of the highlights – the boiling water tap, the fancy wine fridge (fully stocked) and the separate utility room that was bigger than Roz's kitchen – while Roz made a variety of appreciative noises on cue.

At the far end of the room, towards the garden, was a posh conservatory – the 'orangery', Fiona called it – and Roz went for a closer look.

'Actually!' Fiona held up a hand to stop her. 'If you wouldn't mind taking your shoes off in there...'

'Oh, sure, sorry.' Roz kicked off her boots, blushed at the hole in her sock and hoped Fiona wouldn't notice. She tiptoed on and Chloe followed, wiggling her toes into the plush cream carpet.

'It cost a fortune,' said Fiona. 'We've got some offcuts left over. Maybe Chloe could have them for her room? They'll only go to landfill otherwise.'

Chloe nodded hard, but Roz was gripped by the urge to put her boots back on and leave. She wasn't in the mood for domestic chit-chat, still less Fiona's casual boasting and 'Lady Bountiful' act. It was a mistake to have come here and it certainly wasn't the time or the place to bring up Daniel. Apart from anything, the smell of roast chicken had begun to waft down from the kitchen – which meant the family, wherever they were, would soon be sitting down to lunch.

'Oh, look at the time,' said Roz. 'Are you about to eat? We'd better be off. It was only a flying visit. We don't want to—'

'Oh, you're fine. You're fine. Don't worry,' said Fiona. 'I'm trying out Ottolenghi's lemon chicken. It'll be ready in an hour, give or take. Would you like to join us?'

'Oh no,' insisted Roz. 'I wouldn't want to impose.'

'It's alright. There's plenty to go round.' Fiona turned to Chloe. 'And there's pudding too. Chocolate trifle. Home-made.'

'Can we?' Chloe begged.

'Oh, OK then.' Roz gave in. 'If you're sure... It'll save me cooking later on.' And it would save her being at home with her thoughts.

'Of course I'm sure!' said Fiona. 'Now then, Chloe.' She clasped her hands. 'Would you like something to drink? Some squash?'

'Yes, please,' said Chloe and they followed Fiona back to the kitchen.

Fiona opened the fridge. 'Elderflower or rosehip?'

'Erm, elderflower,' said Chloe, unsure, and Roz wondered why Fiona couldn't just have orange or blackcurrant flavours like a normal person.

'And what about you, Roz?' said Fiona, going to the wine fridge. 'I've got fizz and I've got—'

'No. No, thanks,' said Roz. Her head was spinning already and alcohol was the last thing she needed, especially as she had to drive home again. 'Squash is fine for me too.'

While Fiona poured the drinks, her three boys came running downstairs into the room, anxious to see if they were missing out on anything. The eldest, Artie, was wearing a Manchester City top and the three-year-old twins were dressed in matching stripy jumpers, cute as anything.

'Lunch isn't ready yet,' Fiona informed them. 'Why don't you take Chloe upstairs and show her your new bedrooms?' She turned to Roz. 'Artie's got the top floor. The views are amazing. You can see all the way to the Edge.'

The boys didn't look all that keen on showing their big cousin around, but they did as they were told. Chloe followed them upstairs, leaving Roz and Fiona.

'I'll give you the tour of the house after lunch,' Fiona said, as she salted the potatoes, set the table and generally buzzed about like a superwoman.

'Where's Ian?' asked Roz, with fake breeziness. Now she and Fiona were on their own, she'd sensed her chance, but she didn't want Fiona's husband turning up in the middle of it.

'Ugh,' said Fiona in mock annoyance. 'He's doing some triathlon – the Peak District Punisher or something ridiculous like that. If past experience is anything to go by, he'll rock up at six o'clock, covered head-to-toe in mud, asking what's for tea.' She shook her head indulgently. 'Honest to God, it's like having a fourth child sometimes...'

Roz didn't want to hear about Ian. She took a breath, then plunged straight in. 'Do you remember me telling you about the guy I was seeing?' she asked. 'Back in the summer?'

Fiona looked up from basting the chicken. 'D'you know what?' she said, cocking her head at Roz. 'I don't think I do...'

Roz carried on. 'It was at Mum's birthday, remember? At the restaurant in Wilmslow.'

'Oh, right,' said Fiona, wiping her brow with the dish

towel. 'You'd better tell me again. Things have been a bit manic over the last few months. It'll soon come back to me.'

Fuck, thought Roz. This was unbearable. 'OK. Well, anyway. He died on Friday.'

'He *died*?' said Fiona, and stopped what she was doing. 'How? How old was he?'

'Same age as me. They think it was a bleed on the brain.'

'Oh, right,' said Fiona again.

'The thing is, I'm in bits here,' said Roz. 'I'm trying to hide it from Chloe, but I'm struggling and...' She trailed off, conscious she was gabbling.

'Look. Come and sit down,' said Fiona, pulling out a stool and patting it. Then she pulled one out for herself.

'I was about to introduce him to Chloe,' said Roz, sagging under the full beam of Fiona's attention. 'I had so many plans and...'

Fiona handed her a box of tissues and Roz dabbed at her eyes.

'Oh, Roz,' said Fiona, placing a hand on her arm. 'I'm so sorry. I really am. Life can be so bloody, I dunno, *senseless* at times.'

'No, I'm sorry,' said Roz. 'I just wanted a chance of happiness... A proper family.' *What you've got*, she wanted to add. *What everyone else has got.* 'But now...' She looked up at the ceiling, but the tears still came. 'What's the point of anything? Why does everything have to go tits-up for me?'

'How long were you together?' Fiona asked, gently.

'Three months,' sniffed Roz. 'Three and a half actually... But we had a connection, you know? We had a future.'

'Roz...' Fiona sat back in her stool. 'I don't want you to take this the wrong way... But you mustn't make this into a bigger drama than it is. You can't go to pieces over it.' She swallowed hard. 'Not again. For Chloe's sake.'

A noise made them both look up: the click of the conservatory door closing. Then the familiar Scottish voice: 'What have I missed? What's the drama?'

Roz froze and Fiona jumped down from her stool.

'Oh, hi, Mum,' Fiona called out. 'You're early.'

CHAPTER FOUR

Roz wiped her eyes and stuffed the tissue up her sleeve. Christ! Why hadn't Fiona told her *she* was coming?

'Hello, Rosslyn,' said their mother and Roz bristled at the use of her full name. 'What a nice surprise.' As she shook off her trench coat and handed it to Fiona, Roz was struck by how slight she was: she seemed to have shrunk since the last time she'd seen her, her legs quite spindly in flesh-coloured tights and black court shoes. She was probably on one of her diets. Roz hoped she'd just called in on her way home from church and that she wouldn't be hanging around.

'Your dad will be joining us for lunch,' their mother announced. 'He's playing golf with his pals. Although the way they play, it could be dinner time before they're finished...'

Roz tensed up, her mouth suddenly dry. It would be nice to see her dad, but was it too late to make up some excuse, some reason she had to disappear?

Fiona poured their mother a small glass of sherry without having to be asked. 'Have a seat,' she said, pulling out a stool.

'I hope we're not eating our meal around this *island* thing,' their mother sniffed, settling onto her perch, clocking the placemats Fiona had already laid. 'I prefer a nice round table. I like to be able to see you all.'

Roz and Fiona exchanged a look, scarred by the memory of teenage meals when they'd sat there under scrutiny, facing a drip, drip, drip of criticism about their clothes, their friends, their latest school reports. Or worse, being played off against each other.

No problem!' said Fiona, gathering up the cutlery and the white linen napkins in their silver rings. 'We'll switch to the dining room. That'll give us a bit more space seeing as Roz and Chloe are joining us too...'

'Where is Chloe?' their mother asked.

'Just upstairs,' said Fiona before Roz could speak. 'Artie and the twins are showing her their rooms.'

'Lovely,' said their mother, sipping her drink, leaving her usual ring of lipstick. 'So,' she said, smiling at them both in turn. 'What were you talking about when I arrived and rudely interrupted you?'

Roz took a breath to steady herself, but the blood still pounded in her ears. She couldn't face telling the story of Daniel all over again. Not to her mother. But she didn't have to, because Fiona had stepped in to do it for her, putting Roz's 'case' as sympathetically as she could. No wonder Fiona had gone into the law – she was a natural advocate, and Roz felt a stab of gratitude towards her little sister.

Their mother sat listening intently until Fiona had finished, and Roz braced herself, awaiting the verdict. It was a few seconds before it came, although it felt longer. 'You know, Rosslyn... I think you need to toughen up a bit,' said her mother, matter of fact, like she was telling her cleaner how to get stains off the bath. 'Plenty of people have it much worse in life. You know my friend Linda, don't you?'

Roz shook her head.

'Yes you do. She's in that choir with Joyce. You definitely know Joyce – her husband got elected to the council in May...'

Roz couldn't think. 'I'm not sure I—'

'Well, anyway. She's having a terrible time at the moment. Forty-three years married and she's just lost her husband after nursing him through—'

'The husband on the council?' said Fiona.

'No, no,' their mother corrected her. 'That's Joyce's husband. This is Linda I'm talking about.'

'Oh. Right. Sorry,' said Fiona.

'And in the same week her little granddaughter was diagnosed with cancer – some dreadful form of it that attacks the immune system.'

'God,' said Roz. A shiver went through her. 'That's awful.'

'It is, isn't it?' said her mother. 'Puts one's own troubles in perspective, don't you think?'

'That's a bit harsh, Mum,' said Fiona before Roz could reply. 'Roz has had a real shock. She thought she had a future with him. She thought the relationship was potentially—'

'I loved him,' said Roz, quietly.

'She *loved* him,' said her mother after a moment. She looked to the heavens and shook her head, but her lacquered hair didn't move. 'Don't be silly, Rosslyn. You hardly knew him.' She sipped again at her glass. 'And self-pity is such an unattractive quality. This young man dying was bad enough: imagine how his poor mother must feel, losing a child. Don't make it all about you. It's... I don't know... it's *unseemly*.'

Roz bit the inside of her lip. The less she said, the sooner this would be over.

Fiona made a show of looking at her watch. 'I'd better go and sort the vegetables,' she said, and their mother followed her to the sink, with instructions how to slice the carrots – 'batons, not discs'. Fiona fell into line and did as she was told.

'Well!' said their mother, when they were back on their stools. 'What do you make of the *big news*, then?'

Roz and Fiona looked at each other and shrugged.

'I thought *you* would know, Rosslyn?' their mother continued with an air of triumph.

'Know what?' said Roz, weary now.

'About Kate.' Her mother paused for effect. 'She got engaged yesterday. It was a proper down-on-one-knee job – a huge princess-cut diamond apparently. And she's coming back to Buxton for the wedding. Next May it is – a big do, I gather. They're thinking of having the reception at The Old Hall.'

'Ah,' said Fiona. 'That's lovely. I'll have to send her a card. Can you let me have her address in London, Roz?'

'Er, sure.' Roz nodded evenly to hide her turmoil. Why hadn't Kate told her yet – and why did she feel so unsettled by this news? Kate and Sam had been living together for the last few years, sharing the mortgage on their place in Shoreditch. It was hardly a surprise.

'Yes,' their mother was wittering on to Fiona now. 'Kate's mum Jan rang to tell me last night. Sam – that's Kate's partner – fiancée I should say – she's a producer for the BBC. Works on nature documentaries these days. Very good at her job, I'm told. She's worked with David Attenborough apparently.'

'Yeah. You said,' said Fiona. 'Good for her.' Although she

didn't sound all that sincere, maybe because she'd heard it a hundred times before. Fiona had even met Sam once or twice when Kate had been home on visits. But their mother still loved to repeat this sort of thing, basking in the reflected glory of her social web.

The piercing buzz of the front doorbell made the three of them jump.

'Sorry,' said Fiona, rushing to answer it. 'I haven't figured out how to turn down the volume...'

She returned with their dad, who ambled into the room behind her, running a hand through his thick grey hair.

'Sorry I'm late,' he grinned, holding his hands up.

'You're not. Don't worry,' said Fiona.

'Ah, good.' He came straight over to Roz and hugged her. 'Hello, darling! I didn't know you were coming. No-one ever tells me anything...'

Their mother was eyeing him carefully. 'Have you been drinking?' she asked. 'Your face looks more ruddy than usual.'

'Not a drop, Margaret,' he said, the grin now gone. 'The rest of the lads went for a pint, but I've come straight here.' He saluted. 'As per my orders.'

'Hmm,' said their mother, and Roz felt a pang of pity for him. He was kept on a short leash alright. But then he'd opted for the path of appeasement long ago. It was his own choice.

It was after three o'clock when they had sat down to eat, and the meal itself – all three courses of it – took forever. As soon as it was over, Roz had escaped to the kitchen to load the dishwasher and scrub the roasting tins while the rest of them had coffee. She'd stayed another half hour after that, just to be polite, and was now delighted to be back in the car on the way home with Chloe babbling away in the back seat.

There were no cars on the road and the sky was grey and low, but as they followed the fingerpost signs for the A-road, their headlights cast a pleasing glow over gates and barns and hedgerows and the little village shops that were all closed up. Orange lights shone in the windows of the houses they passed. Everyone was home now – watching telly, making tea, doing the last bits of homework before Monday – and Roz was glad they would soon be doing the same. Once she'd sorted out Chloe's school things for the week – her netball skirt and swimming stuff, her blouses that needed ironing – she'd have a nice, long bath followed by a mug of hot tea on the couch. Her rented semi-detached wasn't nearly as fancy as Fiona's 'show-home' – it was definitely at the shabby end of shabby chic – but it was lovely and snug once the lamps were lit and the curtains drawn. Their safe little haven.

By the time the news-at-six came on the car radio, a huge black cloud had scudded in to match the depressing head-lines. And then the rain started, spattering hard against the windscreen, forcing Roz to concentrate.

'Why did Gran say that thing about my hair?' Chloe asked from the back, flicking her loose, dark waves over her shoulders. 'Doesn't she like long hair? It was a bit mean.'

'Oh, I don't think she was being mean,' Roz replied, although she wasn't sure at all. 'She's just a bit old-fashioned sometimes. She thinks little girls should have their hair tied back neatly into pigtails and bunches...'

'I'm not little!' said Chloe.

'No, you're not.' Roz smiled to herself. 'Don't worry. She's the same with everyone. It's just what she's like.' Chloe shrugged and Roz continued. 'You know, when me and Auntie Fiona were young, we always used to have to wear matching outfits.'

'Like the twins?' said Chloe, giggling.

'Exactly,' said Roz. 'Although for us it was girlie little dresses. Cotton sundresses in summer, and in winter, thick velvety ones with little white collars.'

'Seriously?'

'Uh-huh,' said Roz. 'And each outfit had its own set of matching ribbons for our hair. And clasps and bows. The kids at school used to tease us something rotten.'

'What about Artie though?' said Chloe, chewing her nail.

'What about him?'

'His hair's quite long and messy and Gran never has a go at him.'

Roz wondered what to say to her. That Artie was different because he was a boy, Fiona's first-born 'little prince'; that Gran was just using her to get at Roz and that she was an old woman now and nothing on this earth was going to change her?

In the end, she said nothing. She had questions of her own. Like why hadn't she been invited to this cosy family lunch in the first place instead of stumbling into it by accident? Not that she would've accepted. She'd known her mother would scorn her feelings for Daniel. Even so, she'd outdone herself; using her friend's sick granddaughter to make the point was a low blow, even for her. And why hadn't Kate rung her – or even texted – to say she was engaged and that the wedding would be at The Old Hall – the actual hotel where Roz worked? That was weird too.

She stopped at a red light and watched Chloe yawn in the rear view mirror. 'You're a bit quiet, love. Are you tired?'

'A little bit,' said Chloe.

'Don't worry. We'll be home soon,' said Roz, pressing ahead as the lights changed.

Her mother's reaction to Kate's news... that had been ironic to say the least. A few short years ago, she'd been shocked rigid to discover Kate was gay. 'How very modern,' she'd bitched at the time. But now Kate was getting married to a woman who'd met David Attenborough and that trumped everything, apparently. Kate was *respectable* all of a sudden. Someone to be taken seriously. There would be none of that for Roz, though, not now Daniel was gone. There would be no day in the spotlight, no speeches extolling her qualities, no fancy gift list. Roz would be what she always was – on her own, terminally single, the spare prick at someone else's wedding. She'd fix a fake smile on her face and feel like a failure. As though she was 'less than' everyone else. Worse, an object of pity – of judgement.

They passed through Macclesfield, heading back towards the moor and the Cat and Fiddle. It was a slightly different route, which Roz hoped would be quicker and which took them through a dense section of woodland, dark and green like an undersea tunnel.

The chill and the stillness soothed her as the trunks of the trees flashed by hypnotically. Roz breathed out. She was happy for Kate and the wedding would be fun, she told herself. Natasha would be there – and Vicky too – their old friends from school. She remembered Vicky's wedding as if it was yesterday, in that huge marquee in deepest Berkshire. When all Roz's coupled-up friends had left in taxis at the end of the night and she'd emerged from the toilets to find herself alone... Rather than ask for help, she'd stupidly set off walking down a country lane in what she thought was the right direction – trying to call a cab, trying to get a signal – shivering in her flimsy bridesmaid dress. To no avail.

She'd made it back to the hotel eventually. One of the staff had picked her up on their way home, shaking like a stray dog by the side of the road. And everyone had apologised profusely at breakfast the next day – 'We all thought you'd got into one of the other taxis.' It soon became a bit of a laugh – an anecdote trotted out on the rare occasions they were all together – but it hadn't been remotely funny at the time.

'Mu-um, can you turn up the heating?' Chloe whined suddenly, pulling up her hood. 'I'm freezing to death.'

'OK! OK!' said Roz and reached across the controls.

When she looked up, she saw it – the cone of light advancing, blinding her, as an oncoming car crossed the centre line, overtaking a tractor in front. Instinctively, Roz braked hard, swerving towards the muddy verge, avoiding the dry stone wall. The engine cut out and she looked round, expecting crumpled metal and carnage, but there were only red tail lights disappearing in the distance.

The car radio still burbled incongruously – a cheesy show tune that made her feel sick – and she rested her head on the wheel.

Chloe's voice came from the back: 'It's OK, Mum. Don't worry. We're OK.'

Roz reached up her sleeve for her tissue and sat up in her seat. This wasn't how things were supposed to be. Her daughter shouldn't have to be the calm one, having to comfort her like this: it should be the other way around.

'I'm fine, love,' Roz sniffed, pressing her eyes hard with her knuckles to wake herself up. 'I'm fine. It was just a big shock, that's all.' She turned round in her seat and reached for Chloe's hand. 'Let's just get home now, shall we?'

Chloe smiled and nodded, and Roz smiled back.

'Right!' she said. And as she fumbled to start the car, she thought the unthinkable. Maybe her mother was right. Fiona had said the same thing after all, albeit in a nicer way. Maybe she did need to toughen up. To pull herself together and stay in one piece. For Chloe's sake.

CHAPTER FIVE

The following morning, Roz packed Chloe off to before-school club, then left for work. In town, she got off the bus at her usual stop and headed across the cobbles to The Old Hall Hotel. There was something in the solidity of its stone-built façade, glistening in the drizzle, that momentarily comforted her – something in the plaque announcing that Mary Queen of Scots had stayed there in 1576.

Roz stepped into the revolving door and out into the lobby. Mondays in the hotel could be depressing at the best of times. The couples who'd arrived on Friday for 'a romantic weekend in a picturesque spa town on the edge of the Peak District' were all hanging around with their wheelie-cases, hung-over and waiting to leave. And the weekday guests – the middle-aged businessmen in suits – were arriving to take their place.

Angie was already at her desk when Roz pushed open the door to the stuffy back office the two of them shared.

'Morning,' Angie chirruped, tapping at her phone with

long, hot-pink nails that belied her sixty-two years. 'How was the weekend? Get up to anything exciting?'

Roz hung her coat on the back of the door, stalling for time. Angie knew nothing about Daniel – no-one at work did – but she was tempted to tell her the truth about her weekend. The impulse soon passed. Angie would only feign shock and concern, then go round and tell the whole building, from the chef in the restaurant to the girls in house-keeping to the bottle-washer in the residents' bar. To coin a phrase of her mother's, she had 'a mouth like the Clyde Tunnel'.

'Not really,' said Roz, forcing a smile. 'You?'

'Oh, it was pretty low-key,' said Angie. 'I went for a power walk in the Pavilion Gardens on Saturday morning. Then the grandkids came round for a sleep-over – so our Della and Nick could go out for their anniversary and have a few drinks and whatnot – and then we all went to the carvery for Sunday lunch when they came to pick them up.'

'Nice one,' said Roz. She wasn't in the mood for Angie's 'happy families' shtick this morning. 'By the way...' She went over to check the wall-planner. 'Have we got any new wedding bookings for May next year?'

'I don't think so,' said Angie. 'Fancy a brew?'

'Yes please,' said Roz and checked the planner again for today's agenda. Some local lads were coming in for a meeting at ten. They were interested in setting up a monthly comedy night at the hotel and she'd have to take them down to the 'Pauper's Pit' – the tiny little theatre in the basement, which Dalton, their boss, grandly called the 'performance space'.

It was the place she'd first met Daniel – that day back in June, when he'd come in to book it for his band. It was a small charity gig for the local hospice and he'd wanted to ensure it had everything they needed. He'd been so apologetic for taking up her time and had smiled as soon as he saw the place. The little stage would be 'perfect', he'd said, bounding up onto it – and so would the adjoining bar. She'd asked what kind of music they played and was surprised when he said 'folk'. He'd looked a bit clean-cut for that sort of thing, in a white fitted shirt and smart trousers that she later learned were his work clothes.

There was a knock on the office door and Kerry from Reception popped her head in to say that the 'comedy lot' had arrived, a few minutes early. But when Roz stood up, she felt light-headed, unsure she could go through with it.

'Angie?' she said, when Kerry had gone. 'Would you mind going and showing those guys the Pauper's Pit? It's just...' She pointed at the unread emails on her computer screen. 'I've got loads to catch up with...'

'Sure. No problem,' said Angie, brightening at the thought of some new people to talk to.

When she'd gone, Roz ignored her inbox and got straight to typing an email to Kate:

Hi Kate,

Congrats! Thanks for telling me about the engagement – not!

(Was that a bit too passive aggressive? Too sarky? Never mind. She was past caring.)

My mother told me all about it at Fiona's yesterday. God, she was loving having one over on me – knowing something I didn't, relishing the chance to fill me in...
Anyway, I'm really pleased for you and Sam. Obviously!
Which date in May were you thinking of for the wedding, so I

can put it in the calendar? The hotel calendar, I mean. My own social diary isn't exactly packed.

Take care and speak soon,

Roz xxx

P.S. I'm a bit surprised you've decided to come back up here to get married. When you could book some swanky place down south!

Roz pressed send and looked at her watch. Work could wait. Instead, she clicked on the showbiz gossip sections of the Sunday papers she'd missed yesterday. Then she'd have an early lunch.

When she returned twenty minutes later with a Boots-meal-deal, the office was empty. Angie had gone out; Dalton was away on one of his dubious 'business trips'; Kate hadn't replied yet.

Roz threw herself into answering her emails, and when it turned five o'clock, she kept going for an extra half hour till she'd cleared them all. Chloe had a netball game after school this evening – an away match – and wouldn't be back till late.

Back at home, Roz fried off some onions and mushrooms and added a jar of pasta sauce. As it bubbled away on the hob, she settled down to watch a TV gameshow, but the host's lame banter with the contestants was too much and she switched it off.

She got out her phone again. Why wasn't Kate replying

to her? She should've finished work by now. Maybe she was embarrassed she'd forgotten to tell her about the engagement. Or maybe her email had overstepped the mark.

Roz scrolled through her phone reading Daniel's old messages – again. He'd always been so chatty in person, but a man of few words in his texts: *Cheers*; *See you at one*; *I'm sorry I won't be able to make it later, something's come up*. That, and the occasional *Goodnight* text that had warmed her heart, that showed he'd been thinking of her at the end of the day. But that was it. There were no voicemails, so she couldn't listen to his rich, resonant voice. No grinning selfies or photos of them together. Nothing.

Not even on Facebook. Daniel had never even signed up to it. As a teacher, he'd said it would be dangerous for him. The last thing he wanted was to be stalked by the kids at school – or, or even worse, their parents, checking up on him. Not that he had anything to hide: he just didn't want them coming across the odd drunken photo that looked worse than it was – or the sweary comments that his mates would sometimes leave after Derby County got thrashed again at home. Daniel had found the whole concept of Facebook quite sinister: a website that began as a tool for American frat boys to judge women on their looks that had evolved, effectively, into a worldwide surveillance system. And that was before all the 'fake news' stuff came to light – before it became a super-spreader of far-right propaganda that was destroying democracy. He'd got quite animated about it at the time and Roz had vehemently agreed with him.

But she hadn't revealed her real reason for avoiding Facebook: that she didn't want to advertise the fact she was living a sad, boring life in the town she grew up in, and that every attempt to change her life had ended in failure; that she couldn't bear comparing herself with the smug posts and perfect lives of Natasha, Vicky and the rest of them – the 'hashtag blessed' crowd. She'd hoped that things might change with Daniel in her life, but that was out the window now.

To distract herself, she picked up her book from the coffee table. Between the pages was the postcard he'd sent her a couple of weeks ago from the stag weekend – 'Whitby Abbey at Sunset' – which she'd been using as a bookmark. She read his looping, arty handwriting for the hundredth time:

Dear Roz,

You said nobody sends postcards these days, but – ta dah!
It's been a fairly calm one so far – we're all so old and boring these days. Just chilling on the beach now.
You'd love it here, by the way. We'll have to come back some time and explore the place properly.

Yours,

Dx

She sighed, but then her phone buzzed on the couch next to her. It was Kate, replying to her email at last:

Hi Roz,

I'm sooo sorry... My mother and her big mouth! Sam only proposed on Saturday night. We'd gone down to Sussex to see her parents and then, just as we were upstairs getting ready to go out for dinner with them, she produced this ring out of nowhere. I had no idea!!!

I was going to tell you soon – HONEST. It's just… I would have felt a bit shitty ringing up with my 'happy news' – just after you'd had one of the most horrible shocks of your life. Please say you're not upset with me. I'd hate to think I was making things worse for you…

Anyway, I'm looking forward to getting married back in Buxton! The Old Hall's got character – it's not one of those soulless modern venues, all beige carpets and Farrow & Ball paint. Those places are all the same. And Sam agrees with me. She's looking forward to seeing her northern in-laws in their natural habitat. She reckons it'll be like an episode of Gavin & Stacey!

So, we were hoping to have it on the 10th of May (a Friday). Will you be in charge of organising it? And what about planning the menu and all that stuff? When do I need to think about that sort of thing? Not for a while yet, I hope…

Right, I need to go and get on with my packing. I'm off to Budapest in the morning. One of my clients – an investment banker – she's got meetings over there and she's paying me to go with her for a few days to give her personal training. Can you believe it? More money than sense, some people…

You take care of yourself and let's catch up soon.

Kate x

Roz closed the message. Yes, she *would* be in charge of organising the wedding, unfortunately. Her and Angie. It was the part of the job she hated the most. Arranging other people's 'big days' – with entitled, princessy types obsessing over chair sashes and 'lady favours'. At least Kate was sensible and wouldn't be into all that stuff. That was something.

The doorbell rang and Chloe arrived home, rosy-cheeked, filling the house with life and fresh air. 'I'm starving! What's for tea?' she asked, and launched into the details of their netball win over Stockport Primary.

'Hold on! One thing at a time,' laughed Roz, taking her coat and hanging it up. Her own cheerfulness surprised her; maybe things weren't so bad after all.

CHAPTER SIX

On Saturday morning, Roz was cleaning Chloe's room, dusting around the cactus plants on the windowsill. She wondered when the posters of birds and wildlife on the walls would be torn down, to be replaced by pop stars; it surely wouldn't be long.

Roz changed the duvet and pillowcase on the single bed, then lay down on it for a minute. She'd been a zombie all week from lack of sleep; thoughts of Daniel had haunted her every night. Was he still in a fridge at the hospital? How long would it take for the formalities of a 'sudden death' to be completed, before they could move him to a funeral home and lay him to rest? And would she even be invited? Would Daniel's mate Luke think to contact her to let her know the arrangements? She prayed that he would; the idea of not being able to say a proper goodbye was unbearable.

The sounds of car doors slamming and shrill laughter floated up from the street. She went to the window. It was that time of year again: this year's 'intake' being dropped off at the student house next door by their parents. Three girls stood chatting and hugging in the messy garden while the lone male seemed to have a car of his own that he was busy unpacking. The tallest of the girls – striking in a faux-fur coat and flip-flops, her chestnut hair pulled into a high topknot – was sparking up a fag now the last of the parents had gone. She was trying her best to act all confident and sophisticated – they all were – but Roz could still see the child in their faces. Nevertheless she envied them – their potential stretching ahead of them.

Roz let out a sigh and sat down on the bed. Autumn always used to be her favourite season: she'd always loved its back-to-school, fresh-start vibe, like the first page of a new notebook, that sense of new beginnings.

Not any more.

Eventually, a full week later, there was another call from Luke. The results of the inquest had confirmed the doctors' opinion that an aneurysm had been the cause of death. The body would be released and the cremation would be at two thirty on Tuesday the 9th of October, followed by a gathering at Daniel's parents' house at which everyone was welcome.

'*Cremation?*' Roz couldn't hide her dismay that there would be no grave to visit in the future. At the same time, she was ashamed to be almost looking forward to it – the sole landmark on the desert of grief in front of her.

CHAPTER SEVEN

On the day of the funeral, Roz came home from work at lunchtime and headed upstairs. There wasn't much time to change out of her uniform into her black jumper, skirt and boots.

She brushed her hair, fixed her smudgy eye-liner and rifled in the wardrobe for her black velvet coat; it was old, outdated and a bit too long for general wear, but it'd be just right for today. Then she pinned the hare brooch to the lapel and stuck her umbrella in her bag – she'd already decided to leave the car at home so she could have a drink later if she wanted.

She wished she could have one now. The old palpitations she'd thought were a thing of the past were fluttering again in her chest and, if experience was anything to go by, they'd only get worse as the day went on. The thought of meeting his friends and family for the first time, under the worst of circumstances, was overwhelming. The first – and the last – time.

Then she remembered the beta blockers in the bathroom cabinet that she'd needed to get through her driving test a few years ago. They were well past their use-by date, but she downed two of them anyway. They wouldn't do any harm.

Ten minutes later she was on the bus, settling into her seat, wiping the steamed-up window with her cuff. She wasn't sure exactly where she had to get off and the last thing she needed was to miss her stop.

Her phone pinged with a text. It was Angie: *Hope your OK lovey. Thinking of you.* Roz frowned at the grammar, then felt guilty. Dalton was away – again – and it had been good of Angie to cover her work this afternoon; all Roz had told her was that it was a 'family funeral'.

When Roz stepped off the bus, she felt the *smirr* – the fine rain – on her face; it was one of her mother's old Scots words but it seemed to fit perfectly. She pulled up the collar of her coat and began the schlep up the wide, open road to the crematorium, but she was soon sweating from the exertion. A few cars overtook her on the way: a low-slung silver Mercedes, a white Audi hatchback and a couple of VW camper vans that were fashionably dishevelled. God knew how she must appear to these people – a pathetic, lone figure like a heroine from a Hardy novel? One of the cars slowed down as it approached her, but she didn't look up in case they offered her a lift. She wasn't up for small talk with strangers. Not yet.

Roz reached the side gate at the top and stopped for a moment to check the time. Only ten past two. She didn't want to arrive too soon and have to sit there on her own like a lemon. She needed to time it right, arriving just before the start, so she walked a slow lap of the Garden of Remembrance, pausing to read the plaques. They were all from the

39

seventies and eighties, and she wondered where the recent ones were and where Daniel's would go.

She checked her watch again, took a deep breath and switched off her phone to avoid any more texts from Angie beeping away at the wrong moment. Then she headed for the main building and the heavy double doors that were wedged open to show an interior that was modern and light, even on a dingy day like this. Two middle-aged bearded men – Daniel's older brothers? – were standing there, dressed bizarrely in loud shirts under summer blazers, handing out orders of service to the mourners. They smiled kindly at Roz when it was her turn and told her to sit anywhere.

The strains of a traditional ballad came from the PA system as Roz scanned the hall in front of her. It was nearly full, with brightly clad people clustered in groups, all chatting and hugging each other. She started up the aisle like a sorrowful bride until she saw it: a huge photo of Daniel's smiling face on a sturdy wooden easel. To the right of it, in front of the pale blue curtain, sat his light oak coffin under a spray of white lilies. She felt herself shake – a sudden tremor breaking through the protective cordon of the beta blockers – and she stopped to centre herself.

When she dared to look up, she caught the eye of a skinny guy with fair, shaggy hair and glasses, standing up ahead. He too had a beard and seemed to be looking out for her.

'I'm Luke,' he said, stepping forward. 'Are you... Roz?'

'Yes.' Roz smiled, relieved.

'And this is Jenny,' he said, as a shy, slim woman of

similar age and colouring came and joined them. 'We're getting married in a few weeks,' he went on, blushing and taking Jenny's hand. 'Dan would've been best man.'

'Such a shame,' said Roz, realising that the Whitby stag do must have been Luke's, and they both nodded sadly.

'I feel a bit... drab,' said Roz, pointing at her clothes.

'Ah, sorry, that's my fault,' said Luke. 'I forgot to tell you the dress code. The family didn't want the funeral to be all sombre.'

Jenny touched Roz's arm. 'Would you like to sit with us?' she asked.

Roz felt pathetically grateful, less like an interloper. 'That would be great,' she said and followed them to the front.

They took their seats on the bench just behind Daniel's mum. Roz had never met her, but the resemblance was unmistakeable: the same dark hair and cheekbones, the same cleft in her chin. She was wearing a fuchsia trouser suit over a cream blouse, which only emphasised her red-rimmed eyes. Daniel's shell-shocked dad and younger sister were sitting either side of her, arms linked, supporting her. And further along at the end of the row, there was an elderly woman in a wheelchair, who Roz assumed was his grandma.

As two thirty approached, Daniel's mum looked round at the rest of the room. She caught Luke's eye and gave the saddest of smiles. Roz found her dignified stoicism almost unbearable – and Jenny must have felt the same, as she began to sob gently and fished in her bag for a tissue. Luke himself was biting his lip, and Roz stared at the floor in front of her, keeping a tight lid on her own emotions. She had no entitlement – no real right – to break down in front of the family and friends who'd known and loved Daniel forever. She'd do her crying later.

The noise levels were rising, along with the temperature, and Roz discreetly fanned herself with the order of service. There were quite a few teenagers and kids in attendance – young lads in awkward ties and little girls in poignant party dresses. And all the rows were full now, with the latecomers having to congregate at the back: they looked like they were his music pals, dressed in jeans and band T-shirts, most trailing girlfriends behind them.

A couple of indie chicks with long, flowing hair had also just turned up. Wearing crocheted tops and mini-skirts, they were self-consciously holding hands in a way Roz found intensely annoying, as they squeezed themselves in next to some others from a different tribe – solid men in pastel shirts and chinos; kind-faced women in unseasonal floaty tops and heels – most probably Daniel's teacher colleagues from school.

Then the music stopped and the chatter gave away to silence as the female vicar stood up at the front.

The first hymn was a gusty rendition of 'The Lord Is My Shepherd', but Roz's throat wouldn't open to sing it. Likewise, the words of the familiar bible reading were suddenly agonising – 'and the greatest of these is love'.

Daniel's eldest brother was called up to give the eulogy, and the Daniel Roz knew came into view: his love of dogs, his veganism, his passion for music and for passing this on to the children he taught. But so did the side of him she'd never now experience – his flaws that weren't flaws at all. She laughed along, but secretly begrudged the anecdotes of lost passports, missed connections, boozy antics – and the knowing laughs they provoked around the hall. And as the ceremony reached its end, she found herself bristling jeal-ously at his brother's closing words – 'Everyone who met Daniel fell in love with him' – and the rumble of recognition that followed.

It took the slow rise of the little blue curtain – and the disappearance of his coffin through it – to shock her out of it.

CHAPTER EIGHT

After the service, Luke and Jenny gave Roz a lift to the wake at Daniel's parents' house. All Roz's nervousness dissolved when she stepped inside; the high-ceilinged hallway had a cosy, homely, comfortable vibe – full of rugs and wellies and half-chewed dog toys.

'Let's get a drink,' said Luke, and the three of them trailed through to the kitchen where Daniel's mum was removing the clingfilm from a home-made buffet, watched by two hopeful spaniels.

Luke introduced Roz to her – as Daniel's 'good friend' – and Roz was miffed, but immediately realised how ridiculous she was being.

'Lovely to meet you, Roz,' said Daniel's mother.

'It was a beautiful service,' Roz said, cringing at her own platitude. 'And it's such a pretty Garden of Remembrance up there.'

His mother smiled at her. 'Ah, well... We're actually going to scatter his ashes up at Solomon's Temple.'

'Oh?' said Roz, taken aback. The old stone 'tower' that

crowned the hills of the Buxton skyline seemed to her an odd choice – a cold, exposed spot for a final resting place.

'Daniel loved it there,' said his mother. 'He called it his "thinking place".'

Roz nodded, although this was news to her.

'We've got permission to plant a tree up there in his memory,' his mother added.

'Ah, lovely. That's perfect.'

'Thanks, dear,' his mother said, then surprised Roz by hugging her tight. 'Thanks so much for coming today. And remember... I want you all to stay in contact. I don't want to lose touch with all Daniel's friends.' It was mainly directed at Luke, but Roz was touched at being included.

Luke squeezed Daniel's mum's arm and led Roz and Jenny away towards the living room. Standing in the doorway was a tall guy with short dreadlocks and a long waistcoat, who embraced Luke as soon as he saw him. 'Luke, man! Sorry I missed the service. I couldn't get away from work, but I wanted to come here and pay my respects to the family.'

'Hassim!' Luke patted him on the back. 'Jenny, Roz, this is Hassim. He's from Mali originally. He met Daniel when they were running a "world choir" in Manchester – for refugees now living in the city.'

Hassim shook their hands warmly. He had a good energy about him and Roz could easily see how he and Daniel would become friends. She didn't know much about Mali – or choirs – but she was happy to ask questions and Hassim seemed just as happy to answer them. Luke and Jenny drifted off to talk to some friends, but she didn't mind in the slightest. She felt more alive than she had done in years, talking to someone whose life experiences were so different from her own; it was a welcome change from the soul-sucking pleasantries she had to endure at work.

Hassim eventually excused himself to go and fetch something from his car and Roz took herself off to the loo, threading her way through the knots of people in the busy room, catching snippets of conversation here and there: what a shock it had all been; how you never knew what was around the corner; and how important it was to seize the day, live life to the full and not put things off.

She arrived back just as Luke and Jenny were looking for her with more drinks: beer and fizzy water for themselves and another glass of wine for her. They were followed by two young women clutching identical bottles of purple cider – the hand-holding indie chicks from earlier.

Luke introduced them to Roz. 'This is Zoe and Flo. They sometimes join our band on stage when we're doing bigger gigs and need some BVs.'

'BVs?' said Roz.

'Backing vocals!' the girls chorused.

'Ah, yes. Daniel mentioned something about that,' Roz lied, and they smiled sweetly at her. They looked like they were probably sisters – much younger than they first appeared – and Roz regretted her previous unkind thoughts.

'Is Tara here?' Zoe asked Luke.

'Eh, nope,' said Luke quickly. 'She couldn't make it.'

Then Flo spoke up: 'Do you know what's happening with the band? Will you be carrying on, y'know... without Daniel?'

Luke let out a big sigh. 'I don't really know. It's a bit early to say. I'll let you know once we've had a chance to talk about it.'

Jenny threw her arm around his waist just as Hassim

turned up again with some drums that looked like bongos, but bigger. He nodded at Luke, who nodded back, and then the two of them began to sing over the rhythm Hassim was beating out – a sad lament Roz had never heard before. Jenny slipped her arm through Roz's as everyone from the rest of the house drifted into the room to listen. Roz would normally have been mortified by this sort of thing – a spontaneous show of raw emotion, people drawing attention to themselves – but not in this case. Instead, she felt safe, like she belonged.

And she wanted to get drunk. The second glass of wine had hit her bloodstream, warming her up, making her pleasantly light-headed. But it was impossible: she knew she had to prise herself out of this cosy cocoon to get home in time for Chloe.

The singing stopped and Roz turned to the window, watching the wind-blown copper leaves and the grey swirling woodsmoke from the bonfire next door. *Dreich* would be her mother's word for the weather now – drizzly and bleak.

'I need to go,' she said, turning back to Luke and Jenny.

'So soon?' said Jenny, as though she actually cared. 'Do you need a lift home? I've only had mineral water, I can—'

'No. Thanks.' Roz assured her. 'I'm fine. Honestly.'

'OK,' said Jenny and squeezed her hand. 'It's been really nice to meet you, albeit under rubbish circumstances.'

'Likewise,' smiled Roz, and Luke walked her to the front door, where Daniel's mum was welcoming some late arrivals.

'Do you want to borrow an umbrella?' Daniel's mum asked Roz. 'It's looking a bit dodgy out there.'

'Er, yes. Please,' said Roz and took it for some reason, even though she had one in her bag.

Daniel's mum headed back to the kitchen to see to her guests, and Luke gave Roz a peck on the cheek. 'Bye, Roz,' he said. 'And by the way, all Daniel's mates... we're going to have a bit of a memorial "get-together" for him at some point – a night of music and stuff. I'll keep you posted.'

～

Back home that night, with Chloe in bed, Roz went to the kitchen and fixed herself a large whisky. She didn't normally touch the hard stuff, but even her mother had been known to have a dram after a funeral.

Then she slumped down on the sofa. She'd thought she'd feel better after today – that she'd have a sense of closure – but in some ways it was the start of feeling worse. She had the curse of knowledge now – had seen what she was missing out on. A future not only with Daniel, but with his friends and family too. His mum and dad. His friends from the band. Luke and Jenny. She should have been going to their wedding, where she would have *counted* for something as 'the best man's partner'. What a contrast from her own family, where she was just an afterthought for her mother and sister. A shadow of a person who had to fit around the others. The real people. The people who mattered.

She threw back a fiery mouthful and tried her best to cry, but found she couldn't. She was too exhausted, too empty, too damn *disappointed*. Sitting up on her own like this every night. With no-one in her corner. No-one to relax and 'do nothing' with.

Draining the glass, she wondered if the wake was still going and thought about pouring herself another drink. But she decided against it. That wasn't going to help her. She had to do something else. Had to talk to someone. That's what these mental health awareness campaigns always said. *Seek help. Don't suffer in silence. It's good to talk. Reach out to your loved ones. Tell someone.* But that was all bollocks if no-one was interested and your loved ones only pushed you away.

Maybe professional help was the answer. Some counselling. She could try, like she'd tried in the past, but the NHS was so stretched she wouldn't be able to get an appointment for months, if at all. Or she could go private. *Over-indulgent*, her mother would have called it. *Seeing a shrink.* But it didn't matter. She couldn't afford it anyway.

Roz reached for the remote and flicked on the telly – *Newsnight*: a panel of puce-faced men shouting over each other – and switched it off again. Then she picked up her tablet and typed 'bereavement support groups' into Google.

There were loads of websites – pages of them – full of moving stories and testimonials alongside photos of wholesome men and women in brightly coloured anoraks, grinning at the camera, raising money for all sorts of charities. Scrolling through them was comforting and, also, strangely addictive.

One in particular piqued her interest – Grief United – aimed at people in the north-west of England. It seemed more sophisticated and slick – less cheesily earnest – than the others.

Curious, she clicked on the Members' Area for a nosy around, but that was the end of the trail. She couldn't see any more without logging in.

CHAPTER NINE

'I mean, you have to laugh, don't you?' said Angie, ripping open the pile of office post. Loudly.

'You do,' said Roz. Angie had been talking at her all morning, regaling her with the latest hilarious developments on her family WhatsApp group, but Roz wasn't feeling it. Her eyes stung from staring at her screen and her shoulder was stiff from gripping the mouse too tightly, flitting from one boring spreadsheet to another. The last few days had passed in a blur; it was Friday again and she couldn't really remember how she'd got here – couldn't shake the image of Daniel's coffin disappearing through the gap like some God-awful gameshow.

Angie stood up and grabbed her coat. 'I'll hear all about it over lunch no doubt.'

'Oh. Right. Yeah,' said Roz, rolling her eyes as Angie left to go and meet her daughter at Pizza Express. Although if Roz was honest with herself, she envied their easy relation-ship: hardly a day went by that they didn't speak to each other; they holidayed together; spent their weekends together; and generally lived in each other's pockets. Nothing at all like her own experience.

Roz closed her spreadsheet and opened up Instagram, the only social media site she could bear these days. She loved a little glimpse into the unattainable lives of the rich and famous. At least they were unattainable for everyone. Like Angie's glossy celeb magazines, it transported her from the dreary reality of her own existence to a world of alpine chalets, palm-fringed beaches and Cotswold retreats.

In the silence, her mobile sounded, making her jump. It was Kate.

'Hiya,' said Kate, cheerfully. 'I thought I'd give you a quick call. I've got a "window" before my next client at two.'

Roz smiled to herself, as she always did when Kate came out with that daft corporate-speak she'd picked up down south.

'So. How was the funeral?' Kate asked.

'It was... nice.'

'Nice?'

'His friends and family were lovely. Especially his mum. She took the time to be really kind to me – given how upset she was.'

The door opened behind Roz and she could sense it was Dalton. She could also sense his irritation at finding her on the phone; he walked out again, leaving the door wide open. She wondered what he wanted. It wasn't like him to show an interest in anything she was doing. They hardly ever saw him these days.

'So how are you bearing up?' Kate asked her. 'Have you got some, y'know, moral support – someone to talk to?'

'*Moral support?* Oh yeah, Fiona and Mum are always on

the phone, checking to see how I am. No. Not really... I didn't even tell them about the funeral.'

'Oh.' Kate paused. 'Is there anyone else you can talk to then? Someone at work?'

'Definitely not.'

'A neighbour then?' Kate said doubtfully. 'Or, I don't know, one of the other school mums?'

'Hmm,' said Roz. 'The neighbours are a bunch of stoner students that change every year, and all Chloe's friends' mums – well they're nice enough, but they're all "smug marrieds". They don't invite me anywhere in case I steal their husbands. Like *that's* gonna happen.'

'Have you thought about internet dating?' asked Kate. 'To take your mind off things.'

Roz bit her tongue. As if some random off Tinder could replace Daniel. 'Honestly? That's the last thing I'm interested in, I can assure you.'

'Sorry... I'm not sure what to say,' said Kate. 'What is it that agony aunts always suggest – meditation? Voluntary work? Get a dog?' She began to chuckle and stopped herself.

'Well,' said Roz, uncertainly. 'I've been looking at some bereavement groups on the internet and I've found one for widows and widowers. They organise lots of different social events and activities and stuff.'

'That sounds hopeful,' said Kate, encouragingly, although Roz knew 'organised fun' would be Kate's worst nightmare.

'Yeah, well,' said Roz. 'It would be quite tricky for me. Because of Chloe...'

'Even if you just talked to someone online, someone in the same boat who understands. Not a useless bell-end like me!'

Roz laughed. 'That's the thing. I'm *not* in the same position as them, am I? I'm not a widow as such – or a long-term partner. I'm not really entitled. I'd feel like, I dunno, an imposter compared to them.'

'Not entitled?' Kate was unconvinced. 'Look, you can tell them whatever you like. As much or as little as you want. No-one's going to be checking up on you.'

'I think I'd rather just tell the truth.'

'Fine. Do that then,' said Kate. 'It's enough that you, like, *identify* as a widow. So get yourself on there! And anyway, you might find yourself a hunky widower. I was reading about this. Widowers are the gold standard apparently – they've been around the block and completed the course!'

'Kate!' said Roz, shocked. 'What a thing to say...'

Roz sensed that Dalton was looming up behind her again, hovering this time. 'It's one of our new wedding clients,' she muttered to him and he looked sceptical, but disappeared and left her to it.

'Speaking of the wedding,' said Kate. 'I wanted to ask... Would you be my maid of honour?'

'Of course,' said Roz quickly. She was touched, but half-expecting it too, as Kate had no sisters.

'And do you think Chloe would like to be my brides-maid? I only want one. Having loads of bridesmaids would look ridiculous at my age. And anyway, I wouldn't want to offend any friends or family by not including them.'

'Like it?' said Roz. 'She'll be dead chuffed. Thanks, Kate.'

'No, thank *you* both. But listen, I've got to rush off now. My client's trying to get through. With any luck she's cancelling me and I can start the weekend early! Have a good one, OK? Speak soon. Bye... Bye.'

Roz looked at her phone and smiled. Chloe would be

totally delighted at the thought of being Auntie Kate's brides-maid and she couldn't wait to tell her.

But 'maid of honour'? Really? It made Roz sound ancient. Like a maiden aunt. Or an 'old maid'. The spotlight would really be on her – the only one of their group of school friends who'd stayed in their old home town. The single mother of an only child. With no partner in sight.

Unless she could find one by the 10th of May, which was unlikely to say the least. Maybe she could pay someone, she thought grimly.

CHAPTER TEN

Dalton hung around the hotel like a bad smell every day for the next week. His sudden continuous presence was setting off alarm bells for the workforce, helped by a rumour in *The Buxton Courier* that The Old Hall – and the Georgian Crescent that formed the centrepiece of the town – was to be sold off to a big US conglomerate. Roz wasn't surprised. She couldn't believe it hadn't happened years ago: Buxton could easily be the north's answer to Bath, if it was shown the same amount of love, care – and, most of all, money. The hotel staff were naturally worried about the consequences for their jobs – and Roz knew she should be worried as well, but she didn't have the bandwidth for it at the moment. She couldn't think that far ahead. All she knew was she needed to get out for a walk at lunchtime – for some air and a break from the latest round of gossip.

She crossed over the road to the Buxton Opera House side. The exquisite Edwardian theatre – now home to stand-up comedians, juke-box musicals and the much-loved panto at Christmas – glowed like an orb in the drab October light.

She passed through the gate to the Pavilion Gardens, past the bandstand and the mulchy flower beds, mincing carefully down to the River Wye which flowed through them, trying not to slip on the wet yellow leaves. The last time she'd taken this walk was during another lunch hour four months ago – with Daniel. It had been their first sort-of-date, after he'd called her up at work and asked if she'd like to join him for a take-away salad in the park. He'd even brought a rug for them to sit on.

Now, Roz took a seat on a wrought iron bench and pulled her collar up, digging her hands deep in her pockets. That day back in June had been a scorcher, so hot there was a heat haze – very unusual for Buxton. It was, allegedly, the highest town in England and it had been known to snow here in June. Daniel had laughed that day behind his mirrored sunglasses that made him look exotic like a film star. 'I always think of it as England's answer to La Paz in Bolivia – the highest capital city in the world,' he'd joked, telling her how he'd trekked the Inca Trail with Luke back in their youth, constantly touching her arm to make a point. Roz normally couldn't bear gap year stories – they brought back too many painful memories of her own disastrous trip to Australia – but she'd have been happy to listen to him all day long and expected it was the same for his pupils at school. She closed her eyes, recalling the smell of his freshly washed shirt and how she'd imagined his body under it. She remembered his strong, supple hands and tanned forearms and how much she'd looked forward to hearing him play his guitar. Which she now never would.

The park had been crowded that day, full of flowers, spring foliage and families. Mums – and some dads – who looked too young to have two or three kids, some no more than children themselves, had been letting their little darlings run riot, while the older kids queued for the ice-cream van. The older mums – those her own age – had fussed around their offspring more anxiously. And for a moment that day, she'd allowed herself to imagine a fragment of that future for herself.

Roz shivered as the cold metal of the bench radiated through her body, up her spine. She got up and went for a stroll through town, retracing the route she and Daniel had taken that day. The World Cup had been on at that time and all the shops and cafés had had their bunting out, the flags of all the nations fluttering in the breeze. That 'Three Lions' song had floated out from the open doors of every pub and everyone had been in a good mood. So different from today.

The walk back to work took her past La Trattoria, the Italian where she was meant to go with Daniel the day he died. She couldn't look at it though: one glimpse of a lunchtime couple through one of the candlelit arches might set her off again.

She hurried on until a flash of pink and purple caught her eye up ahead: a new craft and gift shop – Serendipity – that had just opened. In the window, there was loads of stuff that Chloe would love: Himalayan salt lamps; bracelets made from 'Blue John', the semi-precious purple stone from the local caverns in Castleton; mugs with different dog breeds printed on the side. She checked her watch and pushed open the door into the warm, womb-like interior, which smelt of musky vanilla. Cheery pop tunes played from a speaker on the wall, but there was no-one behind the till.

Feeling self-conscious, Roz poked around the shelves, stopping by a white Welsh dresser with a full display of coloured pens, pencil cases, post-it notes and other fancy stationery. She would have to bring Chloe down here at the weekend and let her choose something.

Towards the back of the shop, she reached the Hallowe'en section and recoiled. She hated all that stuff and always had: the skeletons, spider webs and fake blood – not the sort of images she needed in her brain, although Chloe would doubtless love them too.

'Can I help you with anything, dear?' said a voice behind her.

Roz turned round. The woman was tall and stately – around her mother's age – with her hair in a pinky-grey bob. She wore a bolero cardigan over dungarees and electric blue glasses on a string.

'Er, no, thank you,' said Roz. 'I have to get back to work. But I'm going to come back at the weekend and bring my daughter. She's ten. *Very* into stationery.'

The woman smiled. 'Aren't they all? My granddaughters helped me choose my stock. I've never seen them so interested in anything!'

Roz smiled at her. Something about her reminded her of Daniel's mum.

'Well, feel free to have a browse any time,' said the woman. 'Any questions, let me know.'

'Thanks,' said Roz. 'Will do.' She felt obliged to hang around a few minutes more, looking at stuff, as it would have felt rude just to leave. At the back, there was a wall with all kinds of signs on it. 'Live, Laugh, Love.' 'I love my hubby and his credit cards.' Who bought these things? Roz wondered. The 'hashtag blessed' crew on social media. People like Angie. Or possibly Fiona. 'This house runs on prosecco and laughter.' Prosecco and passive aggression, more like. 'Dance like no-one's watching' – well, no-one ever *was* watching Roz, except Chloe, covering her eyes in embarrassment usually... 'Best friends stick together like fat thighs!' Bloody hell, thought Roz. Time to go.

She turned away, just as a familiar song came on the radio – 'Shotgun' by George Ezra. It had been everywhere in the summer. She remembered Daniel belting it out in a comedy pub-singer style, acting out the lyrics to make her laugh. But now tears were pricking her eyes and she felt dizzy and faint and the daylight from the window was closing in to a fine point like a distant tunnel.

A hand was supporting her elbow now, guiding her across the room to a chair in the corner she could just make out. 'Come and sit down, dear,' the shop woman was saying. 'You don't look too well. I'll fetch you some water.'

'I'm fine, I'm fine,' insisted Roz. 'It's just... that song... it reminds me of someone. My... my partner... he died a few weeks ago...'

The woman crouched down beside her, taking hold of her hand. 'Oh, love,' she said. 'I'm so sorry to hear that... Leaving you with young children too.'

'It's so hard,' Roz sniffed, fumbling for a tissue. 'No-one understands...'

'I lost my husband a year ago as well,' the woman said. 'It gets easier. I promise.'

'Thank you so much,' Roz said, standing up, embarrassed. 'I'm sorry, but I've really got to get back to work.'

Her cheeks burned bright scarlet as she made for the door. She could never come back here again.

～

That evening, Chloe wanted fish fingers and oven chips for tea, and Roz was happy to oblige as it meant she didn't have to do any proper cooking. Watching Chloe across the table – the sad slope of her shoulders as she chased the peas around her plate – Roz feared her own misery was infecting her daughter.

'Ruby and her little sister are going to Lapland at Christmas,' said Chloe after a while. 'She's so lucky.'

This hit Roz hard. It wasn't just the trip, which she couldn't afford. It was also that Ruby had a sister to do these things with. Chloe often used to ask if she'd ever have a brother or sister, but she'd given up now. She seemed resigned to knocking about on her own. But Roz hadn't given up hope. There was still time. Still the possibility that she'd emulate her mother, who'd had Fiona when she was forty – a 'change baby', to use the old-fashioned term. Sometimes when Roz woke in the night, slick with sweat, she chose to assume it was grief and anxiety because, frankly, it was better than the alternative – the start of the menopause.

Chloe went upstairs to do her homework while Roz washed up at the sink. She re-lived this afternoon's scene with the shop woman, cringing as she recalled the false impression she'd allowed to stand – the woman's assumption that she'd lost her long-term partner, the father of her 'children'. But it had felt good to be taken seriously for once. To have her grief recognised. The woman's sympathy had felt like a warm bath after a long, hard day. She needed more of this. To be heard. To start the healing process.

Roz dried her hands, fetched her tablet and found the Grief United site again. She had to create an account, enter a username, and she really didn't know what to go for – what 'image' she wanted to project – until she decided on 'Rabbit Heart', her favourite song by Florence and the Machine.

In the Members' Area, on the discussion boards, one thread was miles more popular than the others: *The worst things to say to someone who's grieving*. It seemed mostly to be women commenting, she noted, and they were all using acronyms that she had to look up – BRB, AIBU, AITA.

The original poster, 'Mrs. Bee', hadn't held back: *I can't bear the ones who try to be all Zen about it. The Everything Happens For A Reason brigade. Or This Too Shall Pass. They really grind my gears. Or the folk who say, Time's A Great Healer! like it's an original thought they've just come up with. Yeah, well, no shit Sherlock, but that doesn't really help me in the here and now, does it?*

Well bloody said, Roz muttered, giving the post a thumbs up. It was true, people could be so crap sometimes – so lacking in empathy – people like her mother and Fiona.

Most members on Grief United seemed to agree. Mrs. Bee's post had loads of likes and replies, and Roz found a grim pleasure in reading, and agreeing with, every last one of them.

CHAPTER ELEVEN

For the first time in weeks, Roz slept through the night till her alarm went off. She'd forgotten what a full night's rest felt like and what a difference it made. Everything was easier: just putting her feet on the floor, getting in the shower, having a proper breakfast and a chat with Chloe before school. She even got a seat on the bus to work, where she reached for her phone, keen to see the latest chat on Grief United. The thread from last night was still going strong and, although she hadn't really planned to, she was soon typing a post of her own: *Hi everyone. I'm new here and a bit nervous about posting! I just wanted to say 'Hi' to everyone. I lost my partner a few weeks ago and reading all your posts on here has helped me a lot. When it happened, I got zero sympathy from my own mother and 'little miss perfect' sister who's never had a moment's adversity in her life! It was all so hurtful...* Out of habit, she signed off with her real name, but then deleted it; she would stick with her Rabbit Heart pseudonym for now. *Have a good day, everyone xxx,* she wrote and pressed 'send'.

It was a thrill to see her words there on the screen with

all the other posts. She felt real somehow – proper – as if she counted. But she'd arrived at her stop and had to get off. Besides, the florist's van was outside The Old Hall with its cargo of flowers for a small mid-week wedding they were hosting and she should go and help out.

~

All that day, the likes and comments came in on Roz's post – a steady drip at first, then a flood. They were all so kind and thoughtful, welcoming her to the group, and she couldn't stop herself checking her phone every few minutes; every uptick brought its own little frisson – the little hit of dopamine she'd read about.

Some people began to ask questions, as if they were actually interested in the answers, and Roz duly replied: his name was Daniel; he'd died suddenly of a brain aneurysm; no, she didn't really have any other family or friends to talk to – only her ten-year-old daughter who was much too young to understand.

Then, around three in the afternoon, came the question she'd dreaded: *How long had you two been together?*

Roz swallowed hard and went for it. *Four months*, she replied. A little rounding-up wouldn't do any harm.

Oh, love, came the first reply. *You were only married four months? That's so tough...*

Roz was touched, but wanted to be truthful. *Thanks so much*, she wrote. *But we weren't actually married.*

At which point Dalton stuck his head around the door and coughed theatrically. He had his oily accountant in tow, who wanted to talk to her about outstanding invoices.

'If you've got time, Roz,' Dalton said pointedly, 'could you come and join us in my office?'

~

The impromptu finance meeting took over an hour, to Roz's annoyance. When she finally got back to her office and her phone, the likes and sympathy seemed to have dried up, and for a moment she regretted her honesty.

Then a reply from Mrs. Bee flashed up: *Hi Rabbit Heart. It's really tragic what happened to you and I don't want to be **that person**, but maybe your mum and sister have got a point. I'm not being funny, but four months isn't very long. I'm also assuming he wasn't actually your daughter's dad?*

Roz's face fired up and her heart raced at the tone of the message. *He wasn't*, she replied, trying to stay calm. *But I was about to introduce her to him. I wanted to be sure first. Sure of the relationship. And yes, it might just seem a tragic episode to most people, but my entire future was torn away from me.*

Another reply came in, from someone called 'Blue Eyed Girl': *I think you're being a bit unfair, Mrs. Bee. Whatever the circumstances, it's clear Rabbit Heart needs some support and I'm sure we can give it to her. I think it's important we all just #BeKind.*

But this just provoked Mrs. Bee: *Look*, she wrote. *I'm just one of those people – I call it as I see it. There are some folk on here who've been married forty years with children and grand-children – who've been through long illnesses and all manner of shit life has thrown at them. Or who've been together for years but never got married and now they're in legal purga-tory, trying to sort out wills and pensions and all the rest of it.*

People suffering real financial hardship. People like me! I just think it's a bit disrespectful, that's all. Rabbit Heart should count herself lucky. Things could be a lot worse!

The likes were really flooding in for this one: all the little sycophants flocking around their 'alpha'. Roz's hands were shaking. It was Mrs. Bee who should count herself lucky – lucky to have had someone by her side all those years.

'Are you OK, love?' Angie was looking across the desk at her, frowning. 'Have you had some bad news or something?'

'Nope. I'm fine,' said Roz curtly, going back to her phone.

Blue Eyed Girl was back on again like a scalded cat: *Oh, please don't get me wrong, Mrs. Bee. I didn't mean to minimise your lived experience – yours and many others'. I'm sorry if I expressed myself a bit clumsily. I hope I haven't upset you xxx*

Bloody hell, thought Roz. This one must have splinters in her arse from sitting on the fence...

'Roz, sorry, can I borrow you for a second?' Angie was waving a piece of paper at her. 'Would you mind checking over these figures for me?'

'Eh, yeah, sure,' said Roz and closed down the app. Grief United? What a joke! This group was making things worse, not better. She wouldn't be back.

On the bus home, she tried several times to ring Kate for a moan, but the calls went through to voicemail. Kate was probably avoiding her, fed up listening to her no doubt.

Later on at home, with the dinner dishes done and tidied away, she had a long soak in the bath and went straight to bed. Now that her wounded ego had calmed down, she reflected that Mrs. Bee had maybe had a point. She'd only actually met up with Daniel – she counted on her fingers – five times. And their 'dates' had been fleeting, grabbing a quick lunch or a coffee in the park. Of course people in Mrs. Bee's position had it worse. There was no comparison. She should cut her some slack...

Roz picked up her phone from the bedside table and logged back into Grief United. Some other group members had been sticking up for her in her absence and she was gratified.

And Mrs. Bee had replied to her on the thread again: *Rabbit Heart, I just wanted to say – Sorry for being a dick and flying off the handle. I've been having a really shit time of it lately, but I shouldn't have turned grieving into some kind of gross 'competition'. Sorry again. I really hope we can move on from this x*

Roz was flooded with a combination of relief and delight. *I'm sorry too*, she wrote. *To be honest, I've never really had a serious, long-term relationship and I can see now how thoughtless and insensitive my posts might have come across. Anyway, I hope things get better for you soon x*

Mrs. Bee replied with a big red love heart and Roz smiled to herself. She switched off the lamp and pulled the duvet up to her chin, relaxed at last, until a loud bang in the dark outside made her gasp.

It was followed by the nasal whine of a firework and she let out a long sigh. It was only the 23rd of October, but this would be the norm now, all the way to Bonfire Night.

CHAPTER TWELVE

The next morning, Roz opened her eyes and reached for her phone. A major showbiz scandal had broken in the tabloids overnight. Liz Lockhart, 41 (Why did they always have to mention a woman's age?), breakfast TV's star presenter, had lost her husband to suicide only nine months previously. There had been a massive outpouring of sympathy at the time – the public fully invested in her grief – but the story had now taken a new twist: she'd apparently 'found love' with a new – much younger – man and the *Daily Mail* had the pap shots to prove it.

Roz went straight to Grief United, where a spirited debate was already underway. Some posters thought Liz Lockhart had 'moved on' too quickly, that she 'hadn't grieved enough'. Some others disagreed: *People are entitled to grieve how they want. There's no fixed time limit.* That sort of thing.

But Mrs. Bee and her famous honesty were back: *Well I think it's far too soon. It's disrespectful – to her husband's memory and to his blood family.* And Roz was inclined to agree with her.

The male members of the group had been fairly quiet till now, steering clear of the controversy, but now one of them spoke up: *I disagree. Life goes on. Life is for living.*

Another man backed him up: *This is true. And we should be wary of making blanket judgements. You never know what's going on in someone else's life. It's no-one else's business if you ask me...*

Mrs. Bee didn't respond, but 'Bristol Belle' did: *It's easy for men to say that. Men don't get the same shit as women for this sort of thing*, she wrote. *It's sexist if you ask me. Double standards! Look at Josh Larsson, the racing driver. His wife died of cancer and he was married again within a year. Now he's got a baby on the way. No-one said anything about that.*

Moving on is defo different for men, said someone called 'Granny Greyhips'. *Call me cynical, but every man I've known who's lost his wife young has found a replacement in under a year (usually a younger model). That bothers me. In fact, I know someone who shacked up with someone else within six months of the funeral! The wife was barely cold...*

Then Blue Eyed Girl – fence-sitter extraordinaire – waded in with her words of wisdom: *I think a year sounds about right. Time to grieve. Time to reflect. Time to test your resilience. And it also depends on whether you've got children. Seeing your mother or father so rapidly replaced would add to the pain of losing them.*

Roz pulled a face in spite of herself and checked the time – she had to get up in a minute or she'd be late for work.

But there was a new message on the thread now. From 'MarkG (Moderator)': *Just wanted to say – I think that, if people have been happily married before, they're more likely to want to settle down again with someone else. And if they meet the right person, that could happen quite quickly...*

Roz hadn't really considered this, although it echoed something Kate had said to her. A man who'd had a good marriage till the end was bound to be better husband material than one who'd walked out on his wife or was nursing rage towards his ex. By the time you got to middle age, a widower was a better bet than a man who'd never committed before and wasn't likely to now.

Mrs. Bee popped up: *Yeah well, men who've been waited on hand and foot by their wives are often hopeless at looking after themselves... But there is such a thing as a decent interval. And the women they hook up with aren't much better!* Incongruously, she'd added a crying-with-laughter emoji.

Roz's head was spinning. She felt exhausted before the day had begun. This whole terrain was a minefield and she'd be staying out of it in future.

She jumped out of bed, showered, kissed Chloe goodbye and microwaved some porridge, burning her tongue. She was going to miss the bus if she didn't get a wriggle on. Grabbing her coat and bag and phone, she saw she had a notification from Grief United and stopped for a second. It was a direct message – from MarkG (Moderator): *Hi Roz. I hope you don't mind me contacting you. I'm Mark, one of the discussion board moderators as you've probably guessed! I helped set up the group after I was widowed myself a few years ago. I just wanted to say – I hope you're not feeling too bruised by your run-in with Mrs. Bee yesterday. She can be a bit blunt at times, but her heart's in the right place... Anyway, hope to see you back here soon.*

Roz felt touched by his kindness, but also a bit pathetic that he'd felt the need to contact her.

She sent a quick reply: *Thanks so much for your message,*

Mark – I appreciate it – but there's no need to worry. Every-thing's fine. Truly. Roz. Then she ran out the door.

That's good to hear, he replied later. *I'm glad you haven't been put off. We're a nice bunch really!*

Poor guy, thought Roz. Having to play the peace-maker all the time... It had been nice of him to reach out to her like that. He must feel quite a responsibility for people's well-being – a duty of care almost. She didn't envy him. Not at all.

CHAPTER THIRTEEN

Halloween was a low-key affair, much to Roz's relief. Chloe hadn't seemed all that into it this year – had said she found dressing up a bit 'juvenile', which made Roz laugh – but she was excited about the following Saturday when she'd be going with Ruby's family to the bonfire and fireworks display at Buxton Cricket Ground. It started at 5pm and Ruby's mum had suggested that Chloe come round for afternoon tea beforehand, to fill them up for the evening ahead.

Before that, Uncle Ian – Fiona's husband – was coming round with the promised offcuts from their fancy new carpets, for Chloe's bedroom. Fiona had called to say she wanted rid of them 'asap' as they were getting in the way – and what Fiona wanted, Fiona got.

It was half past twelve when Ian rang the bell, catching Roz up to her elbows in flour, making a chocolate cake for Chloe to take to Ruby's. He was dressed head-to-toe in his cycling gear – the classic middle-aged man in Lycra – and Roz couldn't remember the last time she'd seen him in normal clothes.

Ian wasn't a big one for small talk and, after a brief exchange of pleasantries, got on with the job of carting the rolls of carpet upstairs, while Roz wondered how much it would cost to actually get them fitted. Chloe went with him to show him the way, as if he wouldn't be able to find it in their tiny, matchbox house.

When Ian came back down, alone, it was clear he was building up to saying something. 'Er,' he began. 'Fiona asked me to ask what you're doing for Christmas this year?'

'Er,' said Roz, stalling, trying to think. Fiona was nothing if not well-organised. 'Well... I hadn't really given it any thought,' she said, truthfully.

'Ah, right,' said Ian. 'Well, you're welcome to come to us. And you can stay over if you like. The guest bedroom will be done by then.'

Roz smiled at him. 'Thanks,' she said.

'Your mum's insisting on a three-bird-roast,' he added, shrugging his shoulders. 'It's the in-thing apparently.'

And in that instant, Roz knew she couldn't face it. The conspicuous consumption, Fiona showing off, the pretence at family unity – any of it.

'Actually, I forgot,' said Roz, pretending to smack her forehead. 'I promised Chloe we'd go away for a few days over Christmas.'

'Oh, really? OK,' said Ian. 'Fair enough. I'll let Fiona know... Where you off to?'

'To the... To the coast,' said Roz. 'Whitby!' It was the first thing that sprang to mind: what they'd probably be doing for Christmas if things were different and Daniel was still here.

Chloe came down the stairs in time to hear the gist. She gave Roz a funny look, but kept her mouth shut in front of Ian.

'Whitby? Really?' she asked her mother when he'd gone. She didn't look too impressed.

'Yep,' said Roz, briskly. 'I was thinking it might be a nice idea. For a change.'

Bollocks, she thought, as Chloe went up to get changed for going to Ruby's. Now she'd actually have to get on and book some accommodation. Some crappy place that was still available at this late stage. Chloe wouldn't like that either.

Roz had hoped to get something in the diary for herself this afternoon, so she wouldn't have to spend it mooning around the house on her own while Chloe was out. She'd posted on Grief United earlier in the week, to ask if there were any meet-ups or activities planned this weekend, but had drawn a blank. There was a group of them going walking in Keswick, in the Lake District, but that was it. Nothing within striking distance of Buxton. Not for the foreseeable. It was a shame because she fancied the idea of a long walk in the country-side, filling her lungs with fresh air, taking advantage of the bright, sunny weather.

She dropped Chloe at Ruby's house at two o'clock, for an afternoon of eating her own body weight in sandwiches and cakes with Ruby and her sister. Then she got back in the car. She contemplated the hours stretching in front of her – changing the beds, cleaning the oven, doing the ironing – and decided not to bother. It felt wrong to be doing chores indoors on such a luminous day. Instead, she'd head to the other side of town and take a walk up to Solomon's Temple; she could pay a visit to Daniel's memorial tree, which would surely be in place by now.

The weekend traffic was busy and she was grateful when she reached the car park at the bottom of the hill and found it half empty. As she switched the engine off, the sudden silence was a relief; the constant stream of shout-outs for family and friends that were the life-blood of Saturdays on Radio 2 could get exhausting after a while.

She set off up the trail under the trees in the direction of the stone tower – the 'temple' – at the top. She wasn't a hundred per cent sure exactly what it was, though she had a vague memory of her mother making her and Fiona walk all the way up to it when they were tiny.

There were still enough leaves on the beech, ash and elm trees to make the ascent quite gloomy, but the odd spotlight of sun beamed down between them, lighting up the mossy velvet roots that dug deep into the earth.

She would bring Chloe up here sometime soon, she decided. Chloe loved going to 'forest school' after lessons on a Wednesday and would love reading about the birds, wildlife and fossils on the information panels along the path.

The exertion of the climb was bringing Roz out in a sweat even though the gradient wasn't that steep, and she stopped for a rest at the next bench and watched a scruffy-looking robin bathing in a puddle. She imagined he was smartening himself up in time for the festive season and smiled at the idea. What did robins do the rest of the time? she wondered. Where did they go? She'd never really thought about it, but they must go somewhere.

She got up and carried on for a bit, past the dips and pits of some old lime kilns, and a section of young trees that had recently been planted. They each had their own brass plaque and she read the moving inscriptions one by one, to the mums and dads and grandparents – locals and tourists – who had 'loved this place'. Further along, there were a series of wooden sculptures that had been donated by the Rotary Club and Roz thought she must have missed Daniel's tree, but no, there it was – a silver birch sapling. Her heart lurched as she read the dedication. A poem:

We look up at the sky at night
We know that you're not far
We still can see your shining light
Our brightest northern star

Roz pulled a face. It was a bit twee for her taste. Not exactly W. H. Auden... But then she felt guilty. It was obviously sincere and heartfelt and that was the main thing.

She looked around her. Now she was here, she wasn't sure what to do next, so she carried on up the hill, in the direction of the daylight, eventually emerging onto open grass and the final stretch to the summit.

The squat stone Victorian folly at the top was quite plain up close – the biblical connotations of the name had led her to expect something grander – and she questioned what Daniel had seen in it. An information panel told her it wasn't even that old: *built in 1896 to replace an earlier structure constructed by local farmer and land-owner, Solomon Mycock.* Nothing to do with King Solomon or anything like that. It was, however, a site of significance. It rose from the centre of an ancient burial mound and, during the tower's construction, an archaeological dig had uncovered several Bronze Age skeletons, along with later Roman stuff.

She ventured inside the draughty tower and climbed the rickety wooden steps to the top. But the low sun was blinding and she wished she'd brought her sunglasses. It was only when she turned around to come back down that she really saw the view for the first time and realised why Daniel would have loved it so much. The 360-degree panorama was breath-taking. On the horizon, there was Mam Tor – the shivering mountain – towering over the village of Castleton on the edge of the Hope Valley and, further over, she could make out Kinder Scout, the highest point in Derbyshire and the Peak District. Down below, closer to home, she had a bird's-eye view of some man-made landmarks – the carefully sculpted golf course, the impressive dome of the University of Derby and the dignified sprawl of the town of Buxton.

Roz tried to pin-point the crematorium and Daniel's parents' house. In a parallel universe, she'd be having a cosy night at home with Daniel and Chloe this evening, watching telly and having a takeaway. And tomorrow, the three of them would be going to his parents' house for a chilled Sunday lunch, full of laughter and fun – nothing like lunch with her own family. Or else to Luke and Jenny's place – or a snug country pub with wood panelling and an open fire. Looking down on the town, she wondered where Luke and Jenny lived. Their wedding would be happening soon – maybe even today. In the parallel – better – universe, she'd be with Daniel right now at the reception, sipping champagne, cheering on his best man speech, watching him knock them dead with his tasteful, but funny, jokes.

Her hands were a bit chilly and she blew on them for warmth. She'd been up here a while and it would be dark soon; they'd be getting ready to fire up the bonfire at the cricket ground. Setting off down the hill to the car, she passed no-one, save for a dog-walker and a young couple in outdoor gear and head torches who looked at her like she was mad to be out in just a cardigan.

Back at home, she had about three hours to fill till it was time to collect Chloe. She'd have some cereal and watch a film. There was no point making anything special. Chloe wouldn't be hungry after tea at Ruby's and whatever else she'd had to eat at the firework display – hot dogs, toasted marshmallows and the rest of it. That cliché people always came out with about their kids having a better social life than they did – it was definitely true in her case. And it would only get worse as Chloe got older.

'How were the fireworks?' Roz asked her in the car later.

'Good,' said Chloe.

'Is that it?'

'Yeah.' Chloe paused. 'I just hope there weren't any hedgehogs nesting in the bonfire.'

'Don't worry, sweetheart. They'd have checked all that beforehand.'

Chloe said nothing.

'And how was your afternoon tea? Was our chocolate cake nice?'

'I don't know,' said Chloe. 'I didn't have any.'

'Oh. OK,' said Roz. 'What about the other cakes?'

Chloe shifted in her seat. 'I don't know.'

'You don't know?' Roz watched Chloe's grey-green eyes in the rear view mirror, so like her own.

Chloe shrugged. 'I didn't have any.'

'Why not?' asked Roz.

'Because I don't want to get any fatter...'

'Fatter? What are you on about, you daft thing? You're not fat.'

'I'm fatter than Ruby. And her sister.'

Roz sighed, exasperated. 'Don't say that, love. You're gorgeous!'

'No, I'm not.'

'You *so* are!' said Roz, but she felt a lead weight inside her, at the thought of all this crap starting in earnest. It wasn't the first such comment Chloe had made. Her little body had already started to round out a bit, even though she was only ten. Roz herself had been lucky, a late developer, nearly fourteen before all that had begun.

This also explained why Chloe had lost all interest in baking over the last few months, one of the fun activities they used to do together.

Roz wasn't sure what to say.

CHAPTER FOURTEEN

Roz had booked the Monday off work – not for any particular reason; she just fancied a break – and then regretted it when she saw her inbox on Tuesday. It was full of booking inquiries for Christmas parties and lunches, and most of the emails were long, boring rambles about their food intolerances.

Dalton had also tasked her with replying to any faintly negative reviews that the hotel had received on Tripadvisor, and so she spent the morning politely addressing endless moans about the wi-fi, the weather and all manner of other stuff she had no control over, when all she wanted to do was tell them to get a life.

This job wasn't challenging her brain cells any more, not in the slightest, but it somehow still managed to suck the life from her.

Out of the window, she watched a discarded Waitrose bag float across the railings of the Pavilion Gardens, eventually snagging itself on a spike. The browns and yellows of the trees beyond were all greyed out by the mist, with the odd bare, spindly branch poking through. They were heading towards the business end of autumn now: the season of decay and remembrance and wreaths of red poppies. The 'new term' feeling was long gone, but the desire for something more in life hadn't died in her yet.

She needed to do something about the Arctic tundra of her social diary. But mostly she had to do something about her job – before The Old Hall was presenting her with a carriage clock for 'ten years faithful service' or her role was axed completely, if the rumours were true and the place was to be sold.

She needed a *career*. To make a start at least, before it was too late. Maybe it was too late already. She'd be forty in February. That didn't give her long, but maybe it was the kind of deadline she needed. A kick up the backside. A chance to escape her characterless semi and move to a better area away from her student neighbours, who'd kept her awake all night with their thumping, repetitive music.

She should be seeing what roles were out there, sorting her CV, sending it out to recruitment consultants, all of that stuff. Instead, she was staring at her screen, flicking through the 'sidebar of shame' on the *Daily Mail* website to see what various Z-list celebrities and 'influencers' were up to in Dubai. Self-centred and vacuous as these people were, at least they had a life. They weren't spending their existence in an airless room, bored out of their minds.

When she'd had enough of the *Mail*, she switched to Instagram. Natasha – Roz and Kate's old friend from school – was never off it. Her mum had been a dinner lady who'd struggled to make ends meet, but Natasha had always had a charmed life. Even though she had no formal training, she'd managed to score a job as a lifestyle journalist for Condé

Naste over in the US. She was one of those women who had it all: a high-flying husband, four photogenic kids (two boys, two girls) and an equally photogenic home in upstate New York. Although they were rarely at home. Her husband, James, was a manager for a luxury drinks brand and they always seemed to be travelling, posting photos of cocktails and chinking glasses in airport lounges and seven-star hotels. God, it was depressing...

Roz closed down Instagram and went back to the *Mail*, where it was wall-to-wall coverage of Prince William and Kate and *their* perfect family. There was no escape, it seemed.

When five o'clock rolled round at last, she pulled on her coat and headed outside into the rainy blackness. Rivulets were running along the kerbside to the drains and her feet squelched in her shoes all the way to the bus stop. With any luck, she'd catch her death – or at least a nasty cold – and could call in sick tomorrow and spend the day on her laptop at home, searching for a new job. She might have thought it, but she knew she would never do it: she was too conscientious for her own good.

Fighting her way to the back of the bus, she plonked herself down in a seat and checked her phone. There was an alert from Grief United – another message from MarkG (Moderator): *Hi Roz. Just checking in to see how you're doing as I noticed you hadn't posted for a while. Hope all's well? Best, Mark.*

Roz was surprised, but pleasantly so. She wasn't used to being asked how she was. No-one usually cared. *Hiya*, she replied. *The last few days have been a bit shit.* Then she deleted it. It sounded coarse. *Oh, I'm fine*, she typed instead. *Just feeling a bit down.* She deleted this too as it made her sound miserable. *Work's been a bit manic lately*, she lied instead. That was better. It made her sound more dynamic, less pathetic. *Just on my way home now, thank God!*

Nightmare! he replied. *But glad to hear you're OK. Where's home for you?*

She smiled to herself. At least he knew the difference between 'your' and 'you're'.

I'm in Buxton, she answered. *On the edge of the Peak District... If you've heard of it. A lot of people haven't!*

Really? I used to go there on school trips many moons ago. I'm in Manchester. Not so far away.

Many moons ago? How quaint, she thought, and wondered how old he was.

Another message pinged through from him: *Let me know if you ever fancy a coffee some time – or a herbal tea?*

Roz pressed her head against the window, as the rain slid silver down the glass. She hadn't expected that. How could she say 'no' in a friendly way without alienating him? She wanted to be able to go back on Grief United again without feeling awkward.

Don't worry. I'm not an axe murderer or anything! he messaged again, with a smile emoji.

Roz giggled at the naffness of it. She needed to chill out a bit, take herself less seriously. Where was the harm in meeting him for a coffee? It wasn't as if she had much else to do.

OK. That would be nice, she wrote back, before she could change her mind. *When would be good for you?*

How about next Wednesday? he replied. *We could have lunch if you can get away from work. I could come over to Buxton?*

CHAPTER FIFTEEN

Wednesday came and Roz trudged up the hill from The Old Hall to the Columbine – a cosy restaurant close to the Market Place – where she was meeting Mark at half past twelve. It was a place she normally associated with the pre-theatre crowd, re-fuelling on their way to the Opera House, but she'd heard it did a good lunch too. More importantly, she was unlikely to bump into any of her colleagues there.

She checked her watch to find she was slightly early, but went inside in any case. She'd find them a table, get herself settled and wait for him. But as the lithe young waitress stepped forward to take her coat, she saw she wouldn't have to wait after all. Mark was already sitting there, watching for her, having bagged the corner table. He was sporting the long, stripy scarf he told her he'd be wearing for identification purposes. *More subtle than a carnation in the buttonhole*, he'd joked in his text this morning.

Roz felt a flutter of nerves for no good reason as she waved back and went to join him. He looked a few years older than she was – mid-forties? – with light brown hair, and was wearing a smart shirt under a round-necked sweater. His face looked like it wasn't used to smiling, bless him.

'Thanks for coming all the way over here,' she gabbled nervously. 'Did you find somewhere to park?'

Mark had jumped up to pull her chair out for her; he was average height, about five foot ten. 'No problem on both counts!' he assured her. 'There you go.' He sat down again, handing her the menu. 'You said you'd only got an hour?'

'Thanks,' said Roz, noticing his expensive watch. She scanned the specials. 'Yep, I work at The Old Hall Hotel down the road. There are only two of us in the office. I don't want to leave Angie, my colleague, on her own too long.' She turned to the waitress, who was still hovering. 'Could I just have the soup of the day, please? And a roll?'

'So,' said the waitress. 'Today we've got wild mushroom or mixed pepper and chorizo.'

'Wild mushroom would be great,' said Roz. 'Thanks.' She turned to Mark. 'What are you having?' she asked.

'I'll have a steak sandwich and fries, please,' he replied. He looked around himself. 'This place is nice... I don't know Buxton that well – like I said, mainly from geography field trips in the eighties. A visit to Poole's Cavern to see the stalactites, then a route march up to Solomon's Temple after lunch. It was always freezing and throwing it down – even in summer!'

'That sounds about right,' said Roz, buttering her roll. 'Well, you should count yourself lucky! I've lived here all my life. More or less.'

'Really? It seems a nice town from what I've seen of it...'

'It is actually,' she said. 'It's got its good points.'

There was a long pause as he looked at her kindly. 'So, how are things at the moment? Are you coping OK?'

'Things are OK,' she said, steadily. 'One day at a time.' Again, his concern had caught her unawares. She was unused to being the focus of attention. Daniel had always been so scatty, so distracted by his phone.

'It must have been very shocking,' he said, 'what happened to Daniel...'

For Roz, hearing his name spoken aloud was heart-stopping. Like a loud clang only she could hear. Had she used Daniel's name when posting on the discussion boards? She must have done. She took a sip of the water the waitress had brought. 'Er, yes. It was. But I'm coming to terms with it. Slowly.'

He nodded, but didn't press further.

'His family planted a tree for him,' she said. 'At Solomon's Temple actually. I was up there a couple of weeks ago.'

'It's a wild, dramatic – very beautiful – spot.'

'It is,' said Roz, as the waitress arrived with their food. 'How about you?' she asked then, keen to get the spotlight off herself. 'How did you, er, come to set up Grief United?'

Mark rubbed at the empty space on his wedding finger. 'Well... I lost my wife and daughter – Jo and Yasmin – five years ago. It was a car accident. A hit-and-run...' He reached into his wallet and got out a photo of them. Yasmin looked about Chloe's age and was a ringer for her mum – a real 'mini-me', with the same shoulder-length red hair.

'You poor thing,' said Roz, welling up, unable to imagine losing Chloe. 'I'm so sorry to hear that.'

He looked up at her. 'I've got a dog,' he said, forcing a smile.

'Oh, really?' said Roz.

'A black labrador. She's all that's left of my family now. Martina, she's called.'

Roz smiled too. 'Are you a tennis fan, then?'

He looked confused.

'Martina Navratilova...?'

'Ah, I see. No, not really,' he said. 'I just liked the name. It seemed to suit her. I took her on when my neighbours moved to Canada.'

Roz stirred her soup. 'Chloe, my daughter, she's desperate for a dog,' she said, then cringed inside. It felt tactless to mention her own daughter. She changed the subject. 'So you're not at work today then? Obviously!'

'No. I've got the day off... How old is Chloe?' he asked.

'She's ten,' said Roz, nodding. 'Anyway... What is it you do?' She was expecting him to say he was an accountant or something – would have bet money on it.

'I'm an anaesthetist,' said Mark. 'At Stepping Hill Hospital in Stockport – although I haven't been there that long.'

'Oh,' said Roz, thrown by the mention of the hospital where Daniel was taken. At the same time, she was impressed. 'That must be a lot of... responsibility.'

'You get used to it.' He shrugged, humbly. 'It becomes second nature. Like any job.'

'Well, you're very modest,' said Roz. 'And you said you live in Manchester?'

'Yep.' He took a sip of his water. 'South Manchester. Didsbury.'

'Very nice,' said Roz. Even her mother and Fiona would be impressed by that.

Then her phone rang out, embarrassing her with the silly ring-tone Chloe had changed it to last night when they were messing about, watching TV. It was Angie, and Roz pulled a 'sorry' face to Mark. 'I'd better answer it...'

'Please do,' he said.

'Hiya!' said Angie down the line, loud as ever. 'Sorry to bother you, love, but Dalton's on the prowl again. He's called a meeting of all staff for half past one. Right in the middle of lunch – and I was planning on nipping out to Boots for my sun cream and a few other bits. What a knob!'

Roz winced and shot a glance at Mark. 'OK, thanks,' she said. 'I'm on my way back...'

'Sorry, Mark,' said Roz, rummaging in her bag for her purse. 'I think you probably heard that? I've got to go back to work.'

'No problem,' said Mark. 'And there's no need... I'll get this.'

'No. I insist.'

'Honestly,' he said. 'I can stand you a bowl of soup.'

Roz blushed. 'Thanks so much. Maybe I can return the favour some time...'

They both stood up while the waitress fetched Roz's coat.

'Well then,' she said, tying her belt. 'It's been very nice to meet you.'

'Likewise,' he said. 'Actually, I wanted to ask you... The name you use on Grief United. Why Rabbit Heart?'

'Oh, no real significance. It's just the name of a song I like.'

'Ah, right. I don't think I know that one.'

'What does the "G" stand for in yours?' she asked, grabbing her handbag.

'Glaister,' he replied. 'Mark Glaister.'

'Oh that's nice. Unusual. Better than mine – boring old Johnson.'

'Not at all,' he said. 'Roz Johnson has definitely got a ring to it! Look, anyway, I'd better let you go...'

She gave him a peck on the cheek and left with the scent of him in her nose. Not just his aftershave, but something more profound. An almost metallic odour that was quite different from Daniel's – that warm, clean smell with a hint of sweat below, that had been like catnip to her.

Back at The Old Hall, the staff were gathering in the function room waiting for the boss, and Roz and Angie slipped in at the back. When Dalton eventually showed up, he looked dishevelled, like he'd been to the pub for a few sharpeners, which didn't bode well.

'Ah, yeah, OK everyone,' he started, running his hand through his hair. 'Just to say... I know you've probably read the runes in the local press and such. But I wanted you all to be the first to know that The Old Hall's owners have reached an in-principle agreement with the US consortium that wants to acquire the business. Of course, detailed terms still need to be worked out, but it's likely the legal side of things will move quite quickly now...'

There was a resigned mumbling around the room as the news people had expected was finally confirmed.

'What does this mean for us?' Angie called out and everyone turned to look at her. 'Are we all out on our ear then?'

Dalton blew his nose with a massive white handkerchief he'd produced from his trouser pocket. 'Erm. No. I don't believe so. Not at all. Far from it,' he assured her. 'The purchasers have undertaken to retain most of the existing staff – and I hope you derive a degree of comfort from that.'

'Ah. Good!' said Angie, surprised, and the whole room seemed to exhale.

Naïve fools, thought Roz, lying in bed that night, unable to sleep. Her dad, who knew what he was talking about, had told her enough times over the years that these sorts of take-overs rarely worked out as expected. The new owners would want to put their stamp on things – install their own team – if they were going to be spending the eye-watering sums mentioned in the local paper. Her own vague desire for a new, better job had suddenly become a lot more urgent. If she was let go from The Old Hall, the redundancy money would only be a few thousand. It wouldn't last long.

She turned over and closed her eyes. It was bloody annoying, being this dog-tired but unable to sleep. Still, she was past the mid-point of another week. Only two days till the weekend. Till she could put her feet up.

She reached for her phone and had a look on Grief United. Some poor woman was having a late-night meltdown and Mark was trying to help her with some calm, thoughtful advice, not just the usual trite platitudes. Roz felt better all of a sudden: she was lucky to have him in her corner as a real-life friend, not just a disembodied 'messager'.

CHAPTER SIXTEEN

The following week Mark texted Roz to see if she fancied meeting for a coffee. He suggested the 1st of December – a Saturday afternoon – and she'd readily agreed, delighted to have a social engagement to look forward to, however small. She'd planned on packing Chloe off to Ruby's for a couple of hours that day, but it hadn't worked out like that. Ruby wouldn't be around – she was off to visit her cousins in Sheffield – and Roz had no other options. Reluctantly, she texted Mark to cancel, but he wouldn't hear of it and suggested she bring Chloe with her.

'Why, Mum?' Chloe had whined on the day. 'I don't want to go. I thought we were putting up the Christmas decorations...'

'Oh, come on,' coaxed Roz. 'It's just a coffee. It won't take long. We can do the decorations later. And you can choose whatever you like from the menu.'

'Hmm,' said Chloe. 'I suppose...'

When it was time to leave the house, Chloe came downstairs in her padded jacket, beanie hat and gloves. She was wearing thick tights, but had rolled over the waistband of her skirt to hitch it up and make it shorter. Roz had already told her off for doing this with her school skirt and she desperately wanted to say something – to tell her to wear it properly – but the negotiations were still finely balanced and she couldn't risk her refusing to come. Mark would be on his way already.

They could see their breath in front of them in the bright afternoon as they tramped down the pavement to the bus stop. Arriving in town, it was abuzz with festive shoppers and families off to see *Aladdin* at the Opera House. They were meeting Mark at two, at the Cavendish Arcade – home of the old Buxton baths – with its independent shops and quaint tiled interior. Roz had suggested they have coffee at Charlotte's Chocolate Shop and Café, a long-time favourite of hers for relaxing and people-watching.

She spotted Mark immediately, standing at the counter. He was at the head of the queue, pointing at various chocolates that the assistant was picking up with tongs and placing in a shiny red box. Once he'd finished paying, Roz waved across to him.

He came straight over and handed her the box. 'A present! I hope you like them. I got a mixture – white, dark and milk chocolate.'

Roz was delighted – she wasn't used to receiving impromptu gifts, especially not expensive chocolates.

'Thanks. That's so kind. Would you like one?' she asked him.

'No. No. They're for you. Both of you.' He smiled at Chloe, and she wrinkled her nose awkwardly in return.

'So. This is Chloe, my daughter. Obviously.'

'Nice to meet you, Chloe,' said Mark. 'Shall we ask the waitress if we can have that table? It's just become free.'

'Sure,' said Roz.

The three of them took their seats and looked at the drinks list. Roz pointed out of the window, breaking the silence. 'Have you tried the Buxton spa water yet, Mark?' she asked.

'The bottled stuff?'

'No, the real stuff. You see that fountain-type thing out there across the road? St. Anne's Well, it's called. There's a water tap. You can try it.'

'Ugh. Don't!' said Chloe, pulling a face. 'It's horrible. It tastes like rotten eggs!'

'No, it doesn't!' said Roz, slightly annoyed, but Mark found it funny.

'I was telling Chloe about Martina – your black labrador.' Roz changed the subject. 'She loves dogs. But it's not really practical for us at the moment.'

'It wouldn't be fair on the dog,' sighed Chloe, repeating what Roz had told her a hundred times. 'It would be home alone all day.'

'Oh well,' said Mark, kindly. 'Maybe things will change one day and it'll be possible...'

'Maybe,' said Chloe, brightening, and Roz was grateful to him for his kindness. She was cheered too by the thought of crisp winter dog walks in the future, like the families in adverts.

The waitress brought over their drinks: cappuccinos for the adults and a hot chocolate for Chloe that was so stacked with marshmallows and chocolate buttons, it was in danger of toppling over. Chloe made short work of it, picking off the sweets and cream with a long spoon, leaving most of the drink, but Roz didn't tell her off. Chloe yawned, then and asked if she could go and look round the bookshop next door.

'Fine,' said Roz. 'But don't be long. And don't wander off anywhere else.'

'I guess she doesn't want to be here,' said Mark when she'd gone. 'It can't be very exciting for her, hanging out with us.'

'Oh, it's not that,' Roz lied. 'She's, er, annoyed with me because the new carpet for her bedroom arrived a few weeks ago, but I haven't got anyone to fit it yet.'

'Ah,' said Mark. 'I wish I could help you there. I'm not too bad at most DIY jobs, but carpet fitting is skilled work. Above my pay grade, unfortunately!'

Roz noticed his hands – sinewy and strong – as he stirred the froth in his mug. 'It's OK,' she said. 'I wouldn't dream of asking you. I'll have to get someone in. She'll just have to wait.'

Mark spoke again after a moment, his voice thick with emotion. 'Yasmin, my daughter... She was just a bit older than Chloe when she died. She'd be sixteen now.' He looked at the ceiling. 'I miss all that stuff – even the moods.'

Roz reached over and put her hand on his. 'I'm so sorry,' she said. 'I didn't mean to—'

But he'd stopped listening, and was looking over Roz's shoulder.

She turned round to see that Chloe was back, along with Roz's own mother. Kate's mum, Jan, was with them too.

'Look, Mum,' Chloe said. 'Gran's here. She was just doing some shopping and we bumped into each other.'

Roz flushed red and stood up. Her mother was wearing a Cossack hat like Lara's in Doctor Zhivago and an expression on her face that Roz couldn't read; Jan was dressed like a normal person in a long blue puffer coat and jeans.

'Hi, Mum. Hi, Jan,' said Roz, her voice higher than usual.

'Hi, pet,' said Jan, clasping Roz to her. 'Long time no see. My goodness, I didn't recognise Chloe there. She's getting so big...'

'She is, isn't she?' said Roz's mother. Then she turned to Roz. 'I'm sorry, dear. I should have called you to say I was coming to Buxton, but my arrangement with Jan was all a bit last minute. We've just been out for lunch and a catch-up.'

'Oh, don't worry,' said Roz, fixing a smile on her face. 'Next time.'

Her mother switched her attention to Mark then, looking him up and down.

'This is Mark,' said Roz quickly. She hadn't planned to introduce him, but felt she had to.

'Pleased to meet you,' said Mark, standing up out of politeness.

'Hello.' Her mother smiled at him. 'Pleased to meet you too.'

Roz turned to Jan. 'So, then. Are you looking forward to being the mother of the bride? You must be so excited...'

'Oh yes!' Jan gushed. 'I've got half a dozen possible outfits. I'll have real trouble narrowing it down to just one. I need to ask your mum's advice...'

There was some polite laughter, then Roz's mother checked her watch. 'Listen, we just popped in to say hello,' she said. 'We'd better get off.'

'Yep,' said Jan. 'We've a couple of bits of Christmas shopping to do. You can never start too soon.'

'Wow. You're organised,' said Roz, glad they were leaving

before any discussion of 'Christmas arrangements' could happen.

They left and Roz undug her nails from her palms. She turned to Mark as they took their seats again. 'Sorry about that,' she said.

'No problem at all.'

'My mother lives in Alderley Edge now, but she still comes over to see her old friends – her tentacles are everywhere! And that was Jan she was with – my best mate Kate's mum. Kate lives in London now...'

'They seemed very nice,' he said, as Roz watched Chloe, sensing her boredom.

'I think I'd better be getting this one home,' Roz announced. 'I've promised her we'll put up the tree this afternoon.'

Chloe glared at her and hugged herself. She hated it when Roz called her 'this one'.

'Sure.' Mark nodded. 'No problem,' he said, and got out his wallet to pay.

Out on the pavement, they pulled up their collars and scarves against the chill.

'Thanks so much for coming over,' Roz said to Mark, linking her arm through Chloe's. 'It's been nice to see you again.'

'Likewise,' said Mark. 'I was thinking... Maybe we could meet for a drink one evening before Christmas? If you're free, that is?'

'Er, sure,' said Roz. She wasn't *that* sure and it was awkward to be discussing this in front of Chloe, but it would be more awkward to say no. 'That could be good. The next couple of weeks are going to be quite busy... but I'll let you know.'

Back at home, Roz switched on the lamps in the lounge, leaving the curtains open as there was still some light in the sky. She fetched the plastic Christmas tree from the loft and brought it downstairs, Chloe trailing behind her with the tattered box of multi-coloured baubles and flaccid tinsel they'd had for years. Roz had been keen to bin the tinsel and replace the baubles with some tasteful new 'warm white' ones, but Chloe was having none of it.

'What would you like for Christmas?' Roz asked her, untangling the string of lights, nostalgic for the time when Chloe still believed in Santa.

'A phone!' Chloe answered immediately.

Roz frowned. Chloe had been nagging her for a phone for ages, but Roz was keen to keep her out of the snake-pit of social media for as long as possible.

'No,' she said. 'Not yet... Anyway, you can have a little think and let me know what else you'd like.'

Roz was braced for an argument, but Chloe had frozen stock-still, her attention diverted. 'Mum!' she whispered. 'There's someone out there. At the window.'

'No there isn't,' said Roz. 'You're just—' But then a face did appear, rapping on the glass. It was her bloody mother again! What did *she* want?

Roz went to open the door and could tell straight away her mother wasn't happy. Roz turned to Chloe. 'Could you go and fetch the other box of baubles from the spare room, love? The little one.'

'That was very cosy, wasn't it?' said her mother when Chloe was out of earshot. 'The two of you holding hands.'

'What was?' said Roz, baffled.

'Was that your new man?' her mother pressed, spying the box of chocolates on the coffee table. 'Is he the reason you're not coming to Fiona's for Christmas?'

The penny dropped for Roz that she was talking about Mark. 'Hang on a sec,' she said. 'We weren't *holding hands*. We were just having coffee. He's a friend of mine. A doctor actually,' she added, appealing to her mother's snobbery. 'He was just upset about something.'

'I don't care if he's the Dalai Lama,' huffed her mother. 'I don't think it's good for you to be... *consorting* with all these men.'

'All these men?' repeated Roz. 'What men?'

'Well, there was the one you told us about who died and now, a few weeks later, there's this one! If you ask me, you need to concentrate on yourself and your daughter. Set her a good example.'

'Shhh,' said Roz, worried Chloe would hear. 'Keep your voice down. And you know, I've got to say, it's really none of your business in any case.'

Her mother's eyes flashed in anger. 'You know what? You've always been the same, Rosslyn. I've only ever got your best interests at heart, but you never listen...' She pointed at the ceiling. 'And, while we're on the subject, I think Chloe's dressing a bit too...'

'Too what?' Roz challenged her.

'Too... *maturely*. Especially with strange men around. Short skirts and the like.'

'What?' It was one thing for her mother to criticise *her*. She expected it. But it hit differently when directed at her daughter. 'Are you implying what I think you're implying?'

'It happens,' said her mother, matter-of-factly. 'She's becoming a young woman. You should be protecting her.'

'Right,' said Roz, shooing her towards the door. 'That's it. I've heard enough. And don't bother coming round again – or contacting me at all for that matter.'

Roz closed the door behind her, knowing full well her mother would take her at her word – that this would be final – but she didn't care. She should have done this years ago.

Roz turned to see Chloe sitting at the top of the stairs, hugging the cardboard box. 'Is everything OK, Mum?' she asked, her little face all worried.

'Yes, love,' Roz said, and meant it. 'Everything's fine.'

CHAPTER SEVENTEEN

Roz knew what would happen next. Her mother would run to Fiona, telling tales about what a terrible person she was. That she was naïve and rude and a rotten mother. And then, at some point over the next few days, Fiona would ring her up and give her a ticking off, taking their mother's side or – even worse – playing the pious peacemaker. Roz hated that more than anything: her sister seizing the moral high ground, rising above the fray, putting on her irritating, reasonable 'lawyer' voice. Not that it would do any good. Not this time.

But several days passed and no call came. Instead, Mark called while she was in one of Dalton's dull finance meetings. He left a message asking if she fancied a drink on Friday: he was coming over for a work conference at Shrigley Hall – a fancy hotel and conference centre in the Cheshire country-side, not far from Buxton.

Roz was feeling popular that morning, because Kate called her too.

'So, then,' Kate said breathlessly down the phone. 'Spill

the beans… Who's this new guy of yours? This Mark fella? Mum said she ran into you in the Cavendish Arcade.'

'Oh God,' said Roz, relieved Angie wasn't around to hear. 'The jungle drums didn't take long… And he's not *my guy*. He's just a mate. Someone I met through that online group. The grief group.'

'Mum said he was quite dishy,' said Kate, mischievously.

'Really?' said Roz, surprised, but secretly pleased. 'He's not my usual type. He's a few years older than me. He's quite… serious, I suppose.'

'What does he look like?'

'Oh, I dunno,' said Roz, trying to think of someone famous he was similar to – and failing.

'Well, is he tall or short? Fat or thin?'

'Er… None of the above really. He's just… normal, I suppose.'

'Oh well,' said Kate. 'There's a lot to be said for going out with someone normal.'

'I told you, I'm not *going out* with him!' Roz paused. 'Although he's asked me out for a drink on Friday and I'm not sure what his intentions are. Friendship or, y'know, romantic overtones?'

'A drink defo says romance to me…'

Roz bristled. 'It's probably best if I don't go. I don't want to lead him on. And anyway, what would people think?'

'What people?'

'My mother for a start. She gave me some real shit after she saw us on Saturday. Implied I was an unfit mother for seeing *all these men*.'

Kate tutted. 'What's her problem? It's your life, not hers. You should go out with him if you want to.'

'I'm not sure that I do. I mean, he's nice enough, but he's not Daniel.'

'Ah.' Kate sighed. 'Saint Daniel...'

'What do you mean?' said Roz tightly.

'I dunno,' said Kate. 'I just think it's a mistake to hold him up as some sort of perfect being.' She hesitated. 'You did your share of moaning about him, I seem to recall.'

'What moaning?' Roz challenged her.

'That he was always late... Or checking his phone all the time when you were together. You thought it was a bit disrespectful.'

'I don't think it's fair of you to bring that up,' said Roz. 'Not now.'

'He was only human,' said Kate. 'You just never had the chance to get fed up with him. Unlike me with Sam.' She chuckled softly. 'You should count yourself lucky. She's doing my head in at the moment.'

But Roz knew Kate was just trying to make her feel better; Kate and Sam were as solid as anything.

'Maybe you should give this Mark a chance,' said Kate. 'What does he do for a job?'

'He's an anaesthetist. At Stepping Hill.'

'Wowsers!' said Kate. 'He'll be earning a few quid.'

'What are you like?' said Roz. 'Materialistic or what?' But part of her was loving it. 'Well, I have to say, he seems pretty generous. Daniel always seemed to be skint. And he didn't seem to be in any hurry to meet Chloe. Maybe because he had to work with kids all day. Whereas Mark, he encouraged me to bring Chloe along last week.'

'So,' said Kate. 'If you go for a drink with him on Friday, what about Chloe? Can you find a sitter at short notice?'

'It's her school Christmas party,' said Roz. 'They're

having a Scottish ceilidh for some bizarre reason, so I'd be able to go out for a couple of hours.'

'Well, go for it!' said Kate. 'Just remember to take all the usual safety precautions. Meet in a public place. Tell someone where you're going. All that jazz.'

'OK, Mum!' Roz laughed. 'I'm nearly forty. I think I can handle it.'

'And let me know how it goes! Speak soon. Listen, I've got to go. Bye!'

'Will do,' said Roz and turned back to her computer screen. She googled 'Mark Glaister Stepping Hill' and found his name on the NHS website under 'Our People'. He was described as 'Joint Head of Team' alongside a female colleague.

On the spur of the moment, Roz called him back and caught him on a late lunch break.

'I was starting to think you were ignoring me,' he said, pretending to be put out. 'I'd assumed you couldn't make it.'

'Oh no, not at all. I've been in a meeting. Friday's fine for me. But it'll have to be a fairly quick one. Chloe's got a party that evening, but it finishes at nine.'

'Great,' he said. 'How about the Star Bar on the main road through town? That looked nice. Shall I see you at seven?'

'Great,' she said. 'See you there.'

When she hung up, she noticed the knot in her stomach and remembered she hadn't eaten since breakfast. Meetings with Dalton always made her feel like this. She should go and buy a sandwich, but the rain had started and she couldn't face it.

She grabbed her mouse instead and clicked on the *Daily Mail* website. The showbiz section was dominated by more news of 'TV's Liz Lockhart'. Not only had she found love nine months after her husband's suicide, she'd now had the absolute *temerity* to marry the man in question in a 'secret ceremony'. And the comments under the article were the predictable bin-fire of people furious at her, even though it was none of their business.

Roz immediately jumped onto Grief United – this was bound to have caused a stir – and she wasn't disappointed. The usual suspects were all rushing to judgement, condemning Liz Lockhart in their 'black and white' way, and Roz envied them their moral certitude. She shook her head. Nuance was anathema to them.

Then she scrolled down to see if anything else was happening on the discussion boards, but there was nothing much – just a general chat about what people were up to at the weekend. She clicked on it lazily and saw a post from Mark: *Just a boring work conference for me on Friday, although I'm meeting up with a friend in the evening – going out for drinks in Buxton. Should be fun.*

Roz stopped breathing for a second. She had to text him before he said any more: *Hi Mark. Just saw your post on Grief United. PLEASE don't tell them it's me you're meeting up with on Friday! They might get the wrong end of the stick. I don't want Mrs. Bee on my case again, judging me!*

No worries, he replied. *Understood.*

And Roz breathed.

CHAPTER EIGHTEEN

'Ow!' said Chloe, pulling away from her. Roz had made her a tartan sash to wear to the school ceilidh tonight and was pinning it, diagonally, over her party dress.

'Stop fidgeting then,' said Roz. 'We've got to leave in a few minutes. I'm going out too, remember. I don't want to be late.'

Roz's phone buzzed on the dressing table and she hesitated to look, but it was only Fiona. From the sounds of other phones ringing in the background, she was still in the office.

'Hiya,' said Fiona in a sing-song voice. 'I was just calling for a chat.'

'Oh, right. Sorry,' said Roz. 'I'm actually on my way out...'

'Really?' said Fiona, unable to hide her surprise. 'Anywhere interesting?'

I've got a date – with a man! Roz wanted to announce, to show her sister she wasn't nearly as pathetic as she thought she was. That she too had a life. But she didn't, for fear it would go straight back to their mother. 'Nah,' she said instead. 'Just a drink with some workmates. While Chloe's at her school Christmas party.'

'It's such a shame you can't make it to ours at Christmas,' said Fiona. 'We'll miss you.'

'Ah, well. Sorry about that...'

'Here,' said Fiona. 'Can I ask...? What's happened between you and mum? I don't like it when there's bad blood between you two.'

She was obviously fishing for info, but Roz wasn't falling for it; their mother would've told Fiona every last detail of what happened last week. 'Actually,' said Roz. 'It's a long story. I'll call you when I've got more time,' though she had no such intention.

When she'd got rid of Fiona, she walked Chloe down to her party, kissed her goodbye at the school gates and caught the bus to town and the Star Bar. Her irritable mood dissolved when she got off at her stop and felt that sense of anticipation, the fizzing in her stomach. It was a novel sensation to be heading out at this time of the evening, past the glittering frontages of the bars that sat dormant during the day and the people in their after-dark clothes. She was thrilled to be one of them at last, relishing the prospect of some proper, grown-up company – and a proper, grown-up drink. A glass of chilled chablis with condensation on the side. Or a gin with fancy tonic.

She *wasn't* relishing having to walk into the bar on her own. It was ages since she'd had to do that, but in the end she didn't have to: just as she reached the door of the place, Mark was arriving from the other direction. He escorted her into the busy bar, where the combination of spicy 'evening' perfumes and 'Last Christmas' coming from the speakers made Roz feel dizzy. It was bigger than it looked from the outside, but nearly every table was taken. There were a couple of office parties that looked like they'd been drinking since noon and a hen party hovering by the booths in the corner, but the sound levels weren't raucous enough to get in the way of conversation – not yet.

Roz and Mark took the last two stools at the bar and shook off their coats.

'You look nice,' he said.

It was sweet of him to say so, even if her navy jersey dress over leggings made her feel mumsy compared to the glamour-pusses in the corner, with their fake-tanned bare backs, sequinned dresses and stripper shoes.

'What would you like to drink?' Mark asked her, as the flashy barman tossed a couple of optics into the air and round behind his back.

'I think I fancy a cocktail,' said Roz, clapping her hands together.

The barman slipped her a menu and she scanned it quickly, immediately excluding all the ones with rude names she'd be too embarrassed to say out loud. In the end, she went for a dirty martini as she'd never had one before.

The barman placed it squarely in front of her on a crisp, white napkin. A thing of beauty. The sort of thing she would have posted on Instagram if she was that way inclined. She took a quick sip and the sharp, medicinal warmth spread through her, slowing her heartbeat. Mark ordered a coke for himself and gave the barman a tenner.

'Now I feel bad,' said Roz, watching him.

'Bad?'

'That you can't have a drink because you're driving.'

He shook his head. 'I don't drink.'

'Oh,' she said, and waited for him to elaborate. But he

clearly didn't feel the need to explain his choice and she respected him for it.

'I probably drink too much,' she confessed. 'I sometimes worry I'm setting Chloe a bad example...'

He didn't judge her though. 'Well,' he said, looking around himself. 'It's nice to be out on the town for a change.'

'I'll second that,' said Roz, taking another sip of her martini.

'I don't get out much,' he said and chuckled at how pathetic it sounded. 'I blame the job. I'm either working long hours or I'm at home, knackered.'

'Me neither. I blame Chloe,' Roz joked, then regretted it. It was a crass remark to someone who'd lost their own daughter.

'How is she?' he asked. 'Did she get off to her party OK?'

'Yep. All fine,' she said. 'How about Martina? Will she be OK?'

'Yeah,' he said. 'She'll be fine.'

'I guess it must be tricky,' said Roz. 'You work long shifts and labradors need a lot of exercise.'

'I'm lucky,' he said. 'I've got a decent-sized back garden. And there's a local dog-walker – a girl who lives down the road. She comes and takes her out. Or my mum sometimes has her, if I'm away overnight or on holiday.'

Roz popped the green olive in her mouth and stirred what was left of her drink with the cocktail stick. 'So. How was it today?' she asked.

'Today?' He wrinkled his nose at her.

'The conference. At Shrigley Hall. I've heard it's lovely over there.'

'Oh fine. It was fine,' he said. 'You know what these things are like.'

She nodded although she didn't really.

'Lots of sitting around, listening to boring speeches... Lunch was the best bit!' He sipped at his coke. 'How was *your* day?'

'Busy. *Very* busy. My colleague, Angie, she's on a week's holiday to Lanzarote – lucky her – so I'm twice as busy as usual.'

He looked at Roz's empty glass. 'You're thirsty,' he joked. 'Would you like another?'

'I would actually.' She blushed. 'I'd like to try a negroni, please.'

'What's that?'

'Oh, it's very much the drink-of-the-moment. Gin, vermouth and Campari. All the famouses are drinking them!'

'Ah, OK,' he said, and ordered one from the young female server who was now behind the bar. He didn't seem to flirt with fit waitresses or bar staff, and his eyes never strayed to the women around him, unlike Daniel, who'd always tried to charm any passing female, or male for that matter, regardless of age. Mark's attention stayed firmly on Roz, which was almost too much; she didn't feel interesting enough to warrant it.

'What are you having?' she asked him. 'And I'm getting these,' she said, reaching for her purse.

'OK. If you insist,' he grinned. 'I'll push the boat out and have a J2O this time.'

'So then,' he said, when they had their drinks. 'What are you doing for Christmas?'

'That's a bit of a sore point,' said Roz, swirling the spirits in her glass. 'I've been invited to our Fiona's – that's my younger sister. She's just moved to a fancy house in Alderley Edge, not far from our mother.'

'But...?'

'But Chloe and I are going away instead – to Whitby. I've never been before.'

'Me neither.'

'We'd actually planned to go there with Daniel...'

'Ah, I see,' said Mark, softly. 'When are you off?'

'Sunday the 23rd of December. For five days.'

'Oh, that's a shame... I won't see you at Christmas.'

'Yeah,' said Roz, thinking it might be for the best as things were going a bit quickly. 'What about you?' she asked. 'What are your plans?'

'I'm going round to my mum's as usual. Dad's no longer with us. He died a few years ago.'

'Oh. I'm sorry.'

'No need.' He paused. 'It'll just be the two of us. My brother's family... they're spending it with his wife's parents this year.'

'Still, that'll be nice,' said Roz. The drinks had gone straight to her bladder and she had to excuse herself to go to the Ladies. It was even more lively there than it was in the bar – full of women from the office parties who were shrieking and borrowing make-up and planning which pub they were going to next. One of the ring-leaders put her arm around Roz, inviting her to go with them – 'The more the merrier!' It was almost tempting, but she declined politely and headed for a cubicle.

Sitting down, her mood changed as she read the poster and stickers on the door facing her. One gave a number to call if you were a victim of domestic violence. Another a warning about your drinks being spiked. Below that was the instruction to *Go to the bar and ask for Angela* if you were worried about your date turning nasty and needed help from the staff. A good idea, Roz thought, but depressing as hell. She couldn't believe young women were still having to deal with this crap and feared for the world Chloe would inherit.

Back at the bar, the original barman came over to ask her and Mark if they wanted more drinks. Roz wished she could have one. And another. That she could stay out all night and even go dancing. But it wasn't to be. 'I've got to run for the bus,' she said, turning to Mark. 'I've got to pick up Chloe. I don't want to be late.'

Mark touched her elbow. 'There's no need to get the bus. I can drop you off.'

'Are you sure?' she asked.

'Of course. I insist!' he said, offering her his arm, and they left the bright lights of the bar for the car park round the corner. Out in the cold night air, huddled close to him, she caught the same metallic tang as before and, as they reached his dark blue BMW, gleaming under the streetlamp, she realised what it was: the sharp smell of maleness, making her feel safe as he opened the car door for her.

She directed him out of town and up the road to Chloe's school where there was a parking space opposite, much easier than getting the bus. 'Thanks so much,' she said, as he pulled up. 'I'll be fine from here. Our house is just walking distance up the road.'

'Are you sure?' he asked. 'In the dark?'

'I'm sure.' Roz smiled across at him awkwardly. 'Well then. You have a good Christmas. And I guess I'll see you next year?' She winced at her own corniness.

'You too,' he said, turning to her abruptly, taking hold of her shoulders, pressing his lips on her mouth.

Roz pulled away, shocked. 'Sorry,' she said. 'I just... I don't...'

'No, no. Not at all. *I'm* sorry,' he said, raising his hands. 'I totally mis-judged things. I was a bit full-on.'

'Not at all,' she echoed him. 'It's fine. It's just... I'd better go and get Chloe.' She fumbled to open the car door. 'I'll... see you soon. Thanks.'

Roz got out and hurried across the road, down towards the school gates, waiting to hear the padded hush of tyres as he drove off. But he still sat there, watching her, till she was safely through them.

Inside the building, the assembly hall was shaking to the sound of thirty kids jumping up and down to '500 Miles' by The Proclaimers – the evening's finale. Roz was shaking too. Things weren't the same with Mark as they'd been with Daniel. He wasn't as fun – or as charismatic – and he didn't make her laugh like Daniel. Not really. But she'd obviously been giving out signals to the contrary – which Mark had acted on – and now he'd be really upset and everything would be weird between them.

She was an idiot.

CHAPTER NINETEEN

The next couple of weeks were a nightmare, with Chloe stomping round the house like a bear with a sore head. Roz had had the impression for a while that her friendship with Ruby was cooling off and that this was part of the problem. She tried to help by inviting Ruby over for a sleep-over the next weekend and a special 'high tea': assorted sandwiches cut into little triangles, some home-made biscuits and a selection of mini eclairs and custard slices, all washed down with Waitrose's 'Finest' pink lemonade. Afterwards, the girls had watched *Home Alone* and *Elf* – and gone to bed giggling – but things had gone downhill soon after. The students next door were having an end-of-term party, which had started in a civilised fashion – just a small group mulling wine over a fire-pit in the garden – before some lads arrived fresh from the pub and whacked up the music. By eleven o'clock, it had turned into a full-on rave that was making the house vibrate – and Roz's house too. Watching them out of the window, Chloe had been fascinated by this glimpse into the world of 'the big girls' but Ruby had seemed petrified.

When Ruby's mother came to collect her tired daughter early on the Sunday morning, a few 'die-hards' from the party were out in the garden again – including the girl in the fur coat with the topknot – drinking from steaming mugs and smoking. The distinctive aroma of weed filled the air and Ruby's mum was less than impressed. She'd coughed theatrically, waving her hand under her nose – and Roz was quietly mortified.

When Ruby had gone, Chloe was more deflated than ever and Roz wondered why she'd even bothered. Within days, it emerged that Ruby had switched her allegiance to a new best friend, Orla. Orla had a pony and Chloe knew she couldn't compete. Roz tried to be sanguine about it – these things were a rite of passage after all – but it still broke her heart to see her daughter mooning around, miserable, and she wished she could take her pain.

At work, things weren't much better. The sale of the hotel was being pushed through at breakneck speed and, on top of her normal duties, her job had expanded to include answering all sorts of daft questions from Dalton that the American buyers emailed through to him every morning. Her search for a new job had all but hit a brick wall. There was nothing very inspiring out there that fitted around Chloe's school hours – unless you counted stacking shelves at the local Morrisons, which she definitely didn't.

The Thursday before Christmas, Roz spent most of the morning trying to pacify a lawyer sent over by the Americans to review all legal documentation that was kept on the premises – the woman seemed to hold Roz personally responsible for the patchy broadband in the Peak District – and then, in the afternoon, she'd had a string of emails from office Christmas parties that had been held at the hotel, complaining that their complicated dietary requirements hadn't been 'respected' in full. She'd come *that* close to telling them to shove their allergies where the sun don't shine when, finally, five o'clock and home-time arrived.

Back at home, she got straight on with the laundry. They were off to Whitby on Sunday and she needed to get the washing, drying and packing done. Then there was the food to think about: whether she should plan out their meals and take everything with them or wait and go to the supermarket once they'd arrived?

Chloe wasn't helping. She'd decided to whine about the carpet offcuts again, demanding to know when they'd be fitted.

Roz counted to ten. 'I'll say this for you, you don't half pick your moments, Chloe. *Please* can we talk about this after Christmas? I've got a lot to think about at the moment.'

But Chloe was ignoring her now, staring at the floor in alarm. Roz glanced down to see a puddle of water on the floor by the sink. It was getting steadily bigger, and she got down on her knees to investigate but couldn't work out where exactly it was coming from.

She tried calling her usual plumber, but there was no response, and so she googled some others. The place being flooded out was the last thing she needed. Not now.

She tried switching off the washing machine, and pulling out the plug, but it made no difference. And none of the other plumbers were picking up either. But the water was still coming, slowly but surely.

Panicked, she did the only thing she could think of and called Mark.

'I don't know what to do,' she wailed down the phone,

feeling pathetic. She'd become quite good at fixing stuff for herself over the years, but this was beyond her.

'Don't worry,' he said. 'I'm at home, but I'll come right over. What's your address?'

~

Roz ran around the place, hoovering, dusting and plumping cushions – it was probably a tip compared to Mark's place in Didsbury – and when she'd finished titivating the house, she started on herself, brushing her hair and fixing her make-up. Chloe was watching her as if she was mad.

Mark arrived sooner than expected – he must have really bombed it over from Manchester – and she ushered him through to the kitchen.

He put down his tool-bag. 'Have you got any old towels to put down?' he asked, and she fetched some.

He pulled out the washing machine and had a look round the back, then delved in the bag for a spanner. Moments later, he sat back on his heels. 'It's just the drain pipe come loose... I've tightened it up and put a clip round it, so it won't happen again.'

'Phew!' said Roz, relieved. 'Can I repay you with a cuppa?'

'Please,' he smiled. 'A splash of milk, no sugar. Ta.'

They went through to the lounge with their drinks, and Mark noticed her Whitby postcard on the coffee table, next to the book she'd bought to take on holiday. He picked up the card and turned it over.

'From Daniel,' he said, nodding.

Roz nodded too. 'It's all I've got left of him. I don't even have a photo...'

At this, Mark leapt out of his seat and pulled out his phone. 'C'mon,' he said. 'Let's have a selfie together!'

'What?' said Roz. 'I don't think—'

'No, really,' he insisted. 'C'mon.'

Roz smoothed down her hair and straightened her work blouse. 'I feel daft,' she said.

Chloe had come downstairs and poked her head round the door. 'Is the leak fixed? What are you doing?' she asked, horrified.

'Yep,' said Roz. 'Mark's sorted it.'

Mark beckoned to Chloe. 'Come into the photo!'

'No way. That's sad!' said Chloe, laughing, although she seemed to be considering it.

'Come on, love,' said Roz. 'It'll be nice.'

'You're not posting it anywhere, are you?' Chloe asked.

'No way,' said Mark. 'Trust me.'

'O-kay,' said Chloe and, to Roz's surprise, came and joined them.

Mark snapped a couple of shots of the three of them and held them out for their approval.

'Can you delete the first one?' asked Chloe and he duly obliged.

'Right,' he said, checking the time. 'I'd better be getting off. Now, you two, make sure you have a great Christmas, OK?'

'You too,' said Roz, as he packed up his tool-kit and headed out into the night.

When he'd gone, she felt deflated: he hadn't said anything about meeting up again or that he would see her soon or anything, and the house felt strangely empty without him.

Then on Saturday morning, as she packed their things for

Whitby, a courier package arrived for her. She ripped it open and was surprised by what she found: it was the photo Mark had taken, in a posh silver frame, with a note saying *Merry Christmas!*

Roz grimaced. Chloe looked lovely in the picture, but all she could focus on was the beginnings of her own double chin. The whole thing was a bit weird, to be honest.

Then she checked herself. It was a very nice gesture on his part – the postage alone must have cost a fortune – and she should be more appreciative. This is what years of loneliness and disappointment had done to her – made her a miserable, cynical old git.

She let out a sigh and went to find a place for the photo on the sideboard, resolving to be more grateful in future for the good things in life.

CHAPTER TWENTY

On Sunday, Roz and Chloe set off in the car to the North Yorkshire coast. Buffeted by the high winds and rain, it was already dusk when they passed the signs for Filey and Scarborough and dropped down on the A171 into Whitby.

The lit-up Victorian B&Bs on the edge of town had seen better days. They all said 'NO VACANCIES' in their windows, but Roz found that hard to believe – their dining rooms were all deserted, much like the roads.

The Christmas lights in the centre of town were just as depressing, consisting of single white stars hanging from alternate lamp posts. Roz guessed they'd been going for a minimalist effect, but the lights just looked forlorn, like the council had run out of money.

They pulled up outside their accommodation in the dark and found the narrow 'front' door up a lane next-door to a garage: not quite the harbourside or cliff-top cottage she'd imagined sharing with Daniel.

They got out of the car, dragging their luggage behind them, and Roz fumbled with the key-safe, eyes watering from the cold. The wreath on the door was more funereal than festive, while inside, the place smelt airless and fusty.

The kitchen was basic to say the least. It had a small fridge with a tiny freezer compartment and the 'cooking facilities' were a counter-top mini-oven and hot plates – too small to accommodate the M&S turkey crown she'd brought in the cool-bag for Christmas lunch.

The tiny lounge room had a sofa (that was actually a sofa-bed), a TV and an 18-inch Christmas tree. There was no separate bedroom: cut into the lounge was an alcove with a small double bed you could see from the sofa. Chloe announced that she'd be sleeping on the sofa-bed, rather than sharing the double with Roz, and Roz couldn't help thinking that the so-called 'double' would have been no good for Daniel; he'd have been far too tall and there would've been no privacy whatsoever.

The toilet and shower were like something you'd find on a boat, with a few seaside ornaments dotted around. But the place was clean and the towels and sheets smelt reassuringly of washing powder.

Tired from the journey, they went to bed early. Roz had been planning to read her book, but had stupidly managed to leave it at home, so she opened the little visitors' book she'd found and read that instead. There were no recent entries, just a few from last year – from a honeymoon couple (imagine!); an old couple celebrating a seventieth birthday; and two friends who'd come for Whitby Goth Weekend. She sighed, turned over and lay there watching Chloe on the sofa, playing games on Roz's phone. Tomorrow was another – hopefully better – day.

Early next morning, Christmas Eve, Roz was woken by the cry of a baby through the shonky sash window – the sound Chloe used to make as a new-born, which used to pierce her heart like a hot, sharp blade. Only it wasn't a baby, it was a seagull, which made her feel foolish.

She tip-toed in the kitchen, made some tea, then sipped it in bed by the feeble light of the mini-tree, waiting for Chloe to wake.

Coming here had been a terrible idea. She wished they'd stayed in Buxton with all their home comforts, even if that would've meant having to go to Fiona's. She could have gritted her teeth and tolerated it – tolerated her mother – just for one day.

Some more gulls had turned up now, joining in with the first one. They were cackling like crones, laughing at her stupid ruse to avoid seeing her family, waking Chloe up.

'I thought we might go up to Whitby Abbey today,' Roz suggested, keen to make the best of things.

Chloe gave an exaggerated yawn. 'That sounds boring. Can we go to the beach instead?'

The morning sea was grey like molten silver. It hammered on the shore and sucked up the sand, throwing salt in the air.

'Let's walk along the pier,' said Chloe, running ahead of Roz. 'To the lighthouse.'

'No, love. Don't!' Roz shouted after her. 'One freak wave and you'll get swept away. We'll be a story on the evening news, with everyone saying how stupid we were. Let's just stick to the beach.'

'Oh, alright,' huffed Chloe. 'Can I paddle then?'

'No. You'll freeze,' said Roz, then relented. 'Well OK. But don't go in too far.'

Chloe took off her shoes and socks and strode bravely towards the waves. She didn't flinch when she stepped in the water, but Roz did, recalling a family holiday to St. Andrews when she and Fiona were around Chloe's age. Their dad had taken them snorkelling in the sea, which was choppy and Baltic up there, even in August. Fiona had been fine, but the power of the water had scared the life out of Roz, not to mention what was *under* the water. She'd felt something around her ankles, pulling her down, but when she turned to go back, a wave hit the back of her head like a punch, knocking her forward onto her hands and knees. She'd struggled for breath, coughing up salt water, then opened her eyes to see her mother on the beach, gesticulating furiously at her dad to help her, using short, sharp words she'd never heard before. She'd been scarier than the water.

Her mother had rubbed her down with a giant towel – rough like sandpaper – and had refused to speak to Roz's dad for the next two days. After that, their beach activities were confined to rock-pooling and crabbing and going to queue for ice-creams, while their dad eyed up all the pretty young mums, to her mother's annoyance – again.

Once home in Buxton, their mother had enrolled Roz and Fiona in life-saving classes where they had to jump into the pool in their pyjamas to fetch a brick back to the surface. It was all about *survival*, their mother had emphasised. Personal responsibility. Looking after yourself. She wasn't going to *mollycoddle* them. It was a big, scary world out there and life was a series of hazards to be avoided. Like the 'white slave trade', which could be waiting for you around any corner. Or 'saturated fats'.

'Look at my feet, Mum!' Chloe was back and her toes were greeny blue.

'Let's go up to the amusement arcade and get warm,' said Roz. It felt like a subversive act. Her own mother had never allowed them over the threshold of such dens of iniquity; they 'attracted the wrong sort', which made the young Roz want to go there even more.

Roz and Chloe headed for the flashing lights and discordant music and the cloying smell of waffles and doughnuts that there was no-one around to buy.

'Do you want to play the Penny Falls?' asked Roz, reaching in her bag for her purse.

'Not really,' said Chloe, hugging herself. 'I don't really like it here. Can we go somewhere else?'

And so they found a café in the centre of town – run by a cheerful Yorkshirewoman who made all her own cakes – and spent a pleasant hour and a half thawing out. As the only customers, the woman was happy to regale Roz and Chloe with stories of the local tourist attractions, most of which were closed for the winter.

'We really need to find a supermarket,' Roz told the woman. 'We've got nothing for Christmas dinner. Nothing that'll fit in our tiny oven at any rate.'

'Really?' The woman looked horrified. 'There's a Co-op next to the station,' she offered, handing her a leaflet with a map. 'But it shuts early today. Don't leave it too late.'

They took her advice and left (with two free doughnuts the woman gave Chloe in a paper bag) and Roz consulted the map, which threatened to blow out of her hand.

'I think it's this way,' said Chloe, pulling her by the hand along a side street, which turned out to be right.

'Clever girl,' said Roz, as they entered the shop and took a basket. There wasn't much on the shelves and the fridges were even emptier. Only the 'plant-based' shelves were full.

'I don't mind,' said Chloe. 'I'm thinking of going vegan anyway.'

'Are you now?' chuckled Roz.

A member of staff came out from the back with a price-gun, reducing the fresh cream trifles, selection boxes and Christmas cheeses, and Roz threw a few things in the basket, along with a packet of roast chicken, a bottle of white wine and some orange juice for Chloe.

The whole lot came to less than twenty pounds and Roz was pleased with herself as they wound their way home. The metal sign of The Endeavour pub was creaking in the wind up ahead of them and Roz remembered it as one of the places Daniel had raved about after his visit here. Its orange windows cast a rosy glow onto the pavement in front of them, and a rousing rendition of 'Once In Royal David's City' floated from the door.

'The Endeavour,' said Chloe. 'That was the name of Captain Cook's ship,' and Roz pretended not to know. 'We did it at school,' Chloe added proudly.

Back at their little 'hobbit hole', the place was nice and cosy when they walked in, thanks to the storage heaters in the lounge and bathroom. It wasn't quite the Instagrammable open fire she'd originally imagined – with Daniel going to fetch logs from the local farmshop or ironmonger's – but it was good enough for now.

∾

Fiona texted Roz on Christmas morning: *Happy Christmas both! Hope you're having a lovely time xxx*

Same to you x, Roz messaged back, and tried not to think about Fiona swishing around her fancy house in her fancy dressing gown, sipping Bucks Fizz and lighting fancy candles.

She'd half expected a text from Mark – would have welcomed one – but there was nothing. She considered sending one to him, but something stopped her; she didn't want to be seen to be chasing him. Kate would probably tell her do it if she wanted, but Roz's mother had a different saying: *Desperation is the worst cologne.* Her mother won out.

Roz gave Chloe her presents: a purple sparkly jumper she'd asked for; a vast selection pack of coloured pens and other stationery; and the mug with the dogs on it from the Serendipity shop, which Roz had forced herself to brave for a second time.

'I know you'd prefer a real dog,' she said, 'but that'll have to do in the meantime!'

'No problem,' said Chloe, and kissed her on the cheek. She seemed happy enough with her 'haul', as if she knew there was no point wishing for more. If anything, she seemed more excited about the gift she had for Roz. 'Here, this is for you,' she said, and produced it from under a cushion.

'Nice wrapping,' said Roz, carefully tearing it open. It was a book. Two books, in fact. *Hamnet,* by Maggie O'Far-rell, and the latest one by Marian Keyes.

'Thanks, love!' Roz exclaimed, hugging her tight. 'Just what I needed after I forgot to bring my book. Where did you get them?'

'From the bookshop in the Arcade... that day we bumped into Gran. I'd saved my pocket money and Gran gave me an extra fiver so I could get both.'

'Really?' said Roz. 'How did you know what to get?'

'The lady in the shop recommended them.'

'Nice one,' said Roz, touched by her ingenuity. 'Well then. What would you like to do today? We've got a while before Christmas lunch. Such as it is...'

'I think I might want to go to up to the Abbey,' said Chloe. 'I was reading some things about it on the website.'

They began the climb up the 199 steps to the eleventh century Benedictine monastery, set on the headland, high above the town. Within minutes, Roz's thighs were burning and she had to stop, but Chloe wouldn't let her rest for long, dragging her onwards by the hand.

At the top, it was gloriously deserted. The Visitor Centre was closed, but it didn't matter – the atmospheric ruins were reward enough. And the incredible view – even on a dreich day like this – which sloped away to Sandsend further north and Robin Hood's Bay to the south.

They perched on a bench and Roz told Chloe how Bram Stoker, while lodging on the nearby cliffs, had stared out over the coastline and let his imagination run wild, inspiring his famous novel *Dracula*. Chloe had actually gasped at this; as a fan of the darker things in life, she was endlessly impressed.

Then Roz's phone beeped – a text from Mark – and she brightened.

'Who's that?' asked Chloe.

'It's Mark,' said Roz. 'Wishing us Merry Christmas.' She paused. 'Right!' she said. 'Shall we head back down for our Christmas lunch?'

'Have we got any crackers?' asked Chloe.

'We've got both kinds. Crackers for pulling and crackers for cheese!' said Roz, making her laugh.

Back at base, Chloe helped Roz prepare the hodge-podge meal of chicken and mash, which they ate on trays on their knees, wearing their party hats, watching the *Strictly* Christmas special.

Roz turned to Chloe. 'I'm really sorry about this,' she said. 'It's not quite the same as being at home, is it?'

'No. But it's my favourite Christmas ever,' Chloe insisted. 'It's a bit like going camping.'

'C'mon, it's not *that* bad!' said Roz, but she was secretly pleased.

She poured another glass of wine and helped herself to some cheese and crackers, while Chloe tucked into a pot of 'individual trifle' from the Co-op. It was five o'clock now and Roz wondered what they'd all be doing at Fiona's. Getting over-competitive at charades was her best guess. Then she wondered how Mark was getting on at his mum's.

CHAPTER TWENTY-ONE

On Boxing Day the sun came out, bouncing off the red roofs of the town, turning the sea pinky-blue. A couple of hundred hardy souls had come down to the beach for a charity swim, and the promenade was full of families with kids and dogs out for a stroll, blowing away the Christmas cobwebs.

Roz breathed in the sea air as she and Chloe set off on a walk of their own, to the pretty village of Sandsend at the northern end of the beach. The contrast with landlocked Derbyshire couldn't be greater, Roz thought. She sometimes felt that the Peak District landscape – stunning as it was – was suffocating her, closing in on her. But here, under the big coastal sky, it was different. *She* was different.

She stopped abruptly and took her boots and socks off.

'What are you doing, Mum?' asked Chloe, wide-eyed.

'Going paddling,' she answered. 'If all those people can go swimming, the least I can do is go for a paddle!'

Chloe stood guard over her boots, while Roz ran into the sea. The water splashed up over her black velvet coat but she kept going anyway, kicking her legs with abandon.

'Mu-um!' Chloe called after her, embarrassed that people were watching. 'Be careful you don't fall!' she shouted. And Roz had to laugh at how the tables had turned.

Eventually, they turned back in the direction of Whitby, and the famous Magpie Café for fish and chips. They sat on a bench in the sun, crunching through the tangy batter, surrounded by pushy gulls – and Roz was thankful that Chloe's aversion to eating animals didn't stretch to poor old cod or haddock.

That evening, Roz suggested they go out to The Endeavour for a bar snack and a change of scene. 'Seeing as it's our last night.'

'Really?' said Chloe, surprised. 'Will I be allowed in?'

'I think so,' said Roz. 'If you behave yourself.'

Inside the pub, it was cosy, clean and busy, with a roaring fire in the corner. Roz ordered a spiced cider for herself and a lemonade for Chloe, and before they'd had a chance to sit down, they'd been invited to join in with some friendly locals around a piano accordion. They were singing sea shanties this time, and a kind young woman handed Chloe a tambourine to shake, which delighted her.

A pleasant couple of hours passed in no time, but, try as she might, Roz couldn't shake the base note of melancholy. Daniel would have loved this.

In the morning, Roz and Chloe were sad to leave their little house for their last walk on the beach. The weather matched their mood as they scuffed their way along the sand, filled their lungs with air and put off the journey home for as long as possible.

Roz's phone buzzed with a text – from Mark. *Hiya Roz. Are you doing anything for New Year's Eve? They've changed the rota at work and I'm at a loose end now. I could come over? x*

She noted the '*x*' at the end – the first time he'd added a kiss – and her heart lifted. New Year's Eve. She had to think what day that was. Monday. Four days away. She bent to pick up something smooth and shiny that was glinting at her – a tiny tablet of sea glass imprinted by the thinnest of seaweeds – and wondered how to reply.

It would be great not to have to spend another midnight countdown on her own after Chloe had gone to bed. To have plans for new year like everyone else. She reflected on the Liz Lockhart drama and what that guy on Grief United had said: *Life goes on. Life is for living.* It might seem harsh, but the simple fact was that Mark was still here and Daniel wasn't. And he was a decent, solid bloke with a good job. A reason to be hopeful about the year ahead – assuming he didn't have any underlying medical conditions! Maybe that was enough. Something to build on.

Roz texted him back – *That would be great. What time were you thinking? x* – and shoved her phone back in her pocket.

'Was that Mark?' Chloe asked, side-eyeing her.

'Yep,' blushed Roz. 'I've said he can come to ours for New Year's Eve. Is that OK?'

Chloe nodded and kept walking. 'Is he, like, your boyfriend now?'

'No. No. Of course not,' Roz protested, but Chloe just grinned at her.

~

Roz and Chloe arrived home – tired from the drive – and struggled up the path with their luggage. The student neighbours had all gone home for the holidays and next door was in darkness for once.

Once inside the house, Roz pulled the curtains and switched on the lamps.

Chloe spied Roz's book on the coffee table and waved it at her. 'Here it is!' she said. 'Where you left it.'

'Oh, thanks,' said Roz, taking it from her. Only something was missing: the postcard-bookmark.

That was weird. She must be losing it even more than she thought. It had definitely been there on the table, she was sure of it. Mark had picked it up to read it when he was here before Christmas. But it wasn't here now. She might have binned it by accident when she was tidying up, but she doubted it. Maybe she'd put it away somewhere and couldn't remember?

Chloe disappeared upstairs and Roz sank down on the sofa. On the sideboard, she saw the framed photo of Mark, herself and Chloe smiling back at her, calming her down. She was glad it wouldn't be long till she saw him again.

CHAPTER TWENTY-TWO

Mark Laurence Glaister. Look at you... Leaving the building with the junior nurses fussing all over you, falling for your act.

You've only been there five minutes and you've got them dancing to your tune. 'Happy New Year when it comes!' 'See you tomorrow!' Giggling and flirting with you. They don't know you yet. What you're really like.

The quilted jacket and brogues, the college scarf – the new leather man-bag. Was that a Christmas present? Or did you buy it for yourself – your own favourite person?

And that expensive-looking bunch of flowers. Who are they for? Who are you buttering up this time? Or maybe someone gave you them. Maybe they're a 'thank you'. From a grateful patient. You love all that – being the big man, playing God in matters of life and death.

Look at you waving them all goodbye, getting into your flashy car. God, you're a cliché.

They don't know what I know. That you're a sneaky, cheating snake.

CHAPTER TWENTY-THREE

At seven thirty on New Year's Eve, Roz's doorbell rang and it was Mark, exactly on time. She reached up to kiss him on the cheek, taking care not to breathe on him because of the large gin she'd already necked for Dutch courage. She took his jacket and scarf, saw that he was casually dressed underneath – a checked shirt over jeans – and regretted her own choice of a little black dress. Far too formal.

'Did you find a parking spot OK?' she asked, trying to sound nonchalant.

'Yep,' he said. 'No problem. It was nice and empty out in the street.' He fished in the carrier bag he was holding and pulled out a bottle of fizz. 'This is for you.' He handed it over. 'And I brought this for myself.' He produced a bottle of cloudy apple juice. 'It's nicer than it looks,' he grinned. 'Chloe can have some too if she likes.'

'She's upstairs,' said Roz. 'She'll be gracing us with her presence later. She wants to stay up for the big TV count-down this year – and the firework display.'

She led him into the lounge, where she'd laid out some

appetisers on the coffee table: olives and tapenade, mini salmon quiches and a large sushi platter from the deli in town. 'I hope you're hungry,' she said.

'Wow,' he said. 'I sure am. It's all been a bit of a rush. Work's been manic today.'

Roz wondered what the etiquette was, and whether she should ask him what kind of operations he'd been working on, but decided against it.

'I've got some spring rolls and tempura as well,' she said. 'To put in the oven later. Sit yourself down... Here's a plate and a napkin.'

He filled his plate and settled into the armchair while Roz lit some candles and tea lights, to augment the glow from the lamps. She put on some music too: the latest Michael Kiwanuka would do the job – cool, current-ish, sophisticated.

'So. Would you like some ice with your apple juice?' she asked.

'That'd be great.'

Roz went to the kitchen to fix his drink – and another gin for herself.

'This is nice,' he said, through a mouthful of food, when she returned. 'I'm not a big one for parties. I can't remember the last time I went out for New Year.'

'Me neither,' said Roz. 'I think it must be hereditary. My mother's always hated New Year's Eve too – or Hogmanay, as she calls it.'

'Ah yes, of course.' He nodded. 'Being Scottish.'

'Well remembered!' said Roz, and took a swig of her gin.

'Aren't you having anything?' he asked, pointing at the table.

'I'll have something later,' she said. She wasn't all that

hungry. It was probably the nerves. Or that her dress was uncomfortably tight. Or a bit of both.

'So your mum's Scottish, but you grew up in Buxton?'

'Yep,' said Roz. 'We lived in one of the big leafy houses on Macclesfield Road – not like round here.'

'Sounds very nice.'

'Yeah, well. It was nice on paper – to the outside observer. Dad was a lawyer. He still dabbles, does a bit of consultancy work now and again, even though he's getting on a bit. We had a nice house, fancy car, two holidays a year, but the reality...'

'I guess nothing's ever quite as it seems,' he said, knowingly.

'My mother was quite old when she had us,' Roz continued. 'She had me when she was thirty-six and Fiona when she was forty. Old by the standards of the day, I mean – not like now, of course. She was a teacher before that. She should've been a sergeant-major. Controlling doesn't really cover it! I went to Sheffield Uni to escape her, but it wasn't far enough.'

'Oh, really? It's a good university. What did you study?'

'English Lit.'

'Interesting.'

'Not really.'

Mark laughed politely. 'How do you get on with Fiona?' he asked, watching her closely.

'Hmm,' she said. 'Not great. She's my mother's favourite. I mean, they've had their moments, but Fiona was always much better at handling her than me. Much more *straightforward* – d'you know what I mean?'

He nodded vigorously.

'I was always the one who worried silently, who wrote

poetry and couldn't sleep.' She swirled the dregs in her glass. 'Even now we're grown up, Fiona's just... *worth* more somehow. I don't know why. Actually I do. Fiona's a lawyer as well. She might be younger than me, but she's The Successful One.'

Mark frowned deeply and shook his head. 'That's crap, isn't it?' He opened his mouth and closed it again. 'It must really grate.'

'Fiona... Even when she was young, she always *spoke* like a lawyer. She's got all these little phrases. Like spells or incantations or something. *In any way, shape or form. Bona fide. Ad infinitum. De facto...* She's the kind of person who uses a semi-colon in a text, you know?'

Mark's eyes twinkled with amusement. 'I'm more of a plain English guy, myself, I have to say.'

Roz went on. 'Ian, her husband, he's nice enough, but he's *sooo* boring – the definition of a chinless wonder. Actually, I shouldn't say that. But he's a lawyer as well – a tax lawyer. He works in-house with HMRC these days, but our mother thinks the sun shines out of his arse for some reason. All he talks about is triathlons – literally all he talks about. I've never seen him out of Lycra. Maybe on their wedding day. That's it.'

Mark laughed heartily at this and Roz felt guilty. But she was enjoying it too. The sense of unburdening. The unspooling of years of hurt. Her throat was dry now from talking and she got up to fetch more drinks.

'So yeah,' she said, plonking them down on the coffee table and sitting down. 'My mother's a piece of work alright. She came round here, you know, to warn me off you!'

'Really?' Mark seemed genuinely shocked.

'She told me I should stop *consorting* with men and

concentrate on Chloe instead. I mean, the idea of her handing out parenting advice to anyone... She's got a cheek.'

'I'm sorry if I've caused you trouble...'

'Oh God, no, don't worry.' She sipped at her glass. 'It was the same when Daniel died. She just *had* to make me feel bad about it – ashamed of my feelings and my grief. Like, the rug had just been pulled out from under me – my hope of a fresh start with someone I loved – but could she manage a sympathetic word? Of course not. She's a complete empathy bypass.'

Mark shifted in his seat and Roz felt his awkwardness. It might be best if she shut up now about Daniel. 'Anyway,' she said, attempting breeziness. 'I've been rabbiting on for long enough. What about *your* family? Got any skeletons rattling away in the closet?'

'Nah. Sorry.' He smiled ruefully. 'It's all a bit boring really. My brother – Adam – he works in IT. It's one of those jobs where I've no real idea what he does! He's married with two kids and they live down south. A boy and a girl. Thirteen and ten.'

'Nice,' said Roz, although a cloud seemed to come over him at the end. 'Has there...?' she started, then stopped. 'Have you been out with anyone since your wife?'

'Not really.' He rubbed his eyes, looking tired suddenly. 'I usually say it's because of the job, but I think it's because I've never really wanted to before.'

Before? What did he mean by that, she wondered. Before he'd met *her*?

At that point, Chloe came padding down the stairs into the lounge. 'Hiya,' she said, acknowledging Mark, taking a seat beside Roz on the sofa. 'I'm starving,' she moaned.

'I'm not surprised,' said Roz, checking her watch. 'It's

nearly eleven. Anyway, I'm just about to put the tempura and spring rolls in.'

'Would you like some help?' asked Mark.

'No, you're fine,' said Roz. 'You relax. You've been working hard enough today.'

'If you're sure,' said Mark, and Roz went to the kitchen.

As she messed about with the oven trays, she could hear Mark asking Chloe if she'd enjoyed Whitby and Chloe giving him the full run-down of what they'd got up to. It was nice to hear some chatter in the house, she thought, till she burned her wrist on the grill.

Roz tried to eat something, but it felt as if her stomach had shrunk. It didn't really matter though, because Mark and Chloe soon got through the food.

In the run up to midnight, Chloe turned off Roz's background music and switched on the TV. Nile Rodgers and Chic were playing on the massive stage by the river Thames – better than the tired old acts that were usually wheeled out for these things. They'd managed to create some sort of party atmosphere for the shivering audience; Chloe had never heard of them, but was soon won over.

Roz topped up Mark and Chloe with the apple juice and poured herself a glass of fizz, while Chloe glared at her disapprovingly.

'Would you like a small glass? A tiny one?' Roz asked her, but Chloe refused.

Then, when it was time for the big countdown, the three of them stood up. And when Big Ben chimed the arrival of the new year, the three of them sang 'Auld Lang

Syne' and Mark was impressed that Roz knew all the words.

'My mother's influence – again!' she said.

'Well then,' he said, raising a toast. 'Here's to next year. It's going to be our best yet.'

Our? Roz felt a warmth flow through her, as she and Chloe clinked glasses with him.

CHAPTER TWENTY-FOUR

Chloe yawned all through the New Year fireworks and went to bed as soon as they were over. Mark moved to the couch to be closer to Roz, so the sound of their voices wouldn't keep her awake. He kicked off his shoes and spread out, making himself at home.

'So then,' he said. 'Have you made any resolutions?'

Roz sighed heavily. 'All the usual ones. To lose weight.' She held up her glass. 'To drink less... I'll be forty this year.'

'Oh, really? When's your birthday?'

'The 9th of February.' She grimaced. 'I've tried not to think about it.'

'Ah, you're just a youngster,' he said.

'How old are *you* then?' she asked.

'Forty-eight,' he said. 'It's not that bad, I promise.'

'Hmm,' she said. 'Maybe not for a man.' She sipped at her glass again. This was definitely her last drink. Probably. 'My worst nightmare's that I'll end up as a lonely old cat lady – apart from the fact I'm allergic to cats, but you know what I mean.'

He chuckled. 'I do, but that won't happen,' he said.

'I wouldn't be so sure. Even Kate's getting married – my mate I told you about, the one down in London. She always swore she wasn't into all that – always said she'd be the last woman standing. And then Chloe will leave home...'

'Come on,' he said, gently. 'That's a good way off yet.'

'Hmm,' Roz said again. 'It's sooner than you think. And what'll become of me then? I need a new job, a career, a life!'

'What kind of career?' he asked.

It was nice to be able to talk about this stuff with another grown adult. One who actually cared. Or who gave a good impression of caring. 'Well,' she said. 'I'm kind of fascinated by human psychology. The workings of the brain. I'd love to be a therapist of some kind. Helping people with their problems.'

'Interesting,' he said. 'Well, it's never too late to change course...'

'I guess not,' she said, doubtfully.

He paused a moment. 'I was just wondering... about Chloe's dad... You've never really mentioned him.'

'Ugh. It's a long story,' said Roz.

'We've got time.'

'OK then.' She gulped the last of the fizz in her glass and stood up to go and open another bottle.

'Another one?' he asked.

'Seeing as it's New Year,' she said, slightly miffed at him for raining on her parade.

Back in the lounge with a full glass, she carried on with her tale: 'I stayed in Sheffield after uni, messing around, doing a crummy temp job that turned into six years. Then one day I decided to jack it in and go travelling to Australia. I couldn't face another cold winter!'

'I don't blame you,' he said.

'It was amazing to start with. The rippling, velvet air when I got off the plane in Melbourne. The sharp hit of eucalyptus in my nose. The parched ground, so different from the dankness around here. I'd never felt so happy and free. I didn't know a soul, but I got some shifts in a bar and met loads of new people from all over the world. And then after work we'd have a few beers, smoke a joint.' She stopped there. Was that a look of reproach on his face? 'Only once or twice,' she lied.

'To start with?'

'Eh?'

'You said it was amazing to start with...'

'Ah, yeah, so I moved on to Alice Springs and got a job there. In a bar. Again.' Mark looked down at his fingernails and she knew he was bored. 'That's where I met Pete. He was travelling too. A Canadian. Long dark hair, very good-looking, very cool, but he knew it.'

He was listening intently now.

'I was convinced it was true love and imagined our perfect future together, like you do.' She hesitated. 'And then I got pregnant.'

'Ah,' he said.

'Exactly.' She closed one eye and focused on the glass in her hand, embarrassed. She needed to get this story over and done with. He didn't need to know the gory details. 'And, anyway, I... I decided to end things with him. He was too young. Too much of a pothead.'

'Not good.' Mark nodded like he understood.

'The morning sickness was awful. The heat sickened me. It was creepy and stifling – I felt I was suffocating. I had to get away. I still hate Australia to this day.'

'So you came back here?'

'Yep,' she sighed. 'I had to move back in with my parents for a while. It was pretty grim actually. That Christmas...' She shook her head. 'A real low point. My mother was a nightmare. And Fiona... ugh. *She'd* never had to do anything like that of course. She'd always done everything in the right order. She'd never brought shame on the family or had to throw herself on our mother's mercy.' Roz was conscious she was rambling now. 'After Chloe was born, I couldn't get out of there fast enough.'

'So are you still in touch?' he asked. 'With Chloe's dad, I mean.'

'No way! It was a short... *relationship* – hardly worthy of the name. He knows nothing about her – doesn't even know she exists. '

'Sounds like that might be for the best,' said Mark. 'Does Chloe ever ask about him?'

'She did once and I told her the truth – that I didn't know her dad very well and that I don't know where he is.' She breathed out. 'But that's all ancient history, and anyway, I'm grateful to him. Chloe's the best thing that's ever happened to me. I know it's a cliché, but I love the bones of her.' She suppressed a hiccup from the fizz repeating on her. 'As I said, my mate Kate's getting married to her partner, Samantha. It's in May and Chloe's going to be their bridesmaid. I'm so proud of her. I'll probably burst on the day. And I'm maid of honour. Kate hasn't got any sisters or anything so she's just having the two of us.'

She turned to face him square on, steadying herself. 'Tell me... Are you doing anything on the 10th of May? It's a Friday.'

'Eh, no, I don't think so,' said Mark. 'Why?'

'Well, you are now. If you want to, of course. I'd love it if you'd come to the wedding with me.'

'Really?'

'Really. It's in Buxton. At The Old Hall.'

'I'd love to,' he beamed.

And they kissed – properly – for the first time.

Roz opened her eyes and stiffened. Her tongue was furry, her head thumped. She was in bed – on her own – her dress and underwear in a pile on the floor next to her. She picked up her phone to find nothing, except the time, which was six o'clock.

Heart racing, she tried to piece things together. Chloe had gone to bed not long after midnight – tired and probably bored by the two of them talking. There had been a lot of talking. Mainly by herself. She couldn't remember all of it. Or Mark leaving. Or climbing the stairs to bed. Or the order it happened in.

She had a vague memory of a kiss on the couch. Of him being in her room. Maybe he'd had to put her to bed. What if Chloe had seen it? Or maybe things had gone further. Had he slept in her bed and got up before Chloe was awake? Had anything *happened*? A wave of nausea rose up inside her, making her retch. She ran to the bathroom, but it subsided when she got there.

She pulled on her dressing gown to go downstairs and clean everything away before Chloe got up. To get things back to normal.

She was half-expecting to find a note from him. A scribble on a piece of paper. But again – nothing. Just the candles on the sideboard, melted to the bottom like ugly, lumpen fossils, and all her empty glasses, smeared with lipstick. She picked them up, sickened at herself, recalling the amount of booze she'd got through.

She went through to the kitchen and slung the empty gin and prosecco bottles in the recycling. There was still some of the apple juice left, but she chucked that out too: she didn't need a reminder that Mark had been stone cold sober all night. Had he said he was working this morning? She couldn't remember that either.

To distract herself, she did the washing up and dragged the slow cooker out of its cupboard. Her plan had been to make a beef stew for New Year's Day dinner – something simple and straightforward that she could switch on and forget about, while she and Chloe went for a nice walk to the Pavilion Gardens. But the thought of frying off the meat brought back the sick feeling and she couldn't face chopping veg in time with her headache.

She went up for a shower instead, fretting that she'd fucked things up and scared Mark off for good. She'd probably come over as a desperate lush...

When she got out of the shower, she texted him, trying her best to sound casual: *Really enjoyed last night. Hope to see you soon.* She added a kiss, then deleted it. Oh God, this was so lame. She hated this feeling.

Roz hadn't heard her get up, but Chloe was standing in the doorway watching her. 'Can we have pancakes for breakfast?' Chloe asked. 'And syrup?'

'Sure,' said Roz, relieved that she didn't have other questions.

But the relief was short-lived. She was regretting sending

the text now, feeling needy and exposed, like she couldn't relax till he'd replied and everything was normal again.

Then the rain started up and the two of them hung around the house all day doing not very much. By late afternoon, Mark still hadn't responded and Roz convinced herself he *must* be working. He probably had to keep his phone off at work. But it didn't stop her checking every few minutes.

At half past five, Roz made cheesy pasta for dinner, which they ate in front of the TV while Chloe watched *Doctor Who*. Then, still tired from their late night, they went to bed early.

Roz was woken at 10pm by a text from Mark: *It was fun. Thanks for inviting me.*

After the hours of tension – of waiting for his reply – the relief flooded through her. But it departed just as quickly.

Really? That was it? No explanation of where he'd been today, no mention of what happened last night, no mention of meeting up again. Not even a *See you soon*.

CHAPTER TWENTY-FIVE

On the first Monday in January, Angie returned to work after the Christmas holidays and subjected Roz to the usual post-mortem of her festive season in all its technicolour glory. From the Christmas Day food and drink at her daughter's house to the list of the gifts she'd got for her grandchildren – and received in return – no detail was too small. At one point, she opened her blouse to show off the bra her husband had bought her from Rigby & Peller. His generosity had extended to the matching knickers as well – and Roz was happy to take her word on that.

Roz was finding it harder than usual to concentrate on Angie's prattle. She hadn't heard from Mark since the text on New Year's Day and her upset and confusion over his luke-warm response was turning to something else. Anger at feeling used.

'That's where the Queen used to buy her undies,' said Angie.

'Eh?' said Roz. 'Sorry, I was miles away.'

'Are you OK, love?' asked Angie, frowning. 'You look a bit... pre-occupied.'

'Yep, yep.' Roz smiled weakly. 'I'm fine.'

Later in the day, Roz came back from lunch to find an envelope on her chair and Angie sitting waiting for her.

'Did you get one of these?' Roz asked her, tearing it open.

Angie nodded grimly as Roz scanned the letter. The acquisition of the hotel was due to complete in a fortnight. The new owners were 'significantly stream-lining' the workforce. Roz was 'at risk of redundancy'. There would be a three-month consultation period and help in finding a new job for those employees that had to be let go.

Angie started on one of her monologues – telling Roz who else in the hotel had had one, speculating on the amount of the redundancy pay-out – but Roz tuned out. All this was hardly a surprise, but it was moving a bit quickly. She'd grown to loathe her job and redundancy might give her the impetus she needed to find something new. But on the other hand, the work was easy, close to home and close to Chloe's school. Her life might well be boring, but it 'worked' – and now all that could change. She had to talk to someone about what to do for the best.

After she got home from work, when Chloe was in the bath, she considered calling Kate, then decided against it. She was always ringing her with her dramas, whenever something went wrong – always dumping on her with every problem and setback. What was that thing about 'radiators' and 'drains'? Some people are radiators and some people are drains. She'd definitely become a drain on Kate.

Or there was Fiona. Or her dad. They'd be good on the nuts and bolts of it. Advising her on her rights. How much any redundancy payment was likely to be. But she didn't want to go there. She was sick of being the one with all the problems. And it would be like poking her mother with a stick. Inviting more censure, more pity.

Or there was Mark. He would be a good person to talk to, to put some perspective on things.

She'd dialled his number before she could talk herself out of it, but there was no reply, and so she left a message: *I've had some crappy news at work. I was thinking... I feel like I could do with chatting it through. Could you call me back? If you've got time of course. No worries if not...*

Mark surprised her by ringing back straight away. 'Hiya,' he said, as if they spoke every day. 'How can I be of assistance, Madam?'

'Hi,' said Roz and smiled, all her annoyance forgotten. 'It's work,' she said, and told him about the letter. 'I could do with some advice.' She hesitated. 'I was thinking... Maybe we could get together this weekend. I could come over to your place, maybe – to Didsbury?'

'Ah, well now,' he said. 'That might be a bit tricky. I've got this big charity cycle ride coming up.'

'Oh... Right,' said Roz. 'You never said.'

'I mentioned it at New Year, remember?'

'Did you? Sorry.' She flushed bright red. 'I was a bit drunk.'

'Just a bit!' he scoffed.

'So it's this weekend? The cycle ride?' she asked, glossing over her embarrassment.

'Er, no. It's not till the end of the month, but I'm spending all my free time training for it. I'm a bit out of practice.'

'In this weather?' said Roz. 'It's not the best time of year for a bike ride...'

'It's actually in Portugal...'

'Oh... Right,' she said again. She couldn't remember that either.

'Yep, it's a five-day route down the Atlantic coast. To raise funds for a new CT scanner for the hospital.'

'Ah. Nice one,' said Roz.

'A few of us from work are doing it – three guys, two girls. About a hundred miles a day.'

'Sounds like hard work,' said Roz.

'So it's probably best if I give you a shout when I get back,' he said. 'Once I've recovered, that is!'

'Yeah,' said Roz. 'Sure. That's fine.'

'So...' he said. 'What's the issue with work, then?'

'Oh look, it doesn't matter. It can wait till you're back.'

'If you're sure... Wish me luck, then. And see you on the other side!' He laughed and hung up.

So that was it. He was off – and her worries about the redundancy thing would have to wait till she saw him face to face.

She looked down at her thighs. Her New Year resolutions had already bitten the dust, but it wasn't too late to get fit. She'd look into it tomorrow – see what local classes were available. Maybe swimming or something. She and Chloe could go together.

It was nearly dinner time, so she went to the kitchen and opened the fridge, where the remains of a bottle of white wine caught her eye. It had been in there a while, and she felt like a glass, but it was only Monday – a bit early for that.

Her phone beeped on the kitchen counter. It was a text from

Mark with a photo attached: *This was you on NYE when I put you to bed!* it said. He'd added a crying-with-laughter emoji, but it was far from funny. She was lying on her bed with her mouth hanging open, her limbs floppy as a rag-doll. It was humiliating and mortifying – but at least it seemed that 'putting her to bed' was all that had happened. That she hadn't disgraced herself further. *Oh God. Sorry!* was all she could bring herself to reply.

After tea, Chloe asked if she could watch *EastEnders*.

'No,' said Roz, firmly. 'I think you should go and do your homework.'

Chloe whined at her, but Roz stood her ground. She was too young for all that – all the storylines about infidelity, rape, abortion and worse. The adult world would come for her soon enough.

When Chloe had finally gone to do as she was told, Roz struggled to concentrate on the miserable plot line. Her mind was whirring as she replayed her earlier conversation with Mark. Who were the female colleagues he was going away with? Were they *only* colleagues? They must all get pretty close to each other, working in a high-pressured arena like an operating theatre. When exactly was he going to Portugal and when exactly would he be back? All he'd said was it was happening 'at the end of the month', the end of January.

As the days passed, she wondered if it was possible he'd made up the whole bike ride thing. If it was an excuse to let her down gently. If he was ghosting her and she hadn't realised yet.

But why the withdrawal of attention? She'd been worried about the lack of 'spark' she had with him compared to Daniel, but maybe Mark felt no spark with *her*. These things worked both ways. Or maybe she'd been too full-on – too keen, too drunk – and scared him off.

A cold emptiness took hold of her, worse than before. For years, all she'd wanted was a partner in life – a 'significant other' by her side, like everyone else seemed to have. Now she'd managed to lose two in the space of a few months. She needed to accept it – she was clearly cursed.

CHAPTER TWENTY-SIX

My God, you can smell the money round here.

I must be mad, sitting out here in this car, freezing my arse off. The old place is looking good, mind – a 'well-to-do family home'. You've been busy tarting it up – or throwing money at someone else to do it. Still, you're not exactly short of it.

And I see a skip's arrived. More renovations planned?

Those sash windows must've cost a fortune – and the land-scaped garden. The fairy lights along the fence are a nice touch…

Ah, here you come now. You and the dog. Walkies time.

You look flushed, like you've had a few glasses of red with your Sunday roast. Or it's the tan from Portugal. And here comes the wife to wave you off – the lovely Lauren, classy as ever. God, who kisses their wife when they leave to walk the dog?

Where are you going? The fields? The park?

Imagine you were up to something and I found you out. Something that'd ruin your perfect little set-up. I wouldn't put it past you.

I'd follow you if I had the time. One day I will.

CHAPTER TWENTY-SEVEN

January had been a slog, but finally it was coming to an end. At Dalton's request, Roz was working her way along the floors of the hotel, pulling down all the tartan paraphernalia after their 'Burns Night Weekend'. There were a surprising number of Scots who lived in the local area – and an even more surprising number of English people who wanted to eat haggis, turnips and deep fried Mars Bar flavoured ice cream. Or maybe it was the chance of a night on the whisky that drew people in – a staging post in the wintry desert between Christmas and Valentine's Day.

Back at her desk, Angie was lying in wait for Roz, arms folded. 'Oh, you're back,' she said. 'Your phone's been going nineteen to the dozen!'

Roz picked it up to see a couple of missed calls and a text from Mark: *Hiya. Are you around for a quick chat?*

Roz perked right up. She hadn't expected him to call at all and certainly not so soon after his return.

She slipped out into the corridor, to Angie's chagrin, and called him straight back.

'How are you?' she asked. 'Was Portugal fun?'

He laughed. 'Yes and no! The old legs are a bit heavy but apart from that I'm fine... How are *you*?'

'Oh, I'm fine. Keeping busy.'

'Listen,' he said. 'I'm just about to go into theatre, so I'll be quick. I was wondering if you'd like to go out a week on Saturday? For your fortieth. The 9th of February, isn't it?'

'Yes,' said Roz, her stomach bubbling with excitement. He'd remembered!

'I was thinking we could go for a night out in Manchester,' he said. 'For cocktails, then dinner at San Carlo or somewhere. You could stay over at mine. We can get a taxi back to Didsbury.'

'Oh, wow,' said Roz. 'Yep. Definitely. I could really do with something to look forward to. The only issue is—'

'Chloe?'

'Yep, although....' She thought for a moment. 'I could *maybe* ask Fiona if she could have her... Tell you what, I'll ring her and test the water.'

'Excellent,' he said. 'Well, let me know and I'll ring up and book. OK, I've got to run now...'

'No problem,' she said and called her sister straight away while the iron was hot.

Fiona answered with her work voice, nasal and clipped. She sounded busy and Roz felt bad for asking.

'Of course. No problem,' said Fiona. 'Although... I've got a big deal on and the completion date's the following Monday, so I'll probably be at work till early evening that Saturday. If it's easier, you could just bring Chloe to the office?'

'Brilliant!' said Roz. 'You're a gem, Fi. Thanks so much. I owe you one.'

CHAPTER TWENTY-EIGHT

Roz woke early on the morning of her birthday. It was weird. She'd been dreading this day for months – had braced herself for a maelstrom of negative emotions – but now it was here, she felt surprisingly OK about it. She had her health, she had Mark – and a night out in Manchester to look forward to. Just as long as she went steady on the alcohol: she couldn't afford a repeat of New Year's Eve.

Chloe was in a good mood too. She crept into bed with Roz at eight that morning, clutching a massive birthday card she'd made at after-school club. It had a big '40' on the front, made from loads of coloured buttons.

'Wow! That's amazing!' said Roz, hugging her, although everyone at the school would now know how old she was. 'So then...' she said. 'Are you looking forward to staying with Auntie Fiona tonight?'

'Yup!' Chloe nodded eagerly. 'I've already packed my rucksack.' Bless her, thought Roz. She was obviously ready for a break too: it could get pretty claustrophobic here with just the two of them.

Downstairs, there was a birthday card from her mother on the doormat. *Enjoy your special day*, she'd written inside. *From Mum and Dad*. Roz shook her head. Would it have killed her to write *Love?* she wondered. Still, it was more than she'd had from her at Christmas.

Roz shook herself, making a conscious decision to focus on the day ahead. She intended to spend it pampering herself, getting ready for tonight: a face-pack (which would amuse Chloe); a long soak in the bath; and she'd blow-dry her hair properly. Then, like Chloe, she'd pack her overnight bag.

Lying in the bath, she regarded her body with a critical eye, wondering what would happen with Mark at the end of the night and if she was up to date with current pube trends. She decided just to shave her legs, nicking herself with the razor from being out of practice. The cut was tiny, but the blood kept coming, spreading through the water. She'd forgotten about all this palaver, it had been so long. So long since she'd slept with someone. So long since she'd been touched by anyone but the M&S bra-fitter. She wasn't sure she was ready for it – if she'd remember what to do.

Roz and Chloe caught the six o'clock train into Manchester. Arriving at Piccadilly Station, they were swallowed up by the swell of bodies – the shopping crowd going home and the pub crowd just arriving. The night air crackled with poten- tial and Roz realised how much she'd missed the big city buzz.

They marched arm in arm down to Spinningfields – the area of sci-fi glass and chrome towers where the city's banks and offices were located, shimmering in the moonlight like something out of Bladerunner. When they reached Fiona's building, they passed through automatic doors onto a steep escalator, which ascended to a white marble atrium. Its black leather sofas did nothing to humanise the space, nor did the sub-Rothko corporate artwork that hung on the walls.

Chloe stopped and stood there. 'Wow!' she whispered, which somehow rankled with Roz. Maybe because she had never worked anywhere as grand as this and never would.

Roz approached the smart-suited receptionist at the desk, transfixed by her calligraphic eyebrows and plastic pout. 'I'm here to see Ms. Johnson,' said Roz in her poshest voice. 'I'm her sister,' she added proudly. 'She's expecting us.'

If the receptionist was surprised, her face didn't show it. She just nodded and told them to take a seat on the sofas.

It was ten minutes before Fiona emerged from one of the lifts and crossed the shiny floor towards them. She was dressed in jeans and a white shirt, her blonde hair flowing loose. And she didn't acknowledge the receptionist, Roz noticed.

'Happy birthday, old bird!' Fiona trilled at Roz, giving Chloe's shoulders a squeeze. 'So tell me. What does forty feel like?'

'Well, it's better than the alternative,' said Roz.

'Bit morbid,' Fiona chuckled. 'But true.' She handed Roz a birthday card, all efficient as if she was handing over some title deeds. *Let the celebrations be-Gin!* the card said in pink, girlie sparkles under a picture of a cocktail, and Roz feigned amusement. Inside the card was another stiff white envelope.

'That's your present,' said Fiona. 'I really hope you like it. Don't worry if not, though. The receipt's in there in case you want to take it back...'

Roz opened it to find a heart-shaped locket on a fine gold

chain – the last piece of jewellery she'd have chosen for herself.

'What do you think?' asked Fiona, eagerly.

'It's lovely. Really nice. Thank you so much,' said Roz, hugging her tight and putting it in her bag.

'So then,' said Fiona. 'Which *mate* are you going out with? Anyone I know?'

Roz swallowed, pondering her words carefully in front of Chloe. 'It's not actually a mate.'

'Oh.'

'It's a guy I've been seeing for the last few weeks. Mark, he's called.'

'Ah,' said Fiona. '*That* guy...?'

'Oh God,' said Roz exasperated. 'You're as bad as Mum... He's a good guy. An anaesthetist.'

'Yeah. Mum said he was a doctor,' said Fiona, cagily.

'He lives in Didsbury,' Roz boasted.

As expected, Fiona couldn't help being impressed by this and Roz relished it. 'He's into cycling and all that malarkey. He'd get on well with your Ian!'

Fiona checked her watch. 'Where are you off to then? What time's your reservation?'

'Seven thirty,' said Roz. 'At San Carlo.'

Fiona whistled and Roz was gratified.

'I'd better run actually,' said Roz, kissing the top of Chloe's head. 'Have a fab time.'

'We will!' said Fiona, putting her arm round her niece. 'It'll be lovely having another girl in the house for once. We can watch a nice film – your choice, Chloe. And you can choose the snacks too.'

'Well then,' said Roz. 'I'll see you tomorrow.'

Chloe and Fiona waved her off and Roz turned to leave,

missing Chloe already. Although she'd be fine with Fiona, she knew that. And Chloe loved all that girlie stuff.

Sailing back down the escalator, Roz rummaged in her bag for the necklace Fiona had given her and pulled out the receipt. Two hundred pounds it had cost! It was definitely going back to the shop. She could buy something useful with that money – a new coat to replace this old velvet thing...

Out on the pavement, Roz paused a moment for her eyes to adjust to the dark, then pulled out her phone to check the directions to the restaurant.

She had a text, she saw. From Mark: *Really sorry*, it said. *Not going to make it tonight. We're dealing with an RTA at work. Sorry again! I'll make it up to you. Promise x*

What the actual fuck? An RTA? What the hell was that? Something clicked in her brain: a 'road traffic accident'... So was there no one else who could cover for him at work? Seriously?

A volcanic rage began in her stomach, rising up through her chest to her throat. Her hands shook and she felt dizzy, staggering over to a lamp post to steady herself. She couldn't believe this was happening. Every bloody time! Why did she always get thwarted? *Why?*

She took her overnight bag, tossed it into the air and booted it as hard as she could into the road. Then she heard herself scream. A primal shriek of pain from the depths of her being. A sound she'd heard only once before, when she was in labour with Chloe.

After a moment, her rib-cage stopped heaving and she had the strong sense she was being watched. She was. By a homeless guy sitting in a doorway, wrapped in a filthy sleeping bag. He was staring at her now. In concern.

Roz pulled a face and flicked the V's at him, then went to

pick up her bag – and the toothbrush, the spare pair of knickers and all the other stuff that had burst out of it and was strewn across the street. Then she scurried off, sickened by herself.

What now? There was no way she was going back to fetch Chloe. No chance of her going back to Fiona's office, to see the look of pity on her face. There was only so much humiliation she could take. And it wouldn't be fair on Chloe: she'd been so looking forward to this evening.

No. She'd just go home – and collect Chloe tomorrow as planned. She'd pretend that everything was tickety-boo. Like she always fucking did.

Up ahead, Roz's house was in eerie darkness, but the student house next door was lit up like Versailles – every light in the place was on and huge flames were lashing up out of the fire-pit in the front garden. And the garden was crawling with students: they were obviously having another one of their parties.

Roz bowed her head and tried to hurry past, but the tall girl with the topknot wasn't having any of it. 'Hey!' she called to Roz as she passed by their hedge. 'Are you OK?'

'Yes. I'm fine,' said Roz, and paused a moment. She didn't want to be thought of as rude.

'I'm Ellie,' said the girl. She had huge brown eyes and a gentle Welsh accent, and was clutching a bottle of whisky. 'You look like you've been crying,' she said to Roz. 'Where's your little daughter?'

'She's at her auntie's house. My sister's.' Roz hesitated. 'I was meant to be out on a date, but he's stood me up.'

'No way!' said Ellie. 'What a bastard!'

Roz had to laugh. 'I'm Roz, by the way.'

'Would you like a drink, Roz?' asked Ellie, waving the bottle at her.

'You know what?' said Roz, surprising herself. 'I think I would.'

'Well come and have one then,' said Ellie, opening the gate for her. 'We've got enough booze to sink a battleship...'

Roz smiled and followed her up the path to the fire-pit, where Ellie stopped and handed her the bottle. Roz wiped the top of it and took a glug of the cheap whisky. It burned the back of her throat, but a pleasing warmth flooded through her.

Ellie finished off the dregs of it, then coughed theatrically. 'Right!' she said. 'Let's go inside and see if we can find something better than this gut-rot.'

They carried on inside the patchouli-scented house with its lava lamps, rugs and batiks on the walls – the same sort of stuff Roz had had in her own flat at uni – and headed for the fridge.

'It's my birthday today,' Roz mouthed at Ellie over the din of dub reggae. 'I'm forty.'

'No way!' said Ellie. 'We need to do a toast or something.' Then she turned the music down and shouted to her mates. 'Listen up, guys! This is Roz. It's her birthday!'

CHAPTER TWENTY-NINE

Roz woke up under a crocheted blanket on an unfamiliar grubby couch. Her stomach lurched in panic till she remembered where she was – in the student house, next door. *Oh God*, she thought, pressing her painful eyeballs. She was forty years of age – far too old for this kind of thing. Drinking on an empty stomach. Necking whatever she was handed. Rough whisky. Supermarket cider. Vodka jelly shots. Cringe didn't cover it.

She remembered a chorus of 'Happy Birthday' from the girls at the party while the boys stood round looking at her like she was an alien – an alien old enough to be their mother. Then she'd bored the pants off Ellie and a couple of the other girls – Lou and Nia – who'd been really sweet and polite and had sat there, solemn-faced, while she regaled them with various miserable episodes from her life story. They'd been wide-eyed when she'd told them about Daniel and the aneurysm, but lost interest fast when she began whining about her job. One of them had offered her a joint to shut her up and she remembered taking it, thinking how

Mark wouldn't approve. And then she remembered... nothing.

Ellie appeared in the doorway with a mug of tea for her. 'You OK?' she asked.

'Thanks,' said Roz. 'Not really. I'm mortified... You won't tell Chloe about any of this, by the way, will you?'

'Don't worry,' said Ellie. 'Of course not.'

Roz smiled. Then she groaned. 'I've got to go and pick her up from my sister's now. In Alderley Edge...'

'Nightmare!' said Ellie, with a yawn. 'I'll leave you to it.'

Roz went home, had a quick shower and got in the car. She was even more nervy on the drive to Fiona's than last time, taking it as steady as possible, worried she'd still be over the limit.

She rang her sister's doorbell with a horrible sense of déjà-vu and Fiona appeared, bright and breezy as usual, without so much as a shadow under her eyes.

'Here she is, the party animal!' Fiona announced.

Roz gave a thin smile and stepped into the hallway.

'God, you look rough,' said her sister cheerfully.

'Thanks,' said Roz. 'I am. I feel like I might barf.' At least she didn't have to lie about that.

'Did you have a good night?' Fiona asked. 'What was the food like? Was it busy?'

'Yeah. It was really nice,' said Roz. 'Overdid it on the wine though. Also very nice.'

'Chloe's been helping me with Sunday lunch,' said Fiona. 'Come on through...'

'Wait.' Roz grabbed her arm. '*She's* not about to turn up again, is she?'

'What?'

'Mum...'

'No. No, she's not,' said Fiona.

'Thank God for that!'

'Oh for fuck's sake, Roz. Grow up!' Fiona hissed.

Roz was stung into silence.

'Why have you cut Mum off?' Fiona asked her directly. 'She's really upset. She says she hasn't heard from you for ages.'

'*She's* upset?' Roz shook her head, speechless. 'She's always been a complete cow towards me. Why would she even miss me?'

'I think you're being a bit unfair...'

'Unfair?' scoffed Roz.

'Yes. Unfair. You've got a pretty selective memory. Remember when she took you in when you fucked up your life? Coming back from your gap year after two months, knocked up by some dropkick druggie you'd only just met. Who was rough with you and pulled the condom off without telling you, then did a runner. The latest in a long line of disasters...'

'Keep it down,' whispered Roz. 'The kids'll hear.'

But Fiona carried on, her voice like a pneumatic drill through Roz's brain. 'Not to mention the other help she's given you over the years. Looking after Chloe when she was tiny so you could take the job at The Old Hall. Buying you a little car so you could get around.'

Roz tried to speak but Fiona carried on. 'You forget what she went through for the sake of our family. Leaving her home, her family and friends, in Glasgow. Giving up her career when she got married, like you had to in those days.'

'Oh God, don't start,' said Roz. 'She's forever guilt-tripping us about that. Poor Dad, having to listen to it all the time...'

'*Poor Dad?* Never mind *Poor Dad*. He had the life of bloody Reilly. Never at home, always away on business trips, coming home at all hours, leaving everything up to Mum. She must have been so bloody... lonely.'

'Yeah, well,' said Roz. 'It was Dad who was earning the money for the lifestyle she wanted. She turned keeping up with the Joneses into an art form. He might have been a bit of a drinker back in the day, but it was mainly client entertainment.'

'He was a borderline alcoholic, Roz! And the rest...'

'The rest?' Roz asked.

Fiona shook her head.

'C'mon,' said Roz. 'I'm listening...'

'The affairs,' said Fiona quietly.

'No way.' Roz laughed. 'What affairs? When?'

'I saw him once. Caught him in the act. I got home early from school and I found him. *Them*. He was shagging her on the carpet.'

'What? Shagging who?'

'Well, on that occasion, it was one of the secretaries from work... Such a cliché.'

'Really?' said Roz.

Fiona nodded. 'Really.'

'I had no idea...'

'No. Of course you didn't,' said Fiona wearily. 'I told Mum, but she knew about it already. You had just started uni. She asked me not to tell you. You were a bit fragile at the time. About to do your exams.'

Roz stood there, chastened to be told this by her younger sister.

'Dad's not always been the big cuddly bear you think he is,' sighed Fiona. 'Mum kept the worst of his behaviour from us. She did her best. For us. And you need to lay off her.'

Chloe came running through from the kitchen, all wide-eyed. 'What's wrong, Mum?' she asked, looking from Roz to Fiona and back. 'Are you having a row?'

'No love, everything's fine,' they said in unison.

'C'mon, Chloe,' said Roz. 'Grab your things. We need to get back.'

'Why?' asked Chloe, crestfallen.

'Don't argue, love,' said Roz. 'We just do.'

Roz put her foot on the accelerator and seethed all the way home. She couldn't believe Fiona had kept all this stuff from her about their dad – and now had the gall to ambush her with it, shaming her in the process. She didn't need this toxicity in her life. If she had to cut Fiona out of her life as well as her mother, then so be it.

Back home, she ushered Chloe up the path and through the door, head down to avoid being spotted by the students. 'Go upstairs and sort your stuff for school tomorrow,' she told Chloe, who knew better than to resist.

By now, her hangover was really kicking in. Even though it was only mid-afternoon, bed-time couldn't come soon enough. And pizza would have to do for tea, assuming there was one in the freezer.

Her phone rang out on the kitchen counter. It was Mark calling and she nearly didn't answer; she wasn't sure she could mask how pissed off she still was with him for cancelling on her.

She picked it up just in time.

'Hiya,' he said, all cheery, as if nothing was up.

'Hi,' said Roz.

'I would've called you before, but I've just finished work.'

'Uh-huh,' she said.

'It was a very long shift – pretty horrible to be honest.'

Roz felt suddenly guilty: while she'd been getting wasted with a bunch of students, he'd been working all hours trying to save lives.

'Let me make it up to you,' Mark said, before she could say anything.

She sighed down the phone. 'I don't think that'll work. I can't really ask Fiona to babysit again. It's not convenient.'

'No, listen,' he said. 'We could take Chloe with us... To a fancy hotel this coming Saturday – it's the weekend after Valentine's – how does that sound? With a spa and room service – the works! I'll sort it. And somewhere for dinner as well. You just have to bring yourselves.'

CHAPTER THIRTY

On the 14th of February, Valentine's Day itself, a massive bunch of flowers arrived for Roz at The Old Hall, courtesy of Mark. She was stunned and chuffed and pleased he hadn't gone for the hackneyed choice of twelve red roses. The mix of fresh spring blooms and tiger lilies must've cost a fortune and Angie was bursting to know who had sent them, but Roz just winked and let her wonder.

Roz contrasted the bouquet with the posy of marigolds that Daniel had picked for her from the flower beds in the Pavilion Gardens on one of their lunch dates; she'd been quite embarrassed about it at the time and had binned them on her way back to the office.

It was very generous of Mark. She hadn't expected the flowers *as well as* the trip to the hotel this weekend. Chloe had been looking forward to it all week, excited at the thought of a breakfast buffet where everything was 'free' and you could have all the pancakes you wanted – not to mention the toiletries in the bathroom.

But when Chloe woke on Friday morning, she was

running a temperature and said her throat felt like broken glass. Roz was worried it might be tonsillitis again and decided to keep her off school as a precaution. Sadly, the hotel trip would be a no-no as well. Chloe was gutted, but Roz was used to disappointment by now.

She was dreading calling Mark to break the bad news, but he took it in his stride.

'No problem at all,' he said. 'I'll cancel it.'

'Will you lose money?' asked Roz.

'Oh, don't worry,' he said. 'Just the deposit – it's not much.'

'We must be cursed!' Roz joked.

'I know!' he moaned. 'Listen. Why don't I come and visit you tomorrow instead? Even just for a couple of hours. It's been ages since I saw you.'

The next day, Roz felt like she was coming down with something too. She phoned Mark to warn him – to give him the option of not coming over – but he insisted and she was glad.

He arrived at her place just after two and Roz opened the door, dressed in her most flattering pyjamas – a concession to 'making an effort'.

'Hello stranger!' he said, pressing his cold hand against her forehead. 'You look like you need a rest. And maybe a Lemsip or two.'

'You've got a lovely bedside manner,' laughed Roz, as he followed her through to the kitchen where she put the kettle on.

'Here, let me do that,' he offered.

'No, no. You're fine,' she insisted.

'How's Chloe?' he asked.

'Oh, she's through in the lounge. Watching *Frozen* for the hundredth time.'

'So she's on the mend?'

'Yeah. Still not quite herself though. So... How are *you*?' she asked.

'I'm fine,' he said. 'Never better.'

'I've got to say,' said Roz, waiting for the water to boil. 'I really admire you.'

He cocked his head at her.

'All the terrible stuff you've got to deal with at work,' she said. 'That road traffic accident you mentioned. How do you cope with that? After what happened to your wife and daughter...'

An expression crossed his face that she couldn't make out.

'Oh, I dunno.' He looked down at his hands. 'I guess I don't analyse it too much.'

Roz bit her lip. Like soldiers who'd been to war, he obviously preferred not to talk about it and she felt foolish for asking the question.

They took their mugs through to the lounge and Mark sat on the couch next to Chloe – all rugged up in her dressing gown under her pink furry throw – while Roz sat in the chair. Chloe smiled wanly at Mark and carried on watching her film.

'Do you need anything, by the way?' Mark asked Roz. 'From the shops, I mean. Or is there anything that needs doing around the house? I'm happy to help. No job too small!'

She grinned at him. 'No thanks, we're fine,' she said.

'Apart from the fact we should be in that nice hotel now. Swimming and enjoying the spa. Chloe was so disappointed we couldn't go. Weren't you, Chloe?'

Chloe nodded.

'Don't worry,' Mark assured her. 'We'll go another time, OK? When you're feeling better. Somewhere even nicer! In fact...' He dug in his pocket for his phone. 'Remember when I went to Shrigley Hall... for that conference?' He got up and showed the phone to Roz. 'There's a deal on Travelzoo. A two-night stay plus dinner and use of the pool, gym and all the other facilities for £180.'

'Wow!' said Roz. 'That sounds great.'

'I'll forward it to you,' said Mark. 'So you can have a look.'

'Great. Thanks,' said Roz. It was nice to have someone to sit back and relax with, as they passed the time chatting about nothing in particular, their voices low so as not to disturb Chloe.

'Would you like another coffee?' Roz asked him as the afternoon ticked round into early evening.

'No, ta,' said Mark.

'Or something to eat? You must be hungry.'

'No worries,' he said. 'Can I get *you* anything?'

'No, you're OK. I'll make something simple later on. Macaroni cheese or something.'

'OK,' said Mark. 'If you're sure... Listen, I should probably get off and leave you to it.'

'Hold on,' said Roz. 'There's something I want to ask you.' She reached across to the mantelpiece for the wedding invitation from Kate – newly arrived in the morning's post – and handed it to him.

'Very artistic,' he said, admiring the design on the front, which depicted the happy couple in silhouette: Kate, with her trendy long bob, in a long, slim dress, and Sam with her short crop and trouser suit.

'I was wondering if you'd like to come with me?' Roz asked. 'If you're free?'

He furrowed his brow and she assumed the worst.

'But... You've already invited me,' he said.

'What? How d'you—?'

'On New Year's Eve. You asked me if I'd come with you and I said yes.'

'Oh... Did I?' said Roz, flushing.

'Don't you remember?'

'Oh yeah, of course. I'm such an idiot.' She could hardly admit she'd been too drunk to recall it. Not in front of Chloe.

'I'm looking forward to it!' he said.

'Great,' she gushed. 'So glad you can make it.'

He opened up the invite card and read the inside. 'Roz *Plus One* it says? Don't I get a name?' He was smiling as he said it, but Roz felt awkward as hell.

'Ah, well, you see, I've told Kate all about you – obviously – but she's probably a bit busy and stuff and it's slipped her mind.' She was gabbling and she didn't know why. She hadn't spoken to Kate in a while and she wouldn't assume Roz would be bringing him.

'Don't worry. It's fine,' he said, handing back the invitation.

Roz reached up to put it back in its place.

'What's that, by the way?' he asked, peering at her.

'What's what?' she asked.

'That little black thing... on your stomach?'

Roz touched it defensively under her pyjama top. 'It's a tattoo. Of a dolphin. I got it in Australia.'

'A dolphin?' He laughed. 'It looks a bit shrivelled. Like a sea sprat.'

Roz noticed Chloe was sniggering at her. Her face fired up. 'That's pregnancy for you,' she said, brushing it off.

'You won't get a tattoo, will you Chloe?' said Mark.

Chloe shook her head.

'Alright, you two!' said Roz. God, he sounded just like her mother.

'I'm sorry,' he said. 'It's just banter. I was only joking.'

'I know,' said Roz. But she felt wounded all the same; he must have thought it to make a joke about it. Or maybe she was being too sensitive?

She changed the subject. 'I was going to suggest we could meet up next Saturday when I'm feeling better, but I've just realised – it's the 23rd – Kate's coming home to Buxton for a 'wedding planning' meet. Well, I say that... We're going to the spa at The Palace Hotel in town. To chill out and discuss things, then maybe a bit of shopping after. It's just an excuse to get together for a catch-up really.' She had no idea why she was trying to play it down. Maybe out of a sense of disloyalty – that she was going on a nice day out without him, after all the plans they'd made that hadn't worked out.

'Oh, right. No problem,' said Mark, simply, and that was it.

Roz was confused. He didn't seem at all bothered that he wouldn't be seeing her.

The *Frozen* credits were rolling now and Chloe had laid her head on the arm of the couch and closed her eyes.

Roz got up to shut the curtains. 'OK, love,' she said. 'I think it might be time for bed.'

Chloe didn't argue with her – a sure sign she was still

feeling rough. She sat up straight and swung her legs onto the floor, then tried to stand up and wobbled unsteadily.

'Are you OK?' Mark asked her. 'I can carry you up if you like?'

'Really?' Chloe seemed unsure. 'I'm a bit heavy...'

'No you're not. You're as light as a feather,' he laughed, and swept her up easily in his arms.

Roz followed them up the stairs to tuck Chloe in and Mark left them to it.

A few minutes later, Roz saw him out.

'I always used to do that with Yasmin when she was ill,' he said, pulling on his jacket and scarf. 'It's nice to be able to do it again.'

CHAPTER THIRTY-ONE

Saturday the 23rd was one of those murky February days. The sky was grey and heavy, bearing down on the houses opposite Roz, but things were looking up. Chloe was fully recovered from her illness and was also a bit happier with life in general. She'd made a new friend at school – Amy – and the two of them had gone off to Whaley Bridge for the day to play a netball match. And Roz was heading into town to meet Kate, which she'd been looking forward to for ages.

It had been Kate's idea to go to the spa. Roz had been surprised that she hadn't wanted to meet for a long lunch and a few drinks, but Kate had joked she'd need some relaxation after two days staying at her mum's. Roz had laughed along, but was secretly envious of Roz and Jan's relationship.

They met outside The Palace Hotel at ten o'clock. Kate was wearing a smart grey coat with trainers, and her hair was beautifully cut and dyed in a way that screamed 'expensive London salon'.

'You're looking well,' said Roz, as Kate kissed her on both cheeks.

'Fat, you mean?' said Kate.

'No.' Roz tutted. It wasn't like Kate to be so touchy.

They went inside to the spa, where the air was thick with aromatherapy oils and a woman in a white uniform was waiting to greet them. She took their details, then disappeared behind a lacquered Chinese screen with exotic birds on the front.

'She looks like Nurse Ratched,' Kate mouthed to Roz.

'Shush,' said Roz, putting her finger to her lips. 'She'll hear you.'

The woman returned with their fluffy white robes, complimentary slippers and a menu of treatments. 'Can I fetch you ladies a drink from the bar?' she asked.

'Please may I have a glass of cava when you have a moment?' asked Roz, polite to a fault, to make up for Kate's rudeness.

'And could I get a decaf latte?' said Kate.

'Actually, could I change my order?' asked Roz, slightly embarrassed. 'Could I have the same as her? A decaf latte?'

'You should have the fizz if you want,' said Kate.

'No, no,' said Roz. 'It's fine. I'm trying to cut down in any case.'

'No problem,' said the woman impassively. 'If you want to go and get changed, I'll bring your lattes through for you.'

'Are you having any treatments?' Kate asked Roz as they changed into their swimming stuff – Roz in a saggy old bikini, Kate in a Speedo one-piece. 'I'm already down for a pedicure.'

'Sixty pounds?' said Roz, checking the price list on the wall. 'A bit expensive for me. I think I'll stick to the free stuff.'

They went through to the pool area and pulled up some

loungers, where they lay in their robes, sipping their coffees till it was time for Kate's pedicure.

When Kate returned, they went for a dip in the warm water of the pool, which they had all to themselves. Kate, ever focused, did twenty lengths, while Roz splashed about in the shallow end trying not to get her hair wet.

'Fancy a stint in the steam room?' Roz asked, as Kate swam back up to her.

Kate exhaled loudly. 'I'd love to, but I'm afraid I can't.'

'You can't?'

'I was about to tell you earlier. It's not safe for me to use it... I'm pregnant.'

'Pregnant?' Roz was floored.

'It's very early days,' said Kate. 'We haven't told anyone yet – apart from our families.'

Roz's mind raced. 'So, er, how... I mean...?'

'How did we manage it?' Kate laughed, grabbing the side of the pool and kicking her legs. 'We had IVF.'

'You didn't say...'

'Nah. We wanted to keep it quiet – not put any pressure on ourselves. It's a hard enough process without everyone knowing all about it.'

'I can understand that.'

'It's such a nightmare, Roz. It totally fucks with your sanity. My egg count was really low.' She shook her head. 'All these older celebrities who get pregnant... It makes you think it's easy and you've got loads of time, but it's not. It's hard at this age. We had three rounds of it. You want to burrow down till it's all over and you get a happy ending – hopefully. That's why I wasn't home for Christmas or anything – I had to be in and out of the clinic like I was on elastic. I felt like I lived there. *And* it cost a fortune.'

'And the, er...' Roz swallowed.

'The father?' Kate smiled. 'It's Sam's brother, Finn.'

'Ah, that's nice,' said Roz. 'When are you due?'

'Beginning of September.' Kate pulled a face. 'I'm praying we don't have a boiling hot summer again.' She held up her fingers. 'Shall we get out now? My skin's gone all wrinkly.'

They went back to their loungers and lay down to dry off.

'So,' said Roz. 'Are you going ahead with the wedding – or postponing it?'

'Going ahead.' Kate grinned. 'We thought we might as well do it all at once! In for a penny...'

It all sounded so perfect to Roz. Kate's joyful news was such a contrast with her own miserable experience of finding herself pregnant and terrified in a country miles from home. She longed to have the chance to do it all again – properly this time – but time wasn't on her side.

'I doubt I've got any eggs left either,' said Roz, sadly. 'Which is a shame as Chloe would love a sister – before it's too late.' She smiled. 'Even a brother would do...'

Kate turned to her. 'Are you sure it's what *you* want though? It's not just your age – your hormones – doing funny things?'

'Maybe,' said Roz. Although it didn't feel like that. It was more like a profound hunger, growing from the depths of her soul.

Both of their phones pinged at the same time. It was their old school friend, Natasha in New York, on the wedding WhatsApp group. *Hey! I was sooo excited when the wedding invitation popped through the door this morning. I've just booked some flights and am so looking forward to seeing you guys in May – and all your children, partners, significant others, etc. Can't wait! xxx*

Roz and Kate rolled their eyes simultaneously.

'She's just so *American* these days, bless her!' said Kate. 'It'll be really nice to see her too though. And her Stepford husband and children.'

'Kate!' Roz rebuked her, thanking her lucky stars she had Mark now and wouldn't have to go through this wedding by herself. She'd have a partner of her own for once.

Roz and Kate ordered some lunch and two more coffees.

'So,' said Kate. 'How are things going with that grief group – The Merry Widows or whatever they're called? Is it helping you get some closure on Daniel? Are you feeling a bit better about things?'

'Actually,' said Roz. 'I've been seeing some of that other guy I was telling you about. The guy I met on the group, remember?'

'Ah, lemme see, yep. I remember now – the anaesthetist?'

'His name's Mark,' said Roz. She paused. 'We spent New Year's Eve together.'

'Ooh,' said Kate. 'You didn't tell me *that*...'

Roz smiled smugly. 'He really pushed the boat out for my birthday – and for Valentine's Day. Well, he *tried* to... We had to change our plans for a variety of reasons, but it's the thought that counts, right?'

'Totally.'

'*And*...' Roz was enjoying herself now. 'He's coming to the wedding...'

'Wow!' said Kate, sitting bolt upright. 'Nice one. I'll look forward to meeting him.'

Roz chuckled. 'Hmm. You'll be *far* too busy that day to be meeting *anyone*.'

'You know what, I'm really pleased for you,' said Kate.

'Aw, shucks,' said Roz, blushing.

'Seriously, though. You deserve it.'

'Cheers, pal.'

'And I envy you as well,' said Kate. 'A new relationship – so exciting!'

'Oh, come on,' said Roz. 'It's more exciting for you – getting married, having a baby, moving on to the next stage and all that.'

'You reckon?' said Kate. 'Yeah. I suppose.' Her eyes twinkled mischievously. 'Is he a good shag then?'

Roz thought quickly. 'A lady never tells,' she said. Mainly because they hadn't yet slept together and there was nothing to tell.

'What's he like compared to Daniel?' Kate asked.

'You're terrible!' said Roz. She could hardly admit she hadn't slept with Daniel either.

'I don't mean like that,' said Kate. 'I mean... What's he like as a person?'

'Well,' said Roz. 'He's more mature than Daniel. More mature than me too, come to that. Definitely father material. He lost his wife and daughter in a car crash.'

'Oh no. That's awful,' said Kate.

'Yeah,' said Roz. 'I think he'd like another child... He's really good with Chloe.'

'That bodes well,' said Kate.

'It does.' She paused. 'I'm just glad I've got someone to

bring to the wedding. It'll be a relief not to be on my own again – in front of everyone I know!' She looked down at her belly, pulling at her spare tyre. 'I just need to tone up now. Before the wedding. Mark says my dolphin tattoo looks more like a sea sprat.'

'Really?' Kate frowned. 'It sounds a bit like he's negging you.'

'*Negging?*'

'It's a thing apparently...'

Roz shrugged. 'Well, he's right,' she said. 'The skin went all shrivelled after Chloe was born.'

'Even so... It's not very nice. He sounds a bit of a git.'

Roz sighed. 'He didn't say it in a nasty way. Honestly. It was just a joke.' She pulled at her thighs now. 'I could do with joining a gym. I need to lose a stone – at least! – but it's expensive.'

'I can give you some exercises,' said Kate. 'No problem at all.'

'Thanks,' said Roz. 'And I've had the same drab hairstyle for years. I'm forty now. This dark colour is too harsh. I need a make-over!'

'What's brought all this on?' asked Kate. 'Not this guy again?'

'No,' said Roz, indignantly. 'It's me. My choice.'

The woman from the front desk brought them their club sandwiches and Roz brooded as drops of fat rain began to fall on the glass above them. She resolved not to criticise Mark in front of Kate again. She was too uncompromising, too black and white. She didn't really get nuance and Roz wasn't going to let her spoil things with Mark.

Kate carried on, oblivious. 'Oh by the way... There was

something I meant to ask you... Could you let me have Fiona's new address? I need to post her wedding invite.'

'Er, yeah. Sure,' said Roz.

'Your mum was the first person to RSVP out of everyone!' Kate said.

She *would* be, thought Roz. She would be.

CHAPTER THIRTY-TWO

SATURDAY 23RD FEBRUARY – 2PM – OUTSIDE
STOCKPORT TOWN HALL – MAYOR'S
RECEPTION FOR THE WINNERS OF THE
'LOCAL HERO' AWARDS

Look at you, posing with that bike, clutching your little award, smug as you like. So typical of you. You were always such a kiss-ass, a right little do-gooder, a pillar of the community.

I dunno... Asking people to shell out their hard-earned cash to sponsor your trip to Portugal – a free holiday basically, when you're loaded as it is. You could've dug in your pocket and donated the two grand to the scanner appeal yourself. What a scam!

And there's the snapper from the Stockport Express, so we can expect another fawning article in the paper. Christ, folk round here will be sick of the sight of you... And what about your team-mates – your other colleagues? They did the ride too, but they don't get a look-in?

But your son's there, of course – dressed in a suit and tie at his age – a right little 'mini-me'. He'll end up as spoiled as you are. A privileged little shit.

And the wife and daughter too, playing second fiddle in the background – in the 'supportive little women' role. They're just props to you. You don't deserve them.

And now your phone's ringing. Of course it is. And you've got to step away and take it – keep the Mayor, the photographer and everyone else waiting – freezing to death in the rain – just to show how important you are. What is it? An emergency at work?

God, you love yourself.

CHAPTER THIRTY-THREE

'This weather,' Roz moaned to Kate, after the spa lady had collected their lunch plates. 'So bloody depressing...'

'Well,' said Kate. 'I've got something to cheer you up. Something to look forward to...'

'What's that?'

'My hen weekend. In Dubrovnik. Fourteen of us.'

'Hang on.' Roz sat up. 'What? When?'

'At Easter. For the long weekend. Before I'm too pregnant to enjoy it.'

'Dubrovnik?' Roz frowned. 'Why not just Blackpool or somewhere?'

Kate pulled her robe tight around her. 'Blame Vicky! I met up with her last week. She's organising it.'

'Vicky?' Roz hadn't seen their old school friend since that night of Vicky's wedding, when Roz had been left behind on her own, stranded in the middle of nowhere, like an afterthought. Vicky had done well out of that marriage, with two daughters and a townhouse in one of the fashionable bits of south London to show for it.

'You don't mind, do you?' said Kate. 'She's a massive *Game of Thrones* fan and she really wants to go 'cos some of it was filmed there.'

'Oh,' said Roz. 'No, that's fine. I'm relieved not to have the responsibility.' She rubbed her nose. 'Is Sam going?'

'Nah. She'll be in Costa Rica, the lucky cow. Filming for three weeks. She'll have to miss it.'

'So will I, I'm afraid.'

'How come?' said Kate.

'Well, there's the cost for one thing. And also, what would I do with Chloe?'

'Bring Chloe with you! It's hardly going to be a debauched affair. And we're keeping the cost down by sharing rooms. You and Chloe can share with me. We'll get a suite.'

'Even so,' said Roz. 'There's the flights and spending money and—'

'Look, if necessary, we'll all chip in for you to come!'

Roz said nothing. It was a nice offer, but she still had some pride left. She didn't want to be a charity case.

'Anyway, I'm sure we'll sort something out,' said Kate. 'I've asked Vicky to send round an email with all the details. The dates when the deposit and the balance need to be paid and all that jazz.'

'OK,' said Roz. The place was getting busier and she checked her watch. 'Well then. I suppose we should do some wedding planning at some point?'

Kate pretended to yawn, then chuckled. 'OK. Here's the plan. We'll have the ceremony at the bandstand in the Pavilion Gardens at two o'clock on Friday the 10th of May. Then the reception in The Old Hall at four. And, er, that's it. Job done.'

'Well,' laughed Roz. 'There's a *teensy* bit more to it than that. What about your dress?'

'That's all in hand,' said Kate. 'There's a great dressmaker down the road from us in London. You can rest assured it won't be a meringue!'

'I didn't think it would be,' said Roz. 'And what about the catering? Did you get those menus I sent you?'

'Yep. Yep,' said Kate. 'And the list of wine options. We haven't read it all properly yet, but I'll get back to you on Monday once I've discussed it with Sam. Oh and another thing... For the reception, we want to have the formal part first – the speeches and stuff – before the meal. To get them out of the way so everyone can enjoy themselves and have a few drinks without having to worry. Especially my dad!'

'Good idea,' said Roz. 'Now, for the flowers... I was going to suggest our usual florist we use at the hotel. What do you reckon? They're excellent and they'll do you a good deal. I can send you some bumph about it.'

'Fine. Fine,' said Kate.

Roz laughed. Kate was as cool about everything as she'd expected and didn't have a 'bridezilla' bone in her body.

'That just leaves the disco!' said Roz. 'Shall I give Big Dave a call? You can't go wrong with Big Dave's Mobile Disco.'

Kate giggled. 'True. He's a legend – proper old school. Sam's in charge of the playlist though. Dave won't have heard of half the songs...'

They both laughed and Kate clapped her hands together. 'So then. Shall we get changed and have a walk down to the bandstand? Just a short one. The rain's eased off and I could do with some air.'

'Sure,' said Roz. 'Chloe won't be home for a while yet.'

Kate took Roz's arm as they headed back to the changing rooms. 'Then we can go for that glass of fizz – a fizzy water in my case – and discuss the most important issue.'

'What's that?' asked Roz, worried she'd forgotten something.

'Your wedding outfit,' said Kate. 'And, more to the point, Chloe's!'

~

Back home that evening, Roz rang for a takeaway while Chloe was in the bath. Then she called Mark.

'Where are you?' she asked when he answered. 'You sound like you're in an aircraft hangar.'

'Just at work,' he said, briskly.

'Oh, sorry, sorry. I didn't know or I wouldn't have called. Is... Is that music I can hear in the background?'

'Just the radio,' he said. 'I take it you've had a good time with Kate? You sound a bit tipsy.'

'Yeah,' she giggled. 'I've had a couple of wines. We've had an amazing day actually. It was *sooo* good to see her again.'

'Oh, that's nice,' he said.

'And guess what... Kate's pregnant! Due in September.'

'Was she on the wine as well?' he asked.

'Of course not!' said Roz. 'I'm massively relieved actually. I was a bit concerned about mine and Chloe's dresses for the wedding – that she'd ask us to wear something totally unflattering – but I needn't have worried. Kate said she trusted us to choose our own outfits – something that'll feel comfortable on the day – and she's insisted on paying. Chloe's so excited, bless her. She's never been to a wedding before. Hello...?' The line had gone very quiet. 'Are you still there?'

'Yep. Yep. I'm here.'

'Oh, good. Yeah. So, as I was saying, me and Chloe will need to get our skates on and get shopping. The wedding'll soon creep up on us. I don't want to leave it till the last minute. We need to find something nice. I don't want to let Kate down. But look, I've been rambling on long enough and I don't want to disturb you at work.'

'OK,' he said. 'Alright then...'

'Oh, and the other thing Kate mentioned...' She stopped herself.

'Yes?' He sounded impatient. Understandably. 'Tell me.'

'No, it's fine. I'll tell you another time.'

She'd been going to tell him about Dubrovnik, but it wasn't as important as whatever he was doing at work. It could wait.

CHAPTER THIRTY-FOUR

On Monday morning, Roz booked a hair appointment for Thursday after work. Seeing Kate had inspired her to get her hair done professionally instead of dyeing it at home, which gave a dull, matt result that dragged her face down. She'd opted for Salon Alexandria in town, the poshest place Buxton had to offer.

Her stylist, Kirsty, emerged from the back of the shop and introduced herself with a friendly smile. She whipped out a black silk gown for Roz to wear, sat her down in front of the mirror and asked her what she wanted. Roz replied that she didn't know – only that she had a wedding coming up and wanted a change before she met up with a load of old pals. She hadn't relished the prospect of making small talk, but something in Kirsty's easy manner made her want to unburden herself to this complete stranger.

'Well, my love. You've got lovely thick hair,' said Kirsty. 'Let's just take a few inches off the length and, colour-wise, I think we could go a bit lighter.' She produced a massive colour chart with shiny swatches of hair. 'I think number 27 would suit you. Mixed with some number 10.'

Roz thought the samples looked worryingly red, but nodded along anyway, and Kirsty was soon slapping the cold dye onto her head. Roz felt free – happy for the decision to be in someone else's hands for once.

'Now,' Kirsty said, putting the big drier on her. 'I'll just leave you to relax while the colour develops. Can I get you a coffee from the machine? Or a cheeky glass of wine?'

Roz was tempted by the wine but declined, and Kirsty left her with a pile of magazines while she went to make the coffee. They were full of celebrities with bits of their faces highlighted to show the cosmetic 'work' they'd had done. Even Liz Lockhart – a natural beauty by any measure – seemed to have succumbed.

Roz regarded herself in the mirror. The combination of the black gown and the overhead light made her look deathly. Crow's feet. Frown lines. Thin upper lip. Maybe she should consider some 'work' herself? Some botox or subtle fillers. But they'd be far too expensive. She'd just ask Kirsty to give her a fringe – to cover her forehead at least.

Two hours later, after much washing, drying, cutting and straightening, Kirsty was holding up a mirror at the back of Roz's head. She was chuffed with the results – the luxurious caramel swirls – and hoped she'd be able to re-create it for herself at home. The bill at the end was eye-watering, but worth it for the pleasant experience of being cared for and looked after by Kirsty.

When she arrived home, Ellie was outside next door having one of her many smoke breaks. 'You look *gorgeous*,' she called out to Roz – and Chloe was equally appreciative when she got home a few minutes later. Roz hoped Mark would like it too.

Mark. She'd been trying not to think about him. They hadn't spoken since she'd rung him on Saturday night and, although he was probably working, it was niggling away at her. All the same, she didn't want to call him again or come over as needy.

'Hey,' she said to Chloe as they were washing up after tea. 'Do you fancy going to the Trafford Centre on Saturday? See if we can find some outfits for the wedding?'

'Yesss!' said Chloe. 'Can we go to Zara? Amy says its *amazing*.'

'Of course we can,' said Roz. 'We'll go to *all* the shops!'

They set off in the car at half nine on Saturday morning, Chloe beside herself with excitement. The route to the Trafford Centre was quiet, but when they reached the huge car park, it was already half full.

Inside, their first stop was the giant map of the place showing the location of all the shops. Roz studied it, but Chloe was distracted by a central kiosk decked out in stars and stripes that was selling giant cookies. The sickly sweet smell made Roz feel nauseous.

'Can we get one of those later?' asked Chloe. 'Amy's mum always gets her one when they come here.'

'Does she now?' Roz chuckled just as her phone started ringing. She delved into her bag. It was Mark.

'Hiya,' he said brightly. 'How are you?'

Roz strained to hear him over the noise of excited shoppers. 'I'm fine,' she said. 'Well, actually, I'm a bit busy. I'm at the Trafford Centre with Chloe. On a wedding outfit hunt.'

'Ah,' he said. 'I was going to come over and see you this afternoon.'

Roz rubbed at her temple. 'That's – eh. That's a bit awkward actually. We were planning on being here most of the day.' She smiled at Chloe's serious face. 'We've got a *lot* of shops to get through...'

'Aw, really?' he whined. 'C'mon... I haven't seen you for two weeks...'

Roz checked her watch. 'It's eleven o'clock,' she said. 'We've only just got here. What about tomorrow instead?' She turned away from Chloe.

'No can do,' he said. 'I'm working.'

'Or we could come to Didsbury? On our way home?'

'Erm, no. That doesn't really work. I'm having the kitchen remodelled. I've got the fitters in. It's a bit of a bomb-site at the moment.'

'Oh, right... You didn't say,' said Roz.

'No? Well, the cabinets were looking a bit tired and stuff. And I want it to be right the first time you see it. When I'm cooking for you...'

Roz thawed. 'OK then. What time shall I see you?'

'Two o'clock at yours? I'll bring something for lunch.'

'OK then.'

Roz hung up and Chloe's face crumpled. 'I don't want to go home,' she moaned, quietly.

'I'm sorry, love,' said Roz. 'Look, we've still got an hour or two.'

'What about lunch?'

'We can have some at home. Right,' Roz said. 'Let's go to Zara first.'

But there was nothing that met with Chloe's approval in Zara, so Roz suggested Next instead – where the perfect pink dress with silver sequins was hanging on a rack by the door. Best of all, she wouldn't have to buy her a new pair of shoes as Chloe already had some in the right colour. The queue for the fitting room was a mile long – and for the till even longer – but it was worth it to get Chloe sorted.

There wasn't much time left for Roz to find something for herself – only twenty minutes for a 'commando raid' on John Lewis. Nothing was jumping out at her and she was ready to leave empty-handed, but Chloe had other ideas.

'Try this one, Mum!' she said. 'It's lovely and it's sort of the same colour as mine!'

'Really?' said Roz. It was a blush pink satin shift, overlaid with rose gold chiffon – the last thing she'd have chosen – but they were running out of time. And it was in the sale and was surprisingly good value. Kate might be footing the bill, but she still didn't want to spend too much.

Roz tried it on quickly in the changing rooms. It was a good fit and the straps weren't too flimsy, which was good. 'You put yours on too,' said Roz, 'and we'll send a photo to Auntie Kate.'

Kate replied to her text straight away. 'Nice one. You both look fab. Go for it!'

So they paid, then left, and Chloe dragged her heels as she gave a long, last look at the cookie kiosk on the way out.

The journey back home was horrendous; the M60 was nose-to-tail from the football traffic and a coach that was blocking two lanes having its wheel changed.

It was twenty past two when they arrived back in Buxton and half past when they pulled into their street. Roz was already rehearsing her apology for being late, but there was no need for it in the end as there was no sign of Mark at the house.

Roz tried calling him on the way up the path, a slow rage bubbling inside her. She couldn't believe that she'd left the shops early, spoiled Chloe's fun, raced home – and he wasn't even here.

Once inside, she threw down her carrier bags and put the kettle on to calm down, trying to hide her anger from Chloe. But then the doorbell rang and Mark was standing there with a French stick poking out of a carrier bag.

'Hiya. How are you?' he asked, kissing her on the cheek, oblivious to her frown and the tell-tale red spot on her cheeks.

She waited, but there was no hint of an apology from his side.

'I got some pork pie and some nice cheese from the deli near me,' he said, heading through to the kitchen. 'How was the Trafford Centre? Find anything nice?'

'Yep,' said Roz curtly, following him.

'Well then. Are you going to show me?' he asked Chloe.

Chloe shook her head. 'It's a secret.'

'Oh, go on,' said Roz. 'You're lovely in it.'

But Chloe shook her head and ran upstairs.

'Sorry,' said Roz, awkwardly. 'She's stubborn. Like her grandmother...'

'So what about *your* outfit?' twinkled Mark. 'Can I see it? Or is that a secret too?'

Roz blushed. She could hardly say no.

She disappeared upstairs with their shopping bags and

did a quick change. Then, a few minutes later, she was back. She poked her head round the kitchen door, then twirled like a little girl in front of him. 'It'll look better with some strappy sandals and the right underwear,' she said, but his face said it all.

'You hate it, don't you?' she said.

'I don't *hate* it,' he protested. 'It's just a bit... *frumpy* maybe? The material's a bit like my mum's curtains.'

'Your mum's curtains?' Roz's cheeks fired up again.

'I don't know. I just think you'd suit something more... more elegant. Your hair looks lovely though. A lot smarter.'

'*Smarter?*' said Roz. 'Hardly a ringing endorsement!'

'Sorry. That was the wrong word. It's lovely. Lovely and feminine.'

'What are you saying?' she asked. 'That it wasn't feminine before?'

'No. Not at all.' He put his hands together in a praying gesture. 'Listen, I said I'm sorry. I'm just a bloke. I don't know the right words. I was just... I think it looks really nice.'

Roz collected herself. 'No, I'm sorry. I get like this when I'm hungry. My blood sugar drops and I—'

Mark stepped forward and took her hands. 'Why don't you go and get changed and I'll make us some lunch?'

'Thanks.' She smiled. 'That'd be nice.'

When she came back downstairs, he'd laid out a little 'picnic' on the kitchen counter.

'Grab a plate and help yourself,' he said.

'Mmm,' she said. 'This goat's cheese is lovely...'

'It's Croatian... apparently.'

'That's funny,' she said. 'I don't think I've told you. Kate's having her hen weekend in Croatia... in Dubrovnik.'

'Oh great,' he said. 'That sounds like fun.'

'She wants me and Chloe to come – Chloe's never been abroad – but it's expensive. I can't really afford it.'

'How much is it?'

'About £360 for the two of us,' said Roz.

'Is that all?' he said. 'I can give you that.'

'*What?*'

'To make up for the disaster of your birthday. It's the least I can do.'

'Really?'

'Really! It'll be nice for you to have a break.'

'Our mate Vicky – she's organising it – she needs a £100 deposit from everyone – I can manage that myself. But then she needs the balance by the 9th of April. At the latest. And I'll need to sort a passport for Chloe. More expense!'

'Don't worry about that,' he said.

Roz threw her arms around him. 'Chloe!' she shouted up the stairs. 'Come on, love. Come and get some lunch!'

When Chloe mooched in, Roz surprised her with the news that they'd be spending Easter in Dubrovnik. Chloe was speechless with delight – almost. 'Wow, wow, wow!' she said. 'I can't wait to tell Amy on Monday! Everyone else in my class gets to go abroad all the time and I've never even been on a plane before.'

Roz was thrilled too. She couldn't wait to tell Angie at work – for similar reasons. It would be a tiny bit of payback for all the holiday-based bragging she'd had to endure from her over the years.

Chloe went to bed early, completely exhausted, and Roz followed her up to tuck her in. When she came back downstairs, Mark had taken charge of the remote control and was watching something on BBC4 about the rise of the Nazis. Roz sighed inwardly as she flopped on the sofa next to him: she was keen on history programmes, but Saturday night was neither the time nor the place for upsetting programmes like this. All she really wanted was to kick back with an episode of *Casualty* or *Britain's Got Talent* or something equally undemanding, but she couldn't say anything. She felt beholden to him now he was paying for the Dubrovnik trip.

'Would you like something to drink?' she asked him, trying to introduce some conviviality to proceedings.

'No,' he said. 'I'm fine.' And there was something in his tone that made her feel too guilty to have one herself.

Later on, as the bongs of the ten o'clock news rang out, Roz yawned performatively, expecting him to announce he was hitting the road. But he showed no sign of moving.

Instead, he put his hand on her knee and her stomach lurched. Roz looked at her watch. 'What about your dog... Martina? Don't you need to get back?'

Mark was standing up and pulled her gently to her feet. 'I've asked the dog-walker to check in on her,' he said, his voice thick and heavy. 'She'll be fine till the morning.'

A bit presumptuous, thought Roz, as he led her up the stairs. Although it was to be expected, really, that they would sleep together; they'd been seeing each other a while now. But it was weird to think of it happening with Chloe in the room next door. It wasn't how Roz had imagined it – their first time. Now that it was here, she couldn't care less about her thighs, her pubes or whether her underwear was up to the mark. All she could think was that they'd need to be quiet. And that she should try and hide her tattoo.

When it happened, it *was* quiet – almost too quiet – but

at least he'd showed respect for Chloe and that was something.

And when it was over, it occurred to her: they hadn't used a condom. He hadn't offered and she hadn't insisted. What if she got pregnant?

It was pretty unlikely at her age. She knew that from all the articles in every damn magazine – that a woman's fertility fell off a cliff after thirty-five. And anyway, if – *if* – she did end up pregnant, would that be so bad? It might be the perfect outcome.

That night, with Mark lying there next to her, Roz dreamt she was being driven in a plush car, on her way to a wedding. Her own wedding. To Daniel. All the trees were in blossom, but the ground was thick with snow. A vehicle up ahead had broken down and the car could go no further. She had to get out and walk the rest of the way, but the road was treacherous with black ice and she had to tread gingerly. She was freezing cold in her green velvet dress, hair piled high on her head, but nothing would stop her getting to the bandstand. When she made it, Daniel was nowhere to be seen. And there was no congregation. Only a sombre priest like something out of Dickens, who was standing at the front by a Moses basket. He dipped a bony finger in holy water and invited her to present the child for baptism. She did as she was told, but when she bent down and pulled back the soft wool blanket, there was no baby. Just a tiny dolphin, smiling and clicking up at her.

CHAPTER THIRTY-FIVE

Mark was working the next weekend, so Roz wasn't seeing him again till the following Friday night. He was coming to hers again, which was just easier than going to his place: Chloe often had clubs and activities on a Saturday morning and Roz didn't want to drag her over to Didsbury, upsetting her routine.

As Roz tarted up the house – and herself – prior to his arrival, she realised she wasn't that delighted by the prospect. She'd had a crap week at work and would've preferred a quiet night in with Chloe. Then she felt guilty – until he turned up and started monopolising the TV again. He was watching some channel she'd never heard of – the qualifying round of some Grand Prix or other. He explained it all to her at length, but she only pretended to listen. The whizzing whine of engines and the screeching of tyres were doing her head in. At least he would be leaving first thing in the morning – he had to get home for a game of football with some guys from work – and she could get on with some chores.

'Shall we order our takeaway?' Mark suggested after a while.

'Yes, defo. I'm starving,' said Roz. She turned to Chloe. 'What would you like, love?'

'Pizza!' Chloe replied.

Roz laughed. 'Like I had to ask!'

But Mark looked disappointed. 'Aw,' he said. 'I quite fancied Thai.'

'Hmm,' said Roz. 'It's a bit too spicy for Chloe.'

'Really?' he said. 'I'm sure we can find something on the menu she'll like. Some noodles or something.'

'Pizza's her favourite though,' said Roz, digging in.

'Haven't you got one in the freezer you can give her?'

You can give her... Like he was talking about a dog.

'No,' said Roz. 'I don't actually.'

'I don't mind,' said Chloe. 'Noodles are fine.'

'Are you sure?' said Roz, and Chloe nodded.

Roz went to fetch the menu from the drawer in the hall and handed it to Mark. She sat there in silence while he read out what he thought they should have. It was his right after all – he was paying for it.

After they'd eaten, Chloe went straight to her room.

'What's up? Is everything OK?' Mark asked Roz, tenderly.

'Yeah. It's nothing,' she said. 'It's just... She's starting to spend more and more of her time up there.' She let out a sigh. 'I guess it's par for the course at her age.'

Mark nodded in sympathy. 'Come and sit here,' he said, and patted the couch next to him. The Formula One had finished and Jools Holland was just starting up on BBC2. There was peace at last until Roz's phone buzzed on the coffee table.

Roz reached for it and read the text. It was from Daniel's friend, Luke, inviting her to the 'memorial gig' they'd organised for him – at the Pauper's Pit in The Old Hall. The place she'd first met Daniel. Angie must've taken the booking and not mentioned it. Although why would she? She knew nothing about Daniel.

'Who's that?' asked Mark. 'Texting you on a Friday night...?'

'It's Luke – Daniel's best mate. I can't remember if I told you about him...'

Mark frowned. 'No,' he said. 'I don't think you did.'

'Well, they're having a memorial gig, some music and drinks, and he was just inviting me.'

'When is it?' he asked.

'Sunday the 31st of March. Three o'clock.'

She could tell straight away he wasn't happy.

'You're not going, are you?' he said.

She'd been in two minds about it – whether to go or not – but his reaction made her mind up. 'Er, yes, I am actually. I met Luke and the rest of Daniel's friends at the funeral and they were all really nice. Luke's wife too...' She felt the need to mention Jenny, in case jealousy was his problem.

'But this memorial thing,' Mark continued. 'It's on a Sunday.'

'And?'

'It's a school night.'

'Not really,' said Roz. 'It's in the afternoon.' She couldn't believe they were having this conversation, and the boogie-woogie piano coming from the TV made it even more surreal.

'And what about Chloe?' Mark asked. 'I assume you won't be taking her along?'

'No,' said Roz. 'I dunno. She can go to one of her friend's houses.'

'Oh.' He nodded. 'That's great... Pushing her around from pillar to post.'

'Or I can leave her with Ellie,' she said, exasperated. 'She'll only have to go next door.'

'Next door? That bunch of stoners? I wouldn't leave my *dog* with them.'

'That's a bit unfair!' said Roz. 'Like I said, the do's in the afternoon. I'll only be a couple of hours.'

She tensed as he balled his fist and loosened it again. 'Well,' he said. 'Maybe we should call a halt to things – if you're still not over this Daniel.'

'Hang on...' said Roz. 'That's—'

'No, really. Although, as your mother said, you were only with him five minutes. It wasn't a proper relationship. You hardly knew him. You don't know what grief is...'

Roz wished she hadn't told him that about her mother, and a phrase flashed into her mind – something her mother used to say. *Don't give your enemies the arrows to shoot you with.* How ironic. Roz had always thought it was such a negative way to look at the world, but maybe she had a point.

'Actually. Y'know,' Roz faltered. 'Maybe you're right. Maybe we *should* call it a day.'

'OK then. Fine,' said Mark, standing up and storming out, slamming the door behind him.

From the window, Roz watched him disappear down the path. *Pathetic*, she thought. Was he really so fragile he was threatened by a dead guy? And his implication that she was a bad mother... She'd managed fine with Chloe on her own up until now. He had no right to criticise her – for that or anything else. That was the great advantage of her and Chloe being on their own all these years: their home had been a haven – a happy little ship. They hadn't had to deal with this sort of crap.

Roz turned to the sideboard and picked up the framed photo of the three of them. She had every intention of tossing it in the bin, but stopped herself. The frame was too nice to throw out. Instead, she opened the back of it, slid out the photo and tore it up. She'd replace it with one of Chloe's new school photos.

Roz went to the kitchen to make some tea. She wouldn't miss Mark – or his terrible taste in TV. The only downside would be telling Chloe that the Dubrovnik trip was off. She'd be so disappointed, having to tell Amy and the rest of her pals that she wasn't going after all. But Roz couldn't let Kate and the others pay for them. That would be too mortifying. She'd have to lose her deposit, of course, but it was a small price to pay for her pride.

The following morning, Chloe rushed downstairs, late for netball. 'Where's Mark?' she asked first. Then, 'What's that photo of me doing there? I *hate* that photo. My teeth look funny.'

'Don't be silly, love,' Roz assured her. 'Your teeth look fine.'

'What happened to the other one?' Chloe asked. 'The one with Mark?'

'We've fallen out,' said Roz, simply. 'He won't be coming round here again.'

CHAPTER THIRTY-SIX

The thought of going to Daniel's memorial at the end of the month – and catching up with his lovely set of friends – was enough to keep Roz going and stop her brooding on Mark.

When the day itself came, she rose early and put all the clocks an hour forward. The return of the light felt like a new start. It felt right.

She whacked the volume on the radio up and got stuck into the household chores with more gusto than usual. Chloe was surprisingly willing to help, keen to try out the fancy new cleaning products from the supermarket.

After lunch, Roz got changed for the 'party', as Chloe called it. She'd agonised all week over what to wear, but in the end she went for a 'folk vibe' – a purple long-sleeved top over a long black skirt. On her feet she wore a pair of black trainers she'd bought ages ago with the full intention of doing some exercise at some point, but had never actually worn. They would be comfortable if she got involved in any dancing.

At just after three, she dropped Chloe round to Ellie's

next door. Roz produced a tenner from her purse – for them to treat themselves at the shop – but Ellie wouldn't take it. 'It's OK,' Ellie said. 'I've been baking. I've made us some muffins.'

'Alright,' said Roz, warily. 'As long as there's nothing dodgy in them.'

'As if!' grinned Ellie, all angelic, and Roz felt guilty for doubting her.

Roz arrived at The Old Hall half an hour late so as not to look too eager. It was discombobulating to be going into 'work' on a Sunday and she braced herself before heading downstairs to the Pauper's Pit, clutching the banister all the way, as her eyes adjusted to the gloom.

The first thing she saw was the little stage – the spot that Daniel had announced was 'perfect' for his band's charity gig, that day last summer. It was odd. She could remember every word of their conversation, but she was struggling to picture his face.

No-one was on the stage, not yet, but there was plenty of chatter and chinking glasses and tuning-up of various instruments. Already the vibe was different – more relaxed, more joyful – than the wake. There didn't seem to be any family from what she could see, only friends.

Roz headed straight for the bar, where Luke's wife Jenny was standing. She spotted Jenny's new wedding ring immediately and congratulated her on their nuptials.

'Cheers, lovey,' said Jenny, hugging her. 'Thanks so much. It's good to see you again.'

'Likewise.' Roz looked down. The front of Jenny's coat was open and a little pot belly was poking out.

Jenny saw her looking and rubbed her stomach. She grinned sheepishly. 'It's not just a food baby...'

'Really?' said Roz. *Another one pregnant.* 'Aw, that's lovely news.'

'Can I get you a drink?' Jenny asked. 'A proper one. I'm on the lime-soda unfortunately.'

'Yes, please,' said Roz. 'Could I have a white wine?'

'A large one?'

'Oh, go on then,' said Roz. 'Thanks.'

She looked around. All the usual suspects seemed to be in attendance: the folkie crowd, the two indie-girl-backing-singers – Zoe and Flo – and Hassim from Mali, who Roz remembered fondly from the funeral.

'Where's Luke?' she asked Jenny.

'Oh, he's around somewhere,' said Jenny, waving her hand.

'I'm looking forward to seeing Daniel's band,' said Roz. 'I've never heard them before. I could never get away in the evenings because of my daughter.'

Jenny bridled slightly. 'It wasn't *his* band as such. Luke and him started it together. But I know what you mean,' she added hastily. Her tone was warm again. 'What age is your daughter?'

'She's ten,' said Roz. 'Going on twenty.'

'I'll bet,' smiled Jenny, and conversational equilibrium was restored.

Luke came over at that point, clutching a ukelele, and gave Roz a peck on the cheek. 'We're running a bit late, I'm afraid. Waiting for Will...'

'Will?' said Roz.

'He's been filling in for us on guitar since we lost Daniel,' Luke explained. 'His train was cancelled at the last minute. He's on a rail replacement bus. Somewhere...'

'Oh God,' said Roz. 'A fate worse than death.' She

cringed at her words, but they didn't seem to notice the faux pas.

Luke excused himself to go and talk to Hassim, and Roz turned to Jenny. 'Have you been up to Solomon's Temple?' she asked her. 'To see Daniel's tree?'

'Yep,' said Jenny. 'It's a nice tribute, isn't it?'

'It is. Apart from the cheesy poem,' Roz said before she could stop herself.

Jenny frowned. 'His sister wrote it...'

'Oh,' said Roz, flushing with shame. 'Is she here today?' she asked, trying to style it out.

'No,' said Jenny. 'She's away at uni.'

'Oh,' said Roz again. She was saved by Zoe and Flo coming over to say hello and wondered if they went *everywhere* together, even to the toilet.

Then Luke returned. 'Will's twenty minutes away, he reckons. It won't be long now.'

'Oh good,' said Roz, feeling part of something for the first time in ages. Just being around Daniel's friends – breathing the same air – made her realise what had been missing with Mark. She'd been seeing Mark about the same length of time she'd known Daniel, and even before their 'break-up', she hadn't felt the same way about him. She'd thought her feelings might grow – she'd given it a go – but they hadn't. It was a chemistry thing. It was either there or it wasn't. And, with Mark, it definitely wasn't.

A ripple of tension crackled round the room. Someone 'important' had obviously arrived and Roz assumed it must be a member of Daniel's family – or possibly Will – but it turned out to be neither. It was a woman she hadn't seen before, tall and slim with a platinum-blonde pixie cut. She was rocking a cropped biker jacket with jeans and could easily have been a fashion model. She wore sunglasses perched on her head, even though it was grey outside, and her sharp earrings looked as if they might stab her long, slender neck. Roz felt even more dumpy than usual.

Roz watched Luke and Jenny exchange a look and wondered why... Was the woman 'problematic' in some way? Was there a story here?

The woman made a beeline for them. She bent to kiss Luke and Jenny on both cheeks. 'Sorry I'm late. Sorry. Sorry. Sorry,' she said grandly, in a trans-Atlantic twang. 'Well then, this is a nice little performance space...'

'Hi. Hi there,' stuttered Jenny in reply. 'We thought you were still in the States.'

'Well. I had to come over really – after missing the funeral. Toby told me about the do today. I wanted to make the effort for Dan. I managed to get a cheap flight.'

Luke hadn't said anything. He didn't seem that keen on her. Nor did the sainted Jenny, who was normally lovely to a fault.

Roz almost felt sorry for the woman, who turned and looked down her nose at her. 'Hi,' she said to Roz. 'I'm Tara, by the way. I was Dan's S.O.'

'S.O.?'

'Significant other. His girlfriend.'

'Girlfriend?' said Roz. Her stomach dropped. *What?* Luke and Jenny flushed bright pink, which was all the confirmation she needed.

'How did *you* know him?' asked Tara, oblivious.

Roz opened her mouth to say something – God knew what – but this Tara had spotted someone more interesting to talk to and was already excusing herself.

'I'm sorry, Roz,' Luke mumbled when she'd gone. 'She's

been over in Boston doing a music degree... I wasn't expecting her to turn up or I wouldn't have...'

Yeah, you wouldn't have invited me, thought Roz. 'No worries,' she said instead.

'They've had an on-off thing for years,' Luke explained. 'He's never properly split from her. Couldn't quite make the break.'

'She's a bloody nightmare to be honest,' said Jenny, pulling a face. Like that was supposed to make her feel better.

'Me and Daniel... We'd been planning holidays together,' Roz said, exaggerating feebly. 'With my daughter. He never mentioned a girlfriend.'

Luke stared at the floor. 'Daniel was a great guy, but...'

'A great guy,' said Jenny. 'If you weren't *involved* with him.'

Now a bloke in an Oasis T-shirt with a shaved head came lumbering up to them. He threw his meaty arm round Luke's shoulders, as Jenny turned away to avoid his beery breath. The guy squinted into Roz's face in the dim light. 'Are you the one Dan copped off with on the stag do?' he asked.

Roz looked away but he carried on. 'The one from The Endeavour? The one he disappeared with at the end of the night...?'

'Sean...!' Jenny tried to stop him, but it was too late.

'Sorry.' He giggled incongruously. 'It's just... you look a bit like her.'

This was a farce now. With Roz the butt of the joke.

'For God's sake, Sean,' said Luke, grabbing his elbow. 'It's barely half-four and you're pissed already. Come on, I think you need some air...'

Luke led him away up the staircase and Jenny rubbed Roz's arm. 'I'm so sorry,' she said. 'We should've—'

'It's not your fault,' Roz interrupted. Jenny's pity was too much to bear. 'Listen, I'd better go. I've got to collect my daughter.'

Jenny took her hands. 'Are you sure? Are you going to be alright?'

Roz bit her lip and nodded. She had to get out of here before she made a tit of herself by crying. She was foolish and stupid and far too old for all this. Daniel had clearly been a player. And she'd been played.

Back at ground-level on the street outside, she felt like a diver decompressing too quickly. She gripped the railings for a moment and knew she couldn't just go home to Chloe and act like everything was fine. Not this time.

CHAPTER THIRTY-SEVEN

Roz walked, and kept walking, till she reached the path up to Solomon's Temple. Daniel's *thinking place*. Well, fuck him. She could just imagine what he'd been thinking about when he was up there. The various women he was conning and playing for fools. All men were the same when it came down to it – even her own father.

She wasn't as out of breath as the last time she'd come up here, propelled up the hill by rage and shock and disbelief. The new trainers were rubbing at her heels, but she carried on anyway.

All that crap Daniel had fed her... The holier-than-thou sanctimonious bollocks about avoiding Facebook and the rest of it... His high-falutin' ethical views. Now she knew the real reason he avoided social media. He didn't want to leave evidence of his shitty behaviour. He didn't want to get caught out.

If she was angry at him, she was even more livid with herself for ignoring the signs. He'd always been late, was always on his phone, always rushing off, leaving her feeling empty and worthless. He'd always been vain – checking himself out in any reflective surface that happened to be available – and tight with money too, always wanting to meet for a sandwich in some corner of a park, rather than going somewhere 'proper'. She'd noticed this stuff at the time – had told Kate some of it – but it never seemed to stick. Her brain always seemed to over-ride it. Until the next time. Like a love-struck schoolgirl, she'd given him a free pass and only remembered the good stuff – the sunny picnic on the grass. Not the bad stuff – the flies crawling all over it, buzzing in her ears. She'd got carried away with his cheap, empty gestures, like postcards and 'stolen' flowers. As Kate said, she'd elevated him into something he wasn't – and it was utterly cringeworthy.

She wasn't far from his 'tree' now, and that crap poem of his sister's. What did it call him again? *Our brightest northern star.* It made her want to puke. Or pull the thing up by the roots.

But when she reached the tree, she froze. The metal plaque had been daubed with red paint and a word had been sprayed on the ground in front of it: 'TWAT'.

Jeez! thought Roz. Then she let out a laugh and wondered who had done it. It could have been anyone. Some wronged woman probably. There would be no shortage of them.

Roz shivered, suddenly vulnerable. Maybe it was her over-active imagination, but she felt she wasn't alone. She pulled her too-thin jacket close around her and spun round.

She was right; she wasn't alone. A muscular black Labrador stood there on the path, no owner in sight. It stiffened, watching her, and Roz stiffened too. Then a man emerged up ahead, his long scarf flapping around him.

Mark? she thought – she hoped – for a second. But it wasn't him.

Don't be ridiculous, she told herself as the man caught up with the dog and put it on the lead.

'The wind's wild up there,' he said, hurrying past her, down the hill. 'Summat's brewing!'

'Oh. Really?' she said. She wanted nothing more than to turn round and follow him back down through the trees, but her legs carried her on and up towards the light, to the summit. As she surfaced onto the grass at the top, she felt the chill; there might have been an extra hour of daylight, but summer was still a long way off.

The folly was black against the sky now and the only sound was the birds catching their breath in the whipping wind. Her eyes began to stream and the last straw was the sudden sting of hail, stabbing her face like a thousand tiny pins.

She turned and ran back down the path, picking up speed as she went, her legs going faster than was comfortable. She tried to slow down, but it was too late and she hit the ground, landing hard.

The shock of it woke her up, knocked some sense into her. Her only injury was a skinned knee through her tights, like five-year-old. She couldn't just sit here. She had to get back to the main road and a taxi home.

In next door's front garden, Chloe was huddled around the fire-pit with Ellie and the other girls. They were chatting and toasting marshmallows, their cheeks all rosy from the flames. Roz sniffed the air, but couldn't detect any booze or weed: the scene was positively wholesome.

'This looks cosy,' she said, arranging her face into a smile. 'Have you had a nice time?'

CHAPTER THIRTY-EIGHT

By Monday morning, the distress of Sunday's Daniel revelations had died away. Now came the analysis stage. The assessment of the damage. The endless attempts to rationalise. Why had Daniel assumed he could treat her like that? What signals had she been giving out? Maybe he'd sensed her desperation. Maybe he just tried it on with everyone.

At work, Roz refreshed the *Daily Mail* website. Half the 'showbiz' stories were updates on Liz Lockhart's delayed honeymoon, with hundreds of photos of her in Florida. 'All Going Swimmingly,' the headline trumpeted, as she executed a perfect dive off the deck of a superyacht into the lush turquoise waters. In the next pic, she was 'flaunting her curves' (hard not to in a swimsuit), then 'putting on an amorous display' with her fit new husband. Roz sighed and closed the tab before envy overwhelmed her.

Angie was wittering about an April Fool's joke her husband had played on her this morning – about a 'leek' in the bathroom; the vegetable, not an actual leak – and Roz felt she might scream. There was no way she'd get any work done this morning. Her concentration was shot to pieces. She had to get out of here.

'Would you mind if I took an early lunch?' she asked Angie. 'It's just...' she thought of a white lie, 'I've got to go to the bank.'

'Sure,' said Angie, then chuckled. 'I won't be expecting you back any time soon. The queues in there are horrendous.'

'Cheers.' Roz smiled weakly, grabbed her bag and left. She wasn't hungry and she'd had too much coffee already, but it was too cold to hang around outside and so she headed for the comfort of Serendipity and the lure of 'nice things'.

There was an A-board on the pavement outside it today. *Tarot Readings, 12 till 4*, it proclaimed, and Roz raised an eyebrow. She'd never been into all that New Age woo-woo and couldn't remember the last time she'd even read her horoscope, but some instinct forced her inside.

The shop woman was lovely as usual and showed her through to the back. 'There you go,' she said, pulling back the beaded curtain. 'Take a seat and I'll just fetch Jonathan.'

Jonathan? Roz wasn't expecting the reader to be a man – nor the room to be so basic. There were none of the usual fortune-teller's props. No heavy glass ball or velvet tablecloth or flickering lamps. No musky sandalwood scent. Just an IKEA desk, two chairs and the faint whiff of bleach.

When 'Jonathan' turned up – a young guy in polo shirt and jeans, no more than twenty-five – Roz wanted to leave immediately. But he'd sat himself down and launched into his spiel as if he was working in a call-centre: 'Lots of people think the Tarot will tell you the future, but it's not really about making predictions. It's about holding up a mirror to yourself – using the cards to make choices, learn the lessons you need to learn and make positive changes to manifest your goals and dreams. You need to formulate a question in your mind, then meditate on it, using the imagery of the cards to access your inner power and the answer you need.'

He fixed her with his amber eyes – the only 'mystic' thing about him – and she bit her tongue to keep from laughing. Then he produced the cards from a drawer, carefully unwrapping them from a piece of purple silk – his only concession to ceremony. 'So. What's your question?' he asked her.

'Oh. Right,' said Roz. 'Do I need to say it out loud?'

'It works better if you do,' he said, mildly irritated.

'Well... I... er...' This was excruciating. 'Will I ever find what everyone else has got?'

He raised an eyebrow. 'Which is what?'

'A life partner. A proper family? Happiness?' Her stomach curled in on itself, but he didn't react – just shuffled the cards, then fanned them out on the desk, face down in front of her.

'Choose a card that speaks to you,' he said.

Roz studied the ornately patterned backs, waiting for one to jump out at her.

'That one,' she said, tapping it with her nail. She slid it out and flipped it over to reveal a picture of a young man with a knapsack, standing on the edge of a precipice. 'The Fool,' it said underneath.

'Appropriate,' said Roz.

'Eh?'

'Today's date,' she explained. 'April Fool's Day...'

He shrugged, took the card and placed it down in front of her. 'The Fool represents you,' he said.

'Oh,' sighed Roz. 'That figures.'

He shook his head. 'It's actually a very good card. It

means new beginnings, opportunity and potential on your journey through life.'

Roz smiled at him. It was a load of waffle, but he meant well, bless him. Then he got her to choose another card, which had a picture of an angel on it, blowing a trumpet to summon the dead.

He placed it cross-ways over The Fool. 'This is the Judgement card,' he intoned solemnly, and Roz was none the wiser.

'This symbolises the nature of the obstacles that stand in your way. This tells me that you doubt yourself. That you're your own worst critic.'

You've never met my mother, Roz thought, grimly.

He carried on. 'It's a warning not to ignore your inner voice. To trust yourself. To trust your own instincts about situations and people.'

So far, so general. But it was hard not to think of Daniel and all the doubts she'd brushed aside at the time.

Next up was The Empress card.

'This one represents abundance, fruitful labour – feminine energy,' Jonathan said. He set it down on the desk above the first two cards. 'This card represents your aim... your ideal... the best that can happen, although it hasn't fully happened yet. It might relate to your daughter...?'

How did he know she had a daughter – or had he guessed? These types of people were mostly chancers, just really skilled at 'reading' people. Or else he was playing the percentages. Roz just nodded enigmatically. She wasn't going to add anything – wasn't going to make it easy for him.

'Or it could relate to your mother or another female friend or relative.'

He was definitely hedging his bets.

'Or it could mean fertility and motherhood.'

A shiver ran up her; this was more promising. 'So, then... Is that what's in my future?'

'Er, well... I wouldn't put it like that exactly, but it could be. If that's what you're drawn to.'

'Wow,' said Roz and nodded. She checked her watch and he must have taken the hint because he began to speed up. She knew the procedure by now and was quite enjoying it. Eventually she pulled out the tenth – and final – card.

'Ah,' said Jonathan. 'The Hanged Man...'

'*What?*' said Roz, recoiling from the picture.

'It's good news really,' he deadpanned. 'This is the culmination of the influences of all the other cards. He's hanging upside down, seeing the world in a completely different way. It can mean: surrender, letting go, new perspectives on situations. Awareness and enlightenment.'

'Oh,' said Roz, doubtfully. He sounded like he was reading out a shopping list. 'That sounds quite similar to The Fool.'

'It does a bit. I think it's asking you to pause a moment and let go of specific outcomes. You need to compromise and go with the flow of life.'

'So what does *that* mean? In terms of my initial question...'

'Well,' he hesitated. 'It might mean compromising – changing how you think about your relationship with someone already known to you. Seeing a difficult situation in a different way. Or maybe just giving yourself permission to be happy.'

'Cheers. Thanks,' said Roz, and set off back to the office. Jonathan had sure been the master of the cliché, with a fine line in bullshit bingo, but maybe there was something in this card reading stuff. It was certainly making her question things, making her think about life from a fresh angle.

Maybe she'd been too hasty in ending it with Mark. Maybe he wasn't that bad. Maybe she did need to compromise – give him the benefit of the doubt. The truth was, no-one was going to be perfect. She herself wasn't perfect. At the end of the day, the row with Mark had been sparked by the fact he didn't want her to go to Daniel's memorial. By jealousy. No-one had ever wanted her enough to be jealous like that. She wasn't used to it. She herself was used to being the jealous one. She couldn't blame Mark for having the same failings. And she couldn't let a shit like Daniel poison things with him.

More importantly, she shouldn't throw away a chance at love – a baby – a chance at happiness. Maybe her last.

She stopped in the street and texted Mark to ask if he wanted to meet up on Saturday. Nothing ventured, nothing gained.

He'd replied before she got back to her desk: *Yes. Sure. I can come over.*

Great, Roz replied. *Shall we meet in the Pavilion Gardens at 2 o'clock?* They had things to talk about and it was probably best that they met on 'neutral ground'.

CHAPTER THIRTY-NINE

The weather was bright and fine on Saturday, perfect for a stroll in the park. Mark was waiting for Roz, by the bandstand, when she arrived.

'Hi,' he said. 'How are you?'

'Alright,' she said. 'I'm good.'

'And how's Chloe?' he asked, as they set off down the path to the river.

'Yeah. She's good too,' said Roz. 'She's off at this new theatre group in the Opera House.'

'Good for her,' he said.

'They're putting on *The Wind in the Willows*,' said Roz. 'They wanted local children to play the forest animals and Chloe jumped at the idea.'

'Sounds like fun,' he said.

'So then,' she said. 'What have you been up to since I last saw you?'

'Oh, nothing much. This and that.' He stopped suddenly. 'Look,' he said. 'I'm sorry about... everything. The way I reacted about Daniel's memorial. I shouldn't have—'

'No, look, it's fine. I'm sorry too,' she said. 'We were both a bit hasty. Tempers were frayed. And, well, anyway you were right.'

'Really?' he asked, confused.

'About Daniel. I hardly knew him...' She looked at the ground. 'It turns out he had a long-term girlfriend. And a few others for good measure.' She watched Mark's face for his reaction but there was no sign of gloating.

'What a shit,' he said.

'Yup. And I'm not the only one who thinks so. Someone's vandalised his memorial tree – they've spray-painted 'TWAT' underneath it!'

Mark allowed himself a smirk and Roz laughed.

'I did feel a bit like I was competing with a saint,' he said. 'He sounded too good to be true.'

'I know. I'm sorry,' said Roz.

They carried on walking and talking, past the Victorian villas overlooking the pond, where Roz had always imagined living when she was a little girl.

'Do you fancy a stroll up into town for a coffee?' Mark suggested after a while.

'Sure,' said Roz, and he took her hand.

As they approached Serendipity up ahead, Roz told him she'd been for a Tarot reading.

'Really?' he said, looking doubtful.

Roz reddened. 'Yeah, the guy was a bit weird, but it was really helpful actually.' She squeezed his hand. 'It's not really fortune-telling. It's supposed to make you think about your life and I definitely got some clarity on a few things. Anyway,' she said, pointing at the A-board outside the shop. 'Saturday the 6th of April – it's Easter egg painting today!'

'Wow,' said Mark, shaking his head. 'I can't believe it's nearly Easter. Where has the year gone?'

'I know, right?' said Roz as they carried on to the coffee shop.

'When's the balance due for the Dubrovnik trip?' he asked.

'Dubrovnik?' Roz's heart lifted.

He nodded.

'Well, er, Vicky who's organising it – she needs the money by the 9th... That's Tuesday. At the absolute latest.'

'You need to send me her account details,' he said. 'I'll pay it in.'

'Are you sure?'

'Yep.' His phone buzzed in his pocket and he nodded again as he answered it. 'Hello,' he said, wandering into a shop doorway away from the traffic noise. The call sounded serious and Roz wondered who it was. It didn't sound like a social call.

He grimaced over to her when he'd finished. 'That was work,' he said. 'I'm on call. I've got to go in.'

'On a Saturday afternoon?'

'Yup. I'm afraid so. You know how it is. Needs must when the devil drives, as they say.'

'You're too good,' said Roz, reaching up to kiss him on the cheek. 'Well, it's been really nice to see you again. I hope we can put that stupid row behind us and go back to the way things were?'

He surprised her by kissing her hard on the mouth. 'I love you, Roz,' he said. 'You've changed my life for the better. Made me realise I've got something to live for. You're my future. You and Chloe.'

An intense warmth spread through Roz. 'I love you too,'

she said. It wasn't *quite* true right now, but she knew she could make herself love him.

And as he headed off, the disappointment she felt at him leaving turned quickly to pride. This was one of the perils of being the partner of someone with a responsible job – someone who mattered – and she'd have to get used to it.

Roz carried on up the road by herself. She was looking forward to telling Chloe the good news about Dubrovnik – and to posting on the wedding WhatsApp group. The time had come to tell them all about Mark. She'd be sure to milk his status as a doctor. Compared with all their husbands and partners, Mark would have a special cachet. His job was saving lives.

CHAPTER FORTY

God, this car park's a nightmare, even at weekends. Is that a space in the corner? And now here's some git trying to push in... 'Oi, mate! Back off. I was here first.' *Fucking hell, it's Mark...*

'What... What are **you** doing here?'

'I work here, Mark. Long before you did. You've always been the same, though, haven't you – an entitled prick!'

'Right, OK then, I'll move. You can keep the space. I don't want any more trouble. I've told you before. Stay away from me.'

CHAPTER FORTY-ONE

The following week, The Old Hall was close to full capacity. The better weather meant more people were booking short breaks in the Peak District – and Easter would be even busier.

Roz had Dubrovnik to look forward to and it couldn't come soon enough. She didn't know that much about the place, but Rod Stewart and his family had just been there on holiday and the photos in *Hello* magazine were amazing: the city walls of the medieval Old Town; the warm glow of the terracotta rooftops; and the waters of the Adriatic shimmering in the background. Roz imagined cocktails with the girls on the terrace at sunset, the twinkling harbour lights, the smell of sun tan lotion and freshly cooked seafood.

She'd need to plan what clothes she was taking, as she didn't want to be the poor relation compared to the others. Also, the photos Vicky had sent round of the hotel pool were gorgeous and she needed a new swimsuit.

She was about to pop to the shops at lunchtime to look for one when her phone pinged with a WhatsApp from

Vicky: *OK, ladies. Just a quick one to say that I've got everyone's money in my account – except for Roz's!*

What? Roz swallowed. She'd emailed Mark the bank details on Saturday and he knew the urgency. The money should be there by now. She rang his number a couple of times, but there was no answer.

Frustrated, she left a voicemail for him, then checked her junk email folder to see if his reply had got lost – but there was nothing. Just an email from Fiona, date-stamped a few days ago. It was informing Roz of a family party for their dad's retirement: a 'Hoedown and Hog Roast' at his golf club that Fiona was arranging through one of her party-planner friends in Cheshire. The Friday after Easter. Cowboy outfits compulsory!

Yee-bloody-ha, thought Roz, this stuff was never-ending. She'd definitely have to go and make the effort for her dad – it would look terrible if she didn't – even if it meant having to see her mother again. *Argh.* She was dreading it already, but one thing would be different this time: this time she'd have Mark by her side for moral support.

Mark! She tried ringing him again, but got nowhere. Time was marching on and she'd have to reply to Vicky's message; she couldn't put it off any longer. *Really sorry, Vicky,* she wrote. *There must have been some mistake with the money. I'm trying to sort it out. Could you ask them to hold the booking? Just for a day?*

No, Vicky fired back straight away. *I already made that clear in my initial email.*

'Fine,' muttered Roz. The sanctimonious cow. What could she say to that? *I know. Sorry*, she wrote. *I'll just have to drop out and lose the deposit. To be honest, I'm so busy at the moment, I'd struggle to get away anyway...*

227

Roz batted away the rush of sympathy messages that followed and Kate's offer to pay for her, which was embarrassing.

Afterwards, she didn't feel all that sorry for herself – just gutted she'd have to let Chloe down for a second time.

Roz was on the bus home from work when Mark finally called. 'Oh God,' he said. 'I just got your message. I'm really sorry, but I forgot to send the money. It completely slipped my mind. I can do it now if you want?'

'Nah. I'm afraid it's too late,' said Roz, shortly. She hoped he was a bit more organised at work – for his patients' sake.

He continued his apology. 'I've been run off my feet since Saturday. Honestly, I—'

'Look. No worries.' She was too tired for all this. 'I'm just getting off the bus. I'll talk to you later, OK?'

On her way up the path, Roz was chuntering to herself – rehearsing what she would say to Chloe – when Ellie from next door flagged her down. 'Here,' she said, handing her a sheet of paper. 'It's an advert – for a job in student welfare and mental health. At the uni.'

Roz looked blank.

'At our party... you said you were looking for a career change?'

'Ah, yes,' said Roz. 'Of course.'

'This one... It's only an admin job, but I thought it could maybe, I dunno... lead on to something else? A counselling course or something?' Ellie grinned sheepishly. 'I don't know how it all works...'

'Thanks,' said Roz. 'It sounds great. Thanks so much for this. I'll look into it.'

On the sofa that night, Roz read Fiona's email again. There was no mention of an invite to their dad's party for Mark. She hadn't even bothered, just assumed Roz would be on her own as usual.

Roz replied to it, telling her she'd be bringing him. *It'll be good for him to meet my family and get to know some people before Kate's wedding*, she added, pointedly.

What are you doing for Easter? Fiona wrote back. *Do you want to come to ours?*

No, I'll pass, thanks, wrote Roz. *Since I'm seeing you the following weekend. You'll be sick of me otherwise!* In reality, she couldn't bear the thought of Fiona fussing round like the lady of the manor, in full 'Good Housekeeping' mode. The pastel table cloths, Easter egg hunts and family trip to church were more than she could stand.

She turned her attention to the job advert Ellie had given her. The salary wasn't much more than she was earning at the moment but, as Ellie had said, it was a start. The first step to a career as a therapist.

Roz wondered when the start date for this job might be. If she got it, she could avoid having to organise any more weddings – ever. Maybe even Kate's. She'd be able to enjoy the day without watching for things going wrong. Kate would understand.

But she was getting too far ahead of herself. She had to apply for it first.

CHAPTER FORTY-TWO

Mark called her that night to apologise again. And again the following morning. He was so upset about letting her down, she'd ended up feeling worse for him than she had for herself.

She nipped out at lunchtime to buy him something to cheer him up – nothing expensive, just something to make him smile – and ended up with a novelty keyring from Serendipity with 'World's Best Boyfriend' on it. It made her sound like a lovestruck teenager, but it was either that or 'Hubby', which was sick-making and which didn't apply – not yet.

She called him in the afternoon. 'I've just bought you a present,' she said, playfully.

'Really?' He sounded surprised.

'Oh, it's nothing much. Don't get too excited.' She paused. 'I can give it to you at the weekend.'

'Ah, well...' He hesitated.

'You're around, aren't you?'

'Well. Actually. It's the anniversary of the accident. Jo

and Yasmin's...' He trailed off. 'I normally spend the weekend by myself to remember them. And visit the grave.'

Roz froze. He spoke about them so little, it was easy to forget they'd existed – and that they apparently still took precedence over *her*.

Then she checked herself. It was good that Mark wasn't full of self-pity and didn't go on about them all the time. And she couldn't begrudge his need to mourn them. It was to his credit.

'Roz?' he said. 'Roz? Are you there?'

'Yep. Yes I am.'

'Listen, I was wondering... Do you want to meet for a nice lunch in Manchester a week on Saturday?'

'Easter Saturday?' she said, checking the calendar.

'Yeah. It'll be my treat. It's the least I can do for fucking up your Dubrovnik weekend.'

Roz smiled. 'Sure.'

'Excellent,' he said. 'I'll book Malmaison for the three of us – for two o'clock, so you and Chloe can fit in some shopping first. And I *definitely* won't forget this time!'

'Promise?' she said.

'Promise.'

Roz and Chloe had been round the shops and were sitting in the restaurant at Malmaison, waiting for Mark. There was a gaggle of women in the corner getting stuck into a bottomless brunch, getting louder by the minute. Roz tutted her disapproval for Chloe's benefit, although she secretly envied their unselfconsciousness. She wished she could be more like that, but knew it would never happen.

Her phone pinged with a rush of messages on the wedding WhatsApp group. The girls were all in Dubrovnik now: they'd been having a long, lazy lunch by the pool, and were uploading photos of their outfits and of the previous evening's sunset.

'What's up?' asked Chloe in alarm. It was unusual for her mother's phone to be so busy.

'Oh, nothing,' said Roz. 'Just Auntie Kate. Sending some photos of Dubrovnik.'

Chloe glowered at the mention of the word and Roz was relieved when Mark walked through the door.

'How are you both?' he asked, slipping off his jacket to reveal a smart black shirt underneath. 'Get any shopping done?'

'A little bit,' said Roz.

Her phone went off again with another rash of photos and Mark looked quizzical.

'It's Kate and the others on the wedding WhatsApp. They're having fun on the hen weekend.'

He frowned and covered his eyes. 'Oh, God. I still feel awful...'

Roz dug in her bag and pulled out the keyring she'd bought for him, as Chloe rolled her eyes and looked away.

He seemed quite abashed. 'World's Best Boyfriend. Is this ironic or something?'

'Not at all,' said Roz, flustered. 'Just a bit of fun.'

'Well, thank you,' he said. 'I shall cherish it.' He handed it back to her so she could put it in her bag, then turned his attention to the menu.

'The two-course set meal looks good,' he said.

'It does,' Roz agreed.

They both ordered the same thing – goat's cheese salad

and steak – while Chloe pointedly went for the vegetarian option. To drink, Mark ordered a large jug of tap water for the table and Roz confined herself to one decent glass of red.

Once they'd finished, Mark encouraged Roz and Chloe to have dessert. Then he had something better in store.

'I was thinking... To redeem myself for the Dubrovnik thing... How about we take off to the Caribbean for the Christmas holidays – all three of us?'

'Can we go snorkelling?' asked Chloe, before Roz could speak.

'Of course we can!' Mark grinned.

'Although...' Chloe's brows knitted together. 'What about Martina?'

'Oh, don't worry about that.' Mark waved his hand. 'She can go into kennels for a couple of weeks.'

A couple of weeks, thought Roz. In the Caribbean. Wow.

'The hotels there are incredible,' said Mark. 'Five star, all-inclusive.'

'What does that mean?' asked Chloe.

'It means everything's free when you get there!' said Mark. 'So while we're snorkelling, your mum can go in the spa. *And* she won't have to do any cooking. None at all!'

Roz's heart soared. She was trying to be cool, but it was like he was seeing into her soul.

Her phone rang out. It was Kate – Facetiming her now – and Roz struggled to hide her annoyance. She flipped her hair over one shoulder and answered it, mouthing a 'sorry' at Mark.

All the 'hens' were in the background behind Kate, in their floaty dresses and shades. 'Wish you were here!' Kate called out. 'We're all missing you, aren't we, girls?'

'Yeah!' they all agreed, although Vicky was looking

sheepish behind her dark fringe and Ray-Bans. It had obviously been a good lunch: they all seemed pretty tipsy.

'This is the lovely Mark,' Roz announced, leaning across the table to get him in shot. 'We've just had an amazing meal as well.'

Mark waved at them, suddenly shy, which Roz found funny.

Then Natasha appeared on the screen – she'd made it over from New York, last minute – her blonde hair protected by a wide-brimmed hat. Roz knew there would be a blizzard of photos on her Insta later.

'So sorry you couldn't make it over here, Roz,' Natasha drawled. 'Looking forward to seeing you at the wedding though!'

'Aw,' said Roz. 'I'm gutted I can't be there too. But it's sunny here in Manchester. And anyway,' she couldn't stop herself, 'we're off to the Caribbean this winter, aren't we, Mark? That'll make up for it.'

'Wow!' they all chorused, as Mark beamed.

'We can't wait to meet you, Mark!' added Kate.

The rest of them whooped with excitement and, as they said their goodbyes and ended the call, Roz couldn't remember feeling happier.

The feeling lasted all the way home and through the night as she went to bed with Mark and lay in his arms afterwards. It was just over two weeks since her last period, so she was half-way through her cycle. Could she allow herself to dream? She could certainly pray.

CHAPTER FORTY-THREE

The following Friday, Roz rushed home from work to get changed for her dad's 'Hoedown' party. She wasn't feeling the 'country and western' theme at all. She'd never been one of those willowy beauties who could rock a pair of jeans, and had come to accept that she never would be. Instead, she pulled on her denim tunic-dress and ankle boots – the first time she'd worn them since the night Daniel died, the bad vibes a distant memory. On top she wore a red and black checked shirt – a cheap one she'd bought in her lunch hour – which she tied at the waist to give her some shape.

Mark arrived early to pick her up, also in a red and black checked shirt.

'Jinx!' she exclaimed, kissing him on the cheek. 'I'm nearly ready – just need to go up and put some make-up on. Wait here a sec. I won't be long...'

When she came back downstairs, Mark pointed to the sideboard. 'Where is it?' he asked. 'The photo of the three of us?'

There was something in his tone that made her feel it was best to lie. 'I – eh. I broke the glass when I was dusting.'

'No you didn't!' said Chloe, sidling into the room, arms folded. Roz gave her a pleading look, but it was too late. 'You threw it in the bin, remember?' Chloe turned to Mark now. 'It was when you had that row and fell out.'

'Oh,' said Mark. 'I see.'

'Er, well, yes,' Roz stumbled. 'I did, I'm afraid. I found it too... upsetting.'

'Well,' he said. 'We'll have to take another one.'

'We've still got the frame,' Chloe added, trying to make amends. 'It's up in my room, with one of my school photos in it. It's horrible...'

Mark broke into a smile. 'I'm sure it isn't,' he said. And Roz released the breath she was holding.

'What do you think of my outfit?' Roz asked Mark, desperate to change the subject.

'It's great,' he said. 'It shows off your child-bearing hips.'

Her face fell. 'What?'

He pulled her towards him. 'C'mon. Don't be like that. It's a compliment. It's... womanly.'

Roz raised an eyebrow. 'If you say so,' she said, checking the time. 'Right. We'd better be going. It'll take us a while to get to Alderley Edge. I don't want to be late.'

Mark and Roz dropped Chloe off at Fiona's house, where she was staying the night with her cousins. Fiona had booked a babysitter, then Ian was bringing Chloe home on Sunday morning on his way to a cycle race. Roz was looking forward to a whole Saturday on her own with Mark – getting up late, going out for breakfast, taking it easy.

Mark and Roz then carried on to the golf club, where they secured the last space in the car park next to the hog roast van. Inside the clubhouse, it smelt of Middle England – of talc, disinfectant and floral air freshener – with the chintz chairs and regency stripe wallpaper to match. It was full of retired couples standing around self-consciously in waistcoats and stetsons, and Roz was glad of Mark's hand to hold as they walked in.

Fiona waved at them from the corner where she was holding court, dressed as a sexy pink cowgirl. She excused herself and came over to join them, giving all the old guys a better view of her tight pink T-shirt, pink hat with fluffy trim and matching cowboy boots. Their eyes were bulging out of their heads – including Mark's.

Fiona hugged Roz, was perfectly charming to Mark, then excused herself again to go and check on the hog roast and the band – a veritable social butterfly.

Roz scanned the room till she spotted her dad, standing at the bar with his golf buddies, clutching a pint of bitter. Her mother, lurking nearby, had made no concession to fancy dress whatsoever, wearing her usual uniform of a sensible skirt and blouse. Roz wondered if any of her dad's ex-fancy-women were in attendance; there were a few Elaine Paige lookalikes in the house and he'd always been a sucker for a petite blonde.

'Roz!' her dad called out when he saw her. 'By God!' He made a show of looking out the window. 'Have you arrived by plane?'

'What are you on about, Dad?' Roz asked, confused.

He gave her a bear hug. 'Well, I hardly ever see you these days. I assumed you'd left the country!'

'Nice you could make it,' was all her mother said, tight-lipped.

'So... This is Mark,' Roz announced, ignoring her.

'Derek Johnson,' said Roz's dad, offering his hand to Mark.

'Mark Glaister,' said Mark, accepting it.

Her mother just nodded at Mark. 'We've met,' she said. 'Briefly.'

Mark nodded too. 'Nice to see you again.'

Roz produced a bottle of Jack Daniels from the gift bag she'd brought and gave it to her dad. 'Happy Retirement, Dad.'

'Cheers, love!' he exclaimed. He seemed delighted with it, bless him, although her mother looked less than impressed.

Her dad clapped Mark on the back like a son. 'So then, Mark. What do you do?'

'I, eh, work at Stepping Hill Hospital,' said Mark. He seemed uncomfortable with all the attention. 'I'm an anaes-thetist.'

'Ah, yes.' Her dad nodded vehemently. 'I'd heard you were a Gas Man!'

Then he laughed uproariously at his own joke, but Mark didn't get it. Roz couldn't really blame him though: her dad was quite pissed already and slurring a bit.

'Gas Man,' her dad repeated. 'Anaesthetic. Gas. Get it?'

'Ah, yes,' said Mark. 'Of course,' and laughed too.

'I had an op there last year. On my carpal tunnel,' her dad went on. 'I don't suppose you remember me?'

'Er. Well... we do see a lot of patients,' said Mark diplo-matically.

'I'm sure you do... I'm sure you do. Well, you're all doing a great job under very difficult conditions.' Her dad raised his glass. 'Keep up the good work and all that.'

Roz was starting to feel excluded by their chummy boys' act. 'I've applied for a new job,' she found herself declaring. 'At the university. It's in student welfare and mental health.'

Mark turned to her. 'Have you? You didn't say.'

But she had no chance to explain further as Kate's mother Jan had just arrived and was heading in their direction. 'Gosh, you must be very popular, Derek,' Jan said to Roz's dad. 'We couldn't get into the car park. We've had to park half way up the road.'

'Hi, Jan,' said Roz, kissing her on the cheek. 'I think we got the last space! Next to the hog roast van.'

'That tiny little space?' said Jan. 'Well done you for getting into it.'

'Well, it was Mark who did it,' said Roz. 'I'm rubbish at parking.'

Mark nodded and laughed. 'Yeah. It once took her nine attempts to reverse her little car into a huge space outside her house. It was funny. The air was blue, I can tell you.'

A plume of heat rose up in Roz as she tried to make light of it. 'It was actually three attempts and the space wasn't that big,' she said. But no matter how much she protested, they all still laughed. Apart from her mother, which was typical.

'Our Roz has always had a bit of a tongue on her,' said her dad.

'Oh yes!' agreed Mark.

What? Roz couldn't remember swearing in front of him. Certainly never in front of Chloe. But she let it go. It wasn't worth arguing about.

Salvation came from an unlikely place. 'So, Roz.' Her

mother changed the subject. 'Are you all set for Kate's wedding? For your maid of honour duties? And what about Chloe? I bet she's excited.'

'Oh, she is,' said Roz, waiting for a veiled insult that never came.

'That's nice,' said her mother.

The band finished their set to a still-empty dancefloor, and Fiona came over to say that pork sandwiches were being served in the Members' Bar.

'Oh good,' said Roz, as Mark's eyes slid over Fiona's arse in her jeans.

He'd been checking her out – no doubt about it – and Roz had lost her appetite.

In the Members' Bar, Roz introduced Mark to Ian, who was standing on his own like Mr. Personality. Eventually Ian spoke. 'I've heard you do a bit of cycling,' he said to Mark. 'What kind of bike have you got?'

But his reply was interrupted by Roz's dad, who was up at the bar, bashing a teaspoon off his glass, ready to make a speech. He kept it short and sweet, but it wasn't short enough for her mother, who was making a cut-throat gesture at him to wind things up.

Once her dad had finished and everyone had clapped, they all trooped through to the main room for the disco. The lights were turned down and 'YMCA', 'Dancing Queen' and 'Greased Lightning' boomed from the tinny speakers like the wedding disco from hell.

'I hope the music at Kate's do is better than this,' Roz

shouted in Mark's ear. 'Sam's choosing it. She's got good taste.'

The dad-dancing had started now the booze was kicking in, and Fiona came over again. 'Your glasses look empty. Would you like another drink?' she asked Mark, in full hostess mode.

'No, we're fine,' Roz replied.

'Or come and have a dance?' pouted Fiona, wiggling her hips.

'We're just about to leave actually,' said Roz firmly. 'We're keen to spend some time at home on our own for a change.'

'Oh God, don't leave me with these old fossils,' pleaded Fiona, touching Mark's elbow.

'What do you think?' Mark asked Roz. 'Shall we stay for a bit?'

'No, we're going,' said Roz firmly, taking his arm. 'We'll just go and say our goodbyes.'

'Alright then, be like that,' said Fiona. 'I'll be seeing you again soon enough.'

'When?' said Roz.

'The wedding!' Mark reminded her.

Fiona winked. 'Two weeks today.'

'Oh God,' said Roz. 'Of course. We'll see you then.' How great to be able to say 'we' rather than 'I' for once. At long last.

Roz savoured that feeling again when they said goodbye to her parents, conscious of her mother's eyes on her the whole time.

CHAPTER FORTY-FOUR

Back in the car, Roz kicked off her boots. 'Well...' She sighed a long sigh. 'Thank God *that's* over.'

'It wasn't too bad,' said Mark, pulling out of the car park onto the deserted A-road. 'I thought Fiona was nice. Very friendly.'

'Hmm,' said Roz. 'I guess so.'

'You'd never guess you were sisters,' he continued. 'She's very...'

Roz dreaded what he was going to say next.

He smiled as he thought of the word. 'Very polished.'

Roz exhaled with relief. It could've been worse, she supposed.

'Your mother, though,' said Mark. 'She was cold as a witch's tit towards me!'

'Yeah,' said Roz. It was true but, on some level, she felt compelled to defend her. 'I wouldn't take it personally if I were you,' she said. 'She's a bit like that with everyone. It's just her way, I'm afraid.'

Roz pressed her head against the car window, but it was

too dark to see anything out of it. 'Now I've just got to meet *your* family,' said Roz. 'It'll be nice to meet your mum. And your brother.'

'I haven't told my mum about us yet,' said Mark, his eyes straight ahead.

'You're not ashamed of me, are you?' said Roz. She was joking but his face stayed serious.

'It's not that,' he said. 'I just wanted to make sure it was the real thing before introducing someone new.'

The words stung her. *Is this the real thing?* she wanted to ask, but didn't.

'She's never got over the loss of Jo and Yasmin,' he said. 'She was so close to them. She always said Jo was the daughter she never had...'

'Poor thing,' said Roz. 'That's so sad.' Her sympathy was genuine, but her worry that she'd never be able to compete was greater.

She brooded in silence as they left behind the leafy lanes and was glad when they reached the edge of Stockport, with its drinking dens and takeaways and other signs of life.

'Ian's a bit of a wet blanket, isn't he?' she said eventually. 'I thought you and him might have bonded a bit more over cycling and stuff.'

'I thought you might have told me about your new job?' said Mark, sharply. 'I felt an idiot for not knowing.'

'Oh.' Roz waved her hand dismissively. 'It's only an application. They'll get loads of better ones. I don't expect anything to come of it.'

'Even so. You could've told me.'

'I'm sorry, I forgot. It was just something Ellie told me about...'

243

He seemed to bridle at this. 'And do you think you're qualified for it?' he asked. 'Advising young people?'

She turned to him. 'What's that supposed to mean?'

'Just a question,' he said. Then he laughed. Scornfully. 'I mean, you've said it yourself. Your life's been a bit of a disaster.'

'Or you could say I've got some life experience,' said Roz, defiantly. 'I've made some mistakes and learned a few lessons.'

'So that's your qualifications? Going to Australia, taking a load of drugs and getting knocked up?'

'*Taking a load of drugs?*' Roz was blindsided. 'It was only a bit of pot! And it was a lifetime ago.'

'But it's not just that,' he sneered. 'You got sucked in by that Daniel as well.' He shook his head. 'Visiting clairvoyants to sort your life out...'

'I told you, it was a Tarot card reader, not a clairvoyant.'

'Huh? Whatever...'

He was smirking now and something snapped in her. 'You know what?' she said. 'I'm getting a bit fed up of this. You making digs at me all the time.'

'What are you on about?' The smirk disappeared.

'Like what you were saying back there about my parking.' She swallowed. 'Normally I wouldn't make a thing of it, but you made me look a fool in front of my family.'

'Oh, stop exaggerating, will you?' he scoffed. 'You're so bloody sensitive all the time. It was just a joke.'

Roz was trembling now. 'You always say that. *It was just a joke.* It might just be a joke to you, but—'

'Oh for fuck's sake. Why do you have to over-analyse everything?' He pressed hard on the accelerator as he ran the amber light. 'I can't fucking *stand* it!'

Roz's stomach dropped as the speedo hit a hundred. The engine thrust was like an aeroplane at take-off, and she gripped the sides of her seat. She begged him to slow down, but he didn't and she couldn't look. He was going to hit something. A parked car, a bollard, a human. How could he do this after what happened to his wife and child? He was going to kill himself – and her – and someone would have to break the news to Chloe.

She opened her eyes. There was a girl on the pavement ahead, around Ellie's age, clutching a pizza box, waving goodbye to her friends. She was staggering a bit as she stepped into the road and Roz cried out.

Mark blasted his horn, swerving to miss the girl, and the shock of it seemed to jolt him out of his fury, back to reality. He said nothing as he drove the last two miles to Roz's house – impeccably – like he was taking a driving test.

They pulled up outside, got out of the car and headed up the path, still in silence. Roz's hand shook as she struggled with the door key.

Once inside, she went to the kitchen. 'I'll make some tea,' she said, on autopilot.

'OK,' he said, taking a seat on the couch.

When she came back through and set the mugs on the table, it was a minute before he spoke again. 'I'm so, so sorry,' he said, looking at the floor. 'It's just... work's been really stressful lately and I'm totally strung out.' He paused. 'We lost a couple of patients this week. I try not to talk about it away from work, but I've hardly slept...'

Roz sighed in sympathy. 'It's OK,' she said, sitting beside him. 'Don't worry. It's been a long day. I was being irritable and tetchy too... I think it might be my age. I get a bit like that these days.'

She smiled, but he didn't smile back. 'No,' he said. 'I'm not letting you take the blame. I was out of order. Fair and square.' He bit his lip. 'I'm sorry, Roz. It's hard. I need your help. To cope with... all this.'

His eyes glistened now and Roz placed her hand on his. 'I know,' she said, choosing her words carefully. 'And I know you said you try not to talk about this stuff – the stresses of work – but I'm thinking maybe you should.'

He nodded meekly.

'Is there any way you can access counselling at work?' she asked. 'Speak to a professional?'

His tears spilled over and Roz held him tight. 'It's OK. It's OK,' she said, rocking and patting him on the back like a baby. 'I'll help you. We'll get through it together. OK?'

'OK,' he mumbled.

'But, first of all, let's go up and get some sleep. OK?'

He nodded and Roz led him upstairs by the hand. He fell asleep right away, snoring deeply, as she spooned him from behind. But she was wide awake, concentrating on her breathing, waiting for her heart rate to return to normal.

This was another part of his job she'd have to get used to.

CHAPTER FORTY-FIVE

Roz opened her eyes, sensing a shadow over her. She started at the sight of Mark, sitting there on the bed, waiting for her to wake.

'Morning,' he said, kissing her forehead, pushing her hair from her eyes. 'I'm going to make you breakfast in bed.'

'Er... What time is it?' Roz croaked.

'Seven o'clock... There's eggs in the fridge if you like – or else I could go out and get us some pastries or something?'

'I usually just have a mug of tea and a slice of toast with Marmite,' said Roz. 'That'll be fine.'

'OK,' he said, kissed her again, and disappeared downstairs. This attention was over-powering in her still-groggy state, but at least the drama of last night seemed to be forgotten.

He returned a few minutes later with a tray. 'Your breakfast, Madam. Milk, no sugar in the tea – is that right?'

'Yep, thanks.' She pushed herself up to sitting, as he placed the tray in front of her and sat back down.

'Are you having something yourself?' she said.

'No, but I had something else to ask you.' He opened his hand to reveal the keyring she'd bought him, then proceeded to remove the keys from it.

She frowned; she had no idea what he was doing.

'Roz Johnson,' he said, grabbing hold of her hand as she reached for her mug. 'Will you do me the honour of becoming my wife?' Then he pushed the empty 'ring' onto her finger.

'Er...' Roz stumbled. 'Really?'

'I mean it. I want us to be a family. You, me, Chloe and...' He hesitated. 'Who knows? Maybe a sister for Chloe. Or a brother. Oh, and Martina of course!' He sighed. 'I'm tired of rattling around my big, empty house. Or... we could move somewhere else. Start afresh. It doesn't matter where. I just know I want another child. I do. With you.'

Roz knew she should be pleased and she was – really she was. This was what she'd always dreamt of. But the reality of it was weird. This wasn't how she'd imagined it – the thing she'd always wanted, the thing that'd make her life fall into place. There was no going down on one knee. No fancy restaurant, mini-break or other special place. No ring. It was a far cry from the classic proposal.

'Oh, God,' Mark said, eyes twinkling. 'Please say something. Don't leave me hanging.'

'Yes!' said Roz. 'A thousand times yes!' This was something she'd seen some influencer say on Instagram. She'd thought it cringey at the time and had no idea why she was saying it now. Then she threw her arms round him; it was the appropriate thing to do.

'So,' he said, after a moment. 'Why don't we get showered and then go shopping for a proper ring?'

'Now?' said Roz, removing the mock ring from her finger. 'Like, this morning?'

'Yep. Why not?' he said, squeezing her hand. '*Seize the day* and all that.'

'Well...' She cast around for an excuse, not used to this kind of spontaneity. 'I was planning to go to the supermarket. I haven't been for ages.'

'Really?' He cocked his head at her.

'Or we could go over and fetch Chloe. Tell her our news. I don't feel right being without her.'

Mark's face fell like a child's. 'But... I thought Ian was dropping her off tomorrow morning? To give us some time together. I thought that was the idea?'

'Well. OK,' she relented. It was probably for the best. If they went to fetch Chloe, she'd have to see Fiona again, who'd want to know where 'the ring' was.

Roz and Mark strolled down into town, holding hands in the spring sunshine.

'Oh, by the way,' he said. 'Just to warn you...'

'What?' she said. She didn't want any more surprises.

'My mum... She might call me later. She's ordered herself a new TV online and wants me to go over and set it up when it arrives. This is my main role in life!'

'Fair enough,' said Roz, squeezing his hand. 'It's got to be done.' She was grateful she'd never had to do any of that sort of stuff for her parents. Fiona usually took care of it or, more usually, Ian.

When they reached the Cavendish Arcade, he led her

towards a window display of antique rings. 'I like those,' he said.

Roz bit her cheek. *Really?* she thought. These old things? Or maybe it was the price he liked; they were all so much cheaper than a new one.

'Jo's was like that,' he said, pointing one out – emeralds and diamonds set on a thin gold band. 'We bought it on a weekend away in Bath. She was buried with it.'

'Oh,' said Roz, colouring.

'Emeralds were Jo's favourite,' he went on. 'She always said it was the Celt in her – she thought green stones suited her red hair. Oh God, I'm sorry,' he added hastily. 'That was a bit morbid of me.'

'Not at all,' said Roz. 'Not at all. It's fine.'

He turned to her. 'Look, why don't we have our wedding rings specially made? We can give it some thought and have exactly what we want. Our own design.'

Roz cheered up at the thought of having something unique, something no-one else had. 'Yes,' she said. 'I like that idea.'

'Now,' said Mark, putting his arm round her. 'I don't know about you, but I'm starving. I should've had some breakfast.'

They walked out onto the pedestrianised area of Spring Gardens and Mark noticed the vintage tea room up a side street. 'That place looks nice. Shall we go there? Before it gets too busy.'

They chose a window table and ordered eggs benedict for two, chatting away between mouthfuls. Then, as they finished their coffees, they watched the world go by: young lads and their dads coming back from football practice, teenage couples on self-conscious lunch dates, daughters out shopping with their mums.

Mark's phone rang in his pocket. 'It's Mum,' he mouthed to Roz, and answered it.

Roz smiled and nodded. She could hear her muffled voice down the line; she sounded sweet and talkative and, rather charmingly, he called her 'dear'.

'OK,' said Mark down the phone. 'No problem. I'll come over.' But his mum kept talking. 'OK. OK. Bye then,' he said. 'I'll see you in an hour or so. OK. OK. I have to go now. See you later.'

He hung up and pulled a sad face at Roz. 'I'm so sorry about this.'

'No problem at all,' said Roz. 'It's your mum!'

'But listen,' he said. 'Shall we go out for Sunday lunch next weekend? There's a place one of my colleagues recommended. A newly renovated old pub in the Derbyshire Dales. The Black Bull, it's called. The food's meant to be excellent.'

'Sure,' said Roz. 'That would be fab.' She'd been about to suggest they did something in Didsbury for a change, but a pub lunch sounded perfect.

'Great. I'll call you later,' he said, kissing her as he rose to leave.

Roz paid the bill and spent the next hour wafting aimlessly around the usual shops. Later on, back home, she didn't know what to do with herself. For the first time in ages, she thought about posting something on Facebook – the 'exciting news' of her engagement – or telling the girls in the WhatsApp group all about it. But she decided against it. She'd wait a while, till she'd got the ring on her finger and could 'flash her sparkler' in tabloid-speak. She allowed herself a smile at the phrase, which always sounded rude to her.

For now, she just texted Kate – and Kate texted straight back: *Wow! Woop, woop. Weddings are obviously catching! I'm so happy for you x*

You're the first to know, typed Roz. *I'll tell the others when I see them.*

No worries, Kate replied. *My lips are sealed!*

Roz sat back. She'd tell the other girls at the wedding – when she introduced them to Mark – and tell her family at the same time. There would be something triumphant about doing it then. It would be a sign to everyone not to write her off, not to underestimate her. Not least her mother. It wouldn't normally be the done thing at a wedding – pulling focus from the bride by announcing your own engagement – but it wouldn't bother Kate in the slightest.

The house felt empty without Chloe, and a long, lonely evening stretched ahead of Roz. She didn't fancy cooking dinner just for herself. Some left-over quiche and salad would do. Then she browsed some 'design your own wedding ring' sites till she was overwhelmed by the choice available and had to stop.

At six o'clock, she poured a glass of wine and checked her phone. Mark had said he'd call her 'later'. What had he meant by that – literally later tonight? Or just later generally – at some point? She went to bed when he hadn't called by ten.

~

Roz was delighted when Ian dropped Chloe home first thing the next morning – and relieved he drove off once she was safe inside, so she didn't have to talk to him.

Chloe stepped gingerly into the house. 'Is he here?' she asked, in a whisper.

'Mark? No,' said Roz, hugging her close. 'He had to go to his mum's.'

'Oh.' Chloe took off her jacket and hung it up.

'I've got something to tell you, love,' said Roz.

'What's wrong?' said Chloe, wide-eyed.

'It's nothing bad. Don't look so worried. It's just... Me and Mark. Well... we've got engaged.'

'Engaged?' Chloe's mouth hung open as she processed it. 'So... you're getting married?'

'Yep!'

Chloe said nothing. Then, 'Where's your ring?'

'I haven't got one yet.'

'But...' Chloe frowned. 'How can you be engaged if you haven't got a ring?'

'We're going to have some made, love. Our own special design. Maybe you can help me with it? You'd like that, wouldn't you?'

'Yeah.'

'And...' Roz said, hugging her tight. 'It means you can be a bridesmaid again. And go shopping for *another* new dress. Kate's wedding can be a practice run!'

Chloe just nodded.

'So, love. Did you have a nice time at Auntie Fiona's?'

But before she could answer, Roz's phone rang – it was Mark.

'How's my fiancée this morning?' he asked.

Roz giggled. 'Very well. And how's mine?' She watched Chloe disappear upstairs.

'Good, thanks. I stayed over at my mum's – watching the new telly. Talk about a wild night!'

'Sounds very similar to mine!'

'I told mum all about you,' he said. 'She's delighted at our news and is looking forward to meeting you.'

'Likewise!' said Roz. 'We'll have to all go out for a nice meal. Or...' An idea popped into her head. 'She could come with us to The Black Bull next weekend?'

'I thought the same!' he said. 'I asked her, but she's busy next Sunday. A day out with her pals. She's got a better social life than me!'

'Good for her,' laughed Roz. 'Not to worry. Maybe we can get together when Kate's wedding's out of the way?'

'Good idea,' said Mark. 'Sounds like a plan.'

When they'd finished chatting, Roz made a start on the usual round of depressing Sunday chores, although they weren't as depressing as usual somehow. Even the ironing didn't seem so bad.

CHAPTER FORTY-SIX

At work on Monday morning, Roz told Angie she was engaged. She knew it would be all round the building by lunchtime, but she didn't care. They would all know eventually in any case.

'Oh, that's lovely,' said Angie. 'Although it's quite a surprise. I didn't even know you had a boyfriend.'

Roz blushed. 'I didn't want to say anything. Till I was sure...'

'Ah well, it's always the quiet ones,' said Angie. 'You dark horse.'

Roz smiled and Angie leaned across the desk. 'Now then...' she said. 'Lemme see the ring! Where is it?'

Roz's smile disappeared. 'Ah, well,' she said, rubbing awkwardly at her finger. 'I haven't actually got one yet. We're having some made. To our own design.'

'Oh,' said Angie. 'That's nice.' But she was obviously disappointed.

Roz was pretending to do some work, but was secretly

practising her new signature. *Roz Glaister. Roz Glaister. Roz Glaister.* It sounded classy. Better than Roz Johnson.

'I guess I'd better buy a new hat,' said Angie, stretching her arms above her head. 'It's *ages* since I've been to a good wedding.'

It was a bit cheeky of her to assume she'd be invited, but Roz appreciated her enthusiasm. It was more than she would get from her family.

'Will you get married here?' Angie asked. 'At the hotel? Staff discount!'

'I might do,' said Roz, mischievously. 'I might need you to wait the tables and pour the drinks if we're short-staffed...'

'No problem,' said Angie good-naturedly. 'If it comes to that, I'll do it!'

'No, seriously,' said Roz. 'It won't be here. That would be weird – too much like a busman's holiday.'

'So, where then? What do you fancy?'

Roz hesitated. It was strange. On some level, she'd always imagined a big wedding – a traditional day with all the trimmings like Fiona's and all the others she'd been to. But now it came down to it, that wasn't what she wanted.

'I don't know,' she replied, to Angie's surprise. 'Maybe the 'stables courtyard' at Chatsworth House. Something small, stylish – more intimate.'

Angie whistled. 'Very nice. But it'll still cost a few bob. My neighbour's son got married there last Christmas and, let me tell you, it wasn't cheap.'

'Mark can afford it!' sniffed Roz.

'Oh, really?' said Angie. 'What does he do for a job?'

Roz told her and Angie was suitably impressed. 'Actually, I like the idea of a Christmas wedding,' said Roz. 'We're thinking of going to the Caribbean this Christmas. That could be our honeymoon.'

The following day, Angie was still full of questions about the wedding. 'What about the hen night?' she wanted to know. 'Have you thought about that yet?'

'Oh God,' said Roz. 'Not at all.' Would Angie want to come on that as well?

Then, after lunch, Angie came back to the office with a pile of bridal magazines under her arm.

'Thanks,' said Roz, as Angie dumped them on her desk. She was touched as it was such a kind thought and they must have cost a fortune, but she dreaded to think where this would end.

'What about your bridesmaids?' said Angie. 'Who will you have? Chloe? Your sister?'

It was like the Spanish Inquisition and Roz was regretting telling her now.

'Yep, Chloe,' she said. 'And probably Kate – my mate who's getting married here in a couple of weeks. I'm her maid of honour.'

'Oh, that's nice,' said Angie. 'She'll be returning the favour... And the best man?'

'I'm not sure,' said Roz, shuffling some papers, as if she was keen to get on. 'Maybe Mark's brother. Or a colleague from work.'

The next day – Wednesday morning – Angie was waiting for Roz to arrive in the office, clearly bursting to say something, and Roz wondered what today's wedding question would be.

'Your sister called,' Angie announced instead. 'She'd been trying to reach you on your mobile apparently, but couldn't get through. It sounded urgent.'

'Really?' Roz muttered to herself. 'What does *she* want?'

'I asked her, but she didn't say.'

I bet you did, thought Roz, calling Fiona's number. She was probably organising yet another dire family gathering... Well, this time, Roz would get in first with her news and tell her about the engagement. Wrestle the spotlight back from her. For once.

Fiona answered. 'Oh hello. Thanks so much for calling me back,' she said, like she was talking to a client. 'Listen, I'm about to go into a meeting, so I'll have to keep it short.'

'OK. Fine,' said Roz. 'Keep your hair on. What's up?'

'Well....' Fiona was suddenly hesitant. 'I wanted to ask... This guy you've been seeing. Mark.'

'Ye-ah?' said Roz.

'How much do you know about him?'

'I'm sorry?' said Roz, flushing bright red. 'How do you mean?' She was all too conscious of Angie sitting there, ears swivelling like Jodrell Bank.

'Well,' said Fiona. She changed tack, softer now. 'After dad's party the other night... Mum said she was a bit concerned for you and that—'

'Actually.' Roz stopped her. 'Could you hold on a sec?' She got up and left the room, away from Angie. 'Concerned for me?' Roz repeated.

'She said she got a bad vibe from him,' said Fiona.

'A bad vibe? That doesn't sound like something Mum would say.'

'Well, no. I'm paraphrasing... I think she felt he wasn't being all that nice to you. Her antennae were up.'

'Right. I see. So it's OK for her to be mean to me, but not anyone else?'

Fiona swallowed. 'She asked me to do some detective work on him.'

'*Detective work?*' said Roz. 'On Mark? What the actual—?'

'Oh God, wait, that makes it sound worse than it is,' said Fiona. 'Like I said, she was just concerned for you... But Ian's done some digging around at work – at HMRC – and on the face of it, it would appear to be the case that—'

'Look.' Roz gripped the phone. 'Spare me the lawyer speak, just get on with it.'

'Well, his tax records seem to suggest that he's married...'

'His tax records? What?' Roz shook her head. 'Look, I'm sorry. Ian must have got it wrong.'

'I don't think so.' Fiona was suddenly sharp. 'How many Mark Glaisters do you suppose there are, living in Didsbury, who work for the NHS? *This* Mark Glaister lives at 12 Kingsland Road. Is that his address?'

'I don't know,' said Roz.

'You don't know?'

'Er, not off the top of my head.' She *didn't* know. She hadn't been to his house yet, but wasn't going to admit it. 'And anyway, Mark *was* married at one point,' said Roz. 'Married with a daughter. They died in an accident a few years ago. Ian must be mistaken. Or the records are out of date. You know what government departments are like...'

'Well, yes, it's possible they could be out of date, but—'

'Oh fuck off, will you, Fiona? I know what you're doing. It's so transparent. You're trying to turn me against him.'

'Roz, I—'

'Well, I'm telling you. It won't work!'

'OK. Fine,' said Fiona. 'I've said what I had to say.'

'That's good,' said Roz. 'Because I've got to go. You're not the only one who's busy.' She hung up and ran to the Ladies to splash some cold water on her face. *Thanks a bunch, sis,* she thought bitterly. That was Fiona to a 'T'. Always keen to piss on her parade at the first opportunity. She'd had – what? – three full days to enjoy being engaged before Fiona ruined it. It had always been the same. Like the time she broke the chemistry set Roz had pleaded for at Christmas. That had only lasted three days as well.

When Roz returned to her desk, Angie was studying her for clues. 'Is everything OK?' Angie asked.

'Yep. Fine,' said Roz, sitting down. She grabbed the mouse and clicked on Google Street View to check out the address. *Kingsland Road, Didsbury.* It was a wide, tree-lined avenue of Victorian detached houses, all with bay windows and smart gardens, facing onto a park. She tried zooming in as best she could, but couldn't make out number 12.

She could see herself strolling down this street, to the artisanal bakery – or the posh salon or nail bar. Chloe would be attending the local school – a nicer one with well-spoken classmates and a burgundy uniform. Roz wondered how she would get to work. Even if she got this new job, she'd still need to get to Buxton. She'd have to drive. Or she could apply for something in Manchester. That would give her more options. A lot more.

She imagined too the fancy kitchen he'd been having installed – maybe even nicer than Fiona's.

Bloody Fiona. She'd managed to get inside her head and spoil her happiness as usual. Her and their interfering mother.

Roz was desperate to talk to someone about it – to talk to Mark – but couldn't bring herself to ring him. It was all too awkward. She'd bring it up when she saw him on Sunday. It would be easier in person.

Roz looked up as an email from Mark popped in. It was a link to another Travelzoo deal: two weeks in Barbados in December, flying from Manchester – only £10,000 for the three of them, including business class flights.

Only! Roz replied, ironically.

It's a great deal, wrote Mark. *We should get it booked. I don't want to leave it too late and miss out. After what happened the last time!*

Definitely, replied Roz. *Let's discuss it later. Love you x*

CHAPTER FORTY-SEVEN

As the end of the week approached, The Old Hall was crackling with tension behind the scenes. Among the staff, rumours were rife that the results of the redundancy consultation would be announced imminently, and anxiety levels were high as they awaited their fates. Roz, by contrast, felt weirdly calm. She kept her head down and got on with her work. It would be what it would be. *What's for you won't go by you.* Which sounded like her mother. Or one of Angie's inspirational memes that she found on Facebook.

However, her Zen mood was spoiled by a phone call at four, as she was finishing her tasks for the day. It was the secretary at Chloe's school – to say that Chloe had been involved in an 'incident' and that Mrs. Farzad, the head teacher, wanted to speak to her.

'What kind of incident?' asked Roz, fearing the worst.

'I'm, er, afraid I'll have to leave it to Mrs. Farzad to inform you of the circumstances.'

'But she's OK, right?' said Roz.

'Yes,' said the secretary. 'She's fine.'

Roz dropped what she was doing and headed up to the school straight away.

~

Mrs. Farzad – slim, pretty, younger than Roz – was waiting in her office, hands clasped on her spotless wooden desk. Chloe was there too, sitting opposite, her eyes on the floor.

'Thanks for coming in. I appreciate it,' said the head teacher, kindly. 'Please... Take a seat.'

'Thanks. So, er, what's this about?' asked Roz, in no mood for pleasantries. 'What's the matter?'

'Well,' said the head, choosing her words. 'There was a bit of a skirmish at break this afternoon and—'

'A skirmish?' said Roz.

'Chloe lashed out at one of her classmates,' said Mrs. Farzad. 'At Ruby.'

'Lashed out?'

Chloe looked up at her mother. 'I tried to punch her.'

'Tried?' said Roz. 'So she's OK?'

'Yes,' said Mrs. Farzad. 'Ruby's fine.'

'Why though?' Roz asked Chloe, although she suspected she knew the answer. Ruby could be a real spoiled brat at times.

'I told her I was going to Barbados for Christmas, but she laughed at me in front of everyone and said I was a liar. That I was making it up.'

Roz's hackles rose. She glanced at Mrs. Farzad. 'Well that's not very nice. Why would she say that?'

Chloe shuffled her feet. 'She's said it before. She said I lied about Dubrovnik too. That I told everyone I was going when I wasn't.'

Roz wanted to hug her, but stayed in her seat.

'I'm sorry,' Chloe went on. 'I'm sorry. I shouldn't have done it.'

Mrs. Farzad acted quickly to end her torture. 'And that's the main thing,' she said. 'That you've learned from your mistake and that you won't do it again.'

'I won't,' sniffed Chloe.

'OK then,' said the head teacher, standing up. 'I don't think I need keep you much longer.' She turned to Chloe. 'Could you wait in the secretary's office for a minute or two? I'd like to have a word with your mum.'

Chloe left the room and Mrs. Farzad walked Roz to the door of her office. 'I was just wondering... Chloe's usually such a nice girl. This is very out of character for her. Is everything OK? At home, I mean...'

'Yes,' Roz said, indignantly. 'Everything's fine.'

'Oh. OK. I just wondered if anything had changed?'

'Not really,' said Roz. 'Apart from... I've started seeing a new partner – well, fiancé now – in the last few months. But they get on really well.'

Afterwards, on the way home, Roz worried she'd appeared a bit 'flighty' to the head – engaged after just a few months. Would she think she was a Bad Mother?

'You like Mark, don't you?' she asked Chloe as they headed up the hill.

'Yep,' said Chloe. 'Why?'

'And, in future, if there's anything wrong – if you're not happy for any reason – you'll tell me, won't you? Or tell a teacher? I don't want to be called up to the school again, OK?'

'Yep,' said Chloe and carried on walking.

~

Bad things usually came in threes and – after that horrible phone call from Fiona and Chloe's trouble at school – Roz was waiting for the triple whammy, for the third 'anvil' to fall on her head.

She thought it had come when she arrived at work on Friday morning to find a stiff, formal envelope on her chair: her redundancy notice? Angie watched her as she opened it, but the news was good. Her job was safe. The new owners would be keeping her on.

Roz's immediate relief soon gave way to something else, to disappointment on a deeper level. If she'd actually lost her job, it would have forced her to find a new one. Sometimes she felt she'd never break free.

She turned to Angie. 'What about you?'

Angie folded her arms, unusually reticent. 'I didn't want to say anything till it was all done and dusted, but I'm taking voluntary redundancy – early retirement basically.'

'Oh. Right.' Roz was shocked she'd stayed so quiet about it. Even more shocked to realise that she'd miss her.

'I'm old,' laughed Angie. 'If one of us has to lose our job, it should be me rather than a young mum like you who needs it more. But it wasn't just that,' she added before Roz could say anything. 'We want to move to Lanzarote. We've found an apartment we want to buy. It's got sea views, a pool, the works.'

'Sounds amazing,' said Roz, wistfully. 'But what about your daughter? And the grandkids?'

'Between you and me, it can get a bit much sometimes,' said Angie. 'Don't get me wrong, I love them dearly, but they do wear me out. It's like having a second job at times. Sometimes I feel our Della takes advantage a bit...'

Roz was surprised; she'd never heard her criticise her daughter before.

'We've always wanted a place in the sun,' said Angie. 'Before we're too old and decrepit. And anyway, they can come over and stay with us – the kids'll love it – and we'll come back here too obviously.'

'Well,' said Roz, taking it in. 'It won't be the same round here without you. I mean it.'

'Don't be silly,' said Angie. 'It'll be fine. And you can always come and visit once we're settled in. You and Chloe.'

Angie's kindness brought tears to the back of her eyes. 'Thanks,' she said. 'That's so sweet of you.'

When Angie went out at lunchtime, Roz called Mark to tell him her job was safe – getting through to him first time for a change.

'That's great news!' he said.

Roz hesitated.

'Isn't it?' said Mark.

'I suppose,' she said. 'It's just... I've got my heart set on that job at the uni. I feel I'm suffocating here!'

Mark laughed at her melodrama. 'You still might get it,' he said. 'It's always better to start from a position of strength rather than weakness. Better to be in a job – any job – and find a new one from there.'

'I know, I know,' said Roz. 'I'm being an ungrateful cow. I'm lucky to *have* a job I can fit around Chloe. And there are worse places to work. I'm just bored of it. I need a new start. A new challenge.'

'You'll get one. You and me both... We've got loads of

new challenges coming – new adventures. You've got so much to look forward to, Roz.'

'I know,' she said. 'I just want to do something meaningful with my life. I want to help people.'

'And that's why I love you!' he said.

'Aw,' said Roz. 'By the way... Did you manage to speak to anyone at work about, y'know, what we talked about last weekend?'

'How do you mean?' he asked. Then realised. 'Oh, I see. Yes. Yes, I did. I've made an appointment to see a counsellor.'

'Oh, well done,' said Roz. 'I'm so proud of you. The first step is always the hardest.'

'So, then,' he said. 'Any more thoughts on the Barbados holiday? Did you get a chance to look at it?'

'Oh, God, yeah,' said Roz. 'It looked amazing. Maybe we could have our honeymoon there? Depending on when we get married of course.'

'Or we could do both,' he said, eagerly. 'Have that as well as our honeymoon? Or wait – how about this – we could actually get married *in Barbados*?'

'Wow,' said Roz, slightly overwhelmed, and distracted by the arrival of her boss in the room, clutching a folder of documents. Dalton frowned as if he wanted to speak to her, and she wondered what he wanted at this time on a Friday. He was normally in the pub by now.

'Listen. I'm sorry,' she whispered down the phone to Mark. 'I've got to go.'

'OK. No problem. Just to say... The Black Bull... I've booked a table for half one on Sunday. I'll come and pick you up. Say hi to Chloe for me. Bye.'

When she hung up, Dalton launched straight in to his spiel, unburdened by any pleasantries. 'The hotel's new owners want to diversify into offering services for companies and businesses in the local area. Meeting rooms, seminar facilities – that sort of thing. And I've got the Managing Director of Peakland Solutions coming in for a meeting on Monday at one o'clock... but I won't be here unfortunately, so could you take it for me?'

'Peakland Solutions?' said Roz.

'They're a local I.T. company. I need you to put together a pitch, with costings etc, of what we can do for them.'

'A pitch? For Monday morning?'

'Well, afternoon, technically speaking.'

He grinned, but Roz was in no mood to laugh.

'I know it's short notice,' he said, 'but it should only take you five minutes to throw something together. You just need to cover the basics – room hire charges, catering, all that stuff... I hope you don't mind. You mentioned in your last appraisal that you'd like to push yourself a bit – learn some new skills.'

He handed her the file of papers and left in a hurry. Roz sighed as she watched him go. Well, yes. She'd said she wanted a new challenge, more responsibility, but not this. This was the worst of all worlds: boring and nerve wracking at the same time. And she'd have to work on it at home tomorrow, without getting paid any extra. It wasn't just as easy as 'throwing something together'.

She checked the date on her calendar – 3rd May – and wondered when she'd hear back about the student welfare job. If she heard anything at all. They'd probably fill the vacancy internally. It had been brutal what Mark had said to her in the car that night, but there had been truth in it nonetheless. He'd expressed it harshly, but he was right. She didn't have much to offer in the role. In any role, probably.

CHAPTER FORTY-EIGHT

After working on her pitch for most of Saturday, Roz was ready for Sunday and it didn't disappoint. It was the first warm day of the year and the sky was robin egg blue, which boded well for their pub lunch. She'd thought that they could set off early to the Dales, taking Martina with them, so they could have a walk first to give them an appetite, but when she'd phoned Mark, it was a non-starter. Martina hadn't been very well lately – nothing serious, probably just old age – and he was worried about her getting carsick.

Chloe was disappointed and headed out on her bike, while Roz had a leisurely bath and got herself ready. It was warm enough for her stripy green sun-dress, she'd decided, and sunglasses and flip-flops would complete the look.

The dress was tighter than she remembered last year, which was depressing. The peri-menopause probably. Or something else? She worked out the dates in her head. Her last period had started on 5th April, so the next should arrive about now – should, strictly, have already arrived. Roz's heart raced with involuntary excitement and she checked herself. It probably meant nothing: things weren't as regular as they used to be on that front and it wasn't unusual for her to be late these days.

The pleasing burble of voices from downstairs told her Chloe was home and that Mark had arrived. Roz headed down to the kitchen and stood in the doorway, watching the sweet scene in front of her. Chloe's front tyre had got a puncture and Mark was filling a basin with water, trying to fix it for her. Roz was pleased to see them getting on so well after her previous worries.

'I used to have to do this for Yasmin,' Mark was telling Chloe. 'She loved going out on her bike.'

'Luckily it only happened right at the end,' said Chloe.

'That was fortunate,' said Mark. 'Did you go far?'

Chloe mumbled her reply. 'Just the blue lagoon. Up Harpur Hill Quarry...'

'*What?*' Roz couldn't help herself. 'I've told you to stay away from that place, Chloe Johnson.'

Chloe jumped and so did Mark. 'I can look after myself, Mum,' Chloe said, rolling her eyes. 'I'm not a little child any more.'

'You'd better not have gone anywhere near that water,' said Roz. 'Were you on your own?'

'Calm down,' said Chloe. 'I was only throwing stones into it...'

'Calm down?' Roz turned to Mark. 'It's just up the road, this so-called 'lagoon'. It's bright turquoise – like the Caribbean or something – but only because it's toxic from all the chemicals. They have to dye it black every summer, to stop idiots jumping into it. It'd take all your skin off. And the rest.'

'Oh God, don't be so dramatic,' said Chloe, showing off in front of Mark, looking to him for support.

'Actually,' he said. 'I've heard about that on the news. It sounds pretty dangerous. Your mum's right, Chloe. It's probably best to stay away.'

Chloe stared at her feet, not happy, but not prepared to argue any more.

Roz nodded her appreciation at Mark.

'Now go and wash your hands and get changed, love,' she told Chloe. 'We've got to leave in ten minutes.'

Chloe stomped off up the stairs and Roz exhaled, but her relief didn't last long. When Chloe came back down, she was wearing an outfit that was all kinds of wrong: an old pair of denim shorts and vest top that were much too snug on her now, with some black school tights that she'd artfully ripped. She was wearing eye-liner too.

'Oh come on, love, you'll be freezing,' said Roz. Her main worry was that it was far too revealing, but she didn't want to embarrass her in front of Mark by saying it.

'Aw, Mum,' Chloe whined. 'It's boiling out there. You haven't been out yet, but it is...'

'Er, I don't want to interrupt,' said Mark, 'but time's marching on. We don't want to miss our reservation. This place is quite popular.'

'OK. OK,' said Roz, giving in. Chloe had won.

They went outside and got in the car. Roz put on her sunglasses and let the change of scenery wash over her as they reached the rolling Derbyshire Dales. The wildflowers and hedgerows calmed her down, along with the dry stone walls fading to the horizon. There was even a heat haze – unheard of at this time of year.

They pulled into the car park of The Black Bull, a

twelfth century stone inn that had been beautifully restored. The inside was stunning too, with a rugged old fireplace and comfy sofas. It would be a lovely spot to relax after a winter's day walk and Roz made a mental note.

A smart maitre d' in a white shirt and chinos greeted them and showed them to a table in the walled beer garden, where they ordered their food and drinks.

Before long, Roz was sipping a chilled white wine spritzer with condensation on the side. One would be enough, she decided. She'd need a clear head at work tomorrow. And there might be another reason, she thought, running her hand over her belly.

Chloe went off to pet some llamas over the fence of the field next door, chatting away to another family with kids her own age. And Roz kicked off her flip-flops and wiggled her toes in the grass, unable to remember a more perfect day.

'This is gorgeous,' she said to Mark. 'Such a good idea of yours. It's so nice to kick back like this. I had to work most of the day yesterday. Dalton, the boss, he's such an arse. He stitched me up last thing on Friday with a presentation I've got to give tomorrow. The new owners want to diversify into corporate services and all that crap.'

Mark sipped at his mineral water. 'You can't really blame them,' he said. 'The hospitality industry's hard at the moment. No-one's got it easy at work any more.'

'True,' said Roz, sensing a dig. 'Sorry. I probably shouldn't have said anything. The people you work with – NHS workers – they've got it much worse than me.'

She changed the subject to lighten the mood. 'So tell me... Who are you going to have as your best man at our wedding? Your brother or...?'

'I might ask my brother. Or maybe Steve.'

'Steve?'

'One of my pals from work.'

Roz sipped at her drink. 'Talking of work... Have you met with that counsellor yet?'

'Not yet!' He sighed, bristling with irritation. 'You'll be the first to know when I do.'

'Sorry,' said Roz again.

'No, *I'm* sorry,' he said, reaching across the table for her hand.

She'd wanted to mention the call she'd had with Fiona – the issue with HMRC – but she was loath to bring it up now. Mark seemed on edge for some reason and she didn't want to spoil the afternoon. Instead they sat in silence, but for the hum of conversation around them and the chirrup of birdsong.

Roz's phone made a noise and they both smiled; it sounded funny, like it was joining in with the birds. It was a text from Jenny, inviting Roz to her baby shower in a couple of weeks.

'Aw,' said Roz, imagining how sweet Luke and Jenny's baby would be.

'What's that?' asked Mark.

'Just a mate,' said Roz.

'Who?'

'Just Jenny.'

'Jenny?' Mark looked stern, so much so that Roz laughed.

'Luke's wife,' she explained. 'Daniel's mate, remember?'

'I remember. Show me,' he said, holding out his hand for the phone.

He read the text, but said nothing, and Roz wished they'd opted to sit in the dim, cool interior of the pub. The heat out here was oppressive and had brought with it a load of wasps

– crawling over the table, buzzing past her ear, dive-bombing her drink. One was even swimming in it.

'So,' said Mark, after a moment. 'Why is she inviting *you*?'

'I'm sorry?' said Roz, stung by the question.

'This Jenny,' he said. 'Why. Is. She. Inviting. You?' He enunciated each word like she was an idiot.

Roz laughed at him, the combination of the wine and her sunglasses making her brave. 'Not this again,' she said. 'I don't see what your problem is. It's only a baby shower, for goodness sake. What possible harm could it do?'

'I don't want you to go,' he said quietly. 'Daniel and his friends. That's all in the past.'

'Exactly. It's in the past. You're my future.' She swallowed. 'But Jenny's—'

'Look, Roz. It's your choice. You can go... But I'll have nothing more to do with you if you do.'

Their server – a young woman – came out with their meals and Roz called Chloe back to the table. The next few minutes were excruciating, as Chloe chatted away while Roz and Mark said nothing.

'How's the roast lamb?' Mark asked Roz eventually.

'Good,' said Roz, moving it around her plate. She wasn't hungry any more and the smell was making her nauseous.

Chloe pulled a face. 'I don't know how you can eat baby animals like that. It's horrible.'

'You've got meat too,' said Roz. 'Lasagne's made from beef.'

Chloe blushed and shrugged. 'Well... it doesn't look like meat.'

'Do cows not count?' Mark asked her mischievously, trying to make her smile.

But it was too late. The energy had drained from the day. It had wilted, like the carnation in the vase on their table.

Their server came back to clear away their plates. 'Was everything OK?' she asked, clocking the amount of food they'd left.

'Delicious.' Mark beamed at her, charm personified, to Roz's annoyance.

On the drive home, Mark was talkative and chatty, full of questions about Roz's presentation tomorrow. But it was too little, too late. Roz answered him to appear polite in front of Chloe, but her heart wasn't in it.

Mark dropped them outside their house and Chloe jumped out of the car. She'd spotted Ellie sunning herself in next door's garden and wanted to go and see her.

'I'll give you a call,' Mark said to Roz. 'About the wedding arrangements.'

'Wedding arrangements?'

'For Friday.' He grinned. 'Kate's wedding. Remember?'

'Ah, right. OK,' said Roz, and got out too.

Chloe returned from Ellie's to find Roz lying on the couch. 'Are you OK, Mum?' she asked. 'You seem a bit sad.'

Roz sat up and hugged her. 'I'm fine, love.' She took hold of her hand. 'I'm just thinking of all the things I've got to do at work tomorrow. Talking of which, you'd better go and sort your school stuff. You've got a busy week next week.'

'OK,' said Chloe and disappeared upstairs without argument.

Roz picked up her phone and read Jenny's text again. *Let*

me know if you can make it, Jenny had signed off. *It'd be nice to see you again xxx*

She had to reply or Jenny would think she was rude.

Thanks so much for the invite and for thinking of me, Roz typed. *I'm afraid I won't be able to make it, sadly, but hope you all have a lovely time. Oh and best of luck with every-thing...!* She re-read what she'd written. Was it OK – or too rambly?

As soon as she'd pressed send, she knew she'd done the wrong thing. Pushing away the first new friend she'd met in ages. For what? For a man. A man she wasn't sure about. A man who scared her at times.

She went to the fridge for a glass of wine. She had a big day at work tomorrow, but it was only five o'clock and a small one wouldn't hurt.

Chloe came back downstairs and into the kitchen. 'What's for tea?' she asked.

'Tea?' said Roz. 'There's only cheese and biscuits. You've only just had your lunch.'

'OK.' Chloe frowned at the glass on the counter. 'Is that wine – *again*?'

The word pierced Roz in the stomach. As did the look on Chloe's face – the same look Mark gave her when he 'disapproved'.

Roz's phone buzzed in the lounge and she rushed through to get it. It was Jenny replying to her: *Aw, shame you can't make it. Don't worry. Another time! xxx*

'Who was that?' asked Chloe.

'Ah. No-one,' said Roz, lying back down on the couch. It was growing chilly now and she pulled the throw over her. Underneath it, she opened the front buttons of her dress, praying their tightness was pre-menstrual bloating and nothing else.

In some ways, Mark had been good for her. He'd listened to her, they'd had some fun together and he'd ticked a lot of her boxes. Most of all, he'd helped her out of her post-Daniel slump, shown her a future, and she'd always be grateful to him for that. But the red flags were too many to ignore. He had his demons and his reasons – and she sympathised with him, she really did – but life with him would be one long Groundhog Day, skirting around his issues and insecurities, rehashing old arguments. It wasn't what she wanted for herself. It wasn't what she wanted for Chloe. It was over.

Now she just had to tell him.

CHAPTER FORTY-NINE

Roz got into work early on Monday, ready for a nightmare day. Angie was in full 'transmit' mode when she arrived, rabbiting on about her daughter's friend who was opening a new bridal boutique in town. Angie's daughter was anxious to recruit Roz as a customer and had instructed Angie to pass on everything her friend had to offer. It was the subject of 'bridal lingerie' that tipped Roz over the edge.

'Look, I'm sorry,' she snapped, raising her hand as if she was at the dentist and wanted him to stop drilling. 'I've got a lot on my mind today. Can we talk about this later?'

'I know. I know. I'm sorry,' said Angie. 'I didn't think.'

'No, I'm sorry,' said Roz, feeling awful. She sat back in her chair and rubbed her eyes. 'It's just.... I didn't sleep very well last night. I've had a row with Mark.'

'Oh, love,' said Angie. 'I'm sorry to hear that. I'll make us a brew. That'll make things better.'

'I don't think it will,' sighed Roz, as Angie boiled the kettle. 'I've decided I need to call him. I want to break it off.'

'Already?' said Angie. 'You don't think you're being a bit hasty?'

'No,' said Roz, sadly.

Angie placed the mug of tea in front of her. 'What was it about?' she asked. 'The row?'

Roz didn't have the strength to be annoyed by her nosiness. 'Ah, nothing. It doesn't matter.'

Angie wagged her finger at her. 'All I would say is... Be sure to think it through. Good blokes are hard to come by.' The words *at your age* remained unspoken.

'Everyone has rows,' Angie continued. 'All relationships go through bad patches. It might be best to sleep on it.'

Roz just nodded. Angie meant well, but she didn't know the full story. She had no idea how serious it was. How low she felt.

As the meeting with Peakland Solutions drew near, Roz read through her pitch notes for the last time. Angie offered to go out and get her a sandwich and asked her what she would like.

'Nothing,' said Roz. 'I'm not hungry.'

'You've got to have something,' said Angie.

'I don't mind. You choose.'

'Alright. And I'll get you a doughnut too.' Angie winked. 'The sugar will do you good.'

~

Roz's throat was dry and the sharp-edged mouthfuls of prawn baguette scraped their way down it, but the presentation – when it came – went surprisingly well. She'd been expecting a couple of men in suits, but the female Finance Director turned up instead, who was the same age as she was, with a daughter at the same school as Chloe. The office junior she'd brought with her was lovely too, if a bit scared of his own shadow. They obviously liked what Roz had to say, as they indicated there and then that they'd like to sign up with The Old Hall.

Roz returned to her office in triumph, full of energy for her to-do list and all the boring admin tasks she'd been putting off, like emailing Kate to ask for the final numbers and the table plan for Friday. *Friday.* She couldn't believe the wedding was in four days' time. It had come around so fast. Most of all, she was glad she'd had the foresight to book Thursday off work so she could get herself sorted.

She finished up her jobs for the day and looked at the clock. 'God, is that the time?' she muttered, pulling on her jacket. 'Do you mind if I leave a few minutes early?' she asked Angie. 'I need to call in at the supermarket on my way home.'

'No problem,' said Angie. 'And don't forget your doughnut.'

Later on at home, when dinner was done and Chloe was in bed for the night, Roz lit the lamps and put her feet up to watch some TV. Her phone soon pinged with an email from Kate:

Hiya Roz,

I'll keep it brief as things are manic here. This is the plan for the next few days...

I'm coming up to Buxton on Wednesday, staying at my mum's. Sam's coming up on the Thursday. Would it be possible to book her into The Old Hall (to give us some space from each other)? The Mary Queen of Scots room if it's available?! No worries if it's too short notice... Any room will do.

Then on Friday morning – D-Day! – if you and Chloe could get over to my mum's for ten-ish? That should give us plenty of time to get ready...

Hope that's all OK.

Can't wait to see you!!!

Kate xxx

P.S. I've attached the table plan.

Roz opened the attachment, hoping Kate had remembered not to put her on a table with her mother and Fiona. She'd asked for herself and Chloe to be put on the 'girls' table with Natasha and Vicky – Natasha was bringing her husband (the two of them were flying over from New York, leaving the kids at home) and Vicky would be there with her husband and daughters (coming up from London).

Roz quickly found the table with their names: Roz, Chloe, Natasha, Natasha's husband James. But Vicky was listed on her own, with no mention of her family. And then there was the last name: MARK. MARK GLAISTER.

Her heart thudded faster. She had to finish with him. She couldn't put it off. His insecurity – his temper – would ruin the day. She'd be walking on eggshells, watching her every word. He'd be in all the photos as well, preserved for all eternity, well after they'd split up. Which they inevitably would. It was best to do it now.

Roz braced herself, picked up her phone and called him, but he didn't answer. *Fuck.* She let out the breath she was holding, but the adrenaline was still coursing through her body. Where would it go now? How was she supposed to sleep?

It was too late to ring Kate, and anyway Kate had enough on her plate at the moment without a needy mate calling her up. She'd just delete him from the table plan, take him off Kate's bill, and explain everything later.

Roz sat in front of the TV, unable to focus on the drama in front of her for the drama in her head. Mark hadn't been in touch since yesterday – maybe that was a good sign. Maybe, after yesterday's disastrous lunch, he felt the same as her – that they'd reached the end of the road? Maybe she could get away without contacting him at all?

Once the ten o'clock news had finished, she trooped upstairs to bed. Sleep came surprisingly easily.

But at five to midnight a text woke her up: *Sorry to miss your call. Hope your Monday wasn't too bad after all. Sweet dreams. Mx*

Oh God. Roz stiffened and her stomach turned over. He was acting like nothing was up. As if everything was fine. This would make the phone call even harder...

She stuffed the phone under her pillow and curled up into a ball.

She was dreading tomorrow.

∼

'Are you OK?' Angie asked Roz the following day. 'You've hardly said a word all morning.'

'Ah, sorry,' said Roz. 'I hardly slept last night. I just need a coffee.'

Angie frowned at her. 'Why don't we go out for one?' she suggested.

'Go out?'

'Yep,' said Angie, putting on her jacket.

'But... Both of us? What if—?'

'The place won't grind to a halt,' said Angie, firmly. 'Not for twenty minutes.'

They went round the corner to Charlotte's, ordered their drinks and took a seat.

'Now tell me,' said Angie, firmly. 'What's the matter? I've never seen you like this. I'm worried about you.'

Roz thought for a moment, then decided to do what she'd never done before. To tell Angie everything. About Daniel. About Mark. About the text Mark had sent her.

When she got to the night when Mark had almost killed her – and a pedestrian – by driving too fast, Angie had heard enough. 'You need to get out,' she said, simply. 'Trust me. You need to call him. Now.'

Roz nodded. 'I know.' She swirled the dregs in her mug. 'It's just... Doing it by phone feels a bit shitty. I feel like I should tell him face to face.'

Angie looked her in the eye. 'Maybe it's better that you don't, love.'

'How do you mean?' said Roz.

'It's just that sometimes... well... blokes can turn nasty. Some blokes... When you try and break up with them.' She stopped. 'I've probably said enough.'

'OK... OK,' said Roz, her meaning sinking in. 'I'll try him again when I get back to work.'

Angie nodded her approval. *"Twere well it were done quickly...'* she said, quoting Macbeth, surprising Roz. 'I think that's a very good idea.'

Back in the office, Angie disappeared to give her some privacy and Roz steeled herself to call Mark. But it went straight to voicemail. *Again!*

Roz hung up, flooded with short term relief – but no, she had to do something. She couldn't expect Angie to stay away much longer. She felt she might puke, but forced herself to call again and leave a message this time. No rambling, straight to the point, but careful not to antagonise him. 'Hi Mark,' she said, gripping the phone. 'I was just calling to say that, er, I don't think things are really working out between us and I think we should finish it. I'm really sorry, but I need some time and space on my own. I hope you're not too upset with me. I'm really sorry... Bye.'

Oh God, was that a bit blunt? She immediately felt guilty. She should've arranged to meet him and talk to him – done it properly.

Her insides were jagged – her nerves taut – for the rest of the afternoon, as she waited for... *what?* Some kind of response from him. An attempt to talk her round. Or maybe not. She might not hear from him again. He hadn't got in touch when they'd split up the last time. It was she who had contacted him. Stupidly.

Roz got home from work and still there was nothing. He must have got the message by now. Maybe he'd been expecting it. Maybe his pride wouldn't let him contact her. Maybe he was as relieved as she was.

She got on with the job of making dinner – macaroni

cheese and garlic doughballs, which Chloe loved – and they sat down to eat.

Roz cleared her throat. 'Love, I need to tell you something...'

'What?' Chloe looked alarmed. 'You're not having a baby, are you?'

'No, nothing like that,' said Roz, hoping to God that she wasn't. 'It's me and Mark... We've split up.'

'Again?' said Chloe.

'Yep,' said Roz, abashed. 'But for good this time. We won't be seeing him again.'

'Oh. OK,' said Chloe, stabbing her pasta with her fork. Then, 'Does that mean we're not going to Barbados?'

It was the question Roz had been dreading. 'No, love,' she said. 'I'm afraid we won't.'

'OK,' said Chloe again. She didn't seem disappointed or even surprised. Just resigned. 'No-one in school believes I'm going anyway,' she added, matter-of-factly.

Her reaction hurt Roz; she was far too young to be so jaded. But there was something else too. Chloe seemed almost relieved. Glad to see the back of him.

'Mu-um?' said Chloe.

'Yes?' said Roz, full of foreboding.

'Can I watch *EastEnders* tonight?'

'Oh, alright,' said Roz. 'Just this once.' She pointed at Chloe's plate. 'What's up? You've left half your doughballs.'

'Too many carbs.' Chloe shrugged. 'I'm full up.'

CHAPTER FIFTY

The next evening, Chloe was off to swimming practice, but Roz almost had to force her onto the coach that was taking them all to the pool. Roz couldn't understand it – Chloe had always loved swimming – but then the reason came out: she didn't want to wear a swimming costume – to show off her body – in front of her classmates. The reason for last night's 'doughball-aversion' became clear to Roz as she tramped home on her own through the rain.

As she closed the door behind her, her phone buzzed in her bag. A text. Her stomach lurched. From Mark?

But it was Kate: *Just at Euston station, waiting for the train oop north. My last journey as a single woman. Yikes! x*

Roz smiled and messaged back: *Two more sleeps!* She hated that expression, but nothing else seemed appropriate. *Can't wait to see you on Friday! Hope this bloody weather picks up xxx*

She was off work till Monday now and felt she should be in party mode, so she poured a glass of wine, making the most of Chloe's absence. But there would be no lounging here on the sofa. She'd go upstairs and check they had everything for the wedding on Friday. Then, if there was anything she'd missed, she could pop to the shops tomorrow while Chloe was at school. She could also get a wedding gift for Kate and Sam. Kate had been quite adamant they didn't need anything, but she had to get them *something*. It was only manners.

A knock on the door made her jump. It sounded urgent. Had Chloe baled out of the swimming trip and come home? Or was it Ellie next door? Was something up?

Roz opened it to find Mark on the doorstep, hair soaked from the rain. She froze.

'I got your message,' he said. 'I wanted to talk to you. In person.'

Roz nodded. 'OK.' She owed him that.

'Can I, er, come in?' He smiled, wiping his eyes. 'It's biblical out here.'

'Actually,' she resisted for once, 'I'd rather you didn't.'

'Really?' He looked hurt. 'I'm not sure why you're acting like this. Everything was OK on Sunday, wasn't it? We left each other on good terms...'

'Did we?'

'Oh, come on.' His tone was pleading now. 'I deserve an explanation... at least.'

'OK,' she said, tightly, and led him through to the lounge. But she didn't sit down and neither did he.

'I thought things were going great,' he said. He seemed hyper, turning his keys over in his pocket. 'I thought we had something, Roz. Tell me, what have I done wrong?'

'Nothing.' She didn't want to rile him, to make it any harder than necessary. 'Like I said in my message... I've realised I want to be on my own for a while.'

He didn't react, just reached in his jacket pocket for something: a pale blue satin tie. 'I bought this for Kate's wedding.' He said, shaking it out. 'What do you think?'

What? Roz's heart beat faster. 'It's nice,' she said. 'I hope you'll get the chance to wear it to something else.'

'Hang on,' he said, as her meaning dawned. 'But I've booked the next two days off work,' he whined. 'I got them to change the whole rota...'

'I'm sorry, Mark.' This was a nightmare. 'We've split up. You won't be going to the wedding.'

'What?' He shook his head incredulously. 'Who are *you* to tell me where I can and can't go?'

'But it was OK for you to do it to me?' said Roz, quietly.

'Do what?' he asked.

'Telling me I couldn't go to Jenny's. To the baby shower...'

'That's not the same thing,' he scoffed.

'It's exactly the same.'

'I didn't say you couldn't go.'

Roz dug her nails into her palms. 'You said that if I went to it, you'd have nothing more to do with me. I don't want to be with someone who tries to manipulate me like that. To control me.'

'But, hold on, you said it was nothing I'd done. That you just wanted to be on your own. So... which is it?'

She felt exhausted suddenly. 'Look. I don't know...'

'Roz. Are you feeling OK?' He stepped forward and touched her cheek, but she pushed him away.

'I think you need to leave now,' she said. 'Chloe'll be home soon and I don't want you here when she gets back.'

'You know what...' He spat, shoving his face in hers. 'You're a piece of work. You're insane.' Then he laughed.

'She says she wants to be a therapist!' he said, as if addressing an imaginary audience. 'A therapist would have a field day with you. You hate your own mother for a start.'

'No I don't!' said Roz. 'Look, you need to go now. This is—'

'And you're jealous of your successful, better-looking sister.' He pointed at the glass on the coffee table. 'But you've got your wine.' He screwed up his face. 'God... That photo I took of you on New Year's Eve, passed out, drunk and ugly. That should've told me all I needed to know. I should have stayed away from you.' He shook his head in disgust. 'To think you wanted to get pregnant. To have a child. An old soak like you! Nah... You'll be a sad, lonely – old – woman.'

His tirade hit the target. 'At least I've got my daughter,' she replied. 'Which is more than you've got.'

It was too late. The words were out – cruel, like something her mother would say – and he seemed to crumple in front of her. He flopped down onto the couch, grabbed the glass of wine and necked it.

'What are you doing?' Roz cried. 'You don't even drink?'

'No. I don't. Not any more.' He threw the glass across the room, but it didn't smash, only bounced off the carpet.

'I'm sorry,' he said, his eyes filling with tears. 'Jo... Yasmin... It wasn't a hit-and-run...'

Roz tensed, dreading what he might say next.

'Jo had been drinking at lunchtime with her friends. White wine. She got in the car and went to pick up Yas from school. She killed them both. She was three times over the limit.'

Roz released the breath she was holding. He was crying properly now. 'I'm sorry. I'm sorry,' he kept saying, over and over. 'I didn't mean to have a go at you. I shouldn't have said those things I said.'

'Why didn't you tell me all this?' asked Roz. 'Why not be honest?'

'I was ashamed.'

'Ashamed? You had nothing to be ashamed about. It wasn't your fault...'

'I'm *so* sorry, Roz. But I promise... This won't happen again.' He wiped his eyes with his sleeve. 'I've seen the counsellor at work. He thinks I might have complex PTSD because of grief and work stuff. But I'm ready to work on it. I really am. Please don't end it, Roz. Give me a chance. *Please?*'

Her anger – her fear of him – had turned to pity. On a human level, she wanted to go to him – to sit beside him and console him. But she knew that would be a mistake.

'I don't know what to say,' she said, swallowing hard. 'What happened to you – losing your family like that – it's literally the worst thing I can imagine. And people can help you – the counsellor at work or whoever. But not me. I need to put Chloe and me first.' She looked away. This was unbearable. 'I honestly think you need to go home now. Try and get some sleep.'

'Sleep?' he sniffed. 'What's that?'

'Will you be OK to drive home?' she asked. 'Shall I call a cab?'

'Nah. I'll be fine. What's the worst that can happen?' He laughed bitterly. 'I crash the car? Smash it into a wall? There's fuck all to live for anyway. I might as well.'

'Mark...' She tried to reason with him, but he'd stood up and was heading for the front door. It slammed shut behind him and she went to the window, peeping out through the rain. He got in his car and sat there, head slumped on the wheel. Eventually, he started the engine and crawled off into the gloom.

Roz sighed and picked up the glass from the floor. She fetched some kitchen roll to blot the dregs from the carpet; at least it was only white wine and wouldn't stain.

Chloe arrived home from swimming – exhausted, but happy. She ate her hot, homemade soup with crusty bread on a tray on her lap and was none the wiser about the evening's drama.

When Chloe went up to bed, Roz texted Mark: *Let me know you're alright. That you got home OK.* No reply came back, but she was used to that.

That night in bed, Roz replayed the evening's scene in her head. His behaviour had been worrying and erratic and his last words haunted her. The thought that he might do something stupid. She'd read a lot about this. Suicide rarely had a single cause. It was usually a build-up of stuff, until one last thing tipped you over the edge. He had the grief of losing his wife and child, the stress of a demanding job... And now this. Roz breaking up with him. But she'd had no other option. It was the right thing to do. And there would never have been a right time – or a right way – to do it.

Even so, if he did do something stupid, she wouldn't be able to forgive herself.

CHAPTER FIFTY-ONE

The next morning, Mark still hadn't replied. Roz texted him again – more panicked than ever after her poor night's sleep: *Please can you let me know you're alright, Mark? Please?*

She considered calling the police, but decided against it. They had enough to do without checking up on grown adults when there were no suspicious circumstances. They'd either laugh at her or think she was mad.

Then she had an idea: like herself, Mark wouldn't be going into work today – he said he'd got the rota changed. She could go round to his place and check on him herself.

Roz drove Chloe down to school. Then, when she was safely inside, she punched Mark's address into Google Maps. She was clear in her mind that she didn't want to speak to him or anything. Or hold out any hope of reconciliation. She just wanted to know he was OK.

More than once, she nearly turned back. Why was she

doing this? What if she bumped right into him? What if he was angry with her and made a scene? But she carried on.

Eventually, she reached Didsbury and pulled up in a side road by the park. She got out of the car and crept round to Kingsland Road, staying on the odd-numbered side for now. It wasn't a long street and his BMW wasn't parked on it. Had he even made it back here? Then she chided herself for being alarmist. He'd probably gone out. Or arranged to go into work after all.

She stopped behind a cherry tree that was shedding blossom like confetti. It was making her nose fizz and she tried not to sneeze. Number 12 was opposite – a stately property with a solid red door, like something from an old Christmas card. There was no car in the driveway – just a skip that was half-full.

Roz watched the house for five minutes that felt like an hour. She couldn't stay here much longer without attracting attention. She knew she should turn and go back to the car, but found herself crossing the road, opening the gate, heading up the ornate garden path.

She knew she should be bold and just knock on the door, but she didn't. Instead she peered through the bay window into the living room, which was done out in 'generic posh' style like Fiona's – all earthy tones and rich, tasteful fabrics. It was tidy too – suspiciously so – with no signs of life.

She checked over her shoulder, then headed down the side of the house, squeezing past the skip. She wanted a peek through the kitchen window, but was stopped in her tracks by the beauty of the rear garden, where cornflowers, tulips and peonies were breaking into their spring riot. There was a sage-green summerhouse in the middle of it all, a stone pizza oven and – beyond that – some fruit trees and vegetable plots.

A handle clicked somewhere and Roz's heart leapt. She turned back the way she'd come, back towards the path, but a woman had emerged from the front door now, dressed in jeans and a blazer, a designer tote over her shoulder. She had a pair of Ray-Bans perched on her head and a massive rock on her finger. 'Oh. Hello,' she said when she saw Roz. 'Is... Is there something I can help you with?'

'I'm, er... I'm looking for Mark,' said Roz, unsure what else to say. 'Mark Glaister.'

The woman squinted at her. 'I'll just get him,' she said, her expression wary now. 'Darling!' she called into the house. 'There's someone here to see you.'

Roz's stomach dropped. *What was going on? Was this his wife?*

'We're just on our way out,' the woman said, filling the silence till he arrived.

Roz nodded, trying to stay calm.

There was the sound of jangling car keys and a man bounded out of the door. He was around Roz's age, tall and fit with deep brown eyes and hair that was almost black. 'Hello. Yes. How can I help?' he asked, his voice plummy and resonant, as he checked his expensive watch.

'Er, I'm sorry to have bothered you. I think I've got the wrong house,' said Roz.

'You said you were looking for Mark Glaister?' the wife said, sharply. She turned to him now. 'Is there something going on, Mark? Something I should know about?'

'No!' he said, at the same time as Roz. The effect was comical, like a bad sitcom.

Roz tried to explain. 'I've been seeing someone with that

name for the last few months,' she garbled. 'An anaesthetist who works at Stepping Hill. But I must have the wrong address.'

'Well that's me,' he said, confused. 'I'm an anaesthetist. I transferred there last year. I'm fairly certain I'm the only one!'

'Oh,' said Roz. She felt faint, and a whining sound, like feedback, started up in her ears. 'I'm sorry,' she said again. 'I should go. I don't want to take up any more of your time.'

'No. Wait. Hang on!' he said, raising a finger. 'What's going on...? I need to know. Who's this guy you're talking about?'

'I... I dunno. I met him online,' was all she could say.

He shrugged. 'Do you think you're being... catfished by someone?' He turned to his wife. 'Is that what they call it? And he's using my name to do it? Why though?'

'No. It wasn't like that,' said Roz. 'It wasn't a dating site.'

'Are you OK?' his wife asked her now. 'Do you want to come inside and sit down for a moment?'

'No. Seriously. I'm fine... I need to go,' said Roz, backing away.

'No, wait,' he said. 'I need to know who this guy is. He could be doing other stuff in my name. Taking out loans. Running up debts. All sorts... What does he look like?'

'Erm, well.' Roz couldn't think for the noise in her head. 'He's average height, average build. Brown hair. Kind of... tired-looking.'

He gave a hollow laugh. 'That's half the population.'

'Actually,' said Roz. 'I've got a picture of him on my phone...' She fumbled for it in her bag and scrolled through her photos, hands trembling. The two of them were watching her as if she was mad and she couldn't blame them. She kept searching – a second time – sure she had taken one at her dad's party – but she couldn't seem to find it. 'I'm really sorry,' she said eventually. 'I'll find one and send it to you. What's your number?'

He told her and she put it in her phone. Under 'Real Mark'. *Jesus, this was surreal.* 'I'm Roz,' she said, and gave him hers too.

'You'll let me know if you find anything out, won't you?' he said. 'This is a worry.'

'Yes. Yes, I will,' said Roz.

She turned and fled down the path to the gate, but something was following her and beat her to it. A black labrador, old but energetic.

'Martina,' Mark called after it. 'Come here. Now!'

Back in the car, the sweat was sticking to Roz and she wanted to retch. Who *was* he then, this other 'Mark' she'd been seeing, and what was his game? *Had* he been catfishing her? Was he just a liar who'd conned her into a relationship with a fake identity and a sob story? He was probably married. Or on a register somewhere. Just making shit up as he went along.

She was an intelligent woman, who knew that this sort of thing went on. It had happened recently to a couple of high-profile women, who'd been open and honest about their experiences to raise awareness. How could she have been so stupid to take Mark at face value? How fucking desperate had she been to get in tow with him – and what kind of example was she setting for Chloe?

When he'd first contacted her, she should've done more

to check out his background. When he'd used his 'moderator' status to message her privately on Grief United, that should have set alarm bells ringing. She should've ignored him. Or deflected him with a polite one-liner.

She took a few breaths till the shaking stopped and she was calm enough to drive home. She couldn't face going wedding gift shopping at the moment. Not now. There was only one thing she needed to buy.

Roz parked up in the centre of Buxton, close to the shops, hoping to God she didn't bump into Angie. *Angie.* She could never know about this. She'd have an absolute field day. It'd be 'Gossip' with a capital 'G'. Roz might as well take out a full-page ad in *The Buxton Courier*. Everyone would know.

She got out of the car and shot straight to Boots – to buy a pregnancy test.

CHAPTER FIFTY-TWO

The test was negative. Roz sat in her bathroom for a moment, sobbing tears of relief that there was one problem she didn't have.

Her brain raked over the last few months, looking for clues, trying to piece things together. The times she'd met up with Mark. The dates they'd had. The times they *hadn't* met up – when he'd made some excuse for letting her down.

There was so much that made sense now. The fact she'd never actually made it to his house. Or been introduced to his mother or any friends or family. But the questions kept coming. Why had he used a real person's name like that? Why not just make one up?

She clicked on Grief United to see if he'd posted recently, but there had been nothing for ages. Once Kate's wedding was over and she had the brain space, she'd go back on the site and warn them all about him.

She checked the photo gallery on her phone again. Nothing. If only she hadn't chucked out that photo from the frame...

Or maybe it was best that she had. She could let it all drop now. Wash her hands of it. She'd finished with the guy, she'd had a lucky escape and it was best just to leave it now. If Mark Glaister in Didsbury had someone going round impersonating him, that was his problem. He could take whatever action he wanted – inform the police or whatever. It wasn't her problem any more.

Roz pulled her cardigan around her and switched on some mindless TV. It was the usual afternoon fodder – folk buying old junk from auction houses or looking round houses in the country – but she couldn't even concentrate on that. What was wrong with her? First Daniel. Now this guy. Did she give off some vibe that attracted these people, that gave them permission to treat her like dirt? Well that would be the end of it. No fucking more.

Chloe skipped through the door after school, delighted to have the day off for the wedding tomorrow. After dinner, they both washed their hair then settled down in the lounge ahead of an early night. Chloe was keen to watch *Junior Bake Off* and Roz was happy to go along with it. When her phone rang at eight, she was almost scared to look, but it was only Kate. She sounded agitated and Roz was worried.

'Where are you?' asked Roz. 'Is everything OK?'

'Yeah, I'm fine,' said Kate. 'I'm at my mum's... Well no, actually, I'm not. Not fine, I mean.'

'Have you been crying?' asked Roz. 'You don't sound like yourself.'

'Roz, I'm not sure I can go through with this wedding. I'm really stressed and I can't—'

'Hold on,' said Roz. 'Take a breath. It's normal to feel a few nerves. Apparently.'

'It's not just that,' said Kate. 'I'm absolutely knackered from pregnancy hormones and I'm shitting myself about stopping work for a few months. What if my clients leave and don't come back to me? Who wants a flabby, saggy old personal trainer? And I feel terrible sponging off Sam. I've never relied on anyone for money. I've been self-employed my whole life...'

'Oh, love,' said Roz. 'Have you tried talking to Sam? To tell her how you feel?'

'Ugh. There's no point. She thinks I'm overreacting, but it's alright for her. It's not her life – her career – her body – that's being turned upside down. It's taken me years to build up this business... And I can't to talk to my mum. I don't want to upset her. She's on edge as it is. She's doing my head in as well, actually. I just feel I've got nowhere to turn, Roz. D'you know what I mean?'

'I do,' said Roz. 'I do.' She lowered her voice. 'Look, I'd offer to come over and see you, but I've got Chloe...'

Chloe frowned at her.

'Or you could come and stay here tonight?' Roz suggested. 'You're more than welcome. If you want to talk.'

'Nah, it's OK, thanks,' said Kate. 'I don't want anyone here to think anything's wrong. And anyway, I wouldn't want to upset Chloe.'

'Are you sure?' said Roz. 'It's no problem. Chloe won't mind. She'll be off to bed soon.'

Chloe frowned again, harder this time.

'No, seriously, it's fine,' said Kate. 'It's alright. I'm just having a wobble.'

'OK,' said Roz, disappointed. She'd wanted the company for her own benefit as much as Kate's. She was desperate to tell her – tell someone – what had happened this morning. This secret that was corroding her insides. 'What time do you want us to come over in the morning?' she asked instead.

'I've got the make-up artist booked for eleven,' said Kate, clicking back into organised mode. 'So any time before then.'

'Make-up artist? I thought we were doing our own?' said Roz.

'I thought I'd book it as a treat,' said Kate. 'Seeing as we're doing our own hair...'

'Excellent,' said Roz. 'Chloe'll love that!'

Chloe did love it. She was all excited and they sat up till ten, chatting through the plan for tomorrow, all thoughts of an early night forgotten.

'I'd like to be a wedding planner when I grow up,' Chloe announced at one point. 'It sounds an *amazing* job.'

Roz tried not to roll her eyes too obviously. 'Right!' she said. 'Time for your beauty sleep. You've got a big day tomorrow. And so have I!'

Chloe headed upstairs and Roz turned off the TV, tidied the lounge and went to the window. She could still picture him yesterday – 'Mark' – sitting out in his car. Could remember actually feeling sorry for him.

Roz closed the curtains on the memory, then turned off the lamps. In the kitchen, she went to the drawer with the spare keys. Both sets were present and correct. Thank God she'd never given him one.

Then she locked the doors and windows and dragged herself up the stairs, pausing outside Chloe's room, listening to her little-girl snores.

How could she have let herself get into this situation? He could have been a total psycho, yet she'd let him into her home. Her life. Her daughter's life.

Her mother had been right.

CHAPTER FIFTY-THREE

The next morning, Roz and Chloe loaded their outfits and general wedding paraphernalia into a taxi and set off for Kate's mum's house. Chloe was high as a kite, beyond excited by the whole thing, while Roz checked herself in the rear view mirror. She'd had her first decent night's sleep in ages, but still she looked deathly: this make-up artist had better be a genius, she thought.

When they arrived at Jan's, Kate was waiting for them in a Man United onesie and hugged them in welcome. She seemed in good spirits, all yesterday's doubts apparently gone.

'Before we get started,' said Kate, leading them through to the lounge, 'I want to give you these.' She handed Roz and Chloe a velvet box each, containing a silver pendant with a Blue John stone in the centre. 'Thanks so much for doing this today. Both of you.'

Roz squeezed Kate's hand, worried she might cry already. 'These are beautiful – aren't they, Chloe?'

Chloe nodded, delighted.

'We've, eh, got a present for you too,' lied Roz, 'but I've just realised I left it at home...'

'Oh, no worries,' said Kate. 'Now, come and meet Lisa...'

They proceeded up the stairs to Kate's childhood bedroom. Roz had always envied her the light, airy double room at the top of the house with its high ceiling and long Art Deco dressing table. Lisa the make-up artist was busy unpacking all her lotions and potions onto it from her leather case. At the other end, there was an ice bucket and four flutes, a bottle of cava and some orange juice for Chloe.

'Hi, Lisa,' said Roz. 'Nice to meet you.'

'You too, Roz. And you, Chloe.'

'So that's the introductions over,' said Kate. 'Now. Who wants a drink?'

'Could I just have some orange?' said Roz. 'I need to keep my wits about me for later. I don't want to peak too soon.'

'Me too,' said Lisa. 'I need to keep a steady hand.'

'Fair enough,' huffed Kate, 'but I'm having the hard stuff – the world's tiniest Bucks Fizz!'

Kate poured the drinks while Lisa set up a chair by the windowsill, making the most of the watery spring light.

'Now then,' Lisa smiled. 'Who's first?'

Chloe raised her hand and the three of them laughed as she bounced onto the chair. Lisa dabbed her with a tiny bit of blusher and some clear lip gloss, finishing off with a liberal dose of pearly powder from the biggest brush.

'Aw, you look lovely,' said Kate, as Chloe examined herself in the mirror.

'You go next,' said Kate to Roz. 'I'm putting it off till the last minute. My mascara'll only run... I've been on the verge of tears since I got up!'

'So, then,' said Kate, conspiratorially, as Lisa got to work on Roz. 'What's the plan with Mark? Is he coming to the ceremony – or will you just see him at the reception?'

'Er, no. Neither,' said Roz, blushing through the creamy foundation. 'We've split up.'

'What? So... The engagement's off?'

'Yep,' said Roz, keeping her lips still for Lisa's benefit.

'As of when?' said Kate.

'A couple of days ago.'

'But why?' asked Kate. 'What happened?'

'It's a long story,' said Roz. Not one she wanted to go into in front of Chloe. Or Lisa for that matter. 'For another day.'

'Uh. OK,' said Kate. 'Why didn't you tell me last night when I was crying down the phone?'

'Oh,' said Roz, nonchalantly. 'I didn't want to add to your woes.'

'Oh, stuff that!' said Kate, minding her language for once. 'Sometimes it's better to listen to someone else's woes. It makes a refreshing change from your own.'

Roz had to smile.

'So is that definitely it between you two?' said Kate. 'No way back?'

'No,' said Roz, emphatically. 'I *definitely* won't be seeing him again.'

There was a knock on the door, then Kate's mum Jan burst in, resplendent in a coral silk two-piece and matching fascinator. 'Hello girls!' she trilled, and Roz was grateful for the interruption.

'The flowers have just arrived,' said Jan. 'I've got your headdresses here...' She handed them over. 'And I'm available to help if anyone needs it. Just give me a shout, OK?'

'Thanks, Mum,' said Kate, taking the boxes from her.

'Also...' said Jan. 'I've put out some sarnies and pastries

downstairs. You girls need some sustenance. It's going to be a long day.'

'Thanks so much, Jan,' said Roz as Lisa sprayed her face with a fine setting mist. 'We'll come down and have something in a bit.' Although she wasn't that hungry. It would soon be the moment she'd been dreading. Squeezing herself into that pink satin confection of a dress. That she hadn't worn since the day she'd bought it. When she'd tried it on in front of *him* – and his face had contorted at the sight of her.

When Roz pulled it on, she could barely look in the mirror.

'You look great,' Kate said, watching her. 'You should wear that colour more often.'

Really? Roz's first instinct was to say something negative – to reject the compliment – but something stopped her. She needed to ditch this destructive self-talk. Especially in front of Chloe.

'Thanks,' she said simply, and left it at that.

Roz adjourned to the bathroom to put her hair up in a 'messy' bun. Then she brushed out Chloe's long, dark hair, which she'd insisted on wearing down around her shoulders. For the finishing touches, they put on the pendants Kate had given them, and then the flowers in their hair. Roz took a selfie of her and Chloe together, then one of Chloe on her own, posing up a storm. They turned out so well, she considered posting them later on Instagram.

'Gorgeous!' said Kate when the two of them reappeared. 'What a pair of beauts...'

Roz and Chloe curtseyed and Roz went to find the handbag she'd be taking to the ceremony: less a handbag, more a tiny silver purse that held only her phone, lip gloss

and bank card. Totally impractical, but it matched her
strappy sandals.

'Don't worry,' said Kate. 'Leave everything else here. It'll
be safe enough.'

'OK. Right then!' said Roz. 'We'll go downstairs and
leave you to it. Give you some peace to gather yourself.'

Down in the kitchen, Jan was busying herself with the
buttonholes. She was humming away, like in the old days
when Roz used come round after school.

Kate was so lucky. She hadn't had to grow up with a difficult mother or know-it-all sister. She'd been a treasured only
child whose parents thought the sun shone out of her. She
hadn't done as well as Roz at school and hadn't gone to uni or
college. But she always fell on her feet. And look at her now!
She had Sam, a new baby on the way – the world was her
oyster. But it was impossible to resent her. She was a kind,
loyal friend and Roz was lucky to have her.

Jan turned to Roz and Chloe. 'My goodness,' she said.
'Look at you two... a right pair of bobby-dazzlers. I need to get
a photo. Now then...' She pointed to a huge platter on the
kitchen counter. 'Remember to have something to eat. And
you too, Chloe love.' She handed them two small plates, then
ran to the foot of the stairs.

'Katie!' she called up them. 'You don't want to leave it too
late. Time's getting on a bit.' She paused. 'And you, Michael.
What's keeping you?'

'Coming! Coming!' Kate's dad replied, hurrying down
the stairs in his light grey suit.

A few minutes later, Kate followed him into the kitchen.
Her wedding gown was simple and classic – a plain cream
column dress over her neat bump, with a blue velvet trim that
matched the flowers of her head-dress.

Her dad had a tear in his eye and Roz welled up. 'You look amazing,' she said. 'You all do.'

The emotion of the moment was punctured by Kate's phone ringing. 'It's Sam,' she told them, excitedly. 'She's already at the Pavilion Gardens. Just heading to the band-stand. She can't wait to see me.'

'D'you think that's a hint?' said her dad, holding out his hand to take the phone. Then he offered Kate his arm. 'Shall we go then, love?'

CHAPTER FIFTY-FOUR

Kate's dad drove Kate, Roz and Chloe down to the bandstand in his silver Jag. They arrived at ten past two – only ten minutes late.

A sizeable crowd had gathered – of guests and onlookers – mingling and enjoying the mild weather. The light breeze had seen off the morning's clouds, the sun was shining and Roz felt its warmth on her arms as they got out of the car.

Roz helped straighten Kate's dress, fixed Chloe's hair and prepared to follow Kate up the 'aisle', although there was no strict division of bride and groom as such. She was relishing her role, wondering why she'd been so desperate to have a partner at her side to prop her up. So desperate, in fact, that she'd been ready to settle for some creepy imposter. He'd have been a spectre at the feast, watching her, criticising her every move. What a relief to be rid of him. Her biggest worry now was staying upright in her shoes, which were a lot higher than she was used to.

Kate's entrance music struck up – Nick Cave, her

favourite – and their little bridal party started their short journey through the throng, up the steps of the bandstand.

On the left-hand side of the 'congregation', Roz clocked her mother – and Fiona beside her, waving and taking pictures on her phone. Her mother looked almost funereal, in a black and white printed number, wrapped in a grey pashmina, while Fiona wore palest lemon, perilously close to white, which was typical of her. Her dad and Fiona's husband Ian were standing just behind; her dad's tie was already skew-whiff and Ian was trying to control his own kids as if he'd never met them before.

On her right, Roz spotted Natasha and Vicky – and a smartly dressed young lad standing between them. But there was no sign of Natasha's husband, James, who was meant to be attending. Or Vicky's husband and daughters, who hadn't been on the table plan. It was all a bit odd.

The bridal party carried on to the front, where Sam was waiting, dressed in a smart cream trouser suit. She was beaming at Kate, her usual confident self, although Roz thought she could detect a tear behind her trendy glasses. Also waiting was the Humanist celebrant – a woman in her sixties, in a crimson cape and beret – along with the wedding photographer, a lanky hipster with a handle-bar moustache who looked like he'd arrived by penny farthing.

The music subsided, Kate and Sam joined hands and the celebrant took charge of proceedings. Her opening patter suggested she had missed her vocation as a stand-up comedian, but she handled the gear change to the 'serious bit' beautifully and tears pricked Roz's eyes once again. Whether for Kate and Sam, or for herself, it was hard to say. She dabbed at the tear now rolling down her cheek and wished she'd crammed more than one measly tissue into her 'handbag'. She had to widen her eyes and blink several times to stem the flow; ugly crying would be a terrible look on the wedding photos.

After the exchange of vows, there was a spontaneous round of applause, while the photographer clicked away, then took a 'group shot' of the crowd. He was balanced precariously on the metal railings, flapping his arms like a distressed heron, and it was impossible not to laugh.

Moments later, Kate and Sam departed the bandstand as a married couple – shadowed by the photographer again – as Roz and Chloe followed suit. The rest of the guests drifted down the stairs behind them, ready to throw their confetti.

When most of them had wandered off across the cobbles to The Old Hall, Roz felt a tug on her arm.

She turned to see her mother and Fiona. 'Oh. Hi,' she said, posting a smile on her face.

'You and Chloe look nice,' said her mother. 'Gorgeous,' added Fiona, fixing Chloe's fringe.

'Is *he* here, then? Mark?' her mother asked.

'Nope,' said Roz, breezily. 'He couldn't make it.'

'Oh?' said her mother.

Roz shot a 'keep quiet' look at Chloe. She had no intention of doing her usual thing of blurting everything out to them, inviting their censure and their 'told-you-so's'. She would quietly let the whole thing die. Not mention him again unless she had to.

'Well then,' said Roz. 'Shall we go and get some fizz?'

Inside the hotel, the atmosphere was buzzing. The local steel band Kate had booked on a whim were going down a storm.

Glasses were tinkling, the table decorations looked stunning and the scent of spring roses hung sweet in the air. The weekend waiting staff – most of whom Roz didn't know – were neat and attentive in their white shirts and black trousers, deftly doing their jobs, passing round the canapés and champagne in preparation for the 'pre-dinner' speeches.

Kate came over and hugged Roz. 'Everything's amazing!' she whispered in her ear. 'You've done *such* a good job.'

Roz blushed. 'Well, it wasn't just me,' she said, truthfully. 'It was very much a team effort.'

They were interrupted by the photographer, who needed Kate for another shot. Kate pulled a face as she was dragged off, and Roz sympathised. She didn't envy her in the slightest. She would hate it too. All that palaver. All that... *scrutiny*.

Roz turned and went to find her table. She knew which it was, as Natasha was already sitting there, with the smartly dressed young lad from earlier. Natasha was a lot skinnier than Roz remembered, with grey rings under her eyes. Jetlag, presumably.

'Ah good, a friendly face,' Natasha announced when Roz turned up. Her American accent was less strong today. 'This is Josh,' she said, introducing the lad. 'He's my eldest.'

'Very pleased to meet you,' said Josh, and shook Roz's hand.

Roz pulled out a chair to join them.

'I've brought Josh in place of James,' said Natasha, answering Roz's unspoken question as to where her husband was. 'We've split up actually.'

'Oh,' said Roz. She found it hard to compute. Natasha as a single mother. In the same boat as herself. Kind of. Who'd have thought it?

'He's in a very expensive rehab facility at the moment,' Natasha went on. 'In Vermont.'

'Oh,' said Roz again. 'I'm sad to hear that.'

'There's not much I can do at this point.' Natasha shrugged. 'He's got the best care...'

'Well,' said Roz. 'I think you're really strong.'

'It's for the best,' said Natasha. 'It's been a long time coming.'

'I had no idea.'

'No,' said Natasha, sitting on her hands. 'I didn't want to broadcast it.'

'I don't blame you,' said Roz. It was the sort of real-life messiness that had no place on Natasha's carefully curated Instagram.

The sombre mood lifted somewhat when Vicky bounced over to join them. 'Hiya, Roz!' she shrieked, bending down to kiss her on the cheek. Roz could smell that she'd been outside having a crafty fag. She seemed pissed already and Roz noticed she had some startling new veneers that caught the light from the chandelier above.

'Hi, Vicky,' Roz replied. 'How are you? And, er, how are the family?'

Vicky looked her straight in the eye – or tried to. 'You know what?' she slurred. 'I'm at the end of my rope with it all. With domesticity. With London. I just wanted a weekend up here on my own without the bloody husband and kids. A weekend up north to let my hair down!' She cackled. 'And so I've ditched the fam for the sesh.'

Roz spotted Natasha's brief eye-roll.

'Hang on, Roz,' said Vicky, looking around. 'Is your guy here somewhere? Mark, is it?'

'No,' said Roz. 'Actually...'

'Oh good,' said Vicky, before Roz had the chance to explain. 'We might be the smallest table, but we'll definitely be the loudest!' Then, 'Want a drink?' she asked generally – a rhetorical question, as she'd already flagged down a champagne waiter and was negotiating a full bottle.

'Yes, I will,' said Roz, sitting back. 'Now my duties are over!'

Vicky filled their glasses to the brim and Roz felt stupid. Stupid for worrying about coming to the wedding with no partner. For fretting that she and Chloe would be two misfits amid the other, proper, 'nuclear' families. In reality, no-one was judging her. No-one was bothered. Natasha and Vicky... They had their own lives – their own problems. She hadn't realised how much like her they were.

Jan caught Roz's eye from across the room and gave her the thumbs up. Everything was ready for the speeches at four o'clock. Everything was set for the meal afterwards. Everyone was happy and Roz could finally relax and feel a moment's pride.

She let out a breath she'd been holding for years and raised a toast to herself for a job well done.

Her eyes scanned the room for Chloe and eventually found her – sitting with Sam, monopolising her attention. Roz excused herself from Natasha and Vicky and went over to join them. Chloe was bending Sam's ear about a project she'd been doing at school about plastics in the ocean – and Sam was kindly humouring her, answering all her questions about polar bears and what David Attenborough was like.

'Come on, love,' said Roz, taking Chloe by the hand. 'Sam's a bit busy today. Another time maybe...'

'Oh, she's fine. No problem,' Sam assured her. 'Maybe you could come down to London some time, Chloe, and we'll go to the Natural History Museum. I'd love an excuse to go back.'

Chloe nodded like her head might fall off and Roz smiled.

'That would be lovely,' said Roz. She pointed to the table in the corner and turned to Chloe. 'Why don't you go over and play with your little cousins, love? Uncle Ian looks a bit frazzled...'

'Ah. Yeah. OK,' said Chloe. 'He looks like he needs some help with the kids.'

She stomped off self-importantly and Roz chuckled as she sipped at her glass. *The kids.*

She was just a kid herself.

CHAPTER FIFTY-FIVE

FRIDAY 10TH MAY – 3.50PM – WEDDING RECEPTION, THE OLD HALL HOTEL

Christ, it's busy in here. Posher than I thought.

There's the blushing bride over there – Kate, the soppy mate – holding court.

And there's the sister Fiona – looking fit in that tight yellow dress – and the miserable old mother sitting next to her.

Where are you, though, Roz? Where are **you**?

You think you've finished with me, but I'm not finished with you. *'At least I've got my daughter. Which is more than you've got.'* What a thing to say. What a fucking bitch.

Ah... There you are, in that horrible pink meringue. I didn't recognise you with your hair up. Standing on your own, glass in hand as usual...

I'll go over. All smiles. Nice as pie. Here goes...

'Hello Roz. Sorry I'm late – the traffic was terrible for some reason... So, then. Which table are we on?'

CHAPTER FIFTY-SIX

'Mark!' said Roz. *Or whatever your name is...* She was trembling, but she had to act normal. Avoid a scene. *Fuck, though.* He'd actually turned up. In that new tie. *But she had to act normal. Avoid a scene.* Till the formal bit was over. For Kate's sake.

Kate was at her elbow suddenly. 'Roz!' she said, taking her arm. 'I think I've got an issue with my dress. Can you come and take a look?'

'Sure,' said Roz. 'Excuse me a second... Mark.'

'No problem,' he said. 'I'll go and get myself a drink.'

'Are you alright?' Kate whispered when they'd reached a quiet corridor.

Roz nodded. 'Yep,' she said. 'I'm fine.'

'But I thought he wasn't coming?' Kate quizzed her. 'You broke up with him, right?'

'Seriously, everything's fine,' Roz assured her. 'There's nothing to worry about. Go back in and mingle with your public.'

'Hmm. OK,' said Kate. 'If you're sure.'

'I'm sure.'

Kate squeezed her hand. 'Yeah, I'd better go back. Sam'll be wondering where I've got to...'

Kate turned back to the main function room and Roz followed in her wake. *He* was still there – the cheek of him – standing by the bar in the corner, pouring himself some fruit juice from a big glass jug. But he'd spilled some now and was trying to get someone's attention.

An idea came to Roz and she took her phone from her purse. She looked round herself, held it up and snapped a photo of him in profile, but it was too late: he'd turned around and caught her.

'What are you doing?' he demanded, striding up to her, his brow an angry line.

'*Me?*' she scoffed. 'What are *you* doing, more like... turning up here?' She looked round again to check no-one was listening. 'I know you're not Mark Glaister,' she hissed. 'I've met him.'

He didn't answer – he couldn't – and she knew she'd wrong-footed him. *I went to Didsbury*, she wanted to say. *I've seen his house. I've met his wife.* But the familiar cramp in her pelvis stopped her, the trickle inside that would be a gush soon enough. *Fuck*, she thought, *why now?*

She had no option but to run to the Ladies, cursing the tiny handbag again, too small even for some Tampax. There was the machine in the toilets, but she had no loose change. Maybe someone could help?

She was in luck. One of Sam's cousins was at the mirror fixing her make-up and had some pound coins.

'Thank you. Thank you,' said Roz, and made it to the cubicle, just in time.

Sitting there, she got out her phone and scrolled through

for Real Mark's number. She texted him the photo: *I'm at a wedding. He's just turned up. This is him.*

～

When Roz emerged from the toilets, the wedding photographer was up on a chair, waving his arms around, barking instructions. 'Right,' he said, consulting the list in his hand. 'I need to get another one of the bride and the maid of honour – the two old friends together.'

There was a small cheer and Roz stepped forward, embarrassed, as he jumped down to take the shot.

'Now, please stay there,' he told Roz when he'd finished. 'And could the excellent little bridesmaid come here for a photo with her mum?'

Another cheer went up, louder this time.

'What's her name?' he muttered to Roz and she told him. 'Chloe, Chloe!' he called out, cheerfully. 'Where *are* you? You're holding up the speeches!'

A giggle spread round the room, but Roz was mortified at keeping everyone waiting. She hurried over to Fiona's table – where she'd last seen Chloe with the kids – but there was no sign of her. Fiona, her mother and Jan were there, but they all shook their heads: they hadn't seen her for a while.

'She might have gone to the toilet,' suggested Jan. 'I'll go and check.'

'OK. Thanks,' said Roz. Then she realised. 'Mark' was gone too.

～

319

The blood rushed to Roz's head, then away, and she thought she was having a stroke. She had to sit down.

Word had gone round the wedding guests, and some of them had fanned out to search the hotel. Others – Roz's dad, Ian, some of the staff – had run outside to check the surrounding streets.

Jan took charge of the kids while Fiona, cool and articulate, called 999. The police operator advised her – and Roz – to stay put in case Chloe came back.

'No!' Roz was having none of it. She stood up. 'I need to go and find her.'

'Roz,' her mother said, taking her hand. 'You need to sit down, love. I'll get you a whisky or something.'

'No!' yelped Roz, but she didn't move. Kate had come over to try and support her – Natasha and Vicky were there too – but she only wanted her mother. 'I'm such a fucking idiot,' was all she could say, over and over.

'Please. Come and sit down,' said her mother, patting the chair next to her, and Roz did as she was told.

The police arrived within minutes – a senior female officer in plain clothes and a young man and woman, both in uniform. The crowd around Roz melted away, leaving just Roz, her mother and Fiona.

'He's taken her,' Roz cried out to the police. 'He must have tricked her. No-one saw them leaving.'

The senior officer sat down next to Roz and introduced herself. 'Hello. My name's DI Viv Hardy. I know this must be distressing, but we need to take some details from you, Ms. Johnson.'

The questions began and Roz tried to breathe. What age was Chloe? What did she look like? What was she wearing? The last time she had seen her – what time was that? Roz had her phone ready to show them the photo of Chloe in her sweet little dress that she'd taken at Kate's that morning. A lifetime ago.

DI Hardy showed the phone to her colleagues. 'Could you circulate this photo to the team at the station?' she asked the young man, who took the phone away. Then she turned to the young woman. 'Could you check the CCTV, Jess?'

Jess nodded. 'Yes, ma'am.'

'You'll need to speak to Kerry on Reception,' Roz told them. This was taking forever – time she couldn't spare – as Chloe slipped further away from her.

Jess left and the DI carried on. 'Now I'm sorry,' she said to Roz, 'but I have to ask... Is it possible Chloe might have run away?'

'No,' Roz wailed.

'No way.' Roz's mother backed her up. 'That would be *totally* out of character.'

'Look, we've already told you,' said Roz, composing herself. 'She's been abducted. *He's* taken her. There's a photo of him on my phone as well. I can show you.' Her voice shook and she was shivering now.

Her mother took off her own pashmina and wrapped it round Roz's shoulders. 'Just try to stay calm, dear. Just for a few minutes while—'

'I'd actually finished with him,' Roz told DI Hardy. 'Two days ago. Because his behaviour was creepy and controlling and he was scaring me... And then,' she said, 'like a fucking idiot, I actually felt sorry for him. I went round to the house in Didsbury. That I thought was *his* house...'

'And so who is he?' asked the DI, confused. 'This man?'

Roz shook her head. 'He told me his name was Mark Glaister. But when I went to the house, I found the *real* Mark

Glaister.' Roz looked to the ceiling. 'This guy who's taken Chloe... I've no idea who he is. He's punishing me, I know that. But why's he taking it out on her?'

Roz could see the pity in the woman's eyes – the disbelief in her mother's – and felt herself buckle. 'It's all my fault,' she said. 'I should have told Chloe about him. The truth. Instead of hiding it. I should've been honest with her – warned her about him. She wouldn't have gone with him if I'd told her.'

'It's OK, Roz. It's OK. We'll find her,' said her mother, wrapping her arms around her, stroking her hair. 'And then I swear to God I'll kill him. Whoever the hell he is.'

Roz clung to her mother, felt the fierceness in her slight body – the same fury she felt herself.

Some of the guests who'd been searching outside had returned, the search having been fruitless. The young male officer was back too, with Roz's phone. 'It's been ringing,' he said, handing it over.

The phone rang again – it was 'Real Mark' – and Roz pressed to answer. 'This guy. He's taken my daughter,' she stuttered down the line, before he could speak. 'He's got Chloe. She's only ten and—'

'Roz, wait!' he interrupted. 'I got the photo. I know who it is.'

Roz felt her heart might stop altogether.

'It's Adam,' he said. 'My brother.'

'Your *brother*? What the—?

'He's...'

'He's what...? A paedo, a criminal, what?'

'He's not quite right. He's obviously been pretending to be me. I've no idea why.'

'Is he dangerous?'

'I... I really don't know.' He paused. 'Have you called the police?'

'Yep. They're here now.'

'Where are you?' he asked.

'Buxton. The Old Hall Hotel.'

'I know it,' he said, briskly. 'I'm not far away. I'll be there in fifteen minutes.'

The young female officer – Jess – arrived back from Reception. 'The CCTV seems to show her leaving here with a man and getting into a dark saloon car.' She turned to Roz. 'Please could you come and identify them?'

Roz knew he'd taken her, but wasn't prepared for the sight of him on the screen, ushering Chloe out of the door.

Back in the main room, when 'real' Mark Glaister arrived, his dark eyes were grave, his confident manner gone.

He introduced himself to DI Hardy, who invited him to take a seat. She had overheard his conversation with Roz, but was keen to get his version of events. They'd barely started when the police radio crackled into life and the DI answered it. 'OK. OK,' was all she said.

She turned to them all. 'There's been an eye witness account of an adult male, together with a young girl, matching their description. Up at Solomon's Temple.'

'Is she OK?' Roz asked, frantic, as the police got ready to fly out. 'I need to come with you.'

The male officer tried to dissuade her.

'Are you sure, Roz?' asked Fiona, placing a hand on her arm.

'I'm going up there,' said Roz, stuffing her phone in her bra. She looked at DI Hardy. 'Whether it's with you or not.'

The DI nodded her assent. 'Actually,' she said, turning to Mark Glaister. 'It might be a good idea for you to come too, sir.'

'OK,' said Fiona. 'We'll wait here. In case...'

'Thanks,' said Roz and kissed her sister on the cheek.

Roz and Mark followed the DI and Jess outside to the squad car.

'What does he want with her?' Roz asked Mark as they both got in the back. 'He won't hurt her, will he?'

'I don't know,' he sighed. 'I just don't know.'

CHAPTER FIFTY-SEVEN

'Go via Grin Low,' DI Hardy urged Jess from the passenger seat. 'It might be quieter and we'll get closer to the top.'

'Yes, ma'am,' said Jess and set off at speed, blue lights flashing. The scream of the sirens pierced Roz's brain, making her feel queasy, but DI Hardy was impassive, firing questions at Mark about his brother and when he'd last seen him.

'He's actually my half-brother,' Mark corrected her. 'We've got the same dad. My mum's Filipina. My dad – *our* dad, I should say – met her in Hong Kong on business. He left Adam's mother for her. Adam was only six. It wasn't pretty...'

The DI was listening intently and so was Roz. His *half*-brother. It explained why they looked so different from each other.

'He's always had a problem with me,' said Mark. 'In his mind, I've always been the golden child, the successful one... He's bright, Adam, but he's always had a chip on his shoulder. Convinced he didn't get the breaks in life.'

The car slowed to a stop as they hit some traffic, a tail-back from the Morrisons on the edge of the town.

'And then Jo and Yasmin died,' said Mark, as they sat there.

'Jo and Yasmin?' asked the DI.

'His wife and daughter.'

Roz turned to him. 'So that was true? The car accident?'

'Yep.' Mark rubbed at his ring finger. 'The grief... It seemed to send him over the edge. I had the perfect family in his eyes. I still had my wife and children – my George and Daisy. It was like he was obsessed. We tried to help him, but nothing we said or did made any difference.'

Roz sat back, numb.

DI Hardy coughed and asked again, 'When did you last see him, sir?'

'Oh yes, sorry,' he said. 'It was at Stepping Hill Hospital, where I work. About a month ago. I bumped into him in the car park – literally almost. He's working as a porter there now. I didn't know. He used to work in IT. I hadn't seen him for about three years. Not since our dad died. That was another thing...'

'What was?'

'Dad's will. He left everything to my mother. I felt awful, but there was nothing I could do about it. Adam convinced himself it was my fault. Thought I'd cheated him out of his inheritance. Then he got *really* weird and started harassing us to the point where I had to tell him to stay away. I had to protect my family.'

Roz tuned out. She'd spotted a dark blue BMW abandoned on the grass verge of the roadside. 'Look!' she cried, pointing it out. 'That's his car!'

Then she felt a vibration, followed by a rumbling overhead, as if the sky was falling in. 'What's that?' she gasped, grabbing Mark's arm.

'It's OK,' he said, looking out of his window. 'It's the police helicopter.'

'*Fuck*,' whimpered Roz and closed her eyes.

~

The DI told Jess to turn off the sirens as they approached the signs for Grin Low. Then they turned hard right, past the caravan site and up to the car park – both of them full to capacity with tourists, hikers and families on a day out.

The four of them exited the car and approached the two uniformed officers who were stationed at the edge of the trees to stop the public going any further. DI Hardy had a word and they were waved through the cordon, up the hill to the top. Roz tried to stumble on in her sandals, but it was no use and she had stop and take them off. The gravel dug into her feet, but she was past the point of feeling it; she raced to catch up with the others, soon out of breath.

At the summit, three more officers were positioned around the stone folly. And then she saw them. Chloe staring out through the gap in the crenellations, incongruous, like a little pink fairy in her wedding sequins. And Adam standing behind her, his hands on her shoulders.

'Chloe!' Roz cried out, over the roar of the helicopter banking away.

'You don't deserve her!' Adam screamed down at her, tightening his grip on Chloe. 'She's better off with me.'

Roz stiffened. She shot DI Hardy a pleading look as to what she should do next. Then Mark stepped forward and called up to him. 'Come on, Adam. What's all this about? Pretending to be me? Just let the girl go.'

'Please.' DI Hardy fixed him with a stare that told him to shut up.

But Adam's attention was on Mark now – his face twisted, his focus intense. 'This prick here,' he spat, pointing down at Mark. 'He stole my life – and so I stole his!'

Roz's eyes were on Chloe, who was looking straight ahead, staying perfectly still. Her stoic little face made Roz want to cry. But she wouldn't. She couldn't.

Adam was still going. 'Daddy's little favourite, he was. Sent to public school... and med school. But it was the local comp for me.' He wiped his eyes with his jacket sleeve. 'He's got everything. The wife, the kids, the fancy house. He's the award-winning pillar of the community. And I'm living with my mother. In a council flat in Stockport.'

He laughed bitterly and Chloe began to shake. 'He's even got the fucking dog,' Adam shouted, over the noise. His eyes were brimming and a drip fell from his nose onto Chloe. 'It's not fair. My daughter – Yasmin – she wanted a dog. But she'll never have a dog. She'll never be a bridesmaid. Or go to university. She'll never do anything.' He focused on Mark. 'You'll never know how it feels. To be a father without a child. To be one of the damned.'

'And then...' The hollow laugh was back. 'And then he turns up at Stepping Hill Hospital. And now I can't even go to work without bumping into him.'

DI Hardy gave Jess a look, then strode towards the folly, to the foot of its wooden steps. 'Adam!' she called up them. 'Can you hear me? I'm going to come up there and I'm going to fetch Chloe and bring her back down. OK?'

'No!' he shouted, and Roz's heart stopped. 'No,' he said

again, more softly. 'It's a bit slippery up here. I'll bring her down.'

Adam led Chloe down the stairs, one step at a time. At the last – the steepest – he lifted her down and let her go.

~

Chloe ran down the hill into Roz's arms, while the police moved towards Adam.

'I'd never have hurt her,' he sobbed, sinking down onto the grass. 'Never.'

Roz and Chloe turned away and Roz's phone rang out. She pulled it from her bra – it was Kate.

'What's happening?' Kate asked, distraught. 'We can hear a helicopter... Is Chloe OK?'

'She's fine. Everything's fine,' said Roz, squeezing Chloe tight, trying not to cry. 'You can carry on with the speeches now. Everything's OK.'

'Oh, thank God for that.' Kate breathed out. 'Thank God.'

'I'm so sorry, Kate,' said Roz. 'I really am. Spoiling your day like this.'

'Oh, don't be so daft,' said Kate. 'We're all just glad she's OK.'

EPILOGUE
SATURDAY THE 25TH OF MAY

Roz and Chloe took their seats in Nando's at a table near the door. The restaurant was bubbling with lunchtime chatter, and the garlic-and-herb aroma made their mouths water.

At half past one on the dot, Roz's mother wafted in, wearing her trench coat and patent court shoes. 'Hi, both,' she said, as she came over to join them. 'You suit red, you know, Rosslyn – you should wear it more often.'

'Er, thanks,' said Roz, surprised. She searched for a compliment to give her back but, in truth, she looked quite drained. 'How are you?' Roz asked.

'Just dandy,' said her mother, shaking off her coat to reveal a pussy-blow blouse. 'How are *you*, Chloe, more to the point?' she asked, taking her seat opposite.

'I'm fine, Gran,' said Chloe in a sing-song voice.

'That's my girl,' said Roz's mother. 'So,' she looked around herself, eyes twinkling. 'A chicken restaurant? Seems a strange choice for a vegetarian?'

'Oh, they've got veggie stuff too,' said Chloe enthusiastically. 'I'm going to have a halloumi wrap. They're supposed to be really nice.'

At that point, a server approached their table – a cheerful young guy with blue hair and a neck beard. 'Good afternoon,' he greeted them. 'Have you been to Nando's before?'

'You know... I don't believe I have,' said Roz's mother, amused by the question.

He was about to launch into the procedure for ordering when Chloe stepped in and did the job for him. 'You click on the QR code thingy to join the queue,' she explained to her gran. 'And then you choose your food and drinks from the app and then, once it's ready, the man brings them out to you.'

'That's about the size of it,' the server laughed. 'I've got nothing to add.'

'Great. Thank you.' Her mother smiled at him. 'That's what we'll do.'

Bless her, thought Roz. She was trying her best even though she was well out of her comfort zone.

'I was thinking,' said Roz to her mother when he'd gone. 'The two of us... We could just get some peri-peri chicken and a couple of side dishes to share?'

'What's peri-peri chicken?' her mother asked and the three of them laughed.

'So then,' said Roz, when the order had been placed and their drinks brought out. 'Have you spoken to Jan? Has she heard from the honeymooners?'

'Oh, Kate and Sam are having a whale of a time in Ireland apparently. They've certainly been lucky with the weather. It could have been a real wash-out.'

'I still feel bad about ruining their wedding,' said Roz, sipping her lime soda.

'You didn't ruin it,' said her mother. 'You only... interrupted it. They still got to have their party.'

'God knows what Sam must have made of it all,' said Roz.

'Don't worry,' said her mother firmly. 'Sam took it all in her stride. She's a tough cookie, that one. She's used to working on documentaries in the North Pole with—'

'with David Attenborough,' said Roz. 'I know!'

'Oh God,' said her mother. 'Have I started to repeat myself?'

'Only a bit,' said Roz, kindly.

At the back of the restaurant, a young girl had spotted Chloe and was waving over; it was her friend Sayeeda from school, at a table in the corner with her family.

'Mum, can I go over and say hello?' Chloe asked.

'Yes, OK,' said Roz. 'As long as they've finished eating...'

'I think they have,' said Chloe and disappeared off.

Roz's mother watched her. 'Are you sure she's OK after what she's been through?' 'It was quite an ordeal. Does she need to talk to someone or anything? Is there any... any aftercare or whatever? I don't know what they do in these situations.'

'She genuinely seems fine,' Roz assured her. 'She wanted to go back to school right away and for everything to go back to normal. They're keeping an eye on her too. The headteacher's very good.'

'And how are you?' asked her mother. 'Really?'

'I'm alright,' Roz sighed. 'I just keep remembering things. The signs I should've spotted. All the nights out that got cancelled at the last minute. The fact I'd never been invited to his house or met his mother, his brother, any of his friends... The holidays that came to nothing. All a mirage...

I'm so stupid,' she said, bracing herself for it – the inevitable 'I-Told-You-So'.

'Not stupid,' her mother said, swirling the tea in her cup. 'Maybe just a bit too nice. Too trusting.'

'He told me he was going to Portugal on a cycling trip. That was a lie. It was his brother who did it.' She shook her head. 'He cancelled me once – said there had been a road accident and he was stuck at work. How sick is that? How could he trick me into thinking he was an anaesthetist?'

'You said he was a porter. I suppose he picked up the lingo of the hospital – the way they speak?' Her mother tutted. 'What I don't get... This Adam... *Why* did he do it? And why you? You and Chloe?'

'Oh, I've thought about it a lot, believe me,' said Roz. 'A lot. I think he probably targeted me on that Grief United group. He saw I had a daughter the same age as his own daughter when she died...' He would have known Roz had issues with her sister too – the same thing he had with his brother – but it was best to let that lie.

'But where was he going with it all?' said her mother. 'The pretence? He was always going to be found out sooner or later.'

'God knows.' Roz shrugged. 'His grip on reality seems pretty tenuous. I'm not sure he'd have thought that far ahead. It was grief, I suppose – and his brother became the focus for it. It sounds like he'd always been obsessed with him. Comparing himself to him. Wanting to be him. I dunno.'

'Well,' sighed her mother. 'You know what they say...'

'What's that?'

'Comparison is the thief of joy.'

'Don't I know it,' said Roz, watching Chloe chatting excitedly with Sayeeda, her parents and her little brother.

The 'sibling' ship had probably sailed, but maybe being an only child wasn't so bad. Brothers and sisters weren't without their challenges.

'Anyway,' Roz said, turning to her mother. 'I just hope Adam gets the help he needs...'

'That's magnanimous of you,' scoffed her mother. 'After what he did. You'll be well-suited to that therapist job...'

Roz made a face. 'Thanks, but I don't want to get ahead of myself. I've only got an interview. And anyway, even if I got it, I wouldn't actually be a therapist. I'd only be on the first rung. But it would be a start.'

'Well,' said her mother. 'That kind of thing – therapy and all that. It's certainly a growth area for the future, the way things are going...' She looked over her shoulder. 'I have to say, you're a better woman than I. Like I said, I'd have happily killed him.'

'Mum!' Roz looked round to see if anyone had heard.

Her mother was amused. 'What would they do to me? Throw me in jail?' She chuckled. 'At my age? First time offender? With cancer?'

'Cancer?' Roz froze.

Her mother reddened. 'Oh, it's just a wee patch of skin cancer. See here?' She pulled down the collar of her blouse. 'It's nothing. Just a quick op to have it removed. I'm a tough old bird.'

'You are. But tough old birds need support too,' Roz scolded her. 'You should've told me.'

'I didn't want to worry you. You've had enough on your plate.' She shrugged. 'I doubt I'll change my spots at this age. It's just the way I am. An over-protective mother. Some might say carnaptious and over-bearing with it...'

'*Carnaptious?* Is that one of your Scottish words?'

'It is,' said her mother.

Roz reached across the table and took her hand. 'Well, whatever, you were right about him – Adam – from the start. After the chocolate shop, the first time you met him!'

'Call it bitter experience. Or else I got it from my Irish granny. She had *the gift!*' She gave a wry chuckle. 'No. There was just something about him... I didn't take to him. And then again at your dad's party. Fiona wasn't keen either. She was worried for you too.'

'Well,' said Roz. 'You were right, both of you. I need to be more careful who I let into my life. I need to focus on myself and Chloe for a bit. And then... if love comes, it comes.'

'It will,' said her mother, squeezing her hand. 'It will.'

Roz nodded. 'It's a shame Fiona couldn't make it today. She was amazing at the reception. So calm and clear-headed.'

'Well,' said her mother. 'To be totally honest, I didn't actually ask her. I wanted to see you on your own for a change. And anyway... I probably shouldn't say this, but she's got her own troubles at the moment. Her and Ian are having some... *relationship troubles.* They're having counselling.'

'Really? Why?' Roz bit her cheek, guilty at the jolt of pleasure she felt. 'I thought those two were really sound.'

Her mother rolled her eyes. 'Oh, he says she's never at home, that she's always working. And she says *he's* never at home, always doing triathlons or whatever, while she works all the hours God sends. I don't know... I'm sure they'll work it out.'

'I'm sure they will,' said Roz, as their server brought their dishes over.

Chloe came back to the table and the three of them dug into their food.

'This is alright actually,' said Roz's mother, coughing as

the peri-peri kicked in, while Roz and Chloe giggled and passed her some water.

When their plates had been collected, Roz checked her watch and asked for the bill.

'We'd better be going,' she told her mother. 'We're going to the travel agent's. It shuts at three thirty.'

'The travel agent's?' her mother raised an eyebrow. 'How quaint. I thought you did everything online now?'

Roz nodded at Chloe. 'It's to prove to this one that we're definitely going away this time – after all the holidays she was promised that never materialised!'

'Where are you going?' asked her mother.

'To Lanzarote,' said Roz. 'My colleague, Angie – ex-colleague, I should say – she's invited us to stay for a week in the school holidays. We're going in to book our flights.'

'Well I hope you have a lovely time. After everything...'

The server brought the bill and Roz's mother insisted on paying.

'When's your op?' Roz asked, out on the street, as they said their goodbyes.

'Thursday,' said her mother.

'I'll call you before then,' said Roz and hugged her close.

'I'm looking forward to coming to see you at the Opera House,' her mother said to Chloe. 'Auntie Fiona is too. I haven't seen *The Wind in the Willows* for years! Do you know that it was Kenneth Grahame who wrote it? He was Scottish, you know, same as me.'

Chloe gave her a cuddle. 'Our next door neighbours – Ellie and Lou and Nia – they're coming too. You'll be able to meet them, Gran.'

'Oh, that'll be nice.'

Yeah, Roz smiled to herself. As long as they don't spark up a huge joint in front of you.

'They're lovely girls,' said Roz, with a pang of sadness at the thought of them moving out when their exams were over.

Then again, there would be new ones to get to know in the autumn.

'Right then,' said the chatty woman in the travel agent's. 'That's your flights all booked. Just wait a sec while I go and get the card machine...'

Chloe pointed at the poster of Australia on the wall, with turtles, kangaroos and koalas on it. 'Wow!' she said to Roz. 'Can we go there one day? And swim with turtles?'

'Are you sure?' Roz frowned. 'What about the snakes? And the sharks? And the massive spiders?'

'Mu-um!' Chloe laughed at her. 'You're such a scaredy cat!'

The travel agent came back with the machine. 'Here you go, love,' she said, handing Chloe a shiny brochure. 'We've got flights to Sydney for only £675 return. Special offer.' She winked at Roz. 'Maybe you can persuade your mum?'

'Maybe,' said Roz. 'One day. When we've had a chance to save up.'

They left the shop and headed back along the road to the car. Special offer? thought Roz. It was a lot of money just for flights. With accommodation on top, it was a small fortune. But it was a nice thought. Snorkelling on the Great Barrier Reef, relaxing on the beach, watching the sun set over the red earth. It would be great to take Chloe there. Back to her roots. Sort of.

Roz checked herself. Her own thoughts had surprised her. She'd thought she hated Australia – the whole idea of it. But somehow she didn't. Not any more.

She smiled as they got in the car. There was no doubt about it, the brain was a strange old thing.

ACKNOWLEDGEMENTS

I would like to say a huge thank you to Rebecca and Adrian of Hobeck Books for all their efforts in bringing this book to life. Their enthusiasm, hard work and good humour is second to none. I'm grateful, too, to my fellow Hobeck authors for their support.

Thanks also to Sarah Butler, Paul Ledger and Lisa Beard for their encouragement of various kinds – and to my agent, Matthew Smith.

Living in Derbyshire, I love to visit the town of Buxton and surrounding area, whose atmosphere and landscape helped inspire this book. I've employed some artistic licence for the purposes of the story, for which I hope I'm forgiven!

And finally, thanks most of all to Jim and Jazz, my best supporters and lights of my life.

STACEY MURRAY

ACKNOWLEDGEMENTS

ABOUT THE AUTHOR

A native of Glasgow, Stacey Murray was an international finance lawyer in London and Hong Kong, before changing career to become an independent film producer. Her first film, *A Boy Called Dad*, was acquired by the BBC and nominated for the Michael Powell Award for Best British Film at the Edinburgh International Film Festival (which meant she got to chat with Sean Connery). She lives in the dramatic Derbyshire Peak District which is the setting for her tense psychological novel *The Thief of Joy*. Her first novel, *The Curious Case of Maggie Macbeth*, was also set there. You can follow her on X/Twitter @TheStacemeister.

ALSO BY STACEY MURRAY

The Curious Case of Maggie Macbeth

After losing her high-powered job in Hong Kong, forty-something widow and lawyer, Maggie Macbeth, turns up on the doorstep of her old sidekick, Cath, in the sleepy Peak District village of Archdale. A fish out of water, Maggie comes into conflict with everyone and everything – especially Cath's awful best friend, Tiggy – and rock bottom is just around the corner. But it turns out Maggie isn't the only one in trouble.

When a crisis hits the local community, Maggie has a choice: to give up on life, or go back to her legal roots and fight for justice. But can she save the day as well as herself?

This laugh-out loud debut novel shows that no battle is too big when you've got friends on your side.

HOBECK BOOKS – THE HOME OF GREAT STORIES

We hope you've enjoyed reading this novel by Stacey Murray. To keep up to date on Stacey's fiction writing please do follow her on Twitter.

Hobeck Books offers a number of short stories and novellas, free for subscribers in the compilation *Crime Bites*.

- *Echo Rock* by Robert Daws

- *Old Dogs, Old Tricks* by AB Morgan
- *The Silence of the Rabbit* by Wendy Turbin
- *Never Mind the Baubles: An Anthology of Twisted Winter Tales* by the Hobeck Team (including many of the Hobeck authors and Hobeck's two publishers)
- *The Clarice Cliff Vase* by Linda Huber
- *Here She Lies* by Kerena Swan
- *The Macnab Principle* by R.D. Nixon
- *Fatal Beginnings* by Brian Price
- *A Defining Moment* by Lin Le Versha
- *Saviour* by Jennie Ensor
- *You Can't Trust Anyone These Days* by Maureen Myant

Also please visit the Hobeck Books website for details of our other superb authors and their books, and if you would like to get in touch, we would love to hear from you.

Hobeck Books also presents a weekly podcast, the Hobcast, where founders Adrian Hobart and Rebecca Collins discuss all things book related, key issues from each week, including the ups and downs of running a creative business. Each episode includes an interview with one of the people who make Hobeck possible: the editors, the authors, the cover designers. These are the people who help Hobeck bring great stories to life. Without them, Hobeck wouldn't exist. The Hobcast can be listened to from all the usual platforms but it can also be found on the Hobeck website: **www.hobeck.net/hobcast**.

Other Hobeck Books to Explore

Silenced

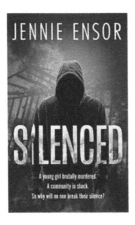

BBNYA (Book Bloggers Novel of the Year Award) SEMI-FINALIST 2022!

A teenage girl is murdered on her way home from school, stabbed through the heart. Her North London community is shocked, but no-one has the courage to help the police, not even her mother. DI Callum Waverley, in his first job as senior investigating officer, tries to break through the code of silence that shrouds the case.

This is a world where the notorious Skull Crew rules through fear. Everyone knows you keep your mouth shut or you'll be silenced – permanently.

This is Luke's world. Reeling from the loss of his mother to cancer, his step-father distant at best, violent at worst, he slides into the Skull Crew's grip.

This is Jez's world too. Her alcoholic mother neither knows nor cares that her 16-year-old daughter is being exploited by V, all-powerful leader of the gang.

Luke and Jez form a bond. Can Callum win their trust, or will his own demons sabotage his investigation? And can anyone stop the Skull Crew ensuring all witnesses are silenced?

Pact of Silence

'What an emotional rollercoaster!'
Jane Isaac

A fresh start for a new life

Newly pregnant, Emma is startled when her husband Luke announces they're swapping homes with his parents, but the rural idyll where Luke grew up is a great place to start their family. Yet Luke's manner suggests something odd is afoot.

Too many secrets, not enough truths

Emma works hard to settle into her new life in the Yorkshire countryside, but a chance discovery increases her suspicions. She decides to dig a little deeper...

Be careful what you uncover

Will Emma find out why the locals are behaving so oddly? Can she discover the truth behind Luke's disturbing behaviour? Will the pact of silence ever be broken?

Best Served Cold

'Vividly-painted scenes and characters but above all terrific storytelling from Hilly Barmby.'
Jennie Ensor

A mystery woman enters Lily's life
At the launch for her latest children's book, a member of the audience asks Lily for an strange inscription in her copy of the book. Why does this unnerve her?

Is Jack the answer to Lily's prayers?
Later, while celebrating in a local bar, Lily, and best friend Alice, spot the same woman. Her name is Rose. Putting aside earlier unease, a new friendship between the three is formed. Rose offers to help Lily re-enter the dating scene after a bad breakup and they come across Jack, Mr Perfect on Paper. Lily quickly falls for handsome Jack. Is he too good to be true?

The past is the past, or is it?

Soon after the pair start dating, bizarre things start to occur to Lily, things are moved or they go missing, and, what's worse, her precious artwork is damaged. Who did this to her? Surely it can't have been her new boyfriend, her new friend Rose, or even oldest friend Alice? They all have a motive. Perhaps Lily did this all herself. Who can she trust, in fact, can she trust herself? Or has a ghost from Lily's past come back to haunt her?